I0526092

SPENCER'S SPIRIT

JESS MOWRY

Copyright © 2020 by Jess Mowry

ISBN-10: 0578634244
ISBN-13: 978-0-578-63424-1

First Anubis Edition 2020

That's My Baby - Walter Donaldson & Gus Kahn
Little Orphant Annie - James Whitcomb Riley
The Walrus And The Carpenter – Lewis Caroll
The Tomb – H.P. Lovecraft
Take In The Sun, Hang Out The Moon – The Clevelanders
Am I A Passing Fancy - Hotel Astor Orchestra

ALL RIGHTS RESERVED - No part of this book or its entirety may be reproduced, distributed, or transmitted in any form or by any means, including photocopying, scanning, recording, or other electronic or mechanical methods, or by any information storage and retrieval system without the prior written consent of the author, except in the case of very brief quotations embodied in critical reviews and certain other noncommercial uses permitted by copyright law.

The scanning, uploading, and distribution of this book via the Internet, or by any other means, without the prior written consent of the author is illegal and punishable by law. Please purchase only authorized electronic editions and do not participate in or encourage electronic piracy – stealing - of copyrighted materials.

This is a work of fiction. Names, characters, businesses, products, places, events and incidents are either the manifestations of the author's imagination or are used in a fictitious context.

OTHER BOOKS BY JESS MOWRY

Rats In The Trees
Children Of The Night
Way Past Cool
Six Out Seven
Ghost Train
Babylon Boyz
Skeleton Key
Phat Acceptance
Voodoo Dawgz
Bones Become Flowers
Tyger Tales
When All Goes Bright
Knights Crossing
The Bridge
Reaps
Magic Rats
Drawing From Life
Midnight Sons
Double Acting
The Coyote Valley Railroad
In The Dead Of Night
Ghost Ship
The Insiders
The Light

To Thorne Smith
For the Spirits

SPENCER'S SPIRIT

Are we still in Oakland?" asked Spencer, gazing out at a forested landscape where tall redwood trees shaded other species whose names he didn't know, along with lush carpets of emerald ivy and secluded nooks of glossy green ferns all sort of roller-coastering over ruggedly corrugated terrain as the narrow road twisted and switch-backed, more often than not becoming a tunnel beneath low overhanging branches, but always, and sometimes steeply, climbing.

"The Oakland a lot of people don't know," Spencer's father, Nathan, replied, at the wheel of his GMC, a 1966 Suburban three-quarter-ton 4X4 he'd bought at an Air Force surplus sale around the time Spencer was born. In contrast to most of today's SUVs, the vehicle seemed as big as a bus, especially towering high off the ground on aggressively mud-tired sixteen-inch wheels. It was well-maintained but not restored – Nathan was an aircraft mechanic -- drably painted primer gray; and a lot of people in Spencer's 'hood had always seemed mystified or amused as to why a black man would drive such a thing instead of rolling a cool city ride. For most of his thirteen years on earth Spencer had heard snarky remarks of, "When y'all movin' up to the hills?"

Those jibes had been laid to rest this morning as, roof rack loaded with boxed possessions, along with the truck's roomy rear section and a U-Haul trailer tagging behind, Spencer and his mom and dad

1

pulled out of their West Oakland bungalow's driveway, stopped at a McDonald's for breakfast, then drove up Broadway Avenue north and headed for those hills.

It was the middle of October, a time often called Indian Summer, when spirits of autumn were spectrally haunting the slowly ever-shortening days with scents of dry grass and falling leaves, which always reminded Spencer of Trick-Or-Treating on Halloween – his favorite holiday next to Christmas despite requiring a lot of walking -- and the mid-morning air was growing hot, though fresher up here beneath the trees without the taints of street tar and exhaust than down in the flatlands they'd left behind after turning onto Moranga Avenue and ascending ever since, and all the truck's windows were open. It didn't have air-conditioning, nor did it have power windows, or power steering, or power brakes, or actually power anything except its gruff-growling engine, a 292 six-cylinder; and Spencer wore only jeans and sneaks, his usual warm weather attire -- though on home turf he mostly went barefoot -- and it felt good to be shirtless with the woodsy-scented breeze blowing in.

Spencer was one of those rolly-fat boys who looked like he weighed a million times more than the number of pounds he actually packed, his upper arms bulked into plump oval shapes, a wobbly torus encircling his waist, and his chest like a pair of bobby balloons inflated to the edge of exploding, their nipples inverted like soft little slits. His belly hung almost halfway to his knees when he was in an upright position, his navel like a yawning cavern tunneling into mysterious depths, though now all that fat spilled into his lap and cascaded over enormous thighs, while his bottom, mostly bare on the seat, suggested a pair of planets colliding. Even his feet were super-size, and his Nikes looked like astronaut boots. His skin was a dusky midnight shade, his face pear-shaped and cherubically cheeked above a chubby second chin, and his lips were full and expressive, perpetually resting partly open displaying a pair of ferocious front teeth in a usually amiable beaver-like smile. His nose was pertly puggy and wide, and his ebony eyes were anime large beneath a cap of soot-colored curls that only nature had ever styled.

The winding road was rough and pot-holed, and Spencer's boy-breasts bobbled about as if possessing life of their own to every jolt and jounce of the truck, while rolls of him rolled upon other rolls and most of the rest of him quivered and quaked upon the Suburban's rear bench seat.

For sound, the truck had an AM-FM his dad had installed years ago. It was tuned to KSAN, a classic-rock station, which Spencer usually listened to – thug-rap not being his thing -- and now playing *Don't Fear The Reaper*, though the signal had started to fade after they'd crossed over Highway 13 and taken this narrower, thickly tree-shadowed, and steeply ever-ascending road. He'd been reading an ancient junk-shop book – reading *was* one of his things – a tattered and musty-smelling hardcover titled *The Jovial Ghosts* and published in 1926, but had lain it aside to observe the surroundings as they continued to serpentine climb seemingly out of the urban present into a wilder rural past. He still saw occasional houses, but usually set far back from the road and mostly hidden by foliage and trees. Some were obviously rich people's cribs, but others weren't much more than rustic cabins like pioneer dwellings he'd read of in books.

He loosened his seat belt a little, its buckle buried under his belly and needing a struggle to reach. "Never knew there was all this to Oakland."

His father down-shifted the four-speed to third as the road snaked up yet another steep grade. "Just 'a grimy industrial city across the bay from San Francisco.' That's what it used to be called when I was around your age."

In contrast to Spencer's profusion of fat, his father was a muscular man in a leanly greyhound-like way, though he was deep dusky black like his son. Today he was clad in jeans and sneaks with a Ford Trimotor T-shirt clinging like paint to his torso, and drove with an arm on the window sill, piloting the truck one-handed, an American Spirit "blue" cigarette ghosting smoke between his fingers.

"That was old-school," said Spencer's mom, Jenny, an opulently full-figured woman with skin-tone of dark chocolate-brown, her face chubby-cheeked and usually cheerful, her hair worn proudly natural, and also dressed in T-shirt and jeans. "It's getting gentrified these days."

"Guess we are, too," said Spencer. "'Movin' on up,' like that old TV show."

"It's not a mansion," said his dad. "But it's all ours and no more rent." He smiled at his son in the rearview mirror. "Now we can start saving up for your college."

"Maybe you won't have to," said Spencer. "Got an email from Stanford last night about a scholarship. That's three collages who might want me 'cause I'm supposedly smart."

"I'm sure that monograph you wrote on The Baker Street Irregulars impressed their literary professors."

"No big thing," said Spencer, his husky voice maturely childlike in a way that could make *Jabberwocky* sound like quantum physics, or inversely The Theory Of Relativity read like a nursery rhyme. "I simply proposed that Sherlock Holmes may have employed them to help solve crimes in many more cases than Watson recorded. It also seems evident Holmes liked kids by his mention of screams of a tortured child in *The Adventure Of The Copper Beeches*, and his expressing hope for the future with new boarding schools in *The Adventure Of The Naval Treaty*. I theorized he might have provided a home for the boys so they didn't have to live on the streets, and may have had a Watsonesque relationship with Wiggins."

His mother said, "Wonder why Doctor Watson didn't write more about them?"

"Perhaps professional jealousy. Kids could help Holmes in ways Watson couldn't... 'go everywhere, see everything, and overhear everyone,' as Holmes said."

"You'll still need money for expenses. Not to mention meals," said Nathan.

"Are you hungry?" asked Jenny, who was master chef in a restaurant that specialized in Italian food. "Prosciutto sandwiches in the cooler. Those so-called 'big breakfasts' with hotcakes weren't much."

"Yeah," agreed Spencer. "I had to have two. But I can survive until lunch."

Nathan snuffed his cigarette in the dashboard ashtray. "That might be late today, Spence; we have to move in and unpack."

"That's gonna take energy." Spencer opened a cooler beside him

4

and took out a big juicy sandwich along with a bottle of Coke. He chomped a huge crescent of bread and meat with lettuce, tomato and succulent sauce, and suggested while messily masticating, "We could move in the kitchen stuff first."

Spencer's mom turned to her mate. "What about gas?"

"The agent said she'd handle that," Spencer's dad replied. "Along with the electricity, but the stove also burns wood."

"We had a wood stove in Mississippi when I was a little girl," said Jenny, "and it cooked better than gas. Might be a blast from the past using one again."

"What about cable?" asked Spencer, around another meaty mouthful and dribbling scarlet sauce on his chest. "I need my computer for home school, you know."

His father shifted to second as the grade grew steeper, the engine grumbling low in its throat propelling the heavily-loaded truck and equally burdened trailer. "The company wants a thousand dollars to run a wire up our lane. I checked with a satellite service and that's a lot cheaper with monthly payments, but they can't set it up for about two weeks so it looks like you'll be on vacation."

"Works for me," said Spencer, after taking a gulp of Coke and politely muting a burp. "There's a bunch of books I want to read... got the *Patches The Paperboy* mysteries series from the 1920s... but that's a long time without Internet access."

His father slowed the truck to a crawl as they approached a narrow dirt lane branching off the road, hardly more than faint twin trails carpeted with leaves and pine needles fallen from overhanging trees. It tunneled even more steeply up through what looked like a little canyon, and hugged the bank of a clear-running brook – if that was the proper name for a stream barely more than six feet wide that bubbled and splashed down a stone-jumbled bed, sparkling brightly here and there in occasional golden shafts of sun, between greenly glistening ranks of ferns. Spencer wondered where the brook went; though obviously on its way to the sea – or more likely the Bay out of sight far below – would it be channeled through grim concrete, consigned to the gloom of an underground crypt to flow unseen in silent darkness under the asphalt of city streets and beneath the feet of thousands of people who didn't even know it existed and had once been free and alive up here?

Nathan switched off the radio and double-clutch shifted to first as he turned the truck up the overgrown lane, bushes and branches brushing its flanks and likewise caressing the trailer as it rocked and pitched along behind. "There's always the great outdoors to explore," he said while waving a hand out the window, "and now we have plenty of that."

Though Spencer wasn't an "outdoor boy" for many more reasons than just being fat -- including drive-bys and other unpleasantries generally involving guns -- and his idea of taking a hike was making a ponderous perambulation to the neighborhood corner market for snacks, he wasn't adverse to trying new things; and having a "great outdoors" to explore was an intriguing concept... as long as it didn't require much walking.

The lane continued tunneling up between the bank of the brook on the left and the slope of foliage and trees to the right, though the canyon – or maybe the right word was gully – seemed to be getting shallower, and there was an eight-foot mossy stone wall, the stones square-cut as if from a quarry, now paralleling the right-hand side.

"What's that?" asked Spencer, swallowing the last of his sandwich and licking sauce from his fingers as they crept past a heavily-rusted and ivy-shrouded iron-barred gateway that looked like an old grave-yard entrance. The two massive gates were shut and secured by a huge rusty padlock and chain. A mossy and almost illegible sign hung askew on one of the gates, readable only as

TRESSPASSERS WILL

Above was a vine-laced iron arch, and under its tangled veil of leaves he could just make out

SHADE

in solemn forged letters.

"The entrance to the old Shade mansion," Spencer's dad replied, guiding the truck through a narrower place where the brook had eroded the lane. "A real mansion, so I've been told."

"We have rich neighbors?" asked Spencer, casually hoisting the spheres of his chest to lick off spatters of sauce. He laughed. "Including Piglet's grandfather."

"If we do, they're ghosts," said Nathan. "According to the agent, the family died out in the 1920s and the place has been empty ever since. Belongs to somebody in England now; a Shade relation named Darkmoor. The agent said she'd written to him several times about selling it... the land is worth a lot these days... but he was never interested. But then, about a month ago, he wrote her to say he'd sell the cottage... used to be for the grounds-keeper... and the half-acre of land it's on to 'suitable residents.'"

Jenny added, "A lucky coincidence for us, because that was when we'd saved enough to look for a home of our own."

CHAPTER TWO

Spencer unbuckled his seat belt, which took a lot of struggle, and squiggled his bulk to the right side window. He pictured an abandoned mansion as something like the Munsters' house, but nothing could be seen through the trees beyond the creeper-covered wall. The canyon, or gully, now opened out into what looked like a forested bowl – the old-fashioned word, "dell," came to mind – about the size of a basketball court with rising slopes to the left and behind, and the wall enclosing the right-hand side.

In the middle of the dell, standing in leaf-dappled sunlight, was a little cottage of square-cut stone, though its walls were mostly covered in ivy, with moss like green fur on its wood-shingled roof. Its windows, deep set in the masonry, were fitted with heavy board shutters, though they all seemed to be open, at least in front and one side he could see. The timber front door also stood open as if to welcome new life. There was a big stone chimney, and Spencer pictured a fireplace and Christmas stockings hung with care. The setting looked very storybook – at least to a boy who read storybooks -- though marring the old-time fairytale scene was a new Lexus SUV parked in front with a magnetic sign on its door:

Oakland Hills Homes
Dwellings For The Discriminating

A short timber bridge spanned the brook, which bubbled past the near side of the house after tumbling over a small stone dam at the upper end of the dell, where a pond glimmered beneath more trees in shafts of leaf-latticed sunlight. The bridge was only about ten feet long above a little waterfall where the brook leapt mistily into the gully creating a miniature rainbow, but barely wide enough for the truck and without any railings, and Nathan crossed it carefully.

"Must have been made for Model Ts," he said when the trailer was safely across and they came to a stop near the Lex. He switched off the ignition and pulled the parking brake, the racheting rasp sounding loud with only the background of water music in the otherwise sleepy silence, and turned around to Spencer. "What do you think so far?"

"Kinda like something under a spell," said Spencer, and gulped the last of his Coke. "Like, from a long time ago." He laughed. "Maybe unicorns play in the pond."

"It does have that feeling," Nathan agreed, getting out of the truck. He went around to the passenger door and assisted Spencer's mom to earth... it was three feet to the ground. Then he took Spencer under the arms -- who didn't just emerge from the truck but rather rollingly avalanched out in undulant ebony profusion -- and sort of bear-hug unloaded him, all Spencer's fat rearranging itself as he settled heavily onto his feet, the huge hemispheres of his mammoth behind still more than half on dusky display since the only thing retaining his jeans was all his belly blubber in front, which created the comical impression of a bib tucked under a vast chubby chin. One might have said he was mostly composed of boy-breasts, belly and bottom.

Having been fat all his life, nature had seemingly concentrated on building a sturdy skeleton instead of reaching for the sky, and though not exceptionally short for his age, his circumference around the middle just about equaled his height.

Despite the compensating effect of the massive moons of his *derrière*, Spencer balanced his belly bulk by leaning rearward from the waist in a rather comical sway-backed stance, his Nike soles sinking into soft loam as his dad released him and added, "The agent said the grounds-keeper left when the last of the Shades passed-away, so I guess nobody's lived here since then."

Again, the storybook scene was sullied as, not three bears or

9

seven dwarves, nor a Hobbit or a young maiden – the latter being a character Spencer would have most preferred -- but a leisure-suited witchy woman who could have gone Trick-Or-Treating as a recently zombified Barbie, her almost theatrical makeup suggesting she might have a fear of the Reaper and hoped by disguise to persuade him she wasn't nearing the halfway point to their rendezvous, a pricey smart phone clasped to an ear, emerged from the cottage's doorway as if she was calling her flying monkeys to kidnap Hansel and Gretel for lunch.

"There were some caretakers," she corrected, mincing grandly up to the truck in what might have been dominatrix boots of nearly knee-length black patent leather, "hired by the English relations, but none of them seem to have stayed very long. According to Mr. Darkmoor, the cottage has been vacant since December, 1926. ...I took the liberty of opening the windows to air it out for you, though the shutters in the smaller bedroom seem to be nailed shut... merely a minor incontinence. ...And here are the keys, Mr. Dray," she added, awarding Spencer's father a pair of big brass skeleton keys – though the proper term was bitt key -- on a huge rusty ring.

"When did the last Shade die?" asked Spencer, who possessed the usual youthful interest in matters of the morbid.

The woman's professional smile faded slightly. "November of 1926 according to property records. Gilbert Grosvenor Shade, who willed the estate to the Darkmoors. ...You must be Spencer," she added, her eyes involuntarily drawn to the lavishly lolling orbs of his chest as if wishing she could have been likewise endowed... at least in voluptuous volume though not, of course, in color.

"Yeah, I'm a boy," said Spencer, who, since around the age of eight, was accustomed to possible confoundings.

The woman may have thought, *what a waste*. "Your parents didn't mention what a... husky... young man you are."

"Is there any reason they would have?" said Spencer, politely resisting an urge to add, *and my eyes are up here*. "And just call me fat, it saves time."

"I'd *never* call anyone that," said the woman, sounding about as convincing as her Cruella De Vil makeup looked. She took the liberty of patting his head, a presumption most kids over three despised; and Spencer decided he disliked her half as much as she deserved.

"I'm Linda Lancaster," she announced, as if he might want her autograph. When he didn't produce a pen, she added, "I imagine you're going to like it up here after all the... hustle and bustle... of living down in the... flatlands."

"'Ghetto' also saves time," said Spencer.

"...And plenty of room to exercise."

"I prefer to work-out the little gray cells, Madame," Spencer replied.

Linda looked blank.

"Natural causes?" asked Spencer.

"...Pardon me?"

"Did Gilbert Shade die of natural causes, such as a heart attack? Perhaps while exercising? ...If inflicting superfluous physical stress upon one's self could be called natural?"

Linda looked nonplussed. "I couldn't find much information about the Shade family's history."

"Doesn't Mr. Darkmoor know?"

"He was reticule on that subject."

"Perhaps you meant reticent? I assume your phone can Google?"

"My field is real estate," said Linda, partly restraining a petulant snap. "Not geology."

"Perhaps you meant genealogy?"

Linda's rouge reddened still more. "It's been so long ago it couldn't possibly matter."

"Sounds like something nasty," said Spencer. "Maybe a murder or suicide."

"You have an active imagination."

"I exercise it frequently."

Linda turned to Spencer's dad. "In matters of the present time – here a scowl at Spencer -- I'm afraid there have been a few *minor* problems with the utilities. The cottage was never wired for a phone, which would have been a luxury in the 1920s and not afforded to grounds-keepers, and its gas and electricity were furnished through the mansion. The meters..." She glanced to the mossy wall. "Wherever they are, are obsolete, and would have to be replaced; but there is no access to the estate. The lane from the gates is too overgrown for vehicles to reach the house... even if Mr. Darkmoor allowed it, which for some reason he won't." She heaved a sigh. "Wealthy people can be difficult."

"Guess when you're rich," said Spencer, "you get to exercise your whims."

"Very perspective," sniffed Linda, then smiled at Spencer's dad. "But, on the bright side, I just spoke with Mr. Darkmoor by phone," (Here a wave of the instrument as if to assure the veracity of trans-Atlantic communication.) "and he offered to disarray the expense of having new lines run up your lane... if you're still willing to take the cottage. ...You do have the option of refusal and full refund of payment based on these unforeseen circumcisions."

"The most unkindest cut..." said Spencer.

Spencer's dad suppressed a smile while turning to Jenny, who was doing likewise. "That's something we didn't expect; no gas or electricity... at least we have wireless phones."

Linda interjected, "The cottage has its own water supply from a spring, as you already know; and I'm sure it would only be a few weeks until new lines could be installed."

"And you wouldn't lose your commission," said Spencer, who, though not being an outdoor boy – or probably because he wasn't –- knew the basics of how the world worked.

"...Er, no," said Linda.

"What do you think?" asked Nathan.

"Kinda like camping," said Spencer. "I'm too fat to be a Boy Scout, but since they discriminate, I wouldn't wanna be."

"I think that's shameful," said Linda.

"Being fat?" asked Spencer.

"Of course not! I meant discrimination. I always work *very* hard finding homes for... minorities."

"Which I guess we are in spades up here," said Spencer, making Linda wince.

Nathan slipped an arm around his son... as much as possible. "Just more of you to love, Spence. But I was asking your mother.

Sounds like you're down with it."

"Tons of great outdoors," said Spencer, scanning the peaceful dell. "If I figure out what to do with it." He smiled at Linda. "Be shameful to waste it on exercise; I imagine one would miss a lot."

"We have water," said Jenny. "And the stove burns wood."

"There's still some in the shed," said Linda. "And very well seasoned by now, I'm sure."

"Age does improve *some* things," said Spencer.

Jenny continued, "We have those kerosene lamps we used in the power shutoff, and we can buy some candles." She paused a moment to look around. "And we won't find anything else this nice for what we can afford."

"It's a once-in-a-lifetime opportunity," Linda added helpfully.

"So is playing Russian Roulette with all chambers loaded," said Spencer.

Linda chose not to hear that. "I'm sure you're aware of property values up here in these exclusive hills; and normally a location like this would cost *much* more than you could afford."

"Well aware," said Nathan.

Linda positively gushed... which wasn't a pleasant sight. "And Mr. Darkmoor *wants* your family to have this quaint old cottage. I told him all about you, of course."

"And he found us suitable?" said Spencer. "I'd think you would have described us as *The Grapes Of Wrath* in blackface."

Linda's makeup threatened to crack as she forced a smile on Spencer that looked like an open wound with teeth. "He seemed very pleased to be informed that there was boy of your age." *Though I can't imagine why*, seemed implied. "In fact, he accepted your parents' offer as soon as I mentioned you." She added to Spencer's father, "He turned down several offers from other prospective buyers, who, to be candidly honest, I thought were more suitable... financially, of course."

"The lady doth protest..." said Spencer. "And 'candidly honest' is redundant."

Linda looked like she'd swallowed something sour. "He asked me to send him a picture of you with your mom and dad... would you

13

all mind posing in front of the cottage?"

Spencer and his parents complied, and Linda snapped a photo.

Nathan patted Spencer's shoulder. "I can get a generator until the power's connected so you can use your computer."

Jenny added, "And we'll get the satellite service so you won't miss very much school."

"Works for me," said Spencer, scanning the storybook setting again.

CHAPTER THREE

"**T**hat rocked, mom," Spencer happily sighed, sprawling back in a chair at the table and pleasurably patting his belly blubber, which wobbled in waves like the Jell-O cliché, his navel suggesting a satisfied smile.

"Just leftover veal parmesan," said Jenny, though looking pleased as always when culinarily complimented. She glanced at the kitchen stove, a magnificent sooty-black cast-iron creature standing on four stout little legs, with nickel-plate trim and white porcelain doors, boasting bread-warmer compartments above and endowed with a duo of gas burners as well as its wood-burning talent. "Of course that was only warming things up; I'll have to practice to really cook with it."

"Practice on me," said Spencer, partially taming a bestial burp. He turned to his dad, who was lighting another American Spirit, and added, "And thanks for the beer," before swigging a bottle of Rolling Rock from a six-pack they'd brought in the cooler.

"You earned it, son," said Nathan, who'd lost his shirt in the afternoon warmth. The cottage's little kitchen, dominated by the stove, fitted with wooden cabinets, a galvanized steel sink and drain board, along with a brass-bound mahogany box that resembled an ancient refrigerator but required ice, was even warmer than the great outdoors because of the fire Spencer's mom had to lit to revive the still-delicious remains of last night's last meal in West Oakland. "Moving in was a lot of work."

"I'll drink to that," said Spencer, polishing off the last of his brew and partially taming another big burp.

It *had* been a lot of hard work carrying in their things, and Spencer had done his fair share, though now his jeans were soaked with sweat and his body glistened like polished onyx. He'd also become aromatic with the earthy scent of a young teen boy enhanced exponentially by his size.

His mom said, "The stove also heats water, but we'll have to tolerate you until I make dinner tonight and there's hot water for baths."

"Works for me," said Spencer, who, like many boys his age, was often remiss in matters of baths.

Nathan glanced at his watch. "Almost two. We need to return the trailer and get your mother's car from the house before somebody boosts it. Want to come along?"

Jenny added, "I have some grocery shopping to do, along with buying candles and some ice for the ice box. We could have dinner at the restaurant. It's my night off, but my assistant cooks very well and there's a meat lasagna special, all you can eat with dessert included."

Spencer was tempted, but yawned. "I wanna take a nap, but you can bring me a doggie-bag and some Florentine cannoli."

"Okay, son," said Nathan, getting up. "And, after you're rested, could you bring in some wood?" He pointed to a bin by the stove. "That'll be one of your chores until we get the gas connected."

"Kinda like *Little House On The Prairie*."

"Or, *In the Big Woods*," said Jenny. "I loved those books."

"Yeah, they're cool," agreed Spencer, with a combination burp and yawn. "Also *Redwood Pioneer*." He glanced to the kitchen windows with their ivy-framed view of forest and ferns. "Guess there's no more bears up here?"

"No lions and tigers either," said Nathan. "Squirrels, possums and raccoons, possibly a deer or two, and maybe coyotes and foxes; but don't surprise a skunk for reasons that should be obvious, and there may be black widows in the wood pile." He glanced at his watch again. "We should be back before dark, but maybe you should unpack the lamps; and call us if you have any problems... but don't use your phone unless it's important since for now there's no way to recharge it except the truck and car."

"What about my laptop?" asked Spencer, while unloading himself from the chair, his bottom as usual mostly bare, his sweat-wet jeans slipping lower, their tumbled cuffs puddling over the floor and hiding all but the toes of his sneaks.

"I'll get a generator today," Nathan replied while donning his shirt. "We can install it in the shed so there won't be very much noise."

"Tons of peace and quiet," yawned Spencer.

Jenny cleared the table and stacked the things by the sink. "You can wash the dishes tonight when I heat the water."

"Home sweet home," said Spencer. "Like we never left."

"Two more sandwiches in the cooler if you get hungry later."

His parents headed for the doorway, and Spencer noticed his father had left his cigarettes on the table. He deftly snitched one before calling, "Hey, dad, you forgot these."

"Oh, thanks," said Nathan, returning.

Spencer suspected his parents knew about his occasional boosts of their smokes when he couldn't shoulder-tap for his own due to a shortage of funds, but considering all the alternatives -- most less expensive than tobacco and much easier to score -- had chosen not to comment. But, he thought of the future: the last store he'd seen on the way up here was a little gas station mini-mart when they'd turned off Moranga Avenue. He didn't know what a mile was – 5,280 feet wasn't helpful – though he assumed about eight blocks, the farthest he'd ever walked in his life… which had *felt* like a mile. Using that for comparison, the store seemed at least five miles away, so it might as well have been on the moon. Which meant no more access to cigarettes without resorting to larceny. He supposed he could simply ask, but that would bring the topic to light with possible negative consequences.

He waddled his way to the front door, belly wobbling, boy-breasts bobbing, while most of the rest of him shimmied and shook… while his inner self strove for economy of movement, his outsides gamboled joyfully with even the slightest change of location. His mammoth thighs got in each-other's way so he had to squeeze one past the other, and he couldn't bring his arms to his sides because of rolls of fat underneath, so in addition to leaning backward he seemed to be constantly balancing upon an invisible tightrope. He watched his parents get in the truck, his dad assisting his mom aboard; and after a little backing and filling – a nautical term he'd read in books – truck and trailer crossed the bridge and disappeared down the tree-tunneled lane.

The growl of the engine faded away, and it was very quiet in the Indian Summer afternoon. ...Quiet, but not silent; besides the soothing splash of the brook there were drowsy insect sounds, the drone of bees amongst wild flowers, the occasional cocky chatter of squirrels, the shrill of blue jays, the caw of a crow, but no mumble of cars in streets or rumble of trucks on freeways, no thumper bumping or barking pit-bulls... though faintly came the toot of a BART train, maybe from the Baypoint line, which tunneled, he'd read, somewhere through these hills.

He closed the door and almost locked it, an automatic thing in West Oakland, but that seemed ridiculous here since all the windows were open... except for one in his new bedroom, which, as Linda Lancaster had said, had its shutters nailed shut.

The cottage was less than half the size of their newly-quitted bungalow; the small living room in which he now stood occupied most of the right side front with its big stone fireplace – which was perfect for Christmas stockings -- while there was a bedroom on the left, which would be his parents'. A short hall led from the living room past the bathroom on the right to the cottage's back door. To the left of that was the kitchen, and the door to his room opposite. They didn't have much furniture beyond what he supposed were the basics; beds, dressers, a dining room set – the latter now installed in the kitchen -- and a sofa with two matching chairs. There was also a big bookcase, though not restocked as yet, a coffee table and a modest TV. Most the things were old but not shabby, prudently purchased at second-hand stores... his mom said she would rather have old, good-quality furniture than tacky modern you-know-what. The sofa and chairs, coffee table and bookcase now occupied the living room in as yet undecided positions; the sofa, though sturdily-made, displaying obvious sagging signs of Spencer's occupation. There was also an elderly brass floor lamp, circa 1920s, which provided good reading light. They hadn't unpacked many other things, lunch taking priority, and the whole place was cluttered with boxes, making it seem even smaller, though Spencer imagined it would look cozy when everything found a home.

The light through the windows was restfully soft, sort of glowing green and gold, and the heat more slumberous than oppressive. Gently bulling his way between boxes, Spencer went into the bathroom, where a massive claw-footed tub took up most of the space. Unlike his former home's more modern tub, there was plenty of room for his mass, and he decided he might rethink baths as something more than parental commands. There was a high-tank toilet with a wooden reservoir, and he now understood why some old people called it "pulling the chain"... this one of brass with a teardrop-shaped knob and a bit greenish with age. There was a small enameled sink, and above it a wooden cabinet with a mirror on its door. The little window over the tub didn't furnish much light, and he automatically reached for the string of an unfrosted overhead bulb that looked like an Edison prototype, though pulling it only produced a click and enlightened nothing.

The cottage had apparently been built before electricity was considered to be essential for life, and the fabric-covered wiring, with porcelain tubes and posts exposed, obviously added later. There was only a ceiling bulb in each room, along with a single outlet, which must have been state-of-the-art in its time, though his dad would probably do some rewiring after new power lines were installed.

Spencer leaned back even farther, hoisted two handfuls of belly blubber, his jeans already half unbuttoned the way he always wore them, and put the toilet to one of the uses for which most toilets are intended for possibly the first time since the 1920s. Then he opened the cabinet.

He and his parents had already found a few relics left by former tenants – a bottle of Mrs. Stewart's Bluing, a somewhat rusty tin wash tub, and a box of Radium Silent Matches, the latter on a shelf by the stove -- and some suggested the grounds-keeper, or maybe one of the caretakers, may have had a family; his mother finding a knitting needle, his father discovering a thimble, while in a corner of

Spencer's room was a tattered old pair of black-and-white sneakers bearing the trademark U.S. Keds, which had likely belonged to a boy though looked large enough for his own chubby feet.

A few more artifacts now came to light when he opened the cabinet... a mostly-squeezed tube of Ipana toothpaste, the tube of soft metal instead of plastic; an empty jar of Pond's Vanishing Cream, which again suggested a past female presence; a little brown bottle of iodine, and a half-used cake of Ivory soap. ...Cake? Well, that was the old-fashioned word, but he wondered why he'd thought of it first when nowadays people called it a bar.

Another yawn exercised his jaw, and he continued to his room. The cottage only having four rooms – not counting the microcosmic bath – each had two windows in their corners at ninety degrees to each other. One of them in Spencer's room overlooked the right side of the dell where the brook bubbled ten feet away, and beyond it, maybe twenty feet more, stood the mossy stone wall. This window was open, its shutters drawn back, liberty of Linda. The other window faced the pond, about two-hundred feet from the rear of the cottage behind the small stone dam, but its shutters were nailed determinedly shut as if never meant to be opened again. Though sleepy and getting sleepier, Spencer gave that a moment of thought: it might have been done for security after the last of the caretakers left... but why just this window and not all the others?

"A little mystery," he yawned. "The Adventure Of The Shut-Up Shutters."

The room was about a third the space of his former flatland den, and with his iron-framed full-size bed – a sturdy antique his mom had bought after his ever-increasing weight collapsed his childhood berth at twelve – junk-shop dresser, desk and chair, plus the unopened boxes of things, there was barely room for him. Maybe not surprisingly – since there had been no television, video games or Internet, and radio was in its infancy when last this room was occupied – there were bookshelves filling a wall with ample space for his library. He and his dad had assembled the bed below the shuttered window, though it was still unmade with only the mattress atop the springs, and he opened a box to get pillows. On the wall beside the open window hung an oval Victorian mirror, another relic left behind -- though it probably would have been worthless by the 1920s -- its gilt frame adorned with a cheerful swarm of opulently chubby cherubs, their little wings spread, and blowing trumpets; and he looked up to see the dust-dimmed shape of a shirtless, sooty-black fat boy in jeans contemplating him from the glass.

He flashed the peace sign. "Hello, friend."

He tossed the pillows on the bed, put the purloined American Spirit and his phone on the nightstand, kicked off his sneaks and mounted the mattress, sprawling at last on his back as only a rolly fat kid can sprawl. The brook sang a liquid lullaby and he was asleep in seconds.

CHAPTER FOUR

Spencer awoke from a sensual dream of having a picnic in silver moonlight on the forested shore of a lake. ...At least it had looked like a lake, though its star-sparkled water had shimmered away seemingly into infinity without any sight of another side. The dream was fast-fading as dreams often do as, lying in the drowsy heat of a sort of Elysian late afternoon, he wistfully tried to recapture it; though like Toyland in the song, once you left you could never return.

It probably wasn't surprising that he often dreamed about eating and food, enjoying in sleep all the textures and tastes and the pleasantly tactile sensations of mouthing, chewing and swallowing; and he'd once dreamt of wallowing in a gigantic bowl of warm mashed potatoes, the rich creamy kind his mom made with milk, half immersed in a pool of gravy while messily stuffing down huge dripping handfuls and getting fatter with every one until his vast body was filling the bowl and he floated in softness surrounding himself as the bowl morphed into a flying saucer and whisked him away amongst the stars -- perhaps to join The Lost Boys gang -- though the only picnics he'd ever been on had been with his parents in Temescal Park. The park had a lake, though based on definitions in books the proper term should have been pond. He smiled, recalling when he'd been eight and playing in the pond, a woman had approached his parents and suggested their "daughter" should wear a top because "she was exciting her son."

He tried again to return to the dream, closing his eyes and lying still, but that only muddled the memory more as his conscious mind tried to make physical sense of its insubstantial subconscious per-

22

ceptions, which was like trying to grasp a ghost.

He'd been with *someone* under the moon, someone friendly and fun to be with, who was not only humorously clever but also conversed intelligently on any number of subjects; but, except for the fabulous food – golden crispy fried chicken still deliciously warm, cool creamy potato salad perfectly spiced with onion and pickles, juicy roast beef sandwiches slathered with succulent Dijon sauce, and melt-in-your-mouth caramel cream pie, which were only a *few* of the foods he recalled – he couldn't remember much more.

...Oh yeah, there had been lemonade to drink in crystal tumblers tinkling with ice; and even in a dreamy dream state, stuffed beyond dreams with dreamy dream food and sprawled on his back on a carpet of leaves with *someone* always offering more from a seemingly bottomless picnic basket, he'd been dreamily sure it was spiked, which had made the dream even dreamier.

...And, maybe that someone had been a girl? A phantasmic fairy-tale princess? A lovely elf-maid from Lothlórien? A winsome water sprite from the lake, or a nubile woods nymph from the forest? He remembered gentle caresses... and the stirring press of lips to his own as that someone lay down to embrace him; and recalled an old superstition he'd read, that kissing somebody while they were asleep could put them under a spell.

Being massively stuffed was often arousing -- he'd found since becoming old enough to appreciate being aroused -- while getting caressed and kissed on the lips had made it all the more exciting; and he realized he'd awakened just before that ethereal dream had come to a physical climax. Not that he would have minded, except for the obvious aftermath... not having full bathing facilities, and he'd have to change his jeans. The source of that possibly pending explosion – which had never suffered the unkindest cut -- was buried beneath his belly blubber and deeply immured between his huge thighs, which was like being massaged when he moved; and he'd learned by his twelfth birthday to subdue what was often on the minds of most boys his age when he walked; though there were more than rare occasions, blamed on what he'd come to call the raunchy randiness of youth, when it simply felt too good not to let it happen.

This seemed to be one of those times, and the anticipatory tingle tempted him to burrow a hand and set off a sensuous surge with a squeeze. He pictured a little cartoon devil sitting on one of his shoulders, and a cherubic angel on the other, and almost gave in to the imp. ...But, he had to bring in some wood. Trying not to wobble too much and undulate an accident, he took his phone off the nightstand and thumbed it on to see the time... almost four o'clock.

He found himself still on the sensitive verge of what promised to be a celestial sensation, and even the angel seemed enticed, but then, as a distraction, thought about Googling Gilbert G. Shade to find out if something sinister had happened to end the family line. But then he recalled what his dad had said, and the battery was down to half.

He lay there a minute trying to chill, though the warm softness surrounding himself combined with the languorous afternoon heat was more inducive to pursuing pleasure and sinking back into sleep for a while – there was plenty of time to bring in the wood, and maybe he could return to the dream -- but started the process of sitting up, bracing his back against the bed's head-rails and levering with his elbows to get his chest above his belly. It was funny that he felt as full as if actually stuffed with all that dream food, but paused to study the shuttered window, again as a ploy to distract his mind from what his body still wanted: someone had used a *lot* of big nails, which seemed like massive overkill since all the shutters in the house had sturdy iron latches sufficient to thwart most attempts at invasion except perhaps an axe attack. The window itself was a wood-framed type with vertical double sashes, each inset with four panes of glass, none of which were broken, so that wasn't a reason to seal the shutters.

He finally achieved a sitting position and raised the lower sash, which, though stiff, didn't resist. A crowbar would extract the nails, and his dad had one in his home set of tools, though they were still packed away somewhere.

He squiggled to the edge of the bed and leaned laboriously over his middle to grope for his sneaks on the floor. Locating one by feel, he started to pull it on, but...

"Damn!" he muttered, finding he'd picked up an old U.S. Keds instead of one of his Nikes, but added, "Oh well, it fits," in lieu of continuing the search.

He finished donning the dusty relic before thinking there might be a spider inside. He warily wiggled his toes, but nothing wiggled back or sank arachnid fangs in his flesh. To be safe, he whacked the other Ked several times on the floor, then turned it upside down like cowboys did with their boots to evict scorpions or tarantulas, but a little key fell out; an old-fashioned barrel type. ...Had it been purposely hidden, or accidentally fallen in? Another little mystery. He put it on the nightstand, puffingly donned the second sneak, then caught an eye-corner glimpse of movement as he avalanched to his feet... but it was just his reflection in the murky old mirror. He regarded the looking-glass boy framed by chubby horn-blowing cherubs, and brushed off the dust for a clearer view. "Wow," he laughed, "you're really fat!"

In fact, he found himself surprised by all that reflected immensity; though except for maintaining the customary parental-commanded clean hands and face, and sometimes annoying his hair, he'd never paid much attention to his physical form. Spencer had weighed at least 300 pounds at his annual checkup a few months before -- the maximum the scale could measure -- his doctor, an old-school family MD, himself possessed of portly proportions, pronouncing him perfectly healthy and rewarding him with a lollipop. Except for occasional treks to the market, mowing the bungalow's front and back yards with a temperamental old gas-powered mower – a chore now thankfully left behind -- expeditions with his dad to shop for books in second-hand stores, and dinners at the restaurant, he'd seldom left the house. He had the whole world to explore in books, as well as the Great Alexandria available on his computer, music, movies, and cyber-friends, including some girls who thought he was cool, and not because they were chubby-chasers... which he regarded as shallow, liking somebody for just how they looked.

But now he took a minute to study the massive midnight boy reflecting on him in return. Though, perhaps ironically, he wasn't good at guessing weights, in comparison to himself the boy could have been a quarter-ton kid. The mirror must have had some distortion like windows in Victorian houses... his breasts looked even more like balloons that might fly away hissing if poked with a pin, while his belly seemed to have reached his knees in pendulous profusion.

He looked down at himself, but he wasn't *that* fat. ...At least on this side of the looking-glass.

Like a cartoon character who thinks he's seeing himself in a mirror while actually looking into a window and being mimicked by someone outside, he first made several goofy faces, which his image reproduced, then fondled his chest, also faithfully followed, and finally pogo-sticked about like an earthquake of himself, which might have registered somewhere on the Richter scale.

"Hello, friend," he puffed at last, as he had formerly greeted the boy, while settling back to a static state, which took several seconds. "Are we gonna have adventures together?"

The reflection only reflected his smile; and of course it was just a funny old mirror and may have been discarded -- possibly from the mansion -- because it made people look fat.

"Or, in this case, a lot fatter," he said to the *very* fat boy in the glass.

The sensation of actually being stuffed slowly began to subside, and he found he was hungry for real, so he went into the kitchen and got a bottle of Coke and a sandwich. There was a trio of Rolling Rocks left, but three weren't enough to get very buzzed, even if he'd wanted to -- which wouldn't have been responsible at the present time -- and one would just make him sleepy again. He considered taking his phone on this venture into the Great Outdoors, though he seldom carried it... hard to dig out of a side pocket over the roll around his middle, easily lost from a back pocket if his jeans abandoned his bottom, and crushed of course if he sat upon it. Besides, he didn't use it much except for parental communications, verifying passwords, and emergencies -- which hadn't yet happened -- so he chugged the Coke for a jolt of caffeine, snagged another bottle, then equipped with sandwich in hand, opened the cottage's back door and waddled out to fetch the wood.

CHAPTER FIVE

The heat had become considerable even in the shady dell, and he started to sweat almost instantly, though sweating was something he did very well... nature's way of keeping cool for many mammalian life-forms. He first went to his shuttered window to check it from the outside, and again he thought it made no sense to nail it shut and not all the others if someone had wanted security.

He glanced across the brook to the wall, but if there was a mansion somewhere beyond it must have been overgrown by trees. About halfway between the cottage and the dam retaining the pond was a wooden foot-bridge spanning the brook and the ghost of a path through waist-high ferns that led to an iron-barred gate in the wall, which of course was logical because the grounds-keeper had to get in.

Taking a massive chomp of sandwich and masticating along the way, he went to the little bridge, its timbers velvet-furred with moss and swayback sagging with age. A slimmer boy could have leapt the brook after a short running start, but for obvious reasons he tested the planking, which though decayed seemed able to bear him. Then, after a gulp of Coke, he carefully crossed the splashing stream treading as lightly as possible, and waded through ferns to the gate. Not surprisingly it was locked and the lock was probably rusted shut. Through the bars could be seen only vine-tangled forest smothering what remained of the path, which dwindled away into sun shafts and shadows.

He swallowed the last of the sandwich and guzzled the rest of the Coke, proclaiming a happy finish with a burp that silenced the blue

28

jays a moment, then cautiously re-crossed the bridge. He glanced at the dam and its cool-looking pond, which seemed to invite a story-book swim as if he were a faun in a forest, but continued on to the shed.

This structure stood to the left of the dell about thirty feet from the cottage, and was made of unpainted planks weathered gray, though mostly cloaked with emerald ivy. There was a four-paned window in front opaquely crusted with dust, and the roof was earth-tone rusted tin, part of it extending over a neatly squared-off stack of wood cut and split long ago. The door wasn't locked, he saw, as, puf-fing a bit, sweaty jeans slipping low, he waded through more waist-high ferns. The latch was just a primitive bar like on a pioneer's cabin; and of course he was tempted to check the place out, but dutifully went to the wood pile. As his father had warned, there were black widow spiders, big fat ones as a matter of fact, and actually kind of pretty in a sort of sinister way with their shiny patent-leather finish and red hourglass decorations; and they had as much right to live as he did, so he let them scurry off one by one as he gathered his arms full of fuel. Then he went back to the cottage and dumped the wood in the bin by the stove. Not sure how much was enough, he made another foray, then brushed bits of bark from his chest and returned to the shed.

Lifting the latch, he pulled the door open, breaking nets of spider web as if they were arcane seals, the rusty hinges shrieking like spooky movie sound effects, while musty scents of dry-rot and dust wafted into his face. The interior was dimly lit by the grimy window, and it took a moment for his eyes to adjust. A big fat rat tried to stare him down, but he said, "Hi, Templeton," and it ambled out of his way.

"The rat-whisperer," he murmured, seeing what one might expect to see in a ground-keeper's shed: there was a wooden wheel-barrow, the flat platform kind with an iron spoked wheel, propped against a wall, along with shovels, rakes and hoes, a pitchfork and other gardening stuff, including a grim-looking Grim Reaper scythe. There was a mammoth old push lawn-mower like some sort of primitive steam-punk machine, which made him very thankful he wouldn't have to push it, and other implements hung on the walls; a sickle that looked like a death-dealing toy for a young Reaper to practice with, several axe-murder axes, two with savage double blades, equally homicidal hatchets, a pair of toothy lumberjack saws, as well as three of the carpenter kind. In a corner stood something he recognized from pictures in books as a treadle grindstone for sharpening things that cut, chopped and slashed. There was a workbench along the front wall, furry with dust, with a big iron vise. Various tools were racked above it; old-fashioned wood-handled screwdrivers, chisels, pliers, assorted files, ball peen, sledge, and claw hammers, clunky-looking monkey wrenches and archaic mechanic's types that might have been used to repair Model Ts. There was also a crowbar, so he could open his shutters. All the metal things were rusty, but could be cleaned and used... Spencer was somewhat mechanically-minded thanks to his capable dad. It occurred to him that everything here had been powered by human hands, so presumably the grounds-keeper, and probably his son – if the boy who'd worn these U.S. Keds had indeed been the grounds-keeper's son – must have been pretty strong. This conjured a hazy vision of a shirtless muscular boy in jeans – though they'd also been called dungarees in those days -- maybe a year or so older than he judging from the size of the sneaks, sawing wood, chopping a tree, or sweatily pushing that monster mower across his wealthy master's lawn.

There was a red-rusted pot-bellied stove, assumably for heat in winter, and near it a stack of old newspapers, probably for starting fires. The top issue was too yellowed to read and so brittle it decomposed in his hands, but after disposing of the remains in a flutter of dust on the floor, he examined several others. All were dated late November, 1926.

He noticed two kerosene lanterns hanging from a rafter, which might be handy to have in the house, and went over to get them, but then a chill ran down his spine when he saw what looked like a little casket -- maybe a baby's coffin! – on a shelf on the shed's rear wall. This froze him for a moment, but then he scanned the ornate wooden case and saw it had numbered dials on the front, and several big black Bakelite knobs like an ancient electric device. Still, he approached it warily, but after a closer inspection decided it must be an old radio. A few moments more examination seemed to confirm that deduction: there was a set of Bakelite headphones attached to a fabric-covered wire, while two more wires were connected to a big square battery on the floor, its terminals fuzzy white with corrosion. He gingerly opened the top of the case, which did disturbingly look like a casket, but saw there were bulb-like tubes inside instead of an infant skeleton. He wiped some dust from the front and saw a brass plate

R.C.A. RADIOLA
PATENTED 1922

"This is cool." He donned the dusty headphones and clicked a knob to ON, but there was nothing but silence, the battery no doubt long deceased.

He considered taking the "Radiola" to his room and cleaning it up – it might be worth something as an antique – but noticed a small wooden box sort of stashed in a corner, mostly concealed by the rotted remains of a canvas tarpaulin, and maybe containing more tools.

…Or maybe something valuable, because it was locked with a big brass lock, the kind shot off by outlaws in movies after robbing a stagecoach. Puffing from the effort of bending over his belly, he pulled the box from under the canvas and found it wasn't heavy.

"No gold, I guess," he laughed.

There were plenty of tools to break the lock, but he remembered the sneaker key, which seemed the right type and size, so he carried the box back to his room, set it on his desk and subsided into his old office chair… another sturdy second-hand buy. The key fit, the lock opened, and he lifted the lid.

For the reason already considered, he hadn't expected treasure, but there *were* valuable things inside, including three packs of cigarettes bearing the name, Fatima, with a veiled lady's face on the fronts… presumably a Turkish lady because it was Turkish tobacco.

He'd never heard of that brand, but maybe they were expensive like Shermans and not to be found in a West Oakland store? They were still sealed in cellophane, and though probably dry as mummy dust, might still be smokable. These lay atop an age-yellowed sheet of quality linen notepaper, and written upon it in fountain-pen ink, though faded to spidery faintness by time, was

See you tonight

"A rendezvous," Spencer conjectured, laying the paper aside. Then he turned to the looking-glass boy. "Wonder if it ever happened?"

Again he reflected upon the boy, so like him yet *so* much fatter. "I can't just keep calling you friend, though I certainly hope you are, but I don't suppose you'll tell me your name?"

Like Dora, he waited a moment with a rather retarded expression, then said, "May I take the liberty of addressing you as Wiggins, for reasons that may be obvious as well as complimentary?"

His reflection made no objection.

"Well then, Wiggins, shall we resume our investigation?"

Spencer turned back to the box: there were some pulp paper magazines, several issues of *Weird Tales*, and some titled *Cap'n Billy's Whiz Bang*... which could have meant a lot of things, though he naturally hoped for the worst, especially since the covers portrayed various pretty young women who, though dressed in old-fashioned clothes, had probably been "racy" back then. And the "flappers," though thin as Barbie dolls, were nevertheless alluring. All were white, of course, but he wasn't prejudiced. The covers also proclaimed, "Explosion Of Pedigreed Bunk," which seemed suggestive of stimulation, if maybe on a higher plane.

Prehistoric *Playboys*? Twenty-five cents hadn't been cheap in the 1920s, so at least, if porn, it was pedigreed. He opened one dated August, 1926:

Do you wish to get away from yourself?

Are you tired of your own company?
If so, let Captain Billy help you.

Spencer wouldn't have said he wanted to get away from himself, who he usually found agreeable; nor was he tired of his own company because it was often all he had, but he was perfectly willing to let Captain Billy help him... and hopefully in enlightening ways that Captain Kangaroo couldn't.

"Save that stuff for later," he said, laying the magazines out on the desk. He winked at Wiggins. "Agreed?"

Wiggins looked agreeable.

Also in the box was an unlabeled flat pint bottle of the type often seen -- empty of course -- lying in alleys and gutters, but this half full of clear liquid. He uncapped it and sniffed. In an English seafaring novel he'd read about pink gin being imbibed by ship officers, and petitioned his mother to make one for him, requiring a trip to Broadway since none of the neighborhood liquor stores stocked angostura bitters or expensive Plymouth gin. He'd imagined it might taste like strawberries... and had been disappointed.

He took a sip and made a face. "Wow, that's nasty!"

Wiggins's expression mirrored nasty, and Spencer set the bottle aside, then remembered the spiked lemonade in his dream. Though it had tasted enchantingly good, gin, which he'd only had once in his life – actually twice, counting just now -- would not have occurred to him as a spirit enhancement to lemonade.

"I think we may presume the box," he concluded to Wiggins, "then fully concealed by the canvas, belonged to the indiscernible boy who might have been the grounds-keeper's son... and who probably spent a lot of time occupying himself in the shed with *Weird Tales*, cigarettes and gin, while listening to the radio with Cap'n Billy's help."

Again, he tried to picture the boy based on these artifacts he'd found and the size twelve sneaks on his feet. He was leaning toward the grounds-keeper's son as the most probable suspect -- the Keds were tattered and dirty as if worn while doing work; and where the box had been hidden suggested someone who knew his turf -- but again only got a hazy impression of a shirtless muscular boy in jeans... though, from what he'd read of the times, the boy had probably been white. Ironically, if there had been a black family on the estate in the 1920s, the father would likely have been the butler, the mother the cook or a maid, while their son helped out around the house and possibly served as a page.

He turned to Wiggins and added, "And, judging from the note beneath the cigarettes... which suggests they were a gift... he had a trusted friend; and they met somewhere at night. ...Which seems to imply a forbidden friendship, or why the necessity of a note arranging a nocturnal rendezvous?"

Wiggins nodded thoughtfully.

"And, since the note is still in the box, and the cigarette packs intact, maybe they didn't meet that night a hundred years ago? ...Which also seems to imply the box has never been opened since then."

He unsealed a Fatima pack, and the cigarettes seemed surprisingly fresh considering their age. Pulling a brass Zippo lighter -- a relic he'd found in a junk-shop and almost as old as the smokes -- from a pocket, he fired one, exhaled a ghost, and settled back in the chair to think as Sherlock Holmes had done with a pipe, Wiggins of course doing the same; and Spencer reflected again:

"You recall Linda Lancaster saying there had been some caretakers in this cottage after the grounds-keeper left when Gilbert Grosvenor Shade died in November of 1926. 'Some' is a word most people use for quantities over two or three... the lesser usually specified. She also said this place has been vacant since December of 1926, which means, in only a month, more than three caretakers quit their jobs and left a very nice little home. ...Why? Presumably, they would have known how much they were going be paid, so a niggardly wage doesn't seem a reason, or they wouldn't have taken the job. It is pretty isolated up here, and probably was a lot more back then, but they would have known that, too. Had there been too much work? But, aren't caretakers just supposed to take care... watch over things, keep trespassers out, and maybe door-rattle the vacant mansion... instead of extensively grooming the grounds?"

Again, Wiggins looked thoughtful.

Spencer had read many ghost stories, including some in *Weird Tales*, so it was probably logical for that explanation to come to mind… the shade of Shade floating around and scaring all the caretakers away. He wasn't sure he believed in ghosts, but wasn't sure he didn't; and Sherlock Holmes had said: "Once you eliminate the impossible, whatever remains, however improbable, must be the truth."

He sighed out another spirit and wished he had Internet access to do some laptop research, and again was tempted to use his phone despite its expiring battery.

As if that thought had set it off, the phone began to beep.

He took it off the nightstand, checked the screen and thumbed it on. "Hi, dad."

"All well up there in the great outdoors?"

"Swell, and I brought in the wood."

His father laughed. "'Swell?' Haven't heard that for a long time, but nice work, Buster Brown."

"Found a crowbar in the shed, so I'm gonna open my shutters."

"Good idea. Can't figure out why those were nailed shut."

"Yeah, and not all the others."

"We're running a little late. Got stopped for a while on the way down; apparently someone called the cops about black people in a truck with a trailer up here in Snow White's hills, which could only mean one thing."

"Guess they didn't shoot you."

"Actually pretty decent after they put their guns away. Said they'd post something at the station so hopefully it won't happen again. We still should be back before dark, but maybe you should unpack the lamps."

Spencer glanced to the window, the daylight dimming in the dell as the sun sank westward. "Okay."

"We're bringing you dinner, but if you get hungry…"

"There's one sandwich left. …And three beers."

"Use your responsible young man discretion."

"That takes all the fun out of it."

"Don't scare a skunk; see you soon."

"Okay. ...Um, you believe in ghosts?"

His father chucked. "I will when I see one. ...Why, did you?"

"Nah, just wondered."

"Logical progression of thought when there's an old abandoned mansion in the neighborhood."

"Yeah, guess so. Even if you can't see it."

"Used to be an old funeral parlor down the block when I was a kid, and we all thought it was haunted."

"Guess that's normal."

"We'll try to be back before dark."

"Aw, don't hurry 'cause of me. Being alone in the 'hood didn't scare me with all the live crackheads, gangsters and thugs, so I don't think a ghost would bother me much unless it took off its face or something. Say hi to mom. ...And don't forget the cannoli."

"Okay, son. Bye."

Spencer shut down the phone, noting its waning battery power, then regarded the box. His parents would probably confiscate the cigarettes and gin -- at least for the sake of parental decorum – so he'd stash it under his bed. He put the bottle back in, picked up the stack of magazines, and something fell onto the desk... a slim silver chain like a necklace. And there was a little pendant attached; a black oval stone, maybe an opal, set in filigreed silver and inset itself with a silver cherub of very rolly-poly proportions, its feathered wings spread as if soaring through space, and chipmunk-cheekily blowing a horn as if heralding something divine.

Spencer had read about mourning jewelry in a ghost story book - - Victorian-age people had worn it in memory of departed loved-ones -- though it had gone out of style by the 1920s. He held it up for Wiggins' inspection, Wiggins, of course, doing the same. "Seems an odd thing for a boy to have, and stranger still to hide it. If a memento of someone he'd known, why didn't he wear it? Or keep it in his room? And he'd have taken it with him when he left this place."

Wiggins reflected reflection.

"He might have boosted it," Spencer went on, "maybe from the mansion; which could explain why he'd hide it, but not why he'd leave it behind. ...Come to think of it, why did he leave all his treasures? That seems to imply a hasty departure, and possibly a furtive flight. ...Curiouser and curiouser, would you not agree?"

Wiggins looked agreeable.

Spencer snuffed the half-smoked cigarette and put it back in the pack for later, then slipped the chain round the roll where a slimmer boy's neck would have been, the pendant nestling between his breasts like a clapper between two bulbous bells, before thinking it might be morbid to wear someone else's memory. But there was no creepy feeling, and it looked kind of cool.

He swiveled the squealingly protesting chair to fully face the mirror and Wiggins now also wearing a cherub. Spencer laughed. "It would be pretty weird if you weren't!"

Again, he noted the daylight dimming. There were still hours until sunset, but it would be getting dark sooner here in the tree-shaded dell, though he might lighten his room a bit longer by dealing with those shutters. He paused before beginning the process of getting to his feet.

"You will, I hope, forgive my curiosity, Wiggins, but may I observe how you manage to rise? It would seem... again, if you will forgive me... you might need the assistance of wings."

But, however incredible, Wiggins unloaded himself from his chair with no more effort than Spencer, and both departed in mirror directions to procure the crowbar.

CHAPTER SIX

The dell was growing darker, slowly becoming shrouded in shadows as if imploding into itself like a gradually forming black hole, though sunlight still burnished the treetops on the slopes above the pond as Spencer pulled the last big nail screaming like a tortured soul from the window frame. Then he pushed open the shutters... also shrieking on rusty hinges and stilling the evening bird-song a moment. This let in a little more light, but it was time to unpack the lamps.

He remembered the lanterns in the shed and went out to get them, opening the creaky door to the now gloomy interior. Carefully crossing the floorboards, which squeaked and groaned beneath his feet, he reached for the pair of lanterns... and thought he heard faint music; a hollow sort of skeletal sound just on the edge of audible. He held his breath for a moment to be sure he was really hearing it, then looked at the dusty old radio, now barely seen in the shadows. He remembered he hadn't turned off the switch when he'd examined it earlier, and tube radios took time to warm up. But...

"No way!" he said, regarding the ancient battery, which couldn't possibly still be alive!

He went over and donned the headphones.

There *was* faint music in them! A tinny but lively dancing beat he almost recognized, sure he'd heard it a long time ago, though he couldn't remember when.

But then it faded away, and the only sound in the darkening dell was the watery rush of the brook.

He opened the radio's casket-like lid, but none of the tubes were glowing. Had that battery's corroded old corpse retained a spark of life all these years and he'd just heard the last of it like a death-rattle out of the æther?

"Spooky," he said to the silence, then removed the headphones and took the lanterns down from the rafter. Toting them into the kitchen, which was also getting dark, he set them on the table. Then he went to the living room and found the box with the hurricane lamps along with a gallon of kerosene in a plastic jug. Using his ancient Zippo, he lighted one of the lamps and set it on a window sill to welcome his parents home. Then he lit the other and took it back to the kitchen. With paper towels and Windex, he cleaned the lanterns' chimneys of dust and spider webs, then filled their tanks with kerosene. He lit one and snagged a beer from the cooler – it was his own discretion, and he was being responsible doing all these archaic chores – considered the last prosciutto sandwich but envisioned a mountain of meat lasagna probably on its way right now, and leaving the lamp on the table, took the lantern into his room to peruse some Whiz Bang.

He set the lantern and beer on the nightstand, took a magazine out of the box, kicked off the battered old Keds, and was about to lie down to read, but decided he better make his bed to be responsible. By the time he'd unpacked the blankets and sheets, tucked everything in and arranged the spread, the daylight had faded to deep purple dusk, and with the golden glow of the lantern softly lighting the room, he could see nothing outside. The air was still on the verge of being a bit too warm, but a breeze began stirring the unseen trees and wafted in through the windows as he finally settled himself to read.

Somewhat to his disappointment, there were no pictures of pretty young women gracing the pages inside, but the funny stories and anecdotes, and often suggestively sexual jokes, though harmless as hamsters by present-day standards, were nevertheless entertaining.

Humor is a peculiar life's potion. It is the relaxing of the nervous system; the bright sunlight into which folk may escape when the sweet singers of calamity begin yodeling and when professional mourners start shedding borrowed tears. It is an invaluable ingredient in the dish of friendship.

Switching the metaphor, it is the grease that keeps the wheels of companionship from creaking. Every once in a while I hear from some section of the country that someone is objecting to several pocket-sized pub-lications and invariably Whiz Bang is included in them. That is because Whiz Bang is the best known. No fanatic ever had a sense of humor. It is the man or woman who cannot see a joke and who has no humor in their makeup who is so apt to make a mountain out of a mole-hill and push a principle to the verge of idiocy. Whiz Bang is not in the world to hurt the sensibilities even of these rare types. Its purpose is to show people the humorous side of life; to be admonitive only when constructive and then without bitterness. In short, Whiz Bang stands for a subtle, wholesome war on Old Man John Yawn and his half-brother, Jim Grouch.

*   *   *

There once was an African family who lived in a little grass hut in a jungle. The father was a good hunter and brought home an abundance of game, which the mother roasted and the children consumed, all them fat and happy. The bones from these feasts were thrown aside, and there were enormous piles of them lying all around the hut. One day the family returned from an outing to the local village and found that a pack of hyenas, attracted by all the bones, had knocked down the hut in a frenzy of feeding. The father sighed and said, "People who live in grass houses shouldn't throw bones."

*   *   *

"At Palm Beach," said mother to daughter,
I hope you'll show pride while down at the water;
For I heard yesterday,
In a roundabout way,
That you really showed more than you oughter."

*   *   *

Touching the question of long skirts vs. short skirts, Lewis Baumer seems to have put a clincher on the whole discussion with his trenchant pronouncement, "It's a question of what's in the skirt."

*　　*　　*

After a dame has paid eight bucks for a pair of stockings, you can't blame her for showing $7.50 worth of them.

The night sounds beyond the windows -- now only rectangles of darkness, though a faint silver glow in the one he'd un-shuttered foretold of a rising full moon – were mostly the soothing splash of the brook, the gentle keening of crickets, the rustle and whisper of leaves in the breeze and occasional calls of nocturnal birds, including the whooing hoots of an owl. Absorbed in 1920s humor, it took a minute to recognize the grumbling growl of the GMC coming up the lane, along with the milder murmur of his mother's elderly Subaru.

He drank the last of the beer, then got up, took the lantern and went to the cottage's front door, opening it in time to see the vehicles crossing the bridge.

"Searching for an honest man?" asked his dad, getting out of the truck as Spencer stood with the lantern in hand.

"I'll settle for supper," said Spencer, seeing his mom emerge from her car with a big hot food delivery bag.

"Sorry we took so long," said Jenny, giving Spencer a kiss on a cheek. "And thanks for the light in the window, makes our new home look very homey."

"The last homely house east of the sea."

"Guess you didn't see any ghosts," said Nathan, ruffling Spencer's hair.

"No shades of the Shades," said Spencer, his nose haunted by savory scents as his mom took the bag to the kitchen.

His father laughed. "Guess we're the only spooks in these hills."

Spencer's stomach growled, but he asked, "Want me to help bring in stuff?"

"Just the groceries and ice," said Jenny. "The rest can wait until morning."

Nathan patted Spencer's shoulder. "Go eat, son, I'll handle it."

"Works for me," said Spencer, eagerly following his mom.

A minute later in the lamp-lit kitchen, he was gobbling three-meat lasagna – his mom's recipe of beef, pork and lamb with three melted cheeses and rich spicy sauce -- as fast as he could shovel it down, accompanied by gulps of normal milk – as opposed to the watery no-fat kind – from a tall glass tumbler. It felt almost as good as the feast in his dream.

Jenny said, "Something new has been added," palming the pendant on Spencer's chest. "Where did you get this?"

"Found it in the shed," muffed Spencer, around a massive mouthful.

"Funny place for something like that," said Nathan, also checking the necklace.

"Thought so, too," said Spencer. Not wanting to mention the treasure box for reasons already considered, he added, "Guess somebody lost it."

"Reminds me of you as a baby," said Jenny. "Except for the wings, of course."

"Think it's okay to wear it?" asked Spencer, after another gulp of milk. "Like, not bad luck or something?"

"Don't see why it would be," said Jenny, refilling his glass from a gallon jug. "It looks nice on you."

Spencer paused with fork in one hand to take the pendant in the other. "Think it was for a little kid... like, in memory of?"

"Might have been," said his mom, she and his dad sort of dancing around like Tom Bombadil and Goldberry stocking the cupboards and ice box. "But also may have signified a cherub announcing a new soul in heaven, which could have been an older child."

Nathan said, "'Except ye become as little children, ye shall not enter into the kingdom of heaven.'"

"That sounds cool," said Spencer. "Like, when you die you're a kid again. Like a whole new beginning."

"Nice thought," said his mom. "Who'd want to spend eternity old and feeble like me and your dad?"

Spencer laughed. "You still have a few years to go before you need hearing-aids and walkers."

"He saved us two beers," said Nathan, delving into the cooler and handing a bottle to Jenny. "What a responsible son we have."

Spencer reloaded his plate with lasagna. "Hope you got some more."

"Yeah, but not cold yet," said Nathan, slipping a sixer of Rolling Rock into the now well-filled ice box.

"Save some room for cannoli," said Jenny.

"I'll ravish it in bed," said Spencer, around another mouthful. "And probably read awhile."

"It's been a long day," said his dad with a yawn. "And I have to be back at work tomorrow. Guess we'll turn in early."

"Works for me," said Jenny.

"Guess baths have been postponed?" said Spencer. "Or will I regret asking that?"

"I married a hard-working man," said Jenny, "and I have a hard-working son, so those benefits… at least for tonight… outweigh the aromatics. But, wash up a little, please, before you get between the sheets; I'll have to find a laundromat until we get electricity to use our washer and dryer."

"How about that old tin tub and Mrs. Stewart's Bluing?"

"If you want to be in charge of the laundry."

"No thanks."

"And don't forget to brush your teeth."

"Guess the water's safe?" asked Spencer. "To put in your mouth, I mean?"

"Probably safer than down in the city," Nathan said, and finished his beer. "Linda showed me the spring house when I first came to look at this place, though she said the key to its door was lost. It also sup-plied the mansion with water, and, as she assured me, 'was considered quite hygienic in the 1920s.'" He laughed. "However old Gilbert Shade turned up his toes, it probably wasn't from drinking bad water."

"Speaking of whom," said Spencer, his fork performing the function for which most forks are intended. "Can you put my phone on your charger? I want to Google about him and find out how he died."

"Ask his ghost," said Jenny. "If you see it ghosting around."

"Ha, ha."

"Sherlock Spencer," said his dad.

"Sherlock Holmes didn't believe in ghosts," said Spencer around yet another mouthful. "Which probably wasn't surprising because Mr. Doyle didn't believe when he wrote the stories; though by the 1920s Doyle had become a spiritualist due to the death of his son, who he tried to contact beyond the grave."

"Sounds like good material for another monograph. …Your phone should be charged by morning, and I'll leave it in the living room." Nathan yawned again and added, "I'll be leaving early. Don't want to be late for work if I get stopped for Driving While Black up in these 'their' hills again."

"How close are our nearest neighbors?" asked Spencer. "Assuming there aren't any ghosts in the mansion."

"According to Linda," said Nathan, "half a mile to the north with nothing but woods in between, and about the same east above the pond. West down our lane is the road, and no one beyond for about a mile. The mansion sits on several acres, so it's even farther to anyone living south of us."

Spencer sighed. "Guess Trick-or-Treating won't happen up here."

"I'll take you to Montclair," said Jenny. "I'm sure those treats will far surpass your usual Dollar Store haul in the 'hood. …What are you going as this year?"

Spencer laughed. "A ghost again, since a sheet is about the only thing to convincingly costume someone of my size."

Jenny closed a cupboard door. "You have everything you need tonight?"

"I will when I finish all this," said Spencer, around another mouthful. "And top it off with cannoli."

Nathan kissed Spencer's forehead and took the lamp from the table. "'Night, Spence."

"'Night dad."

"'Night, son, and sweet dreams," said Jenny, kissing Spencer's cheek.

His parents left, the kitchen a little darker now with only the light of the lantern. Spencer gulped the last of his milk, burped, then unloaded himself from the chair and put his plate and glass on the drain board… he'd be washing them in the morning, along with the lunch dishes from today. …And the breakfast dishes tomorrow after his mom heated water.

"Sometimes being responsible sucks."

"We heard that," called his dad.

Taking the lantern, Spencer went to his room, now softy bathed in a silvery glow by the gentle light of the rising moon. He unpacked his toothbrush and paste from a box, proceeded to the bathroom and responsibly washed… a little Then he regarded the tube of Ipana, curious about the taste. Did toothpaste ever go bad? He opened the cap and touched it with the tip of his tongue. The stuff seemed okay, sort of wintergreen flavored, so he brushed with it and rinsed his mouth with cool spring water from the tap, which tasted a whole lot better than what came out of a flatland faucet. Then, though oxymoronic, he got the cannoli container off the kitchen table and returned to his room. He closed the door behind him, set the lantern and dessert on the bedside stand, peeled off his jeans, tossed them onto the chair and, grunting a bit from the effort of moving after a massive meal, pulled the box from under the bed and snagged an issue of *Whiz Bang*. The room was still comfortably warm, its stone walls infused with the heat of the day, so he settled onto his back on the bed without pulling up the covers. He reached for a creamy cannoli and scanned the moonlit dell through the rear-facing window, smiling when he saw a deer daintily drinking from the pond… no, it wasn't a unicorn. Then he read for a while, absorbing more 1920s humor as he consumed the cannoli, the only sounds outside in the night the rush of the brook and the hoots of an owl backed by a chorus of crickets. He wouldn't have called the reading material more than mildly stimulating, but found the mood coming over him, enhanced by being thoroughly stuffed, to do what he'd postponed after his afternoon nap. He'd been doing it at least once a day since around the time he'd turned thirteen, and it ranked after eating and reading on his list of favorite things. After licking his fingers, he lay the magazine aside, lifted the lantern's chimney and blew out the flame, then burrowed a hand beneath his belly, though for the last few months the objective was getting harder to reach, but at last got a grip with a finger and thumb. He glanced at the dimly-seen looking-glass boy, who seemed to be equally occupied making wobbly waves of himself, and traded smiles with him. "Masturbation by moonlight."

CHAPTER SEVEN

"**W**ooooooooooooooooooooo."
Spencer's eyes flew open to the silvery glow of the moon shining in through the pond-facing window.

"Woooooo, woooooo… woo-OOOOOOOOOOO!"

Was that an over-inquisitive owl? He turned his head on the pillow…

Right outside was a ghost!

"YOW!" he cried, for lack of a better expression of fright, and scrambled frantically out of bed, scuttling fearfully backward and butting his bottom into the desk… which wasn't even a *fraction* as far as he wanted to get from that window!

He was sure his eyes were as wide as saucers, and couldn't seem to pull them away from the wooing white shape in the moonlight.

Of course he'd seen ghosts in movies and read their many descriptions in books, and this one – a slightly less terrified part of his mind began to analyze – might have been called a classic; a specter of rippling, shimmering white like spirits in Halloween decorations, with two black empty holes for eyes, its flowing arms waving eerily over its shapeless shrouded head as it sort of capered around wooing all the while.

He was about to yell for his parents and make a lumbering bust for the door… but then began to realize this shade was a little shady. Instead of fleeing the phantom, he flung himself back on the bed and scrabbled to the window. The figure, still wooing and waving its arms, continued to gyrate around, and below its flapping ectoplasm were glimpses of jean cuffs and pale bare feet.

For a second Spencer wondered if his dad was playing a joke, but

47

the shape beneath what was *surely* a sheet wasn't tall enough, and his father's feet were far from pale.

Spencer wouldn't have called himself brave, and he'd always wisely surrendered his money when somebody shoved a gun in his face, but the shock of seeing a spirit now flashed into fury at being scared by a wooing weirdo. Without thinking who it might have been, or whether they had malign motivations — such as the local KKK trying to spook away spooks from their hills — he sort of torpedoed himself out the window with a rocket boost of adrenaline, the rolls of his sides compressed by the frame like a champagne cork popping out of a bottle, and seized the specter's sheeted shoulders, crashing it with a THUD to the ground beneath his massive material mass.

There was an *oof* of earthly breath strongly scented with gin, and Spencer struggled to a sitting position astride a writhing body, grasping what felt like muscular arms and pinning it under his bulk.

"Hey! Get off!" gasped a young male voice. "I can't breathe under here!"

"Why would a ghost need to breathe, Tom Swift!" It dawned on Spencer that, while he'd caught a perpetrator of something at least a little unlawful — if maybe only trespassing -- he didn't know what to do with him. Should he yell for his dad? The boy — he was almost sure of that — was possibly a head taller and, from what he felt of those arms, definitely stronger. At the moment his weight was his only advantage. ...And what if the dude had a gun or a knife?

He almost did yell for his dad, but the sheeted boy puffed, "I strike my colors, Nelson."

Spencer considered strategies, but finally unloaded himself from the boy, rolling off to sit on the ground, as the boy, still panting for breath, sat up and pulled off the linen.

He was maybe fifteen, Spencer guessed, barefoot in only old-school jeans; a long-bodied slenderly-muscular boy who looked like an artist's anatomy model with high jutting pecs, baseball-size biceps, and a solidly-sculpted six-pack. His face was still more youthfully cute than adolescently handsome, with a sassy snub nose, small elvin chin, front teeth big and beaver-like in a way that would usually show, and the kind of wide, full-lipped mouth slightly upturned at the corners that would always suggest a smile. His eyes were winsomely large, and blue, though almost buried under a mop of shaggy shoulder-length blond hair; and his skin in the moonlight was pale enough to play a ghost without a sheet, though his scents were scruffily earthy to an aggressively feral degree, of male teen sweat, tobacco and gin, with maybe a specter of recent self-love.

Spencer, puffing a little himself from such unaccustomed exertion, watched the boy pull a flat pint bottle half full of clear liquid from a pocket.

"This may soothe your spirit." The boy uncapped and offered the flask.

Spencer accepted and took a sip, not too surprised by the same nasty taste as the liquefied smut he'd found in the box. Whatever this "gin" had been flavored with bore no relation to juniper berries... or anything else in nature.

The boy smiled like a friendly fox as Spencer made a pukey face. "Coffin varnish, huh?"

"More like embalming fluid," Spencer improved, forcing himself to take a swallow, deciding he needed it after the scare.

"The formula does need refinement," said the boy, as Spencer returned the vile stuff. His voice, like his face, was still childlike in a sort of innocent choir-boy way, but he leaned back and took a manly gulp, making Spencer wince, and was obviously a bit more than buzzed. "A seven-percent solution of something."

Except for his cute face and long shaggy hair, few boys could have looked any more male, yet there seemed to be something – what was the word? – androgynous about him in a way Spencer might have described as intriguing. "Guess the logical question...?" said Spencer.

"Call me Dodger," said the boy, offering a long-fingered hand, which, though looking delicate, was adolescently overlarge like his big puppy-feet.

"As in The Artful?" asked Spencer, grasping slim white in plump ebony.

"A *surnom* bestowed by my father because of my artful

avoidance of baths in my younger days."

"Spencer," said Spencer, while thinking it airily obvious that Dodger was still dodging baths. "But, my first question would have been, what in hell were you doing?"

Dodger offered the flask again. "I suspected you might want to see a ghost."

Spencer took another swallow -- the stuff may have been formaldehyde but left a happy finish -- and passed the bottle back. "Why would I want to see a ghost?"

"To confirm one of your suppositions in regard to why all the caretakers left."

"How did you know I was wondering that?"

"Logical progression of thought." Dodger palmed the silver cherub between the spheres of Spencer's chest. "I was hoping you'd find it."

"You knew it was in that box?"

"Elementary, I put it there."

Spencer had a new thought. "Have you been watching me all day?"

Another friendly-fox smile. "Ever since you opened the shutters."

"...Okay," said Spencer. "But, why were they nailed shut?"

"Because it's the only window at which the ghost appears."

"...So, there is a ghost? ...A real one?"

Dodger took another drink and smiled enigmatically... an expression his face seemed well-suited for. "*Something* was obviously real enough to frighten all the caretakers away. The last one sealed the shutters, but..." He made a spooky face and fluttered his fingers over his head, "he still knew the ghost was there."

"...Yeah, that *would* be scary," said Spencer, picturing someone in his room shrinking away from the shutters while *something* outside went wooing around. "...But, how do you know all that?"

Dodger passed the bottle. "Also elementary; I read the newspapers in the shed, which feature several accounts... though of course treated skeptically... of hauntings at the Shade estate."

"...Oh," said Spencer, after another smutty swallow. "Sounds like you've read some Sherlock Holmes stories."

"Every one, he's my favorite detective besides Carnacki."

"Mine, too. ...What about Auguste Dupin?"

"Not enough material to make a proper comparison, but Poe did create the detective genre and Holmes employed his methods."

"I'd agree with that," said Spencer, passing back the flask. "What about Hercule Poirot?"

"Promising," said Dodger. "Judging from his debut in *The Mysterious Affair At Styles* and *The Murder On The Links.*"

"Then *The Murder Of Roger Ackroyd.*"

"Haven't gotten to that one yet."

"Where do you live?" asked Spencer.

"Around," said Dodger, waving vaguely skyward while taking another gulp of gin... to dignify it as such.

"How come you're only wearing jeans?"

Dodger smiled mischievously... he seemed to have all sorts of smiles. "How come you're *au naturel?* Not to say it doesn't become you."

"'Cause I was asleep before you showed up and started that wacky wooing. ...Were you watching me... before?"

"Did you think you invented that pleasurable pastime?" said Dodger, his smile turning wry.

"It's *au naturel*, too!" Spencer snapped.

Dodger held up his hands. "I have indulged since the age of twelve and no hirsute palms, as you observe." Then he made spectacles with his fingers. "Nor is my vision failing."

"Ha, ha," said Spencer.

Dodger offered the bottle again. "I often swim in the pond, hence my informal attire."

"...You do realize it's my pond now?"

"I'm sure you'll be a gracious host."

Spencer sipped more coffin varnish and turned toward the moon-shimmered water. "Isn't it cold at night?"

"Just right at this time. Care to go for a dip?"

Spencer glanced at the cottage. His "yow" had been fairly loud, and he and Dodger were conversing in normal tones of voice, but there were no flickers of light in the windows to indicate his parents had heard… though the rush of the brook was like natural white noise masking many other sounds. He didn't know the time, though it felt like hours after midnight, but found he wasn't sleepy. "Okay."

"Swell," said Dodger, getting up, his jeans slipping comically low in the shamelessly careless way a little kid would wear them, just about baring the base of his shaft, their cuffs hiding all but his dirt-begrimed toes. Also like a younger boy, there was still a childlike sway to his back.

Spencer returned the bottle and began the struggle of rising, but Dodger grasped him under the arms and lifted him easily to his feet, confirming he was as strong as he looked. Then, after bundling the sheet, he led the way through the jungle of ferns along the brook to the base of the dam, taking Spencer's hand and towing him up the dell's left slope to the shore of the pond. The pond was sort of triangular shaped with the dam on its lower side, the mossy stone wall on the right, and the tree-shadowed shore to the left. Above it, the dell narrowed sharply into a steep-sided gully or gulch heavily shrouded with leafy foliage and overhung by vine-tangled branches through which the brook bubbled mostly unseen except for an occasional sparkle. Far above and barely discerned in the leaf-dappled moonlight, stood what looked like the massive timbers of a railroad trestle.

"What's that?" asked Spencer, pointing up while puffing from the climb.

"The O, A and E," said Dodger. "Oakland, Antioch and Eastern Railway."

"Didn't know that," said Spencer. "'Course, I don't know anything about living up in these hills."

"Runs through downtown Oakland," said Dodger. "I often catch a ride. …We could do that if you wish? Perhaps go see a movie some time?"

"That would be cool," said Spencer. "…I haven't heard any trains today."

"It's an electric railroad," said Dodger. "The trains are very quiet." He theatrically cupped a hand to an ear. "Here comes one now, and right on time."

Spencer heard a faint whine approaching, obviously an electric sound, and the metallic click-clacking of wheels. A few seconds later he saw a ghostly blue-white glow flickering through the trees above as a train rumbled slowly over the trestle. A few moments more, and again the only sounds in the dell were the gurgles of water and hoots of an owl backed by cheerfully chirping crickets.

"Just freights at this time of night," said Dodger. "But they're the best way to get to town without requiring coin of the realm."

"Sounds very Artful," said Spencer.

Dodger dropped the sheet in a little clear space underneath the trees and unbuttoned and lost his jeans, looking like some sort of boy-god from a long time ago -- who had also not suffered the unkindest cut -- yet also, as Spencer had noted, somehow intriguingly something else. "Shall we?"

Spencer dipped a toe in the water, which was comfortably warm despite the wee hour. Except for the picnics in Temescal Park, he'd never gone swimming anywhere, but his experience in the lake had proved he could float without any effort, so he waded in with Dodger, who took his hand again and warned:

"Careful, there's a drop-off into a very dark place."

CHAPTER EIGHT

"Spencer! Breakfast!" called his mom.

Spencer awoke in morning sunlight and sleepily answered, "Coming."

Then he muttered, "Damn!" finding – his mind making the pun - - he apparently already had. That hadn't been happening often as long as he did it consciously, or he might have said conscientiously, once or twice a day; but though such surging events in his sleep were probably pleasurable in dreams, he usually felt as if he'd missed something he should have been awake to enjoy.

He lay there a minute on his back, head on crossed arms on the pillows, the sun beaming sensually warm on his body through the pond-facing window, while trying to remember what had happened last night.

Or, had anything happened... besides the moistly obvious?

Had it just been a dream... being awakened and scared by a boy pretending to be a ghost, then going up to the pond with him, the train crossing over the trestle, and their nocturnal swim in the moonlight?

Those details were still distinct as if they had actually happened, but then memories began getting hazy... though maybe due to the coffin varnish they had sipped sitting on the shore, the Indian Summer night still warm, the stars shining silvery over the trees, while smoking Fatima cigarettes from a fresh pack provided by Dodger and talking of things he couldn't recall, though Dodger had seemed a lot more well-read and smarter than any boy of his age Spencer had ever met. ...He *sort* of recalled coming down from the pond with their arms over each-other's shoulders like boys in *The Little Rascals* –

though more for mutual support resulting from copious libations --
and Dodger boosting him back through the window and stuffing and
tucking his rolls past the frame. ...And, he had a recollection of
asking Dodger to spend the night – what was left of it by then – and
of lying side-by-side, sharing more Fatimas while reading to each
other in whispers from *Cap'n Billy's Whiz Bang* in the glow of
lantern light until he must have fallen asleep. And Dodger had
apparently left between whenever that was and now.

He glanced at the boy in the mirror, who would have witnessed
everything – had there been anything to see -- but Wiggins was looking just as bemused.

He heaved himself to a sitting position and scanned the slopes
above the pond, but saw no railroad trestle spanning the overgrown
gully... though maybe it couldn't be seen from down here? He
squig-gled to the window and studied the ferns below: there *might*
have been signs of a midnight scuffle -- Sherlock Holmes would have
spot-ted them -- but Spencer couldn't be sure. And, probably since
they'd been swimming, there was no earthy scent of Dodger on the
pillows or sheets.

He addressed his looking-glass Boswell as Holmes may have
sounded Watson, "If we assume it wasn't a dream, then who is
Dodger, we may wonder? A boy who lives 'around,' as he said; a
neighbor kid, presumably wealthy... at least compared to us... who
might have grown up adventuring on the abandoned Shade estate?
...Or, perhaps a homeless boy who found a peaceful place to live?"

Spencer recalled the "ghost" sheet, with which they had dried
themselves after swimming. "I'm not an expert in fabrics, but it sort
of felt expensive compared to what we are presently on. Egyptian
cotton maybe? Of course it could have been boosted... but why
would a homeless kid want a sheet when a blanket would be more
practical?"

Wiggins only looked reflective.

"Spencer!" called his mom again. "Come and get it or I'll throw it
away!"

"...Coming." *Ha, ha,* laughed Spencer's mind, aware again of the
slipperiness beneath his belly between his thighs. "Gonna wash first."

"That *would* be a first," remarked his mom.

Spencer cascaded out of bed and, taking his jeans from the chair, opened the door and looked into the kitchen across the narrow hall, the scents of hot metal and wood smoke, along with those of sizzling sausages, frying eggs and steaming hash-browns welcoming him to a brand new day with spirits of an older past. His mother stood at the stove clad in one of her white chef's aprons and tending black cast-iron pans.

"What time is it?" asked Spencer, lumbering to the bathroom.

"Does anybody really know what time it is? …About nine. How do you want your eggs?"

"Preferably cooked… over-medium as usual, please."

In the bathroom he found that one of the faucets was now dispensing stove-heated water. Using the ancient cake of Ivory, he washed where washing was necessary, a process requiring considerable effort, then donned his jeans and went to the kitchen, climbing aboard his chair at the table.

His mom set a plate before him loaded with six plump sausages, a trio of eggs over-medium, and a mountain of golden-brown potatoes crisp from frying in butter. To drink there were glasses of orange juice and milk.

"Dad left?" asked Spencer, salt-and-peppering his eggs and adding dashes of Crystal hot sauce to the sausages.

"Yes, and your phone's in the living room." Jenny poured an enamel mug full of coffee from a big pot – she made "classic coffee" instead of using modern methods like percolators and filters – and seated herself across from Spencer with a breakfast plate of her own. "Pleasant dreams in our new home?"

Spencer wasn't secretive – at least when being secretive wasn't more convenient or less hazardous than not – but since he wasn't sure if the adventure with Dodger last night had actually been material, decided not to mention it. Instead, he asked while attacking his eggs, "Guess there's a lot of work to do?"

Jenny sipped coffee and seasoned her food. "I'll handle most of the unpacking; you arrange your room, though I might need help moving furniture. Your dad left the generator outside and asked if you'd set it up in the shed. And, could you clear away some ferns from the front and back doors? No massive environmental destructtion... I like ferns... just pathways please. I guess there are tools in the shed?"

"Tons of 'em," said Spencer, around a mouthful of sausage and eggs. "Shouldn't be hard to clean 'em up with dad's WD-40." He glanced at the dishes on the drain board. "I assume you want me to wash those?"

"Until we get a maid."

Spencer took a gulp of orange juice. "Hopefully a hotsy."

"Returning from Fantasy Land," said Jenny, "I'd like to plant an herb garden out back."

"Should I start growing dreadlocks?"

"You'll have plenty of thyme."

"A sage observation," Spencer returned, "though I'm more parsley to rosemary."

"How oregano. Could you clear a space about twenty feet square?"

"A command concealed in a question."

"Could be construed as a thinly-veiled threat."

"Sure," sighed Spencer. "But you'll need chicken wire or something to go around and over it, or the birds and beasts will be banqueting."

"Good thinking, botanical boy."

"Yeah, swell," said Spencer. "Guess I can always be a grounds-keeper if higher aspirations fail."

"I seriously doubt if they will."

Spencer laughed. "There's a saying, 'never give up on your dreams,' so maybe I should go back to sleep."

His mother smiled. "Must have been pleasant dreams indeed."

"I assume I'm back in the waking world despite this dreamy breakfast, so I'll have a cup of coffee, please. Feels like I'm gonna need it for all the forced labor today."

"I'll be leaving at one," said Jenny, rising to get another mug and pouring it full from the pot. "Have to be at the restaurant to start the sauces for dinner, but I'll make you a nice big lunch."

Spencer creamed and sugared his coffee. "A *très grand* lunch, I hope; feels like I'm gonna need that, too."

Jenny sat down to continue her breakfast. "Are you adding the speaking of French to your many other charms, *chérie?*"

"Just came to mind, must have read it somewhere. ...Want me to milk our herd of cows, shear the sheep, shoe the horses, and plow the forty with our mule?"

"You could install a new mail box... your father bought one... down at the road."

"That's gotta be about three blocks, or maybe a quarter mile."

"I'll drive you down when I leave."

Spencer sighed again. "Down is the easy part. ...I'm gonna need an ATV to ride around our extensive estate."

"Send an email to Santa."

"What about child labor laws?"

"They only apply to Elmo's kids."

"Yeah," said Spencer. "Who go out and play for an hour every day without having to worry about getting shot... unless they go to public school... and whose parents don't get stopped at gunpoint for Driving While Black in a nice neighborhood."

"My, what a smart young black man you are; but you don't have to do it all in a day."

"Maybe I'll go out and play for an hour."

"Take one of the spirited horses and survey our extensive estate."

"I'd rather do that on an ATV."

"I'd rather be Princess Fancy-Fanny riding a unicorn over the rainbow, but for the present I'm satisfied to be driving a second-hand Subaru... which is more than ninety percent of this planet's population can say."

"Okay, point taken," said Spencer. "...Would you really rather be a princess?"

"I married a king, which makes me a queen, and I have a charming prince for a son, but I wouldn't say no to a unicorn ride."

"But, wouldn't you have to be a...?"

"Guess I gave up that dream gifting you to the world."

"Oh swell, now I'm gonna need therapy."

"Just buy me a second-hand unicorn after you make your fortune. ...Your dad said he might work overtime: candles, ice and kerosene cost a lot more than they used to back in the days of the Shades. And the generator was three-hundred dollars. ...I hope Mr. Darkmoor is true to his word about paying for new utility lines."

Spencer stabbed a sausage, deftly dodging a juicy spurt. "Why not, he seems to like us. Especially a boy of my age."

"Maybe he'll ask for naked pictures."

"I draw the line at interacting with goats dressed in rubber and pink party hats."

"I knew we should have installed parental controls on your computer."

"Most of the so-called normal news a boy of my age is subjected to is more confusing than sumo wrestlers who cross-dress and marry transsexual squirrels." Spencer fork-lifted a load of hash-browns. "But I like to think there are still a few people who do nice things for other people without asking them to take off their clothes and cover them-selves with chocolate syrup."

"Whipped-cream would go better with your complexion."

"I'll keep that in mind if asked to perform and sacrifice my innocence for the sake of gas and electricity."

"Be sure to record it for future blackmail." His mom sipped more coffee. "Your dad will call if he's going to be late, and I should be home by midnight. I'll leave you dinner in the ice box: I assume you can master the rocket science of lighting a fire to warm it up."

"There must be an app for that."

"Any requests for dessert?"

"Half a dozen cream-filled zeppole, the ones with cherries on top."

"I'll make it a dozen if you start on the garden."

"Consider it debuted." Spencer drank the last of his milk. "Did Linda Lancaster mention a railroad above the pond?"

"No. Is there?"

"I... heard a train go by last night... 'least I think I did."

"Your father and I didn't hear anything... it's so peaceful up here compared to the city. Maybe it was BART? I've never been on the Baypoint line, but I've heard it runs through these hills."

"Yeah, me too," said Spencer, after sipping coffee. "But there weren't any lights in the cars, just the engine's headlight."

"Might have been a maintenance train, especially late at night."

"...Yeah," said Spencer, reflectively. "And Linda might not have told us because it's not a good selling point to have a railroad nearby."

"You could always climb up there and see, my very inquisitive lad."

Spencer thought of the overgrown gully slanting steeply skyward. "I'm not that inquisitive."

CHAPTER NINE

It was around two o'clock on another hot autumn afternoon when Spencer, panting and pouring sweat, swung a sledge hammer a final time, pounding a metal mail box post several more inches into the ground at the shady entrance to Shade Lane. Then, using wrenches from the shed, he attached the box to the post with the supplied nuts and bolts. He'd found the decomposed remains of two other boxes amongst the ferns, which must have fallen ages ago; and his new address was 2 Shade Lane... the mansion presumably 1. He applied stick-on letters spelling DRAY, added the numeral 2, then regarded the tree-tunneled grade he had to ascend to get home.

"Swell," he muttered.

He fired an ancient Fatima that tasted as fresh as yesterday and sat on a rock beside the brook to rest a bit before the ordeal, then ground the cigarette safely out beneath a venerable Ked – which he'd found more comfortable than his new-age Nikes as if custom-conformed to his fat-padded feet -- and finally got back to a vertical plane. Pocketing the wrenches, he slung the hammer over a shoulder and started trudging up the lane, jiggling, quivering, bobbling, quaking, and feeling like John Henry after a day of driving steel. "My kingdom for a horse," he puffed. "Or, better yet, an ATV."

He stopped at the massive ivy-laced gates to peer between their rusty bars up the even more overgrown drive that led to the abandoned mansion, but there was nothing to be seen except vine-tangled foliage, shadows and trees; not even a glimpse of a tottering tower, collapsed cupola or batty belfry. Then he resumed his ponderous pace, pausing often to pull up his jeans, along the bank of the bubbling brook, until finally crossing the little bridge above the rainbow-misted falls and arriving at the cottage.

After washing the dishes, he'd spent most of the morning unpacking his things, stocking the shelves with his library of mostly old-time junk-shop books, putting stuff in his desk drawers and his clothes in his dresser... though his wardrobe wasn't extensive, consisting mainly of T-shirts and jeans with socks and a few pairs of boxers reserved for formal occasions. He'd helped his mom arrange furniture, flattened the empty moving boxes to be burned in the fireplace – a task he was well-suited for -- then, following the instructions, installed the generator in the shed, bored a hole in a wall for its exhaust with an ancient brace-and-bitt, filled its tank with gasoline from a gallon can, checked its crankcase oil level and given it a test run.

The cottage's rusty fuse box on the wall beside the back door was a primitive two-wire type, and he'd clipped the female plug from one of his dad's extension cords, stripped its wires and screwed them in. Then he'd restarted the generator and ascertained the antique light bulbs worked. He'd turned them all off – there was plenty of daylight – but the generator still sounded labored as if under load when he'd come back outside. He'd glanced at a pair of moss-bearded wires drooping up to a tottering pole on the other side of the mansion grounds wall: was he now powering the mansion... and possibly awakening things in places where only shadows and darkness had ruled for a century? That conjured a kind of spooky scene of spider-webbed halls and dead silent rooms with dusty sheet-shrouded furniture now again seeing light. He'd remembered reading a story proposing live wires provided a path for spirits to travel along.   The generator had a charging feature, and he'd thought of trying to resurrect the Radiola's battery, but found the cells were all bone-dry. ...How could it have played music last night?

He'd shut the generator down and, after regarding the Grim Reaper scythe and finding it too intimidating, cleaned up a G.R. Junior sickle with a rag and WD-40 to slash away ferns from the cottage's doors. Then, after a hefty lunch of saucy meatball sandwiches, he'd ridden down to the road with his mom to plant the box like a flag of conquest on a foreign shore.

The fact that he was an alien here had been confirmed by suspicious looks from paler people in passing cars of mostly Teutonic manufacture; and a millennial mountain biker had pointedly paused to take his picture with a pricey Chinese phone as if to verify a Sighting.

Now, leaving the hammer outside the front door, he went to the kitchen, got a Coke from the ice box, chugged down half and blasted a burp. His body was gleaming as if he'd gone swimming -- which seemed like a cool idea – but he considered some Googling about the late Gilbert Shade. There was probably a lot of data about someone who'd been so rich, and there would surely be mentions of him in the *Oakland Tribune* archives – at the very least an obituary about the last of the Shades – but research would be tedious on his phone's tiny screen. He thought of the newspapers in the shed: Dodger had learned something from them – assuming there really was a Dodger -- enough to know why the caretakers had left... though the ghost explanation, as Dodger had said – assuming there really was a Dodger -- would have been skeptically treated in print.

Again, he contemplated a swim, but was tired from the uphill hike, so decided to take a nap. He checked the time on his phone: almost three. His mother didn't expect him to do everything today, but after a snooze and maybe a swim, he could make a start on her garden. He gulped the rest of the Coke, then went to his room, sprawled on the bed and set his phone to beep in an hour.

"The game is afoot."

Spencer opened his eyes. The Elysian afternoon sunlight suggested he hadn't slept for long; and Dodger stood at the window still barely clad in careless jeans, though with a towel draped over a shoulder and a huge picnic basket in hand – an old-fashioned two-lidded wicker type -- his body peaches-and-cream in the sun, his shag-gy mop of hair pale gold, and smiling his friendly-fox smile.

Spencer heaved himself up on his elbows. "Guess I didn't dream you." He laughed. "Unless I'm dreaming you now."

"Or, perhaps I'm dreaming you."

"Never thought of that."

"Or perhaps," said Dodger, "we're both beyond the wall of

sleep."

"That's an H.P. Lovecraft story. You read him, too?"

"Another of my favorite authors." Dodger reached in and pinched Spencer's arm. "Is that sufficient proof you're not dreaming?"

"Guess it proves one of us isn't."

"Care to go for a dip?"

"Sure," said Spencer, yawning. "But then I have to clear some space; mom wants to plant an herb garden out there."

"I can do that in no time," said Dodger. "There's a scythe in the shed."

"Yeah, but it looks pretty scary. ...You know how to use it?"

"I was taught by a master reaper. ...Shall we...? I brought some refreshments." Dodger indicated the basket. "There's cold chicken, cold tongue, cold ham, cold beef, pickled-herring, chicken salad, French rolls, potted meat, lemonade..."

Spencer laughed. "That's The Water Rat's lunch in *The Wind In The Willows*."

"Along with my own additions such as..."

"You had me at refreshments." Spencer started to roll out of bed, but Dodger took his hand. "This is the entrance to the egress, quoting the late Mr. Barnum."

Spencer maneuvered himself around to make a frontal exit, extending his legs out the portal, but found without the rush of rage propelling him as it had last night, or Dodger's stuff and tuck assistance, the rolls of his sides wouldn't fit through the frame. "Guess I'm too fat to enter this egress."

"You underestimate yourself." Dodger set the basket down and, taking Spencer under the arms, gently sort of squiggled him out – the bottle cork analogy came to Spencer's mind -- and lowered him to earth with a hug. Despite their moonlit swim, Dodger again radiated an aura of scruffy-boy sweat, tobacco and gin with a faint spirit of personal pleasure. Then as he'd done last night, he palmed the cherub on Spencer's chest. "It fits you like the cat's meow."

"About the only thing that does," laughed Spencer while hoisting recalcitrant jeans. "Except these old Keds I found. ...What do you know about it?"

Dodger seemed to look thoughtful. "A memento of a child departed." Then he led the way through ferns along the brook to the base of the dam and again took Spencer's hand, helping him ascend the slope to the tree-shaded shore of the pond.

"There is a trestle," puffed Spencer, gazing up at the vine-laced timbers, which, as he'd wondered that morning, evidently couldn't be seen from a lower perspective.

Dodger set down the basket and towel. "Did you think that was also a dream?"

"Too much coffin varnish, I guess."

"It can be dream-inducing, though I've found such dreams enlightening as well as entertaining."

"Yeah, last night was fun." Spencer noticed a little stone structure almost buried in ivy and looking like a graveyard crypt mostly dug into the dell's left slope about thirty feet above the shore. He hadn't seen it last night in the dark; and there was a rusty pipe at its base from which water trickled into the pond. Another pipe angled down toward the cottage, while a third crossed over the top of the dam and disappeared under the wall, presumably supplying the mansion.

"Guess that's a spring house?"

"My secret hide-out," said Dodger. "In my younger days with Water Rat, Mowgli, Kim, and Huck Finn, to name just a few dream companions." Then he turned to the pond and looked sad. "Before wise and gentle childhood was murdered by the ignorance and savagery adults call life."

Spencer nodded. "Sometimes not knowing how the world works seems better than knowing how it does."

"An accurate summation," sighed Dodger, still gazing at the pond, its placid surface like a mirror reflecting two boys on the shore. "I know many things now I wish I didn't, but I suppose that's called growing up."

Spencer touched Dodger's shoulder. "'Wherever they go, and whatever happens to them on the way, in that enchanted place on the top of the forest, a little boy and his Bear will always be playing.'"

Dodger's smile rekindled and he took Spencer's hand again. "Welcome to my house at Pooh Corner."

He assisted Spencer up to the spring house, pausing at its heavy plank door to pull a barrel-key from a pocket and unlock a big brass padlock that looked like another Wells Fargo relic, then pushed the door open on spooky hinges. The interior was about twelve feet square and softly lit by forest light filtering in through narrow screened spaces between the stone walls and timber roof. The floor was also stone; and maybe a third of the uphill side was filled by a big stone basin. From a pipe in the wall above it, clear water trinkled into the font; and the pipe running down to the pond kept it from overflowing. Incongruously, there was a claw-footed bathtub crouching against the right-hand wall. On the floor was a trio of big glass containers like those in bottled-water dispensers but these encased in wicker matting... the old-fashioned term was carboys. There were also a lot of small bottles, several of the "bitters" type used in the early 1900s, and at least two dozen flat pint flasks.

"Is this what I think it is?" said Spencer.

"Christopher Robin has grown up a little."

"But, why make gin?" asked Spencer.

"No distilling process with all its required apparatus and dangers of fire and explosion." Dodger indicated the carboys. "One only needs alcohol... preferably grain... water and flavorings." He picked up one of the bitters bottles. "Though the right formula for the latter continues to evade me." He presented one of the pint flasks. "But I think I'm getting closer."

Spencer took a sip and grimaced. "No offense, but not much."

"I'm hoping practice makes perfect." Dodger offered another flask. "Try this one."

"It's even worse!"

"That's an older batch, so I am improving."

"Ever tasted real gin?"

"It's hard to recapture the memory."

"I've got most of a bottle of Plymouth; I'll give it to you later," said Spencer. "But, I meant why make your own? Why not just go shoulder-tapping?"

"I'm afraid I don't know that expression," said Dodger, also taking a sip from the flask and making a nasty face.

Spencer explained, and Dodger smiled. "Most of this isn't for my consumption, though I do consume a lot."

"People actually pay for this?" said Spencer, taking another taste to verify the vileness.

"My shoulder gets tapped quite often."

"I would have thought the kids up here could afford Hennessy." Spencer had another thought. "How come you have a key? The real estate agent said it was lost."

"It's in the shed on a nail by the door any time you want it."

"I don't think my parents are gonna approve of Christopher Robin's gin mill in here."

"I assure you that won't be a problem," said Dodger.

"You're gonna take all this stuff out?"

"Consider it already done."

Spencer noticed a lantern atop a wooden Ivory Soap box, along with a stack of magazines. "Hey, you have some *Whiz Bangs*... and *Weird Tales*."

"I like Cap'n Billy's humor," said Dodger. "Especially since it's deemed improper for a stripling of my age."

"Do you mind if I read...?"

"Consider them yours."

"Thanks! ...These are in pretty good shape. ...You've got the 1924 issue of *Weird Tales* with H.P. Lovecraft's story, *Imprisoned With The Pharaohs*."

Dodger nodded. "Ghost-written by him for Harry Houdini. As I mentioned, Mr. Lovecraft is one of my favorite authors."

"Mine too," said Spencer. "My favorite story by him is *The Shadow Over Innsmouth*."

"Haven't read that one," said Dodger.

"It was published in 1936."

"I'm afraid I haven't read anything later than 1926."

"Wow, you missed a lot of good stuff."

"Perhaps you'll help me catch up on my reading?"

"Sure, I have tons of books."

"Swell," said Dodger. "And for now..." He bowed Spencer out, re-locked the door and led the way back down to the pond.

Seen in sunlight the sparkling water was almost crystal clear, yet though the bottom was visible sloping away ten feet from the shore, beyond was only a drop into darkness, as Dodger had warned last night.

"Must be really deep," said Spencer, kicking off his Keds and shedding his jeans along with Dodger.

"Formerly a quarry," said Dodger, stretching faun-like in a shaft of sun, though except for golden down in appropriate places, his body was childishly smooth. "From whence came the stone to build the mansion, the wall, spring house, and your cottage."

"So, if the mansion is made of stone, guess it hasn't fallen?"

"Why would you think it had fallen?"

Spencer pointed beyond the wall. "I can't see anything but trees."

"If you only look at trees you'll never see a forest." Dodger shaded his eyes like an Indian boy and raised his face to the heavens. "I see only sky, so the stars must have fallen."

"Point taken," said Spencer.

"Perhaps you'd like to visit?"

"The mansion? Sure," said Spencer. "...If it's not too far away. As you may have deduced, walking is not one of my *fortés*."

"Merely a ramble," said Dodger.

Spencer laughed. "There's no such thing as a ramble for me."

"You underestimate yourself."

"Is it spooky?" asked Spencer.

"Some, I'm sure, would find it so."

"I would like to see it, but maybe some other time."

"We have all the time in the universe."

Spencer looked back at the pond. "How deep is it?"

Dodger's smile faded. "Deeper than one might imagine when seen from the present perspective." He indicated the drop into shadow. "I've only been down there once: it's dark, cold, and lonely."

"Guess it would be," said Spencer. "And 'lonely' does go with dark and cold. At least I've never read of a place being 'light, warm, and lonely.'"

"Robinson Crusoe might disagree... at least until he found Friday." Dodger gazed skyward again. "But, looking for light, the faintest glimmer, no matter how hopeless it may seem, is better than resigning one's self to dwelling forever in darkness."

Spencer asked half playfully, "Even with friends in the dark?"

Dodger answered seriously, "There are no friends in the dark."

Spencer shivered despite the warmth and light in which he stood not alone. "Sounds like you almost drowned down there."

Dodger regarded the lightless place. "I almost did sink into darkness."

Spencer said to lighten-up, "I couldn't sink if I wanted to."

Dodger's smile re-lighted. "You have a very buoyant spirit."

"Are you religious?" asked Spencer.

"Religion is often an assurance that one will never find any light, because it seems safer to dwell in the dark, which though itself may be frightening, conceals what one may fear more to see, including their own naked soul."

"That's a deep thought," said Spencer.

"Perhaps too deep," said Dodger, "for the present time. Shall we just say all children are angels and therefore have no need of religion."

"Until they fall?"

"In order to fall," said Dodger, "one must be taught to forget they can fly." Then he laughed. "Please forgive my pontificating; I tend to run on if unrestrained."

"I like talking with you," said Spencer. "You're cool and smart at the same time."

Dodger laughed again. "I wasn't aware those terms were mutually incompatible. ...But, flying comes later in the program, and for the moment a swim will suffice."

As on the night before in the moonlight, the water was just the right temperature as they waded away from the shore, Spencer's vast belly and torus of middle becoming more buoyant the deeper he went and rising up to support him until, when he came to the drop into dark, he was suspended in liquid space, the balloons of his breasts engulfing his chins, and propelling himself with a languid back-stroke while Dodger glided along at his side. Reaching the center of the pond beneath blue sky above green trees with an almost underneath view of the trestle looming high overhead, he drifted quietly for a time as Dodger tread water beside him, then asked:

"Don't you ever get scared here alone? After what happened, I mean?"

Dodger shook his hair from his eyes, scattering sparkles like diamond drops. "I'm not alone, you're here."

"I meant when I wasn't."

"One should learn from the past, no matter how dark, to enlighten the future." Dodger looked down into darkness. "One cherishes warmth if one has been cold, and light if one has been lost in the dark. And..." He gripped Spencer's shoulder. "One realizes how precious is friendship after being alone."

Spencer spread his arms. "Climb aboard if you get tired, I'm buoy-ant enough for both of us."

"Indeed a gracious host," laughed Dodger, slipping aboard as if mounting a mattress – making Spencer think wryly of a scene in *The Graduate* -- and like a cat on Spencer's chest, seeming to slowly increase in weight as if bestowing all of himself by fully materializing. "There is nothing half so much worth doing as simply messing about in boats."

"Do you have a boat?"

"My father has a forty-foot schooner. I'm going to sail her around the world and have a lot of adventures."

"Alone?" asked Spencer.

"Adventures are always more fun with friends."

"That will be cool." Spencer laughed. "If Jim had been as fat as me, Huck wouldn't have needed a raft."

Dodger rested his chin on Spencer's shoulder as if dancing cheek-to-cheek in a watery horizontal plane. "Good friends adventuring into The Great Beyond."

Again, Spencer felt an androgynous intrigue, and maybe an urge to explore it, but told of his dream of becoming so fat he filled an enormous bowl with himself, transforming into a flying saucer and soaring away to the stars.

"When you remember how to fly you'll have no need of a saucer," said Dodger.

"You know a lot about metaphysics."

"All one needs to know about metaphysics can be found in *Alice In Wonderland*."

Spencer gazed into the infinite sky, knowing it filled with stars beyond number no matter they couldn't be presently seen, lulled by the soothing splash of water tumbling over the dam, hearing occasional calls of birds and other subtle sleepy sounds of an afternoon in a peaceful place of which, before yesterday, he'd only gotten glimpses in dreams inspired by what he'd read in books. "Kinda wish we could stay here forever."

"A bide a wee," said Dodger. "A rest a while to contemplate perhaps what came before. ...But, what about adventures?" He extended a phantom telescope as if to scan a distant horizon. "To launch a new ship, to hoist a new sail, and voyage into The Great Beyond. For-ever, don't you think, would get rather boring after a while unless one went messing about with it."

Spencer smiled. "Can we mess with our Water Rat lunch?"

CHAPTER TEN

"**W**hat the devil do you think you're doing!"

Spencer opened his eyes to an azure sky and the goldening light of late afternoon.

After drying themselves with the towel – which, Spencer had noted, seemed just as expensive as Dodger's spook sheet -- they had lounged bare on the tree-shaded shore and Dodger debuted the picnic basket, which did contain all of Water Rat's wonders, along with a marvelous myriad of others including a scrumptious caramel-cream pie.

"Wow!" Spencer had exclaimed in delight, not even knowing where to begin as Dodger continued conjuring comestibles out of the seemingly bottomless basket and spreading them on a checkered cloth of the type often pictured in picnic scenes, along with a jug of iced lemonade… which of course had been charmingly spiked with Dodger's juvenile version of gin. It was like a phantasmagoric feast in one of his erotic eating dreams, and Spencer wanted everything, but began with analytical portions of foods he'd never tried before – the cold tongue, which was quite appetizing despite its rather off-putting name; as were the pickled herring and the steak-and-mutton pie – then he'd attacked the crispy fried chicken, followed by tasty roast beef on rolls, honey-basted ham on same, cool, creamy potato salad, along with so many other good things he'd soon stopped trying to count them. Spencer had eaten some massive meals in his short sojourn on Planet Earth, but this was a banquet surpassing them all, an outright orgy of regal repasting, not only in the incredible volume of vivacious victuals consumed, but also in the palate pleasure of seemingly infinite textures and tastes, every one tantalizing his tongue into a rapturous raving for more; and finally after delicious desserts consisting not only of the pie but including shamelessly messy cream puffs, Napoleons and chocolate éclairs, all washed down with lemonade in tall glass tumblers tinkling with ice, he'd sprawled in absolute ecstasy, arms out-flung like a crucified kid and belly bulging in blubbery bliss, while the part of him deeply buried below was also engorged to the verge of explosion.

It seemed almost supernatural that Dodger had eaten – or so it seemed – every bit as much, his muscled middle as proudly tumescent as a carefree little kid's as he'd graciously offered the last cream puff, slipping it into Spencer's mouth where it vanished in untidy bites. Then he'd gently stroked Spencer's belly, sensually soothing away its strain, a forefinger circling its cavern of navel as if being drawn inexorably into the depths of a midnight maelstrom; and Spencer had managed to pant, even so stuffed he could barely breathe, "Oh, wow, don't do that or I'll… you know."

Dodger had smiled. "Wouldn't that be a perfect climax to a perfectly pleasurable dream?"

Spencer had laughed, though the squiggles it caused surrounding himself were almost enough to set off a surge. "I think I had this dream last night."

Dodger had leaned over Spencer's chest, pert pecs sinking in soft hemispheres, and met Spencer's lips with his own.

"Wow!" Spencer had sighed, for lack of a more expressive expression, when Dodger transformed the boyish buss into something defying a known definition… at least in Spencer's abridged dictionary. Then, silly as it had sounded – or maybe not – Spencer had said, "You *do* know I'm a boy?"

"That has been obvious to me ever since you opened the shutters."

More childishly than anything else -- Spencer had thought of cherubs at play unabashedly unaware of any TRESSPASSERS WILL taboos -- Dodger had gently burrowed a hand beneath Spencer's over-rolling bulk until a questing fingertip resolved any possible doubt.

It took every bit of Spencer's will to resist what Dodger's

innocent touch came close to a heartbeat of unleashing; and he wondered why he did, when it *would* have been the perfect climax to a perfectly pleasurable dream.

...But, would he become someone else, he'd wondered, not the boy he'd been before, if he gave in to this temptation, which seemed like the final and ultimate in an increasingly sensual series. He'd thought of things he'd found on the Web, usually presented as porn, of older boys "turning out" younger ones, as if there was always an alternate self — better, worse, or maybe just different — existing some-where in the cosmos of psyche. Or, perhaps in fairytale context, awaiting a kiss from a prince to awaken... and Dodger had given him one. He'd remembered Dodger's remark about children being angels and having to be taught how to fall — presumably by one who had fallen -- reminding him of something he'd read about angels being androgynous though mostly portrayed as physically male.

Then, perhaps in ambivalent effort to either prevent or prolong a plunge, Spencer had asked, "Do you like me 'cause I'm fat?"

"Friends come in all shapes, colors and sizes." Dodger had dis-interred his hand without making the most miniscule of moves, which would have -- at least in the physical sense -- denied Spencer of free will.

"Guess they do," Spencer had panted. "But... I'm not sure if it's... I don't know... maybe *necessary* to say... I've never had a white friend."

Dodger had replied, "It *shouldn't* have to be said. And rest assured there are times and places when it never was and never will be." Then he'd smiled and regarded Spencer as if making a memory. "But, one doesn't like a book, do they, merely because of a hand-some cover?"

"Garsh," Spencer said in a goofy voice. "He done called me hand-some."

"As any enlightened spirit would." Then Dodger had raised his face to the sky. "The pleasures of earthy existence are relatively fleeting and few, and so... at least in my grubby opinion... should be cherished to their fullest in the short time allotted."

"I think I agree with that," Spencer had said after a moment. "But maybe some shouldn't happen too fast or else you can't fully appreciate them."

"Did I take a liberty?" Dodger had asked, in genuine juvenile innocence.

"It was just... unexpected." Then, sounding silly, Spencer had added, "There's a lot more to it than that."

Dodger had smiled again. "There's a lot more to everything than only five physical senses perceive." Then he'd lain down beside Spencer, head on crossed arms, gazing up at the sky. "But, like my running-on about things, I tend to get wild if unrestrained... my father calls me his *enfant sauvage*."

Spencer had finally found himself cooling, perhaps slipping back from the edge of a fall -- though wasn't sure he wanted to — and wondered why denying himself a purely physical pleasure should seem to symbolize anything. In fact, it seemed rather absurd that loving himself should be natural but allowing another to share that love was supposed to mean something else. ...Or maybe supposed to mean something else if that someone else was a boy. For a moment he'd pictured Huck Finn surprising a prudish Tom Sawyer; but the present time for this adventure seemed to have become the past.

"So, you're not homeless," he'd said, now just enjoying the pleasure of fullness along with someone to talk with. "Sounds like your father loves you; and that food didn't come from Grocery Outlet, so I assume you're rich."

Dodger had shrugged, still regarding the sky. "I have everything anyone can have as soon as they realize they can have it." He'd turned to Spencer and smiled once more. "And therefore also realize it's not at all what they wanted."

*   *   *

That smile, seeing to fade away like the Cheshire Cat's, was the last thing Spencer remembered before waking up hearing a rancorous voice he found he liked not at all. Still feeling almost helplessly stuffed, he managed to heave himself onto his elbows and scan the dell below.

The first thing he saw was Dodger, still *enfant sauvage* naked, his body shiny with sweat in the sun, and armed with the fearsome Grim Reaper scythe with which he was expertly reaping ferns, presumably for the garden. He must have polished and sharpened the blade, because it gleamed a deadly blue-white as it smoothly swathed mass herbicide.

"I said," the unknown voice repeated... a man's, and sounding twice as much not likeable at all. "What the devil do you think you're doing?"

Dodger neither paused nor even deigned to turn his head. "I know precisely what I'm doing, and the devil has nothing to do with it."

"That's work for the boy!"

"What would you know about work?" replied Dodger, slashing another swath of ferns.

Spencer spotted the source of the voice, a rather cadaverous-looking man with a ghoulish gaunt face and moldy complexion, possibly middle forties of age and dressed in a formally old-fashioned style. Though his clothes didn't date that far in the past, Spencer thought of Mr. Murdstone... whom he'd tagged Mr. *Merde*-stone after making his churlish acquaintance in print.

Apparently he'd been wrong in assuming the lock was rusted shut, because the gate in the wall stood open, and the man was darkly framed in shadow, though technically not trespassing since he hadn't come out in the light. "The boy," Spencer found with surprise, referred to no other than himself, as the man's out-flung arm and long bony finger indisputably indicated. For a moment he felt naked, and not in the physical sense, but then a flash of anger overrode uncertainty: it seemed submissive to just sit there as if being accused of something nasty by someone who seemed the embodiment of everything nasty that ever was. For once in his life he regretted not being able to leap to his feet, but his struggle to rise was ignored by the man, who turned again to Dodger.

"Don't think I don't suspect," he said in a snidely sinister tone, "all your low and wicked ways. Of which your father should be informed but... for whose sake entirely... I have *so far* chosen not to."

Dodger cleared a last clump of ferns to stand in a neat square of future garden and finally face the malevolent man. The scythe, held upright at his side, was considerably taller than he, and its glittering six-foot blade curved simultaneously halo-like and menacingly overhead. "And I more than suspect your own, which my father, I am sure, will doubtless soon discern."

"You dare threaten me?" roared the man.

"Unlike you," replied Dodger, and impertinently spreading his arms, "I have no need to hide anything."

For a moment the man appeared on the verge of maybe spontaneously combusting, but managed to contain himself and yanked a big gold watch from his vest. "Supper will be at eight; and dress... for a change... appropriately. We are entertaining the Havens and will be discussing future investments in the streetcar system... of which, of course, you'll have no interest. Young Albert will be present, and you might, at least, learn something from him about being a manly man of your station."

"That experience," Dodger returned, "will be neither entertaining nor in the slightest enlightening."

Spencer, meantime, had descended the slope below the dam and was lumbering down the path through ferns. He'd considered donning his jeans, at least as a token formality, but Dodger obviously didn't need raiment to face what seemed a nemesis. Spencer had planned to confront the man, even if for nothing more than being called a boy -- which, though he certainly was, had not, of course, been meant as a reference to his age or sex – but the man, after flushing at Dodger's retorts -- at least as much as possible considering his rancid tone -- spun on a heel and stalked away, slamming the gate behind him, its iron clank stilling the bird-song a moment and echoing over the water music.

Spencer reached the foot-bridge and peered across to the gate, but the man had vanished into the shadows of foliage and trees beyond the wall.

"Who was *that*?" he asked, as Dodger, casually toting the scythe over a shoulder, joined him.

Dodger chuckled. "My wicked uncle Ebenezer."

"Scrooge or Balfour?"

"Possessed of the worst qualities of both, but, unlike Scrooge, unredeemable."

"Thought you lived with your dad?"

"My father's greatest fault," said Dodger, "is being too kind to the unkind who don't deserve any kindness." He glanced to the iron-barred gateway. "I often find it hard to believe that *he* and my father share the same source… he has been, no offense, the black sheep of our family, squandering his share of wealth on various reckless investments and fraudulent money-changing schemes, which not only left him penniless but would have led to imprisonment had not my father intervened. He is now… unfortunately… an occupant of our domicile, having nowhere of his own to dwell, and growing ever more hateful like something continually licking its wounds while refusing the fact they were self-inflicted, perceiving himself ill-used by life, the universe and everything." Dodger chuckled again. "And of course he is direfully jealous that I inherit my father's estate, although he does receive a share, which is more, in my opinion, than he rightfully deserves."

Spencer also glanced to the gate. "Think he spies on you? Like, for something to use against you so your dad won't love you anymore?"

"No doubt of him spying," Dodger replied. "As you just observed. But I'm sure my father is cognizant of most of my 'low and wicked ways.' And, having once been a boy himself whom Mr. Holmes might have enlisted as a Baker Street Irregular, but who worked his way to worldly success though all the grime of his urchin origins, I'm confident of his understanding any of which he is still unaware."

"I take it *you're* aware," said Spencer, "of what David Balfour's wicked uncle tried to do to him?"

"I do watch my step in dark places."

Spencer again regarded the gate. "Is that like a shortcut to where you live?"

"Apparently it was for my uncle."

Spencer indicated the pond. "Think he saw us up there?"

"Were we doing anything low and wicked?"

"Nah," said Spencer, smiling. "And thanks for reaping my mom's garden." He gingerly touched the scythe blade, its gleaming edge as sharp as a razor. "I couldn't have done it with that."

"Just takes a little practice," said Dodger, smoothly decapitating a thistle with a hissing swing. "I can teach you in no time... here..."

Putting the scythe in Spencer's hands and showing him the proper grip, Dodger positioned himself behind, and like a lesson in grisly golf, guided him through a series of swings that cleared a convenient path to the bridge. "Speaking of time," he said, as Spencer grew more proficient, "would you like to see a movie tonight?"

"Ride a train into town?" puffed Spencer, at last relinquishing the blade.

"I could have the chauffeur drive us, but that wouldn't be as fun."

"Sure," said Spencer. "...But, didn't your uncle say you had to be at dinner?"

"That won't be a problem. Expect me at the stroke of seven." Dodger took Spencer's shoulder and ushered him to the cottage. "I'll boost you back through your window."

"That's okay, I'll go in the door."

"Windows, don't you think, are more fun? Suggesting adventures and naughtiness of which one's parents may not approve?"

Spencer considered that: while his parents would doubtless approve of him seeing a movie with a new friend – and, being racially realistic, a friend who was also white and rich would surely assure their approval -- they probably would at least inquire about the means of transportation, which left the choices of telling a lie or slipping naughtily out on the sly.

"Windows are more fun," he agreed.

Standing the scythe against the wall, Dodger hoisted Spencer, stuffing him gently through the window and tumbling him onto the bed.

"Want to come in?" asked Spencer, after rearranging himself. "I got all my books on the shelves, and we could start catching you up on your reading."

"I have a few chores to perform," said Dodger, shouldering the scythe again, his boy-scent strong in the afternoon heat mingled with those of tobacco and gin along with the woodsy fragrance of ferns. "Despite what may seem like a dissolute, debauched, dissipated or decadent air, I... unlike my uncle... am required to earn my exist-ence."

"I deduced that," said Spencer. "How would a spoiled rich kid know how to swing that thing like you. ...So, see you tonight?"

"I left you a note in case you forget."

Spencer laughed. "The note in the box? That has to be a hundred years old."

Dodger looked thoughtful. "Sometimes I forget."

"Forget what?" asked Spencer.

"Oh," said Dodger carelessly, "time can get a bit muddled some-times if one goes messing about with it. ...But for now, *à la prochaine.*" He turned around and walked away along the brook toward the pond.

Taking his phone off the nightstand, Spencer checked the time, finding, despite an eventful and seemingly timeless afternoon, it was only nearing five o'clock. He'd accomplished all his chores for the day – with Dodger's help, of course – and had earned another nap. Then he'd indulge in the dinner his mom had left in the ice box. He rolled lazily onto his back and relaxed to the soothing song of the brook, but then another thought came to mind and he avalanched to his knees on the floor to pull the box from under the bed and examine the note

See you tonight

Settling into the chair at his desk, he faced the boy in the looking-glass, who had also seated himself in rolly-poly majesty. "At first glance, as we see, Wiggins, a seemingly simple request... or perhaps a confirmation... for or of a rendezvous, obviously taking place in an evening; but you know my methods, so what more can we glean from it?"

He held it up to the window light, Wiggins doing the same. "It is, we observe, expensive notepaper, not foolscap or torn from a pad, and watermarked with an impressive design, possibly a family crest, though now all but illegible to the naked eye. The message has faded to sepia, indicating iron-gall ink of the type written with in Victorian times, though was still in extensive use well into the twentieth century... viable ballpoint pens not becoming available until the late 1930s. The ink has flowed smoothly and evenly, suggesting superior quality, and the nib hasn't spluttered or skipped, which is much more probable with a proletarian pen. The writing, though gracefully elegant, indicative of a practiced hand groomed in proper penmanship... and therefore presumably educated above a common level... is also rather boyishly bold and, though no longer childish, has not yet matured to a more restrained and stolidly consistent style one would expect in adulthood, so we may infer adolescence. And, despite being a casual note likely regarded as simply a scribble by its teenage author, is neatly centered on the page, evincing at least an orderly mind, if not above-average intelligence."

Wiggins seemed to acquiesce, and Spencer went on:

"No doubt there are other minutiae which more modern and scientific examination would reveal; but may I assume we are in agreement that, despite Dodger's curious remark... and in our brief acquaintance we have found him Puckishly enigmatic when something seems to amuse him... this note was almost certainly written in 1926, consistent with the magazine dates?"

Wiggins, not surprisingly, nodded.

Spencer tossed the note on the desk and steepled his fingers over his chest. "Now that, within the parameters of our admittedly limited means, we are satisfied that Dodger... despite his *surely* jesting remark... could not have written the note, perhaps we may delve a bit deeper into what it seems to reveal about its actual author and why he thought it necessary to place it in the box?"

Wiggins looked attentive.

"A one-pipe problem," said Spencer, taking a Fatima from the open pack in the box, but then ejaculating, "damn," because his lighter was in his jeans, which were still up at the pond.

"*Excusez-moi.*" Relieving the chair of his presence, he waddled into the kitchen for the box of Radium Silent Matches then re-settled at his desk and lit the cigarette. Waiting until Wiggins reflectively also arranged himself, he exhaled a ghost and continued:

"We, as I'm sure you recall, made some speculations when first opening the box yesterday afternoon; at least one of which we have found to be wrong… that the box had not been opened since 1926." He fingered the cherub necklace, Wiggins doing likewise. "Because Dodger stated last night he'd left this jewelry in the box, which explains how he knew about the note."

He glanced to the pond-facing window, its light dimming now as evening approached and shadows crept into the dell. "I confess a curiosity as to why he placed it there, in hope… as he said… I would find it. Why hope instead of certainty? If he wanted to give it to me, perhaps as a welcoming gift, why not after he'd scared me to death… figuratively speaking… with that silly sheet? But, of course, I can always ask him."

Wiggins looked a duh.

Spencer produced another spirit. "But, shall we return to the past? We have concluded from the note that its writer was teenage and most likely male, well-educated as well as intelligent… the latter not always synonymous with an education… and from a wealthy family prestigious enough to posses its own crest. To indulge in more speculation, and considering the time, it seems rather improbable this boy would have been anything but white, and probably in the genetic realm of Anglo-Saxon or Celtic. …Would you not also presume?"

Wiggins nodded.

"So now," continued Spencer, after freeing another phantom, "shall we consider the circumstances surrounding the missive in question? As we hypothesized yesterday, the box being concealed in the shed, secured with a sturdy padlock, and containing mainly things of naughty-boyish nature, would suggest it belonged to the grounds-keeper's son. This theory seems further reinforced by our finding a key to the box in this room, either hidden intentionally, or maybe accidentally dropped in the type of sneaker a boy would have worn in the 1920s. And, because of the size of the sneak, it seems safe to assume he was also a teen. That he had a trusted friend seems clear since that friend had a key to the box... how else could the friend have left the note? And, if assuming the cigarettes... and maybe the gin and magazines... were gifts to the grounds-keeper's son, his friend must have had more money to spend on naughty luxuries. It seems incidental to add that he was a *good* friend, sharing his wealth."

Spencer paused to produce another spirit. "Proceeding along that line of deduction, since they seemingly had to communicate through secreted notes and arrange their rendezvous at night, it still seems very probable... as we conjectured yesterday... their friendship was, if not forbidden, at least parentally frowned-upon, most likely by the wealthy family. ...Seems elementary, does it not?"

Once more Wiggins seemed to agree.

"Of course," Spencer added modestly, "I have been known to make mistakes." He snuffed his cigarette and flipped the stub out the window, then cocked his head, almost sure in an eye-corner glimpse he'd seen Wiggins take a last puff on *his* smoke before flipping it out. "You didn't just do what I thought you did?"

Wiggins looked quizzical... which of course was how Spencer was looking. But then both shrugged.

"Anyway," Spencer went on, "what else may we infer from logical progression of thought, except that friendship may have been..." He raised a forefinger into the air. "I dare to go further... most *likely* had been, between a son of Gilbert Shade and a son of the grounds-keeper?"

Spencer didn't expect applause, but Wiggins looked impressed.

"It seems plausible," Spencer added, "that such a friendship during those times might have been forbidden because of social status." He glanced at his laptop. "No doubt we could Google to ascertain if Gilbert Shade had progeny... though, according to Linda Lancaster, he was the last of the Shades. But we don't have Internet access. ...However..." He picked up his phone.

Which began to ring.

He checked the number. "Hi, dad."

"Still haven't seen any ghosts?"

"Did you expect me to?"

"Must be a little spooky up there."

"Not to the point of seeing them; and I'm kinda liking the peace and quiet as opposed to thug-rap and gunshots." Spencer thought about mentioning Dodger, but that might have led to questions he wasn't informed enough to answer. "I performed all the chores requested of me."

"Good man," said his dad. "I'm impressed."

"Remember that at Christmas. Guess you're working overtime?"

"Yes, but your mom should be home by midnight."

"I'll leave a lamp in the window again."

"You could run the generator; must be spooky after dark with only kerosene lights."

Spencer laughed. "You seem more concerned about ghosts than I am."

"I wasn't as brave at your age about things that might have gone bump in the night."

"Oh, yeah, the old funeral parlor."

"Explore the haunted mansion yet?"

"...Why would you think I would?"

"I detect a channeling of Holmes."

"Guess I eventually will," said Spencer, recalling Dodger's invitation. "When I have *time* for adventures... hint."

"Being benevolent masters, your mom and I only work you eighteen hours a day."

Spencer thought of tonight's adventure; would he be back by midnight? Best to play it safe. "Despite your very humane treatment, I am a bit tired and will retire early, so I probably won't be up to greet mom."

"Okay, son, pleasant dreams."

"Bye, dad."

The daylight continued to fade, shadows deepening in the dell and stealthily invading the cottage as Spencer went into the kitchen to see what his mom had left him for supper... a massive plate of angel-hair pasta smothered with creamy mushroom sauce and loaded with big beefy meatballs. Also a salad with Caesar dressing, along with Tiramisu for dessert. He glanced at the microwave oven his mother had set near the sink and the kitchen's only electric plug, and thought about the generator; but why disturb the evening peace just to warm up dinner?

He opened the stove's firebox door; and it didn't take a PhD to start a blaze with yesterday's *Tribune* and kindling split with a hatchet, to which he added larger wood as it flared to life, soon crackling cheerfully and beginning to roar up the flue. He adjusted the damper, then paused to consider how he'd known how... probably read it somewhere. He placed the plate on the oven rack, lit the lamp on the table as daylight continued to wane, poured a tumbler of milk and sat down to the salad. By the time he'd consumed the tasty greens, the pasta plate was perfectly warmed and, using his mom's oven mitts, he presented it to the table, added a blizzard of Parmesan cheese, and seated himself for feasting.

Dusk was settling in by the time he finished dessert, quaffed the last of the milk and climaxed with a blasted burp. Through the doorway to his room he could see the looking-glass boy also in a soft pool of light and blissfully overflowing a chair in blubbery abundance. That reminded him of their speculations about the grounds-keeper's son and his possible friendship with a youthful Shade... which resurrected the question of *had* there been a younger Shade? Dodger might have known -- he seemed well-acquainted with the past and history of the Shade estate, maybe from reading the old newspapers and/or exploring the derelict mansion – but there was an Oakland wiki simple to navigate by phone. Taking the lamp, he returned to his desk and powered up his phone.

"I'm sure Mr. Holmes would have found this a useful detection device," he said to the looking-glass boy.

"Ah, here we are: Gilbert Grosvenor Shade... Damn, the battery's low again! ...Maybe time to skim. ...1875 to 1926... only fifty-one when he died. ...Son of English emigrants, Garrett and Gwendolyn Shade, who settled in Oakland... No time for ancient history. ...Gilbert Shade, early years... newspaper boy at eight... went to

85

sea at age thirteen on cargo steamer, *S.S. Robin*... something about salvage rights to another ship found abandoned, and shares to *Robin's* crew... apparently how he got money. ...Prudent investments in Oakland shipbuilding... logical, but no time for that. ...Married Dorothy Laura Boyer, of the coal and ice Boyers, in June of 1910. ...Here we are! *Son*, Gavin Garrett Shade, born in 1911. ... Damn! Battery's going! ...Dorothy Shade died in the 1919 Oakland flu epidemic. ...Wait! ...Gavin Shade *drowned* in an accident in 1926! ...Shit! Battery's dead!"

He lay the phone on the desk and picked up the time-faded note.

See you tonight

"This could have been the last thing Gavin Shade ever wrote. And we know his father was the last of the Shades. ...Who died the same year as his son. ...Was it because he'd lost his son? People did that in those days... dying of grief it was called."

The looking-glass boy looked sad.

Spencer looked out the window, where the pond glimmered like polished gunmetal under the darkening sky. "Gavin Shade drowned," he repeated, and for a second he shivered. "Think it could have been in the pond?"

Wiggins, of course, didn't reply, though sadly continued to gaze at the pond.

"Dodger might know," said Spencer. "But that could explain why the caretakers either saw Gavin Shade's ghost, or maybe only thought they did because they expected to. ...Power of suggestion, you know?"

Wiggins looked reflective.

"Sad, but it fits our theory," said Spencer, "about the boys being friends... rich Gavin Shade and his grounds-keeper's son. A friendship of which Gavin's father may have not approved. ...Guess he might have become a snob despite his own poor beginnings. ...And I think we may also assume this window was used as a portal for the boys' nocturnal adventures. ...Which would explain, if we grant

Gavin's ghost, why it might be the only window where it would appear... Gavin coming to meet his friend. And so the shutters were nailed shut. ...And I think we may assume, unless he's well over a hundred years old, Gavin's friend would be dead by now; and maybe they finally hooked up again in The Great Beyond." He laughed. "Which might explain why the only 'ghost' still haunting this place was Dodger in that sheet."

Wiggins looked amused.

"Speaking of whom," said Spencer, "It must be a little after six, so we better get dressed for adventure."

CHAPTER ELEVEN

"**T**he game is afoot."

Spencer, again in the chair at his desk but clad in his newest pair of jeans, a white T-shirt and the ancient Keds, opened his eyes to dusky twilight and saw a pale shape at the window seemingly materializing out of a silvery mist. "Sorry, Dodger," he yawned. "Didn't mean to fall asleep, but I ate a lot for supper and it usually has that effect."

Dodger smiled. "Little Nemo In Slumberland. But I hope you'll be hungry after the movie; I planned on taking us to dine."

"I can always manage to eat," said Spencer, blinking his eyes for a moment and noting there really was a mist settling into the dell. He also saw with puzzlement that Dodger was still just in jeans.

As if deducing his thoughts, Dodger said, "I have some clothes in the spring house appropriate to the occasion."

"I'll leave this for mom," said Spencer, unloading himself from the chair, belly spilling out of his shirt like a typical cartoonish fat kid's, and taking the lamp off the desk. "Be back in a minute."

"We have plenty of time," said Dodger. "The movie doesn't start until eight."

Spencer went to the living room and set the lamp in the window, then returned and arranged his bedding into a bulky slumberous shape. "In case we're not back before midnight," he explained to Dodger, who stood outside with chin in hands and elbows on the window sill. "I told dad I wouldn't be up, but mom might look in on me."

"We could return before we left, but that wouldn't be as much fun as a bit of naughty deception," said Dodger.

"...Huh?" said Spencer, then laughed. "Sometimes I don't understand what you say."

"I understand what I say," said Dodger, "but of course I've heard it before. ...Here are the jeans you left at the pond," he added, tossing them in neatly folded.

"Thanks, I need my lighter." Spencer pocketed his Zippo, then took a paper bag off the desk.

"What have you there?" asked Dodger.

"A surprise for you," said Spencer, squiggling out through the window with Dodger providing embracing assistance.

Dodger retained his hug, suspending Spencer in space chest to chest. "The best surprise you've given me was seeing you open these shutters."

Spencer's arms went around Dodger, also prolonging the hug. "Thanks, but you've been a cool surprise. You're the first physical friend I've had since I was eleven."

Dodger cocked his head. "I can't imagine why; you're smart, cool, and fun to be with."

"I assume it's my physical form that puts a lot of people off."

"Only those who think physical form is anything more than transitory... and, I assure you, very brief in the natural order of things."

"I'm sure you understand that."

"Have your other friends been imaginary like many of mine in the past?"

"Just when I was little, now they're mostly in cyber-space."

"Sounds a bit spooky," said Dodger. "Like disembodied spirits in some vast indiscernible void calling to each other but never able to touch."

Spencer held the hug a bit longer. "Being able to touch someone is cool."

Dodger settled Spencer to earth. "There are deeper ways to touch, but..." He smiled. "For the moment we're just two grubby things messing about on a speck of dust."

"Ever read Aleister Crowley?"

Dodger laughed. "One would learn more about life, the universe and everything from The Yellow Kid."

Spencer looked around in the mist, its slowly swirling shroud of gray suggesting an indiscernible void. There was also a humid scent in the air that often foretold of rain. "Maybe I should bring my coat… if I can still get into it; haven't worn it since last winter."

"I have one that will fit you," said Dodger. "Also appropriate to our adventure."

He led the way to the dam and assisted Spencer up to the spring house, then took the key from a pocket, unlocked the lock, pushed the door open and disappeared into darkness. There came the rasp of wooden match, a momentary yellow flare, and the screech of a lantern's chimney lifted, then golden light infused the void and Spencer joined Dodger inside, seeing everything the same as earlier that day -- the bathtub, the bottles, the alcohol carboys -- though now there was also a Gladstone bag, of scuffed brown leather and rather battered.

Setting the lantern on the soap box and pocketing a little box of Radium Silent Matches, Dodger unbuckled the bag, taking out a pair of Keds in slightly better condition than those on Spencer's feet, along with socks and the kind of white shirt Spencer associated with funerals… since the last time he'd worn one was when he'd been ten at his grandfather's service. Dodger donned the sneaks and shirt, along with a nondescript rat-colored coat, and added a floppy over-size cap atop his shaggy mane, which made him look like a scruffy newsboy in a 1920s movie. Then he delved into the bag again and presented Spencer a brown canvas coat like a workman would wear, along with a somewhat shabby black derby.

Spencer laughed. "Trick-or-treat is still two weeks away. Or is it some kind of Halloween movie?"

"That will be my surprise for you."

Spencer donned the derby and coat, the latter not only fitting his bulk but actually a little too large although it couldn't be buttoned, and studied his reflection in the water basin. There was a rippling distortion caused by the trickling pipe, which made him resemble the much fatter boy in the cherub mirror. "I look like a super-size Stymie in *The Little Rascals*."

"Hal Roach's rascals?" said Dodger. "In the *Our Gang* films? I can't recall a Stymie, but I haven't seen them all."

"Here's your surprise," said Spencer, taking bottles out of his bag. "Plymouth gin... real gin... and Angostura bitters. You use that to make pink gin, but it doesn't taste like strawberries."

Dodger uncapped the gin, took a sip and smacked his lips. "That's the oyster's earrings!" He leaned back and tilted the bottle.

"Woah!" said Spencer, grabbing his arm. "Don't drink it all, I had an idea."

"I'm your donkey," said Dodger, making Candlewick ears.

"What if we added a little of that to the... concoction... you made?"

"Swell!" said Dodger. "And maybe a dash of that pink stuff, too. That'll start a panic! ...I was planning on doing some business after our evening's entertainment. ...Would you mind?"

"Not at all," said Spencer. "Let's try this." He picked up one of the pint bottles, took a swallow and made a face. "That's for comparison."

"Now we're on the trolley," said Dodger, adding a dollop of Plymouth. "After you, Alphonse."

Spencer took another taste. "That's a *little* more like it." He passed the bottle back.

"A vast improvement, I'd say." Dodger added a few drops of bitters. "How about now?"

Spencer sipped. "It wouldn't fool anybody who knows how gin is supposed to taste, but if people have been buying your stuff..."

"Ain't no flies on me," said Dodger. "Let's hokus-pokus the rest of the batch."

The boys got busy, first dispatching a swallow from each of the many bottles, then adding a bit of the Plymouth and bitters, followed by another sip to be sure the taste was consistent; and Spencer was a little buzzed by the time they finished. Dodger packed the bottles into the Gladstone, except for one he stashed in his coat, then drew a big silver watch from a pocket like The White Rabbit consulting the time. "We have a train to catch."

It was now full night outside, though the mist-shrouded sky

above the trees was faintly glowing a slight shade of pale from the rising moon. Dodger, toting the Gladstone, took Spencer's arm to steady him as they went down to the shore of the pond, then led the way to the narrow gully through which the brook gurgled and splashed. Spencer's eyes had adjusted to the softly spectral light, and he saw a torturous-looking trail slanting steeply skyward.

"I can't get up there," he said. "Guess I'm too fat for adventures."

"Adventurers, like their adventures," said Dodger, "come in infinite sizes, and I'm sure this one will fit just right." He knelt. "Climb on my back."

"I know you're strong," said Spencer. "But..."

"Smell isn't everything."

"Seriously."

"Would you doubt Peter Pan if he said you could fly?"

"He had fairy dust."

"And we have coffin varnish." Dodger pulled out the bottle, offered it to Spencer, then also took a swallow. "All aboard."

Still doubtful, Spencer mounted Dodger as he'd done in his younger and lighter years for pony rides with his dad; and though it seemed almost impossible, Dodger rose, picked up the bag and began ascending the path, which switch-backed through foliage along the brook now mostly a series of small waterfalls. Spencer held on tight as they climbed, seeing the pond slowly receding into misty distance below; and though puffing a little and more aromatic, Dodger at last reached the top of the trail where railroad tracks crossed the trestle.

Spencer slid off and hoisted his jeans, which had abandoned his bottom during the arduous climb. The mist was thicker up here, but the moon rising over the slopes above provided a little more light, and he regarded the rails, which, polished from the wheels of trains, glimmered beneath a tunnel of trees and curved around a hillside to the right, while running across the trestle and burrowing under more trees on the left. Overhead were wires on poles. Dodger set the bag on the ground and offered the flask again, both boys taking liberal draughts; then came the *wooo* of a distant whistle.

"Right on time," said Dodger, consulting his watch again. "Just coming out of the Redwood Tunnel."

Spencer gazed up the tracks. "I assume the train won't stop for us and, in case you haven't deduced it already, running isn't one my things."

Dodger picked up the bag. "It's downgrade with curves all the way into town, so the trains don't go very fast, and they slow even more for the trestle. I'll get you aboard like a Pullman porter given a two-dollar tip."

Spencer laughed. "You could make me believe I could fly."

"That, as I said this afternoon, comes later in the program." Dodger cocked his head as there came another, nearer, *wooo*, and a faint rumble sounded around the curve. He knelt beside the tracks. "Mount your trusty steed, Sir Knight."

The oncoming rumble grew louder, and now came a distant click-clacking of wheels. Then a ghostly blue-white glow began to flicker through the trees and fluoresce the mist. Then there were squeals of brakes applied and the hum of a huge electric motor. The sounds increased in volume, the overheard wires began to thrum, and then the tracks were flooded with light as a train slowly rounded the curve.

Spencer's eyes were dazzled and he couldn't see many details, the engine only a mammoth black shape behind the Cyclops glare of its light, and there were faint blue sparks above where a skeletal structure contacted the wires. The brakes continued to squeal as the locomotive rumbled past and started over the trestle, and there were scents of hot asbestos from the clamping shoes, while dimly discerned on the engine's side were old-fashioned letters in white:

OAKLAND ANTIOCH & EASTERN RAILWAY

There followed a line of freight cars -- flats, tankers several gondolas -- click-clacking by at a walking pace, including an empty boxcar with an open door; and Dodger heaved Spencer in though its doorway like loading rolly-poly cargo, then tossed in the bag and scrambled aboard, turning to dangle his legs outside. Spencer joined him a moment later as they crossed the trestle, catching a glimpse through swirling mist of the dimly glimmering pond far below.

Dodger offered the flask, and pulled a Fatima pack from his shirt. "Let the midnight special shine her light on me," he sang in his choir-boy voice, then added, "Or, I should say, us."

"Credence Clearwater?" asked Spencer, passing back the bottle and accepting a cigarette as the train rumbled downward under the trees snaking its squealy way around curves.

"Haven't heard of him," said Dodger, firing a match. "But the song was written by Howard Odum in 1905." He exhaled a ghost. "Before my time, of course."

Spencer also puffed out a spirit and watched the landscape passing by, the trees thinning out as they reached lower ground, the boxcar rocking over the rails as the train continued its slow descent with frequent applications of brakes. "Thought a lot of people lived in these hills," said Spencer, scanning the nighted slopes. "But I don't see very many lights."

Dodger's face looked thoughtful in the ruby glow of his cigarette ember. "Perhaps a different perspective?"

"Yeah," said Spencer. "I've been looking up at these hills all my life, but now I'm looking down."

Dodger offered the bottle again and Spencer took another sip. He'd been drinking, mostly beer, with and without parental consent since the age of eight, and recognized his current state as that slightly out-of-body sensation of seeing the world with a careless detachment where distant details were indistinct and only the closest things were clear.

The mist appeared to be getting denser, swirling in through the doorway and further dimming distant sights, though he began to see more lights as the train seemed to enter an urban scene at a now sedately pedestrian pace, the rails running down a concrete street lined with buildings, shops and stores. He wasn't sure whether his vision was hazed by the mist or alcohol – most likely a combination of both -- but the lights all around seemed different somehow, oxymoronically brighter yet dimmer than any he'd seen before in the city. There were a few colored neon signs, but...

He looked up at a street lamp as they passed and saw it was an incandescent, a brightly-burning filament bulb, as were most of the lights in the buildings. There were no softer shades of fluorescents in any storefront or window. Also oxymoronic were the figures of people on the sidewalks; normal enough at a glance, if seemingly a bit out of focus, yet also somehow different, possibly in modes of clothing; and everyone – men, women and kids -- wearing some kind of hat... though maybe just dressed for the weather. He noticed a street sign, SHAFTER AVENUE, which they were rolling down.

Dodger lay a hand on his shoulder. "You're looking a little curious, if I may presume."

"Never been in this part of Oakland. ...Oh, this must be Old Oakland, huh? The part of the city they kept preserved?"

"That's a perspective," said Dodger.

"This is cool!" Spencer scanned around. "Is that a Model-T?"

"1920 Auburn. And that truck is a '21 Reo Speedwagon."

"And the hearse in front of that funeral parlor?"

"1919 Buick."

"I heard about this place but I've never been here before. ...Is this the surprise you were talking about?"

"The universe is full of surprises." Dodger leaned out and looked down the street. "Hang on to your hat and jump."

Spencer laughed. "Can I fly yet?"

"A small leap will suffice at this time."

Taking the bag, Dodger slid out and landed lightly on the pavement, Spencer ungracefully following and alighting a light-year from lightly. He stumbled, but Dodger grabbed his arm to keep him on his feet. Spencer recovered and looked around as the rest of the train went rumbling past tailed by a caboose with a ruby rear light, and saw they were on a corner of Shafter and College Avenues. An overcoated middle-aged woman topped with a floppy *faux*-flowered hat and retaining a big shaggy dog on a leash seemed to have seen their arrival; and Dodger tipped his cap to her, offering a "Good evening, ma'am," while Spencer doffed his derby as seemed appropriate.

The woman shook her head but smiled. "Boys will be boys."

She continued on her way after her dog had anointed a lamp

post, and Spencer donned his hat. "Didn't know it went this deep...
like some sort of theme park."

"You seem in comfortable character," said Dodger.

"'When in Rome.'"

"Indeed, Antony." Dodger glanced up Collage, which like Shafter
had rails in the middle, and Spencer saw a streetcar emerging from
the mist, the classic kind he'd seen in old movies. Dodger took his
arm again. "Our next entrance into an egress."

Spencer laughed. "Do I have to ride in back?"

"Oakland is a bit more enlightened than many other parts of this
land, though, unfortunately, you may encounter prejudice which,
though officially unlawful, is still considered acceptable by those
with less-enlightened souls."

"That hasn't changed much," said Spencer, "since whenever this
was."

The streetcar arrived and stopped for them as Dodger raised a
hand, its doors opening with a hiss and clatter. Dodger led Spencer
up the steps and dropped two nickels in the coin box. The car's
interior was lighted by yellowish bulbs that flickered as it continued
on. Above the windows were advertisements, some for things that
were still around, like Coca-Cola and Hershey's chocolate, others for
items he'd never seen, like Bixby's ShuWhite and Black Cat Stove
Polish, along with archaic cigarette brands. The varnished wooden
seats were unpadded, and there were brass poles and overhead rails
for a standing crowd, but not many people aboard at this time, and
all of them seemingly in costume; the motorman wearing a uniform
appropriate to the period – which Spencer assumed was the 1920s
from what he'd seen so far – a woman, maybe forty or so, in ankle-
length coat, severe-looking shoes, a hat drably decorated with feath-
ers that might have come from a crow, and some sort of pin on her
lapel displaying the letters WCTU. A boy beside her, maybe seven
and presumably her son, was clad in white shirt, gray tweed jacket,
knee-length pants, long wool socks, clunky oxfords, and a cap. There
was a portly man in a suit -- who made Spencer think of Orson Wells
-- topped with a black fedora and smoking an aromatic cigar while
perusing a newspaper; and Spencer got the impression of a few

other figures randomly seated while following Dodger up the aisle. He tried to read the paper's date as they passed the suited man, but the lights went out for a moment as the car jolted over a junction.

When they came back to life, he noticed a girl of maybe fourteen possessed of a winsomely pixie-like face, her lips enhanced with lush cherry red, who might have been a junior model for one of the *Whiz Bang* flappers, wearing a knee-length pleated blue skirt, a black blouse involving lots of lace, and a short, cream-colored, fur-collared jacket, her shapely legs sheathed in wide-mesh stockings, her feet in moderately high-heeled shoes, her raven hair bobbed like a perky page-boy's beneath a blue velvet helmet-like hat adorned with an artificial rose. She also sported a long string of beads, pretty but unabashedly glass, above-the-elbow ebony gloves, and was smoking a cigarette in a possibly Bakelite holder. The only flaw in her costume – at least in Spencer's opinion – was that it understated her breasts, which were doubtless deserving of better display.

It wasn't surprising she smiled at Dodger, who was doubtlessly drop-dead handsome even though clad in what would have been lower-class garb in these times; but her big brown eyes remained just as warm as they inspected Spencer and gave him an equally charming smile... which gave him a pleasant tingle of warmth. Then she glanced at Dodger's Gladstone:

"In the undertaking profession?"

"I've varnished quite a few coffins," said Dodger.

"How much for embalming?" asked the girl.

"A Tom for a pint. Care for a toot?"

"Don't mind if I do."

Dodger presented the flask from his coat, the girl first daintily taking a sniff like a kitten offered questionable cream, followed by a cautious sip as if anticipating icky. Spencer expected her pert nose to wrinkle, but she smiled again. "This must be the real McCoy I've been hearing about since my dollie days."

"It'll coat your casket," said Dodger, and lay a hand on Spencer's shoulder. "My friend perfected the formula."

"Worth twice the price," said the girl, reaching into a little purse. "But don't get any ideas, Rockefeller."

Dodger nudged Spencer, who opened the bag and offered a flask. The girl wisely took a sip from that before passing a two-dollar bill to Dodger.

"May I know my embalmers?"

"Dodger," said Dodger, tipping his cap. "And my *protégé* Spencer."

"Dodger and Spencer," said the girl, as Spencer doffed his derby. "No offense meant, gentlemen, but you sound like a vaudeville act."

"Did I ever mention," said Dodger to Spencer, "a man with a wooden leg named Smith?"

"I don't recall," returned Spencer. "What was the name of his other leg?"

The girl laughed... she had a nice laugh. "Annie," she said, her eyes, unless Spencer mistook it, giving him a twinkle. "Though I'm not an orphan. But with my bluenose mom and pops I often wish I were." She flicked the stub of her cigarette out of the holder onto the floor and snuffed it under a heel. "I'm out on the lam tonight when I should be entombed in my room drearily studying Laughing and Grief."

"What about Reeling and Writhing?" asked Spencer.

"And Ambition," said Dodger. "Distraction, Uglification, and of course Derision."

Annie laughed again. "There's more to you two than just handsome faces and actually drinkable gin. Do please have seats."

Another surprise to Spencer was Annie making room for him while Dodger took a seat ahead and lounged sideways to face them. The woman in the feathered hat was looking prudishly disapproving, her son observing with interest until she snatched him by an ear and turned his face away.

Spencer had thought a lot about girls since he'd turned thirteen – girls of all colors, sizes and shapes – but this was the first time in his life he'd been in close proximity in an engaging physical way. Annie smelled nice, a bit like jasmine, with just a sufficient hint of tobacco to make her seem wise enough to the world not to be thought a babe in the woods yet still qualify for a unicorn ride. He supposed it was only natural – a survival-of-the-species thing – that he felt a rudimentary urge to somehow compete with Dodger for the young lady's attentions. ...Which of course was ridiculous since Dodger, in any culture or time, fitted with skin of any color and hair of any genetic origin, or eyes of any alternate hue, was a perfect example of strapping young male; the handsome hero of classic boys stories made all the more perfect by being a *real* boy of snips and snails and puppy-dog tails – which were only decorous adult euphemisms for sweat, dirt and randiness -- flaunted the flaws of smoking and drinking, and had no regard for TRESSPASSERS WILL. And, in tales for the opposite sex -- also properly bowdlerized -- he would be the young knight in shining armor in all the chivalrous incarnations.

So how, asked the practical part of his mind, could he possibly "compete" with Dodger? He was neither stronger, fleeter of foot, nor – at least in the present context – more cleverly gifted with gab. And, completely disregarding the blatantly obvious handicaps of being black and fat – and both to an extreme degree – he suspected, despite being rather well-read and accomplished enough in composition to attract the attention of college professors, he might not even be as smart.

And, bringing it down to modern methods of attracting companionship, Dodger possessed more material wealth.

Spencer had also occasionally – generally when involved with himself and pleasurably plying a finger and thumb -- pondered the potential problem of his "equipment" buried in blubber with not enough accessible to put to one of the primary uses nature had intended. In short, there didn't seem much of a chance he'd be disqualifying young maidens from mounting mythical mono-horns. Still, since the time when such an event seemed far in the unforeseeable future, it hadn't been more than a minor concern. ...And, he thought now – reverting again to practical mode -- meeting a pretty girl on a streetcar, even if she seemed to like him, didn't – or maybe shouldn't have – brought *that* matter to mind.

"Going up to the Claremont?" asked Dodger, offering a Fatima, which Annie inserted into the holder while Spencer fired his lighter for her.

"What a clever thing," said Annie, taking Spencer's hand to admire the battered old Zippo. "Very modern-looking and much less clumsy than others I've seen, though I still use my granny's strike-lighter." Then she turned to Dodger. "The Claremont's too swanky for my taste, even if I could afford it." She exhaled a specter of smoke, took a lady-like sip from her flask and offered it to Spencer.

"Thanks, but you just bought it," said Spencer. "And we have a lot."

"Fun is for sharing," said Annie. "Go on, wind your watch."

"This is really cool," said Spencer, his instinctive urge to compete with Dodger fading like a ghost into fog. "Like, you get to interact."

"An interesting term," said Annie. "But, what else does it resemble?"

"Huh?" said Spencer.

"Why is it only 'like' interacting instead of whatever it actually is?"

"Oh," said Spencer. "It's just an expression."

"Seems a bit confusing," said Annie. "If something is only similar to what it may actually be."

Dodger added, "Also not quite of a muchness to what it actually may not be."

"My, a philosopher," said Annie.

"...Um, yeah," said Spencer, taking a nip while trying to work that out. "Guess they didn't say cool either."

"'Holmes was as cool as ever,'" said Annie, also taking a nip when Spencer passed the bottle back.

"Oh, yeah," said Spencer. *The Disappearance of Lady Frances Carfax.*"

"Written in 1911," said Annie.

"And I seem to recall," said Dodger. "A 'you are very cool, Mr. Holmes' in another of his stories."

"Yeah, but it kinda meant calm," said Spencer.

"Only 'kinda?'" said Annie, with a mischievous look. "As in something is only kinda-like whatever it really may be?"

"Or may not be," said Dodger.

"Which makes it be twice not really," said Annie.

Spencer laughed. "A be by any other name."

"I be, therefore I am," said Annie. "Even if only kinda-like."

"To be, or not to be," said Dodger. "Or kinda-like being, but not actually."

"Or inversely," said Annie. "Not quite actually kinda-like being."

"Things are of two natures," said Dodger. "Either being what they appear to be as opposed to what they actually aren't, or not being what they appear to be as opposed to what they actually are."

"But throw in kinda-like," said Annie, "and nothing will ever actually be whatever it actually is."

"Or inversely," said Dodger, "whatever it actually may not be."

"I be confused," said Spencer.

"Try some more kinda-like gin," said Annie, cheerfully passing the flask.

"Substitute swell in most cases," said Dodger, "and you'll be kinda-like cool."

"Though not amongst swells," added Annie. "Or they won't think you're kinda-like either."

Spencer shook his head. "This sounds like a Thorne Smith conversation."

"As in *The Jovial Ghosts*?" said Dodger. "One of the last books I read."

"I've just read it," said Annie. "My parents forbade me to, of course, which made it be all the more swell."

"I'm reading it now," said Spencer. "But I be kinda-like feeling I'm in it."

Dodger offered his flask. "This'll clear the bees out of your bonnet."

Annie laughed. "I've fallen in with intelligent beings."

"You'll fall a lot farther if you're not careful!" warned the feather-hatted woman, towing her son down the aisle as the car creaked to a stop at a corner. "A young lady like you dressed like *that*... if one could call it dressed at all... out and unchaperoned at this hour and imbibing the devil's drink with a common newsboy and a shine!"

"Oh, go haunt a house," said Annie, and the little boy giggled.

"Preferably," added Dodger, "long ago and far away."

Annie wiped steam from her window to scan a street sign as they passed. "I'm getting off at the next corner; going to the Chimes."

"Swell," said Dodger. "So are we."

Annie clapped her hands. "What a swell fall."

Spencer laughed. "I be like kinda liking this being."

CHAPTER TWELVE

The mist had morphed into a feathery drizzle, further obscuring distant sights and giving the pavement a shimmery sheen as they disembarked and took shelter under a store-front awning. Annie flicked her cigarette stub away and slipped the holder into her purse. "I hope we won't be late."

Dodger consulted his White Rabbit watch. "Nah, we're right on time."

"Sounds like you come here a lot," said Spencer.

Dodger pocketed his watch. "This is the first time in a long time I've had such spirited company."

"You've both raised my spirit," said Annie, offering an arm to Spencer, who gentlemanly took it, Dodger claiming the other, as they strolled to a movie theater, its brightly-lit sign proclaiming CHIMES, its marquee displaying

THE PHANTOM OF THE OPERA

"This is swell!" exclaimed Spencer, scanning the posters on the walls as they strode arm-in-arm to the ticket booth like the quartet, less one, in *The Wizard Of Oz*. "The original starring Lon Chaney."

"I should hope it's original," said Annie, "not just kinda-like."

"Seems *apropos*," said Dodger.

"I hope it isn't too scary," said Annie. "I have a rather low threshold of fright when it comes to spooky things."

"I'll hold your hand," offered Spencer, before he had time to consider it might sound a little forward, but Annie gave his arm a squeeze. "I'm sure that will strengthen my spirit."

At first Spencer thought the girl in the booth, looking possibly seventeen in a frilly-fronted dress, might be an old-time automaton dispensing penny fortunes, but she gave the trio a wistful smile as if wishing she might have been part of their party as Dodger bought three tickets at twenty-five cents apiece. Spencer pointed to a poster as they continued to the doors:

"There's an *Our Gang* matinee on Saturday afternoon; *The Sundown Limited* and *Seein' Things*."

"The trains run all the time," said Dodger. "We can return whenever you wish."

Annie asked, "You gentlemen from out of town? You don't strike me as butter and egg men."

"I'd never strike a lady," said Dodger. "Unless she struck me first."

"Just up in the hills," said Spencer.

"Princes playing paupers?" said Anne.

"We turn back into mice at midnight," said Dodger.

A man in a stiffly high-collared suit, resembling H.P. Lovecraft though looking a lot less benign, was tearing tickets at the door and gave the group a gimlet eye. "Peanut gallery," he snapped, snatching the tickets from Dodger and ripping them like Jack. "One little peep and you're out on your ears... and check that bag in the parcel room."

"Was that because of me?" asked Spencer, as they proceeded toward a snack bar across a palatial lobby with sparkling chandeliers on the ceiling and cushy carpet on the floor, in which most of the older people were formally dressed as if for a ball, the eldest men wearing top-hats, the women in long dresses and gowns, though all looking slightly hazy to Spencer, who, probably due to the kinda-like gin, was still seeing things as if through a mist where details more than a few feet away wouldn't quite come into focus. There seemed to be many figures around him, but like the shapes on the streetcar and sidewalks, they gave the impression of movie extras only populating the background and not taking part in the plot. There was a murmur of conversation, but melded into a sort of white noise like the ambiguous rush of the brook.

He also still felt a bit out-of-body – the only description that seemed to fit -- in a pleasantly careless way but notable since, for obvious reasons, he was usually well aware of himself, especially when ambulatory… there being inertia to maintain, shifts of mass to counterbalance and clearances to be gauged ahead, not to mention retaining his jeans. And then, for just a moment, he felt a sort of slipping sensation like partly awakening from sleep with a feeling he might have forgotten something, even if only as minor as taking out the garbage. …Or, it might have been better described as being intensely absorbed in a book but having his mind interrupt the story by feeling he'd missed some essential detail that should have been logically obvious.

"Nah, we're all flaming youth," said Dodger, drawing Spencer back into the scene. "Flagrantly flaunting our lack of morals and blatant disdain for social norms… many of which we regard as abnormal if not downright disgustingly wrong… dancing and drinking in shameless abandon, petting, necking, French-kissing in public, frolicking naked in fountains and such."

"Does a pond rate the same as a fountain?" asked Spencer, forgetting whatever he thought he'd forgotten including whatever he might have missed.

"Oh, do tell," said Annie.

"Actually just swimming with Dodger; I've never tried to frolic."

"I'm sure you'd be very good at it," said Annie, giving Spencer's belly a playful pat, "having so much to frolic with; but I picture a Norman Rockwell scene of boys being boys at 'the ol' swimmin' hole,' idyllically suitable for *Boy's Life*."

"You read *Boy's Life*?" asked Dodger.

"I've sneaked a few peeks in the library until the librarian caught me, but I'd hoped a boy's life was more exciting than Pee-wee Harris prudery and toasting hapless marshmallows on sticks while singing *Tenting Tonight*."

Dodger laughed. "Pee-wee Harris would faint dead away if his manly companions suggested something more stimulating around a campfire."

"Oh, double do tell," said Annie.

"Let's just say it involves a circle, but you won't find it in *Boy's Life*."

"When adults write about boys," added Spencer, recalling his thoughts on the streetcar, "they never mention what's usually an important part of their lives."

"Do you think it's any different," asked Annie, "when adults write about girls?"

"...Guess not."

"It's a shame how little informed we are about what should be perfectly natural things." Annie sighed theatrically. "No doubt there are *many* things in this world which even an entire year in Miss Penelope's finishing school has not prepared me for."

"I'm sure you learned something useful," said Dodger, "if you ever find it necessary to balance a book on your head."

"I must catch up on my racy reading to be informed in these modern times in regard to young manly activities."

"Don't get ahead of yourself," said Dodger.

"Mind your manners, Buster Brown."

"I'm pretty advanced for my age," said Spencer.

"Maybe too far for this one," said Annie.

"I don't think I could dance," added Spencer. "But the other flaunting stuff sounds swell."

Annie squeezed his arm again. "I'd enjoy seeing you frolic."

"I don't think Norman Rockwell would have."

"More's the pity."

"Don't get out much, do you?" said Dodger.

Annie threw an arm in front of her eyes in a gesture of silent movie despair. "'Yet still she strains the aching clasp...'"

"Now whose manners need minding."

"Let me pay for the popcorn," said Spencer, as they reached a glass-fronted counter displaying many candy bars, some of which, like the streetcar ad items, would still be around in what part of his mind was starting to think was the future – Butterfinger, Baby Ruth, Hersheys, and Bit-O-Honey -- but also Love Nest, Goo Goo Clusters, and, intriguingly, Chicken Dinner.

"Hey, it's only five cents a bag instead of five dollars."

"Who without birds on their aerial," said Annie, "would pay a fin for a bag of popcorn?"

Spencer dug in a pocket, but Dodger stayed his hand. "Your money's no good here, this is my treat."

"Okay, Diamond Jim," said Annie. "What besides popcorn goes well with gin?"

"Maybe a Chicken Dinner?" said Spencer.

"Call me a cat," said Annie.

Each now equipped with a bag of popcorn generously drizzled with actual butter, along with Chicken Dinner bars, they approached the theater doors, where slouched a cartoonishly pot-bellied boy of possibly Dodger's age clad in a bell-hoppish blue uniform. He had tomcat green eyes and red porcupine hair, the latter bristling electrically from under a silly pillbox hat, his face like Mickey's in *Our Gang*, very fluently freckled, equipped with bottle-opener teeth, and was armed with a brass torpedo flashlight.

"Let's see them tickets," he commanded, and added when Dodger presented them, "Peanut gallery, an' no peeps."

"Seems to be an echo in here," said Annie.

"Didn't see any peanuts for sale," said Spencer.

"Make too much noise an' mess up the carpet. ...An' don't crack wise with me, bub; I got no grudge against you people... got a good friend of your persuasion... but the boss won't have no shenanigans upsettin' the hoity-toitys. ...An' ya gotta hock that bag."

Dodger undid a buckle and stealthily offered a flask, which the boy stealthily stashed in a pocket.

"Let's see them tickets again. ...Oh, my mistake, you got loges. C'mon an' I'll assort ya."

He ushered the trio to comfortable seating just as the lights went down, and Spencer and Dodger flanked Annie. "But, hey, no Katzenjammer capers or it's my neck, y'know."

"We came for the movie," said Dodger. "No phonus balonus, Jonas."

The boy patted his pocket. "An' this is decent hooch? Ain't gonna make me get naked an' howl at the moon or nothin' like that?"

"Probably not," said Annie. "Though I wouldn't mind seeing that show."

"Hey, you're okay."

Annie un-pursed her bottle, and the boy took a nip.

"That's the elephant's eyebrows! ...Name's Mickey, just axe if ya need anything."

"Let me know when you're going to howl."

"That clasp must really be aching," said Dodger, as the screen curtains parted and a live organist played an overture.

"Oh, hush and pretend you're a Rover Boy."

"Want me to rover all over?"

"Want to learn to play dead without playing?"

Spencer had seen the movie before, but only the tiny version on YouTube grainy and faded with age; and despite its relative tameness compared to something like *Nightmare On Elm Street* in gory color with spine-chilling sound and all its gruesome computer FX, was still more than sufficiently shocked when Christine snatched off Erik's mask accompanied by the organ's shriek, while Annie's grip almost compacted his hand.

The clock in the lobby was nearing ten as they left the theater, Spencer again holding Annie's arm, Dodger clasping her other; and probably due to consumption of gin, which did go well with Chicken Dinners – composed, despite their peculiar name, of marshmallow, peanuts, caramel and chocolate -- the crowd all around was still hazy, though Mickey appeared crystal clear for a moment as if in a spot-light across the room and foxily flashed an OK sign.

The drizzle seemed to have ceased as they emerged beneath the marquee, but the mist had thickened to full-fledged fog, shrouding the street in ghostly gray with spectral haloes around the lights and creating a sort of pocket effect as if the world was only composed of what could be seen within a small sphere, the rest fading into infinity. There was a bray of an ooo-gah horn as another old-time car clattered past; and a real Knickerbockered newsboy, black and pos-sibly eight, crowned with a comically oversize cap, a cigarette cornered in his mouth, was hawking *Tribune* editions and actually bawling, "Extra!"

Spotting Dodger and eyeing the bag, the boy stalked over and, reaching high, jabbed Dodger's chest with a finger. "Beat it, I'm workin' this side of the street!"

"No beef from me," said Dodger.

The boy seemed to reconsider with another glance at the Gladstone. "Bet them ain't papers you peddlin'. How much for the coffin varnish?"

"How much have you made tonight?" asked Dodger.

"Almost two bucks."

Dodger unbuckled the bag and slipped a pint into the boy's coat pocket. "It's on me, go get embalmed."

"Hey, you're okay!"

"Well," said Annie, as the boy walked away and seemed to vanish into the fog along with other departing figures. "I can appreciate your kindness, but I had to pay for my casket coating."

"Perhaps a late supper will compensate? Shall we have some sustenance to further fuel our frolicking?"

"I must have missed something," said Annie. "Except for being scared out of my wits by dastardly Erik's malfeasance, it's been quite a proper evening so far with you spirited gentlemen, but of course the night is still young."

"What shall we have?" asked Dodger. He smiled at Spencer. "If I may assume you now have room?"

Spencer laughed. "For me every meal is like Chinese food."

"I'm game for just about anything that doesn't bite back or scream," said Annie. "Though I shan't have any Welsh rarebit as I'm sure I already have a nightmare scheduled for the wee and small."

Spencer squinted into the fog. "Looks like a burger joint over there."

"Jake by me," said Annie. "I usually dine a bit more refined but you Baker Street Irregulars aren't attired for Delmonico's."

Several more old-time cars clattered past, materializing and then disappearing, along with a big chugging truck with

HYGENIC DOG FOOD COMPANY

painted on its side. There followed a whirring streetcar, then the trio crossed the street.

The café was a little storefront displaying a Coca-Cola sign beneath a Chinese-hatted light bulb with

WATSON'S DINER

lettered below. Its window was steamed to pale opaqueness, its interior taller than it was wide and lighted by ceiling fixtures that might have once been gas. There was a counter along one side with a row of leather-padded stools, and high-backed booths on the opposite. Spencer's stomach rumbled from the tempting aromas of frying meat as they entered the open doorway. He got the impression of figures occupying stools and booths, but only the white-aproned counterman, a rolly fat chocolate-colored boy of possibly his age, though maybe only two-thirds his weight, breast balloons bulging half bare in a 'beater – or maybe the period word was singlet -- a paper cap topping his bushy mane, appeared as entirely "there."

The boy gave the group a welcoming smile with an extra brotherly spark for Spencer. "Evenin', folks."

"Evening," said Dodger, and turned to Annie. "Would the lady prefer a booth?"

The boy, who'd been tending a grill where big juicy patties were sizzling, apologetically cleared his throat and aimed his spatula at a sign:

TIPS ARE APPRECIATED FROM
TABLE SEATED PATRONS

"No worries," said Dodger, "we're rolling in dough."

"Nah, I'm just part of the gang," said Annie, lithely boarding one of the stools.

Spencer struggled to mount another but couldn't manage to hoist what seemed like a sudden abundance of blubber, as if the out-of-body sensation he'd been feeling for most of the evening had vanished. He supposed, most things being relative, he was only again aware of his weight because he'd been unaware for a while. But now, despite all his efforts, he couldn't climb onto the stool. Dodger noticed his discomfiture and lifted him under the arms.

"Funny," puffed Spencer, arranging himself with a lot of his bottom suspended in space, "I feel fatter tonight."

"I think you're cherubically charming," said Annie, cheerfully chucking his chins.

"I'm not as innocent as I might look."

"I should hope not," Annie laughed. "Many cherubs are naughty; frolicking in fountains... or in your case apparently ponds... feasting to overstuffed ecstasy, imbibing wine from amphorae and playing Puckish pranks on mortals."

"I could be that kind of cherub."

"Maybe you already are."

Dodger hopped onto a stool on the other side of Annie. "You look the same to me as when you opened the shutters."

Spencer looked down at himself, recalling the fatter boy in the mirror and wondering if he *had* gotten that fat and, being inside looking out, so to speak, simply never noticed.

The boy behind the counter set up three glasses of water, but Dodger asked, "Have any tonic?"

"Got White Rock."

"Split a bottle into these glasses, please, and add another for yourself."

The boy smiled. "Hey, you're okay." He poured the water into a sink, uncapped a bottle with an opener and divided it into four glasses, to which Dodger added gin.

"To high spirits," said Dodger, raising his glass in salute.

"I'll drink to that," said the boy, and everyone happily did.

"May we make your acquaintance?" asked Annie.

"My friends call me Willie; my pops owns this place." The boy puffed his chest, nearly bursting his shirt. "First colored-owned business in this part of town."

"That gives me hope for the future," said Annie.

Spencer almost said, "Don't hope too high," but didn't want to lower her spirit.

Annie introduced herself, along with Dodger and Spencer; and Willie asked, "What'll it be for you folks?"

Spencer scanned the menu board suspended on chains above the grill. There weren't a lot of selections, though some were as intriguing as Chicken Dinner candy bars... Pig's Feet In Batter for 25¢, Stewed Veal, 25¢, and Mutton Chops for 35¢. More prosaically, there were chili and hash for 20¢, succotash for 15¢, and Cod Cakes for 30¢. Some of the burger descriptions were also a little unusual, like Ham-burger Smothered With Spaghetti, and Hamburger Whipped With One Egg. Besides ice-cream at 5¢ a scoop – chocolate, vanilla or strawberry -- dessert was Apple Pie, 10¢ a slice, or a-la-mode for 15¢.

"What's the blue plate special?" asked Dodger.

Willie took another nip from his glass. "Me, I'd have the Double Deluxe; that's two burger patties with all the trimmin's... lettuce, tomato, pickle an' onion... served on a buttered an' mayonaised bun... we can hold the mayo... an' comes with French style spuds. Thirty-five cents but you won't leave hungry. Beverages another nickel... glass of milk, Coca-Cola, root beer, Orange Crush, ginger ale, or Bevo."

Spencer regarded some ads on the walls... Wards Orange Crush, Vernor's Ginger Ale, White Rock Sparkling Tonic Water. There were also a few cardboard placards:

WE'LL CRANK YOUR CAR AND HOLD YOUR BABY
BUT WE WON'T TAKE YOUR CHECK
AND WE DON'T MEAN MAYBE

IF YOUR WIFE IS A BUM COOK
KEEP HER FOR A PET AND EAT HERE

IF YOU DON'T LIKE OUR FOOD TRY THE
GREEK'S DOWN THE STREET

"What's Bevo?" he asked.

"Why bother beer," said Willie.

"...Oh, I forgot," said Spencer. "This is Prohibition, huh?"

Dodger raised his glass again. "I'm surprised you hadn't deduced that already when all around you see the results of the Noble Experiment."

"Here's to the Volstead Act," said Willie, taking a noble gulp from his glass.

"Speaking of which," said Annie, "I'll stick to the gin and White Rock. ...I'll have that Double Deluxe, please, and don't hold the mayo."

"That's a relief," said Willie. "Holding mayo is messy."

"I'll have what the lady is having," said Dodger. "As long as it isn't a fit."

"Me, too," said Spencer. "But make it a cheeseburger, please."

"What's a cheeseburger?" asked Willie, with a cock of his head.

"...Huh?" said Spencer.

"I should think a burger with cheese," said Dodger. "Rather than solely composed of cheese."

"Which would be a patty-melt," said Annie.

"Learn that in finishing school?" asked Dodger.

"We had a special class in how to balance them on our heads."

"Okay," said Willie. "But how?"

"Want me to show you?" asked Spencer.

Willie made spectacles with his fingers. "Look, I'm an owl."

"Got any slices of cheese?" asked Spencer, unloading himself from the stool and coming around behind the counter. He found he was less aware of his weight, or maybe becoming accustomed again.

"Here's some cheddar for sandwiches."

"Just do this," said Spencer, dropping a slice on a sizzling patty. "Wait till it mostly melts, then..." He borrowed the spatula from Willie and slid the patty onto a bun. "For a double do it twice."

Willie picked up the bun, gave it a puff to cool it a bit, then took an analytical bite. "Hey, that's swell!" He chomped a huge crescent of meat and cheese and added around the mouthful, "I shoulda thought of that."

Spencer laughed. "Maybe you did."

"May I?" asked Annie, and took a nibble when Willie passed it over. "Mmmm! Delicious! I shall have one."

"Double cheeseburgers for all," said Dodger, after mouthing a sample. "And don't forget yourself."

"I'd like to," said Willie. "But according to pops I been eatin' the profits."

"Add it to my tab and join our gang."

"I'll drink to that," said Spencer, returning the spatula to Willie, who began grilling his new creations.

As if now an understood thing, Dodger helped Spencer back on the stool. There was a rumble and clanking outside as another big van-bodied truck, its cab a C-type – so Spencer had read – rolled up to the curb on six solid tires. Hazily seen through the steamy window was a fish painted on the side of its box smiling mischievously, along with the words

FINN'S FRESH FISH
YOU'LL WANT TO SLAP THEIR FACES

"What kind of truck is that?" asked Spencer.

"1919 Mack AC. Also called a Bulldog," said Dodger. "Chain-drive, four-cylinder engine developing 37 horsepower."

"Men do love their machines," said Annie.

"I read *The Boy Mechanic*," said Dodger.

"I prefer *Cap'n Billy's Whiz Bang*," said Annie.

"We read those, too," said Spencer.

"That's encouraging."

Willie, meantime, had loaded four plates with steaming cheeseburgers and all the trimmings, along with golden mountains of crispy "French-style" potatoes. "I made yours a triple," he said to Spencer, setting the plates on the counter. "No extra charge."

"Hey, thanks," said Spencer.

"Thanks to you, brother. Got a feelin' these things are gonna catch on."

Spencer lowered his voice. "Some white guy will say he invented them."

Willie shrugged. "Ain't news to me, but that's life on the dark side. The French Army gave pops a medal for doin' somethin' like Sergeant York... captured a whole bunch of Huns single-handed."

"In World War One?" asked Spencer.

"Did I miss somethin'?" said Willie. "When was there another world war?"

"...Oh, yeah," said Spencer, I keep forgetting. ...Your dad was in the French Army?"

"Nah, the U.S. Army... which wouldn't admit he got a medal; said it would demoralize the troops if they rewarded a colored man for doin' somethin' brave, an' put him to peelin' potatoes for the rest of the war."

Spencer sighed. "I hear that."

Willie smiled. "Looks like you got some *Our Gang* friends, an' that gives me hope for the future."

Again, Spencer almost said, "Don't hope too high," but again didn't want to lower a spirit.

Outside, the truck's engine coughed into silence, and a coal-black boy of maybe fourteen, clad in ragged dungarees, what might have been Army-surplus boots, and shirtless beneath a blue denim coat -- also tattered, way too large, and apparently missing its buttons be-cause it was belted with a rope – and of course equipped with a newsboy cap, descended from the lofty cab. It was hard to tell in his oversize coat and seen though the misted window, but he seemed to posses a muscular build, slenderly so like Dodger, below a still-childlike impish face shadowed by a halo of hair. He went around to the rear of the truck and unloaded a wooden box, which he carried in.

"Got your cod cakes, Willie," he called, then, "Hey, what's cook-in'? Smells pretty swell."

"His new invention," said Spencer. "Cheeseburgers."

"Make me one, please," said the boy, toting the box behind the counter, then mounting a stool beside Spencer and offering a hand. "Name's Finn... Junior... an' no jokes, okay?"

"Spencer," said Spencer, shaking hands. "And I won't say nice hooking up with you."

"Gee, thanks," said Finn, his voice sort of little-kid husky, his "thanks" sounding more like "thags." He would have pronounced the "B" in lamb, and if he ever said "valentine" it would probably come out "balentine."

115

"And this is Annie and Dodger."

Finn hesitated a moment when Annie offered her hand. "I's a little fishy, Biss."

There was indeed an aquatic aroma emanating from Finn, which no doubt H. P. Lovecraft -- of whom it was said detested fish -- would have found distressing; though maybe because Finn's Fresh Fish were notably impertinent, Spencer thought of fish tacos and other piscine pleasantries such as fish-and-chips.

"I prefer men a bit fishy," said Annie, as Finn shyly took her hand. "They're usually much more interesting than those who always tow the line."

"Slip me a... well, you know," said Dodger, dismounting his stool to shake with Finn. He flashed his flask. "May we raise your spirit?"

Finn spread his arms. "I is risen!"

Willie uncapped another White Rock and partly filled a glass, which Dodger topped off, and Finn sampled.

"Must be da real McCoy, huh?"

"My friend created it," said Dodger, laying a hand on Spencer's shoulder.

"What's da wholesale?" asked Finn, after a full-on gulp. "Folks on my route is always fishin'."

"Thought you said no jokes," said Spencer.

"So are people in here," said Willie, around a mouthful of juicy cheeseburger while starting another sizzling creation. "I'll take a few if the price is right."

"We could give you both a half-dozen for a dollar a pint," said Dodger. "But we have to save some for the high-rollers later."

"I was hoping there would be a later," said Annie, who, despite the big dripping burger, looked quite ladylike consuming it.

"As you said, the night is still young," said Dodger.

CHAPTER THIRTEEN

"**S**hall we indulge in dessert?" asked Dodger, dipping his last French style potato into a dollop of Blue Label ketchup before dispensing it into his mouth. "Perhaps apple pie?"

Spencer sighed and patted his belly, which did its usual Jell-O jiggle, and all the more so since it still seemed to him an amazing new abundance of blubber. "I'd like to, but I'm not sure I can."

"I'll say," sighed Finn, who'd un-roped his coat in the room's steamy warmth, revealing a chest like a pair of small bricks, and now patted a six-pack of anthracite abs that bulged a bit over his jeans.

Dodger suggested, "Must be a corner that still needs filling."

"I might be able to find it," said Spencer, unsuccessfully stifling a burp.

"Me too," said Annie, also dispatching a last potato after cloaking it with ketchup.

"I'm in," said Willie.

"Make it a-la-mode," said Dodger.

Spencer muffled another burp. The combination of kinda-like gin, even tamed a bit by tonic, along with the enormous cheese-burger, had made the surroundings hazy again and resurrected the impression that things going on at edges of sight were only there to fill the background, which otherwise might have been featureless void. Like his perception when first coming in that figures were sitting on stools and in booths, and presumably dining, they only suggested movie extras not meant to be interacted with or individually recognized.

Or maybe they were in other movies, metaphorically speaking?

He'd been vaguely aware while eating that shapes were sometimes in motion around him – patrons entering or leaving, paying their tabs at a brass register, which he dimly heard ringing – and Willie occasionally seemed to fade into some vanishing-point perspective while serving a phantom customer, taking a plate of food to a booth, or departing to clear a table.

As when he'd felt the slipping sensation in the theater lobby, a part of his mind momentarily seemed to come drowsily out of a dream with a feeling of either forgetting something or missing what might have been obvious. But Willie set a plate before him loaded with a huge slice of pie topped with a generous scoop of ice-cream; and Annie's voice brought him back, asking Dodger:

"What are your plans for this still youthful night? Assuming we ever finish this feast. ...Not that I mind; I could stay here forever if given a choice of eternities."

"So could I," said Spencer, shelving his analytical musing and digging into ice-cream and pie, the ice cream the thick old-fashioned kind that hadn't been frothed full of air.

"Wouldn't mind neither," Finn put in, while also putting a fork to sweet use. "If I got to choose a foreber, now would be a mighty good time. But, I still got deliberies down on Cypress Street."

"Have you heard of Hogan's Alley?" asked Dodger. "In that neighborhood."

Finn chased his pie with gin. "Eberbody who anybody know 'bout Hogan's Alley."

"How strange," said Annie, spooning ice cream. "I never once heard it mentioned at Miss Penelope's."

Finn returned to his dessert. "I be droppin' a crate of oysters dere; give y'all a ride if you don't bind fishy."

"We've already laid that to rest," said Annie.

"You left your lights on," said Spencer. "Isn't that running the battery down?"

"Nah, dey acetylene," said Finn, glancing out at his truck. "An' da taillight's kerosene."

Dodger said, "I thought that model came equipped with electric lights and a self-starter?"

"Dem was options," said Finn, "but we couldn't afford 'em."

"Thoroughly modern men," said Annie.

"What are your current interests?" asked Dodger. "Besides putting patty-melts on your head?"

"Mostly thoroughly modern men."

Spencer smiled. "You have us at your pleasure tonight."

"So far it has been very pleasurable."

Finn asked, "Why would you put patty-melts on your head?"

"She's also thoroughly modern," said Dodger.

"Any chance I could join you?" asked Willie. "Take me no time to close up."

"High spirits are always welcome," said Dodger.

"Do please further elevate mine," said Annie.

"Patty-melts optional," added Dodger.

"I be habin' cheeseburgers from now on," said Finn, "but I can't see puttin' 'em on my head."

"Might be a white thing," Spencer said wryly.

"Dat could explain it," said Finn.

Dodger plied his fork. "Plenty of time to finish our pie and have an after-supper smoke."

"I's feelin' like whitefolks," laughed Finn.

"What do whitefolks feel like?" asked Spencer.

"I 'magine good as dis most of da time 'stead of just in dribbles an' bits."

"We're all kindred spirits here," said Annie, leaning past Spencer to touch Finn's arm.

"And souls are composed of all colors," said Dodger, "which means they're clear as crystal light and immaculate as newborn stars." He flashed his foxy smile to Spencer. "Unless, of course, they fall."

A clock was showing close to eleven – IT'S ALWAYS TIME FOR COCA-COLA -- when Willie, after paying the difference between Dodger's tab and six pints of gin, ringing NO SALE on the register, and cleaning up the counter and grill, disappeared for a minute – presumably he lived upstairs -- and materialized minus his apron and clad in gray coat and cap.

"All aboard!" said Finn, crushing his cigarette stub in an ashtray and re-securing his coat with the rope.

The others also disposed of remains, Annie pursing her holder, and followed Finn out to the truck as Willie doused the café lights and locked the door with a skeleton key.

"I get her started," said Finn, climbing into the cab and adjusting two levers – spark advance and throttle, as Spencer had read in an old book for boys – on the steering column. Spencer also noted

Lulibelle

painted on the side of the hood, and recalled reading it had once been common for people to name their cars and trucks.

"I'll twist her tail," said Dodger, going to the vehicle's front and unfolding a heavy crank handle, while Willie and Annie assisted Spencer up onto the seat.

Finn shifted the transmission to neutral and flipped a switch on the dashboard. "Contact, but sometimes she touchy, Dodger. Careful she don't bust your arm."

"I'd bust an arm, too," said Annie, "if anyone tried to twist my tail."

Spencer laughed. "Try putting a patty-melt on her hood."

"Still can't figure dat out," said Finn.

Dodger gave the crank a pull and the engine grumbled to life like a sleepy lion clearing its throat, settling into a rhythmic idle as Finn retarded the throttle and spark.

The truck sat higher off the ground than Spencer's father's GMC. Its van box was possibly seven feet wide, ten feet long and eight feet high, but the cab was relatively small. The seat, though roomy in relation and comfortably padded with diamond-tucked leather, was mostly filled by Spencer. Finn, despite probably being fourteen – Spencer remembered reading it had once been the legal driving age - - was only of average American size for a twenty-first century twelve-year-old, his feet just able to reach the pedals, his eye-level just sufficient to see above the huge steering wheel, which was lucky because, even though partly engulfed in Spencer, he had enough

space to man the controls.

Annie was squeezed between Spencer and Willie, the latter riding shotgun, which completely filled the cab, so Dodger with the Gladstone in hand mounted the right side running-board. "And they're off!" he announced.

Finn released the parking brake, shifted the transmission to first, let out the clutch and up-throttled the engine while advancing the spark, wrestling with the steering wheel and watching the little rearview mirror mounted outside from the roof of the cab as Lulibelle lumbered away from the curb, her drive chains metallically clattering like Marley's ghost haunting Scrooge. The pale bluish glow of the headlights didn't project very far, and again there was a pocket-effect with the feathery fog all around in which only the closest things could be seen – various old-fashioned storefronts, all apparently closed at this time, the lights of their signs mostly dark; vehicles going the opposite way, though there weren't very many; and spectrally-haloed street lamps -- fading in as they rolled along and fading out behind. Figures on the sidewalks were few and far between. There didn't seem to be any who looked as if they were homeless, all appearing bound somewhere and on their way with purposeful strides instead of doing the lost-soul shuffle; and a cop in a vintage uniform was sportily twirling his billy club while rattling a door.

The truck didn't have a windshield, but the night was not uncomfortably cold and the mist felt refreshing on Spencer's face as if recharging his battery for new adventures lying ahead on what, so far in his life, had been the most adventurous time.

Lulibelle, not surprisingly, was possessed of a piscine aroma, though sufficiently sassy to anyone fond of seafood. The scent h_ been more noticeable with the vehicle stationary, but there was open hatch on the van behind the cab's unglazed rear window, the gentle breeze of chugging along at maybe twenty-miles-an-h_ after Finn had double-clutched up to fourth gear -- wafted mo_ out the back, which was flappingly curtained by canvas. _ glanced through the opening, seeing several wooden bo_ ming with glistening specimens obviously newly-departe_

they jiggled about to the solid tire jolts as if not fully convinced.

Like most young people who didn't yet drive, Spencer was only familiar with a few blocks of his former turf, which was less than many his age because, except for the marathon of walking eight blocks when he'd been twelve, he'd seldom self-propelled himself beyond the corner market. Likewise, the only sights he'd seen outside of his old neighborhood had been from his parents' transport, mostly traveling to and from the restaurant for dinners, and with his mother on shopping trips to Safeway and Grocery Outlet -- usually with lunches included at Church's Chicken, KFC, McDonalds, Jack In The Box or Wendy's – and occasionally to the Salvation Army where he mostly bought old books while his mom searched the racks for T-shirts and jeans to fit his ever-expanding form. There had been the vehicular expeditions for junk-shop reading material; the journey to Broadway for bitters and gin; and an annual visit to Pill Hill to earn a lollipop. Also the picnics in Temescal Park; a barbecue at Lake Merritt; a dimly-remembered excursion to Children's Fairyland when he'd been five; and he'd gone numerous times with his parents to the Paramount, Grand, and Fox theaters. He'd never been on a bus or BART; and while he'd read a lot about Oakland, he hadn't actually seen much of it. Of course he'd heard of many street names – they were now chugging and clattering, exhaust smoke melding into the mist, back up College Avenue, then Finn turned left onto Alcatraz, adjusting the spark as Lulibelle loafed on what seemed to be a slight downgrade – but he'd never been on most of them.

Annie, though rather overwhelmed by Spencer and Willie's abundance, managed to un-purse a pack of Old Gold and offer smokes to all, which Spencer fired with his Zippo after Annie had loaded her holder.

"Wouldn't it be so jolly," she said, after exhaling a spirit and draping her arms around the boys' shoulders, "if we were taking a country excursion on a sunny afternoon, perhaps to a picnic by a pond, and all you men were shirtless in the pleasant warmth."

"My, how that clasp must be aching," said Dodger, secured by Willie's arm around him, the Gladstone in his other hand while dragging on his cigarette. "I'm surprised you'd only settle for shirtless."

"I wasn't suggesting something improper."

"That in itself is suggestive."

"Are you suggesting a frolic?" asked Spencer.

"Sounds like a swell suggestion," said Willie. "Ain't done no frolickin' for a long time."

"Ain't sure what frolickin' is," said Finn, readjusting the spark as they seemed to reach level terrain and the engine took over from gravity. "But I think I be suggestible."

Dodger offered his flask, everyone taking a nip. "Free spirits aren't restricted to only frolicking at night."

"And I happen to have a pond," said Spencer.

"A prince indeed playing a pauper," said Annie. "I surmised there was a lot more about you than just a cherubic feast for my eyes."

"Careful, Miss," said Dodger. "Flattery may get you somewhere."

"And such a jolly lot of somewhere," said Annie, giving Spencer a jolly squeeze as if he had a squeaker inside.

The cheerful conversation and playful banter continued, Spencer only infrequently noting their hazy immediate surroundings and occasionally seeing a sign, one reading SAN PABLO AVENUE, where Finn made another left turn, and PERALTA STREET on which he turned right.

"'Spect she getting' thirsty," he said, slowing as a Gilmore Gas station, one of the few establishments still open at this time, materialized out of the mist ahead, its lighted sign suggesting that motorists

Roar With Gilmore

There were only two pumps on the concrete island in front of a small stucco building, the sort that Spencer had seen in old photos, conical cast-iron mechanisms topped by tall glass cylinders. Both displayed logos of roaring lions, one touting Gilmore Red Lion goaded with Tetraethylene at 22¢ a gallon, the other assumably less ferocious at 20¢ a gallon. A sign on one of the posts supporting the overhanging roof requested:

PLEASE STOP MOTOR
NO SMOKING
PLEASE EXTINGUISH YOUR LIGHTS

Finn pulled up to the pumps, the mechanical rear wheel brakes squealing softy, shut off the ignition switch and pinched out his half-smoked cigarette, interring the remains in a pocket; the others also snuffing their stubs as a lanky black boy of around Dodger's age though several inches taller, clad in blue denim coveralls, a matching cap on his untamed curls, emerged from the building's doorway, smiling and raising a welcoming hand.

"What's up, Finn?" he called, while ambling to the truck.

"Did people say that now?" asked Spencer.

"'What's up, your majesty?'" Dodger quoted. "And 'did' and 'now' are oxymoronic when paired in the present context."

"*Tik-Tok Of Oz*," added Annie. "Published in 1914. ...And I was taught it was rude to correct other people's English."

"Weren't you also taught it was rude to suggest other people remove their clothing to titillate your aching clasp?"

"I must have missed that etiquette lesson while putting patty-melts on my head."

"Still can't figure dat out," said Finn.

"Oh," said Spencer. "I haven't read that Oz book yet."

"I have," chuckled Willie. "Everybody puts patty-melts on their heads."

"Why?" asked Finn.

"So they can live happily ever after."

"How would...?" Finn began, but Annie gave Willie a poke and said:

"They do live happily ever after, but they never have patty-melts again."

"Only cheeseburgers," said Spencer.

"I can understand dat," said Finn. "From now on dey part of my eber after."

"What have you been reading?" asked Annie.

"Started *Doctor Dolittle*, 'till I come to da nigger part."

124

"That put me off, too," said Dodger. "Spoiled, I thought, what was otherwise a very amusing story."

"Readin' *Great Expectations* now."

"I like Dickens," said Spencer. "He knew how to write about kids."

"Probably 'cause he'd been one," said Willie.

The lanky boy had reached the truck, apparently not concerned by the steady flames of its lights, and Finn greeted him with, "Hi, Dreyfus. She wantin' ten gallons, I 'spect."

"Check her water an' oil?"

"Probably needin' a quart. I take a can of carbide, too."

"Carbide?" asked Spencer.

"Acetylene generator," said Finn.

Dreyfus went to the less feral pump and began cranking a big iron handle, the cylinder slowly filling with honey-colored gasoline, rising up gallon gradient marks until the level reached ten.

"Don't 'spose you could make a mistake," said Finn, "an' add an inch by accident?"

"Boss checks the tanks with an eyedropper."

"Well, don't leave none in da hose."

Dreyfus chucked, removing Lulibelle's fuel-filler cap and inserting the pump hose nozzle. "Only do that to upstage swells." He undid the latches and raised the hood. "Y'all branchin' into the taxi business?"

"Forgettin' my manners," said Finn. "Dis Annie, Spencer, Willie an' Dodger. ...Dis here my good friend Dreyfus. ...Takin' 'em to Hogan's."

"Miss an' gentlemen," said Dreyfus, tipping his cap to Annie. "Wouldn't mind goin' myself." He pulled the engine's dipstick and wiped it with a rag... carried presumably for that purpose in one of his back pockets. "But, I got graveyard shift tonight 'top of my other ten hours."

"You gonna get rich," said Finn.

"The boss sure is. An' the company's raisin' prices another penny a gallon, but I still makin' fifteen cents an hour."

"Dey calls it Capitalism," said Finn.

"I call it greedy whitefolks," said Dreyfus. "No 'fence meant to company present."

"None taken, sir," said Annie.

"Likewise," said Dodger. "One of these days they'll suck all the oil out of the ground."

"Then they corner the market on hay." Dreyfus re-inserted the stick, then again drew it out and checked the level. "You right, Finn, she wantin' a quart."

"Just give her da bulk," said Finn. "Gonna rebuild her engine soon."

"May I use the facilities?" asked Annie.

"'Round back, Miss," Dreyfus replied, tipping his cap again. "Light switch right inside the door."

Dodger dismounted the running-board and Willie clambered down after him, both boys taking Annie's hands and assisting her to earth.

"Got any snacks?" asked Spencer, as Annie vanished around the building.

"This a gas station, brother," said Dreyfus. "Y'all wantin' eats try the Greek's down the street."

Spencer reflexively turned to the street, but there seemed to be nothing but pearly mist beyond the station's island of light. Nor, looking up, could he see any sky, only more featureless fog. With the truck's engine off it was very quiet, not eerily so but peacefully so; no rumble and rush of traffic on freeways, no screaming sirens, no honking horns, or all the other city sounds he'd been hearing at night all his life.

"They's a soda machine inside," said Dreyfus, hanging the gas hose back on the pump after draining the last drop into the truck.

Spencer turned to Dodger. "Wonder if something else goes with gin?"

"Somebody say gin?" asked Dreyfus.

Dodger offered his flask to Dreyfus as Spencer unloaded himself from the cab and perambulated into the building, its interior lighted by a bare bulb, a pyramid of Lion Head Oil cans filling most of the front window. A row of fan belts hung on a wall above a rack of old-fashioned tools like those he'd found in the shed, the other walls mostly lined with shelves stocked with automotive things along with cans of Union Carbide; and there were various advertisements for items such as Apollo Spark Plugs, Sure Fire ignition parts and Willard batteries. A poster depicted a little boy clad in a footie pajama suit, obviously sleepy, and yawning. A car tire was slung on his shoulder, and in one hand was a candle. The caption read

Time to Retire
Get A Fisk

There was a wooden desk and chair, and an issue of *Whiz Bang* lay on the desk next to a candlestick telephone. By the door stood a trunk-sized steel box brightly painted black and red with the suggestion to Drink Double Cola.

Spencer lifted the casket-like lid, revealing rows of bottles immersed in ice-cold water, their necks imprisoned by angle-irons. He deduced the bottles could be removed by sliding them along the irons to a release mechanism apparently nickel-operated and probably freeing one bottle per coin. He scanned the selections: Double Cola, Big Chief Root Beer, Bireley's Orange Soda, and Bubble Up Lemon-Lime. The latter seemed most likely to be compatible with gin, and he dug a nickel out of a pocket.

"Please allow me," said Dodger, entering just as Spencer dropped the coin in the slot.

"Thanks, but I got it," said Spencer, as he extracted the bottle. "It was only a nickel."

Dodger drew a coin from a pocket and held it out between finger and thumb. "This is a nickel."

Spencer noted the buffalo, though the only ones he'd ever seen had been worn almost illegible, while this looked nearly new. "Did I break some kinda rule?"

Dodger regarded the coin box, which was secured by a padlock. "Someone may soon be pondering the mysteries of The Great Beyond."

CHAPTER FOURTEEN

"**D**id I miss something?" asked Annie, appearing in the doorway, her lipstick looking freshened and a new blush of rouge on her cheeks.

"Oh, nothing much," said Dodger. "Just that our charmingly cherubic friend may have altered the universe, space, time and everything."

"How exciting! ...What did you do?"

"Bought a soda," said Spencer.

"How nice. Shall we have it with gin?"

Spencer glanced at Dodger. "I bought it with my own nickel... I mean a nickel I brought with me."

"Was it a wooden nickel?" asked Annie. "That would have been a bit naughty."

"...No." Spencer glanced at Dodger again, who'd donned his enigmatic smile. "But I guess it doesn't belong here."

"An honest mistake, I'm sure," said Annie, and un-pursed her flask. "Open the Bubble Up, please, and we'll make a cocktail."

"Did someone say cocktail?" asked Willie, appearing along with Dreyfus and Finn.

Spencer used the machine's opener to pop the cap off the bottle. "What about altering the universe, space, time and everything?"

"Perhaps no one will notice," said Annie, offering her flask to be cocktailed.

"Did we miss somethin'?" asked Finn.

"Oh, nothing much," said Dodger, presenting his bottle to Spencer.

"Seems to be an echo in here," said Annie. "Spencer just altered the universe… grains of sand, drops of water, that sort of metaphysical stuff."

"I didn't do it on purpose," said Spencer, adding soda to Dodger's flask.

"Mistakes," said Dodger, after tasting the mix and nodding approval, "are seldom made on purpose, unless in hope of short-term profit." He Puckishly wagged a finger. "But I did say your money was no good here."

"I didn't think you meant catastrophic."

"Oh, piffle," said Annie. "It probably isn't as bad as all that… perhaps a few galaxies rearranged, an angel falling here and there, and minor apocalyptic events, perhaps only one or two horsemen." She took a sip from her bottle and offered it to Willie. "Rather tasty, have a nip."

Willie imbibed a swallow and passed the flask to Finn. "That'll crank your motor."

"On the other hand," said Dodger. "Perhaps world peace and cheeseburgers for all."

"Hopefully not on our heads," said Finn, glancing heavenward.

"What did you do?" asked Dreyfus, after also taking a taste.

Spencer repeated his transgression, and Willie said, "If you did alter the universe, it's probably only this one."

"An' maybe nobody will notice," said Dreyfus.

"My thought exactly," said Annie. "Even apocalyptic events are beginning to seem rather normal these days, what with the Great War and 'In flew Enza.'"

"There are other universes?" asked Spencer.

"Bags of 'em," said Finn. "Maybe a tad more Bubble Up?"

Spencer regarded the coin box, then turned to Dreyfus. "Don't you have a key? We could take my nickel out."

"You're assuming it's in there," said Dodger. "An assumption not worthy of Mr. Holmes."

"Of course it's in there, I just put it in there."

"No, you put it in the slot, but you don't know where it went after that or what mischief it might be making."

"I shot an arrow into the air…" Annie added helpfully.

"Learn that at Miss Penelope's?" asked Dodger.

"Right after the patty-melt lesson."

"Still can't figure dat out," said Finn.

"My dad say my feet are poetic," said Dreyfus.

"Why?" asked Annie.

"'Cause they long fellows."

"So now it a non-nickel," said Finn.

"Like Schrödinger's cat?" asked Spencer.

"That rings a bell," said Annie.

"That was Pavlov's dog," said Willie.

"No relation to Cowper's hare," said Dreyfus.

"Neither hare nor there," said Annie.

"Shoulda put a string on it," said Finn.

"That don't work with these new machines." Dreyfus took another drink after Willie added more soda. "Just about right for my taste." He indicated a small brass plate

OUROBOROS
AMUSEMENTS & VENDING

"Machine belong to the company so I don't gots a key."

"…Well…" Spencer pointed to the tools. "There's a hacksaw, you could cut off the lock and at least we could see. …I mean if I altered the universe…?"

"And space, time, and everything," Dodger wryly reminded.

"You don't have to rub it in," said Annie. "It was, after all, a mistake, and I daresay you've probably made a few."

Dodger circled a finger over his head. "And so, you observe, my lack of a halo."

"I get fired," said Dreyfus. "An' probably prostituted."

"Truly a fallen angel," said Dodger.

"In my opinion," said Annie, "*this* world, at least, would be a lot better if men spent more time frolicking and less trying to alter universes."

"I wasn't trying," said Spencer. "And I wish I was frolicking now."

"Wouldn't that be so jolly."

"But, what about the universe? . . .Even if it's only this one?"

"Maybe nobody will notice," said Finn.

The peaceful night stillness was broken by the approaching snarl of a motor, and everyone stepped outside to watch as a racy-looking topless car materialized out of the mist, came careening off the street and, rear wheels locked and tires shrieking, skidded to a stop at the pumps. It was a two-seater, Spencer saw, a luxury sports car for this time, and occupied by fur-coated figures who looked like circus bears capped with tweed.

"What kinda car is that?" he asked.

"Stuz Bearcat," said Dreyfus, which seemed appropriate.

"Guess it's expensive?"

"'Bout two-thousand oysters," said Finn.

"I thought the term was clams?" said Annie.

"Only got oysters tonight."

"Yes, we have no clams," said Dodger.

"I've heard about oysters," said Annie. "And their effects when consumed by boys."

"Surely not at Miss Penelope's."

Annie laughed. "I've never found watercress sandwiches to be effective at anything except producing gas."

Dodger added to Spencer, "You could buy three Model Ts for that and still have a basket of bivalves left."

"Men do love their machines," said Annie.

"Gives us something to play with when we're not altering universes."

"He didn't do it on purpose," said Willie.

The car's occupants, though bulked by their coats to ursine proportions, seemed to be boys of eighteen or so, their hair slicked with pomade as if painted on. Both were equipped with whisky bottles that may have been the real McCoy and were putting them to copious use. The driver killed the engine, flipped his cigarette away, and squalled like a petulant child to Dreyfus:

"Hey Licorice Stick, fill 'er up with ethyl! C'mon, shag it boy, chop chop!"

Dreyfus rolled his eyes and ambled to the pumps. "Don't seem like this universe altered much."

"Hey, shine!" the other boy yelled to Spencer. "Bring your box and gimmie some wax!"

Spencer almost made a suggestion he would have offered to anyone who'd ordered him to shine their shoes – impossible anatomically though interesting to watch in attempt – but refrained by reminding himself he might have altered a universe by introducing something new, and he couldn't recall that rude remark in anything published before World War Two.

"I'll take an evening edition, newsy!" the driver squalled to Dodger.

His companion glanced at the truck, then to Finn. "And flip me a flounder, fish-boy!"

Annie flipped him something else – credited to the ancient Greeks, though probably purloined from Egypt. "Twenty-three skidoo, small change!"

The driver laughed. "Poop-poopy-doop! Flap yourself into this hepmobile, doll, and we'll fly you away from the low-life."

"You can ride on my lap," said the other boy, "since you seem to like coon skin."

Annie made the rude remark Spencer had restrained, seeming to prove it *had* been in use before the 1940s.

The driver laughed again. "Little Miss Hotsy-tot's got spirit, gotta give her that."

His companion made the kind of face that should have been instantly slapped. "I'd like to give her something!"

"That would be small change indeed," said Annie.

"No little tramp talks to me like that!" The boy made a move to get out of the car, but the driver grabbed his arm. "Stow it, Charlie, we don't have time." He turned to Dreyfus. "Hurry up, boy, we got places to go!"

Dodger consulted his watch. "You're due for a haunting on Telegraph Road at twenty-eight minutes past midnight... Deadman's Curve, if memory serves."

"Go peddle your papers!" yelled Charlie.

"You'll be in the morning edition," laughed Dodger.

Charlie broke loose from the driver's grip and burst from the car in a flurry of fur. Beneath his partly open coat he was clad in a bow-tied evening suit cut for a build more beefy than fat, and was about a head taller than Dodger, who didn't look in the least concerned as Charlie stalked toward him with ham-fists clenched.

Maybe because of Dodger nonchalantly standing his ground, Charlie's focus shifted to Annie and he made another slappable face. "Into the struggle-buggy, kitten! Newsy can't do nothin', an' none of these jigs will touch a white man!"

Except for launching himself onto Dodger for masquerading as a ghost, Spencer had never been in a fight, but he started to step between Charlie and Annie to at least offer his bulk for a shield as Charlie reached to grab Annie's arm. But Annie lashed out with a delicate fist, mashing it square into Charlie's nose with a sound like squashing a hamburger patty.

"Ow!" The boy looked surprised for a moment, a hand going to his proboscis, from which blood dribbled down his chin to sully his snow-white shirt. Then his face flashed lobster red. "You little slut!"

Again, Spencer moved to intervene for whatever good he might do, eye-corner seeing that Willie and Finn were also about to break a rule and maybe alter a universe by laying hands on a rich Caucasian, while wondering why Dodger, astoundingly strong, seemed to be only observing.

But, again it was Annie who touched a white man – more accurately a nasty white boy – or rather the toe of her shoe making contact with Charlie's most intimate parts.

The big boy yelped and doubled-over, forgetting his disrespected nose to clutch with both hands his mistreated treasures.

"I'm sure," said Dodger, smiling, as Charlie tottered back a few paces and seemed to be pondering a puke, "Miss Penelope didn't teach that."

Annie adjusted her skirt. "My Victorian granny did; said it might come in handy some day."

"A woman ahead of her time," said Willie.

"A woman for all ages," said Annie. "As I aspire to be."

"Forever thoroughly modern," said Dodger.

133

The Bearcat's driver, not quite as beefy as now moaning Charlie though still considerably larger than Dodger, had witnessed his friend's ignoble defeat and tried to scramble to his aid, but Dreyfus, also disregarding a possible cataclysmic event, seized his shoulders and held him seated. "That be two dollars an' eighty-six cents."

The boy struggled to free himself, but Dodger came over and said, "Pay up and be on your way... *boy.*"

"And take this nasty brat with you," said Annie, following with Spencer as Willie and Finn escorted Charlie none too gently back to the car as if frog-marching a bent-over bear.

The driver tried to break free again, but stopped his struggles and stared. "...Dodger?"

Dodger smiled. "Hello, Albert."

"I'll tell your father!" squalled Albert.

"That you won't be doing," said Dodger, "because you never did. But once again I advise you not to drive up to the inn tonight. Nothing is preordained, and you have free will... even if not, apparently, the sentience to use it. Now pay the man and dearly depart."

"I won't forget this, Dodger!"

"But you might finally learn from it... though, if I may paraphrase, a stupid soul dies a thousand deaths."

Willie and Finn got Charlie aboard as Albert dug out a wallet and surrendered three dollar bills to Dreyfus, who counted back fourteen cents in change.

"Roar with Gilmore," said Dreyfus, politely touching his cap as Albert engaged the self-starter and the engine snotted to life.

Albert popped the clutch, and the car squealed away into the mist, its engine roar rapidly fading until there was peaceful silence again.

"You know him?" asked Spencer.

"Albert?" said Dodger. "Our fathers are acquainted through business; and Albert once dismembered a cherished Teddy of mine when inflicted on me as a nursery playmate; though thankfully our succeeding contacts have been confined to social events, which, I'm happy to say, have been few."

"Is that the Albert your uncle said could teach you how to be manly?"

Dodger chuckled. "The very spirit."

"It seems obvious," said Annie, "he wasn't as well-bred as you."

"On the contrary, very well-bred. One of Oakland's first families," said Dodger. "Just, apparently, not well brought up."

"All children," said Spencer, "are born knowing how to love, but they have to be taught how to hate."

"Couldn't have said it better," said Willie. "That some kinda quote?"

"I don't know, my dad told me that."

"You was well brought up," said Finn. He pulled a big nickel watch from a pocket and consulted the time. "It been fun but we best be goin'; dem oysters ain't gettin' no fresher."

Annie, Willie and Dodger boosted Spencer into the cab as Dreyfus poured a quart of oil from a tin-spouted jar into Lulibelle's engine. Then he closed and latched the hood, went into the building and returned with a can of carbide, which he tossed to Finn, who climbed behind the steering wheel to adjust the spark and throttle and flip the ignition switch.

Dreyfus gave the crank a pull and Lulibelle's engine lioned to life. "Give my regards to the gang at Hogan's; wish I was goin' with you."

"Another time I'm sure," said Dodger, delving into the Gladstone and presenting a pint to Dreyfus, then mounting the running-board and pointing into the mist. "An infinity of adventures ahead."

CHAPTER FIFTEEN

Finn engaged the clutch and Lulibelle rumbled onto the street, the gas station melting into the mist with the figure of Dreyfus under its lights raising a toast in farewell as Finn double-clutched through the gears up to fourth and maybe twenty-five-miles-an-hour. Spencer looked back through the hatch, catching a last glimpse of Dreyfus framed in a gap in the van's rear canvas.

"Looks like a lonely job," he remarked.

Finn smiled and, surprisingly, said, "'Spose he could be on a asteroid pumpin' fusion fuel into starships."

Again there was a pocket-effect as if nothing existed around them except what could be dimly discerned in the pale glow of the head-lights and an occasional street lamp fading in and out as they passed and for moments illuminating a small isolated city scene. From what Spencer could see, after Dodger had shared cigarettes with all and a bottle was jovially passed around, the surroundings seemed more industrial now as they turned onto Cypress Street, the buildings utilitarian in various old-fashioned masonry styles, and most of their windows dark, the street lamps fewer and farther between, and Spencer catching glimpses of signs involving warehouses, ironworks, machine shops, manufactories, along with suppliers of coal and ice. Most of the streets had rails in the middle, and boxcars, gondolas and tankers stood on sidings at loading docks. They overtook a big wooden wagon drawn by a slowly plodding mule and driven by a work-coated black boy of possibly eight or nine topped of course with a cap. The wagon was loaded with junk -- rusty bed frames, parts of old stoves, fenders and doors from cars and trucks, battered washtubs, buckets and such -- and a red lantern served as a tail light.

The boy smiled and waved to Finn as Lulibelle clattered past.

Finn remarked as they lumbered on, "Little Vulcan got him another load of ol' gived-up on dreams."

"What does he do with them?" asked Annie.

"Dey be melted into new ones for kids."

It occurred to Spencer they must be in West Oakland and -- at least relatively -- close to his former neighborhood. But, nothing in the fog looked familiar; and while he knew of a Cypress Park, he'd never heard of a Cypress Street. They rumbled past a barricade lit by a red warning lantern around an open manhole cover, and he caught a glimpse down the opening of what appeared to be starry space -- though must have been lights for workmen -- and again he felt the slipping sensation of partly waking from a dream with a feeling he'd forgotten something, but Annie's voice brought him back:

"You mentioned you have your own pond?"

"Yeah," said Willie. "You rich?"

"Far from it," said Spencer, accepting the busy bottle from Finn. "I grew up around here... I think it was here... but now we live in a little stone cottage... me and my parents... and there is a pond."

"Sounds very storybook," said Annie.

"Any fish in dat pond?" asked Finn.

"Big fat trout," said Dodger.

"I didn't know that," said Spencer. "We just moved in two days ago. Guess Dodger's been there a long time."

"You two have just met?" said Annie. "I would have thought you'd been friends forever."

Spencer laughed. "Maybe we met in a former life."

"I would think more than one," said Annie.

"What's the pond like?" asked Willie.

Spencer began to describe the setting, but Finn shifted to a lower gear and turned the truck, jolting over rails, into an alley between brick buildings that seemed to be no longer in use, their ground floor windows boarded, and one with a sign saying

ESSEX COACH WORKS

The passage was claustrophobically narrow with less than two feet to spare on each side and, except for the headlight glow, almost totally dark. A rusty, riveted iron door with traces of faded green paint remaining came into view on the right-hand building; and Spencer saw several bicycles of the old balloon-tire type leaning against the wall beside it, along with a homemade wooden scooter that might have belonged to a Little Rascal. Finn stopped the truck just beyond the door, shut off the ignition switch, and peaceful silence settled. Then Spencer heard faint music... the same lively beat he'd heard yesterday in the ancient Radiola's headphones.

Annie snuffed her cigarette and tucked the holder into her purse. "Is *this* the Hogan's Alley that 'everybody who's anybody' reputedly knows about?"

"Don't judge a book by its cover," said Dodger.

"If I did I wouldn't have joined this gang."

"Well," said Finn, climbing down from the cab. "Ain't da ballroom at da Oakland Hotel, but I thinks you might like it." He went to the back of the truck and added while pulling out a box, "An' dey gots da best fried oysters in all da universes I knows."

Dodger and Willie dismounted and offered hands to Annie, assisting her into the narrow space between Lulibelle and the building. Then all helped Spencer down, though he was barely able to move with his bottom pressed to the building's wall and his belly squeezed against the truck, so he had to squirm and squiggle sideways back to the rusty door, where Finn and the others waited in the ruby glow of the tail light.

Dodger knuckle-rapped the door with the "shave-and-a-haircut" signal. A moment later a small panel opened, revealing the cautious face of a boy, perhaps a year older than Dodger, beneath a tousle of shaggy brown hair, along with the louder sound of music.

"Joe sent us," said Dodger.

The boy laughed. "Clap hands, here comes Dodger. ...An' there's Finn with the oysters. Good thing you got here, we're runnin' low."

The panel closed with a clank, and there were rasps of bolts being drawn. Then the door creaked open, the music growing louder again, coming from beyond an old blanket that curtained-off a small alcove dimly lit by a bulb on frayed wires. The walls were rough-mortared brick, and there was a Little Rascalish sign painted on a piece of wood.

HOGAN2 ALLEY
COVER CHARGE 10¢

Dodger dug in a pocket, but the brown-haired boy said, "G'wan, no charge, but I'll take a gasper if you got one."

"Here you go, Harvey," said Dodger, producing a Fatima, which Spencer fired with his lighter.

"Thanks." Harvey drew the blanket aside, and the others stepped back to let Finn proceed with the dripping box.

At first Spencer thought they were back in the mist, though now glowing ethereally gold, but it was tobacco smoke hazing the air; and there was a lusciously succulent scent that seemed to confirm what Finn had said about which universe fried the best oysters. Spencer had read about speakeasies and of course had seen them in films, but this place, like the childish sign, looked like a movie set for *Our Gang*, except for being in color. The room was possibly fifty feet square and bare brick-walled without any windows, its lofty ceiling blackened with soot from maybe a former industrial use, and like the alcove was dimly lit by doubtful bulbs on dangerous wires, their yellow-orange filaments suggesting the power might be purloined. The floor was grimy concrete almost as black as the ceiling, the tables and chairs not related by birth – those that weren't formerly big wooden spools that might have once held rope -- and so deplorably battered no junk shop would have embarrassed itself by offering them for sale. At the rear of the room was a packing-crate bar with several de-silvering mirrors behind it in juvenile imitation of an old-fashioned saloon, and rough board shelves lined with castaway glasses, repurposed bottles and Mason jars. There was also a five-gallon lard can perched on a blue-flaming iron gas ring and emitting a feathery cloud of steam along with the tantalizing aroma of possibly egg-battered oysters being deliciously deep-fried.

As in the theater lobby and Willie Watson's café, he got the impression of figures around him – most of the tables seemed occupied and some of the shapes were dancing – but they only came into focus if he concentrated on them. The bar was staffed by a dusky black boy of possibly sixteen who looked like an African version of a Charles Atlas "after" ad, clad in white T-shirt and coal-colored vest, a derby like Spencer's crowning his curls, the stub of a chunky unlit cigar accessorizing a pugnacious face which, while idling in neutral, looked just as ready to smile as snarl.

Tending the oysters was a tubby white boy who could have played Chubby in *Our Gang* wearing a greasy apron and an equally oily newspaper cap. To the right of the bar was a plank bandstand spotlighted by an acetylene lamp that might have come off a truck. A shabby, frontless upright piano stood against the wall, and another black boy of around Spencer's age and a very close second in rolly fat size, his midnight mass only partly contained within a straining sweat-soaked singlet – the air was very warm, as well as steamy with cookery – was smothering a shipping box while skillfully coaxing a tinny but very voluminous romping tune from the old instrument's ivories. Another boy, possibly fourteen, wiry, white, and moppy blond-haired, his singlet so large it bared most of his torso, was pounding a percussion set with equal degrees of perspiration and proficiency, accompanied on a yakety sax by a copper-toned boy of slender build who may have been Native American and looked about thirteen; while a cherubically-chubby lad with a Gypsy air about him – suggested by baubles, bangles and beads adorning his wrists, ankles and chest – and possibly eleven years old, his belly like a plump loincloth far over-rolling his low-riding jeans, his bobby-breasted torso bare and gleaming goldenly under the light, his hair a silky raven cascade rippling over his shoulders, was sounding his soul on a tarnished trumpet; all backed by a small Chinese boy, maybe ten, his singlet so large it looked like a dress, his face mostly hidden by sheep-dog hair, whose diminutive size was further enhanced by an enormous bull fiddle. There were no speakers or microphones but the sound was more than adequate to possibly wake the dead.

Painted on the bass drum was

THE LOST
BOYS

"I've heard that tune before," said Spencer, as Dodger led the way to a table while Finn took the oysters behind the bar.

"The Charleston?" said Annie, as Spencer politely seated her, taking her jacket as she removed it and draping it over the back of her chair. "You'd have to be recently resurrected not to have heard it before; it came out in 1923."

Spencer turned to Dodger. "You know that old radio in the shed?"

"Hum a few bars and I'll fake it," said Dodger.

"Seriously," said Spencer.

"The Radiola?" said Dodger, taking a seat and shedding his coat. "Somewhat obsolete by this time and replaced by a Grebe with a speaker."

"My pops just bought a Crosley," said Annie, un-pursing her holder and loading a smoke. The feeble electric lighting was supplemented by candles in wax-webbed bottles on every table, and she lit-up from a flame. "I was hoping I'd get our old Westinghouse for exclusive use in my room, but he used it for trade-in."

Willie plopped down and took off his coat. "We got an ol' Atwater-Kent, but it brings in KLX pretty good."

"Built me a crystal set," said Finn, appearing along with the bartender boy, who greeted Dodger by name and asked:

"Got any casket coatin' tonight?"

"Hi Louis." Dodger opened his bag and offered a pint, which Louis uncapped and cautiously sniffed.

"Smells a lot better than last time," said Louis, and took a wary taste. "That's the bee's knees!" He sampled again. "Almost like the real McCoy."

"My friend Spencer perfected it," said Dodger, patting Spencer's shoulder.

"Pleased to meet ya, professor," said Louis, as Spencer doffed his

141

coat and sat down.

"Likewise," said Spencer, shaking hands.

Dodger introduced Annie and Willie, and after greetings were exchanged, Louis turned to Dodger again. "I take all ya got. But, guess ya want more for this star-shine?"

"For you, same price," said Dodger, and began pulling bottles out of the bag and lining them up on the table. "I can let you have a dozen; already promised six to Finn."

"Swell," said Louis, producing some bills, which Spencer noted looked larger and different than "future" money.

Finn loaded his coat's baggy pockets with pints. "Real nice meetin' you all."

"You're not leaving us?" said Annie. "It feels like the fun has just begun."

"Wish I could stay, but I still gots three boxes of cod to deliber, an' Finn's always guarantee fresh. ...Got to, bein' colored, y'know."

"Surely they'll stay impertinent a little while longer?" said Dodger.

Annie added while taking Finn's hand, "Do stay and be part of our gang this time."

Finn considered. "Well, dey on ice, so dey still be smarty a while."

Dodger consulted his watch. "Plenty of time for fun." He added to Spencer, "Last train going our way before sunrise passes at 1:57."

"Swell!" said Annie. "Do remove your coat and join us."

"Coat's all I got," said Finn, seating himself between Dodger and Spencer.

"Yes, I know," said Annie.

"That pesky clasp again?" asked Dodger, offering a Fatima to Finn.

"I find shirtless boys adorable," said Annie, adoring the chubby Gypsy lad gleamingly pumping his trumpet on stage.

"You've exposed that already," said Dodger.

"I wouldn't mind more exposure."

"How about this?" suggested Spencer. "We'll take off our shirts if you do."

"How naughty," laughed Annie. "Tell me please, and honestly, do boys only want one thing from girls?"

Dodger said, "We could ask the same question of you, inversely."

"Good cookin' come to mind," said Willie, then added diplomatically, "But I help do the dishes."

"I likes 'telligent conversation, long's it ain't over my head," said Finn.

Louis gathered the bottles. "Hang around a while, Miss, an' your wish might get granted. Things tend to get lively after midnight an' formal dress ain't required. ...Now what can I get for you all, since you already got the best coffin varnish I been exposed to in ages?"

"Oysters all around," said Dodger. "Glasses, and two White Rocks, please."

Louis called to the tubby boy, "Norman, five orders here."

Using a wire basket, Norman began scooping gold-battered oysters out of the steaming can.

"Oh, they smell delicious!" cried Annie.

"Mind that clasp," said Dodger.

"Gotta get that recipe," said Willie.

Louis laughed. "I could tell ya, but then I gotta snuff ya out."

Spencer took a cigarette from Dodger's offered pack, lit it from the candle and scanned the smoke-filled room. As he had already noticed, the figures around were indistinct unless he consciously focused on them. There may have been close to fifty, with white the predominant shade of skin, black the next most numerous, various hues of coppers and browns, and a scatter of Asian. None appeared to be over eighteen, while a few seemed as youthful as ten. Maybe two-thirds were male, all garbed about the same as Dodger, Willie, Finn and himself in what were blue-collar clothes for this time; nowhere were suits like Charlie and Albert's, or any raccoon coats. The girls wore mostly flapper styles, though some were in working-class dresses that brought the term, shop girls, to mind. Everyone seated had bottles and glasses, though some of the younger were sipping Cokes. He wondered if there was an age limit here, but that seemed absurd since alcohol was illegal for everyone in this time.

He focused his eyes on the dancing figures in front of the make-shift bandstand -- maybe five couples of various ages -- and he recognized Mickey, though mostly from his porcupine hair, fluent freckles and basketball belly, since he was now clad in singlet and jeans and teamed with a very attractive girl who might have been Japanese. As if sensing Spencer, he grinned and flashed an OK sign.

Two boys of possibly fourteen, one slender black, one muscular white, and both with shirts body-baring unbuttoned – as Annie had obviously noticed -- were intimately dancing together unabashedly cheek-to-cheek.

"Guess they're gay," Spencer remarked. "…But, I thought that was illegal… now."

Dodger shrugged. "It's always illegal to be gay, especially to be young and gay, when most of a society isn't."

"They look very gay," said Annie. "I hope we can all be as gay tonight."

"I feel pretty gay," said Willie, as Norman appeared with a big wooden tray loaded with five steaming mountains of oysters piled on newspaper sheets, along with a shaker of pepper and a bottle of vinegar.

"I feels some gay comin' on," said Finn, sprinkling an oyster with seasonings and chomping a big messy bite. "Mmmm! Yeah, I's def'tly gettin' gay!"

"The '90s were very gay," said Annie, "according to my granny."

"My dad said Paris was gay," said Willie. "'Specially since the French folks treated him like a human bein'.'"

Spencer laughed, taking an oyster from his pile and adding pepper and vinegar. "No, I meant…" He didn't know what word to use – the textbook term seemed too clinical and the common either cretinish or maybe still just meaning odd in this time – and took a moment to eat the oyster, which tasted like food meant for gods, tender and juicy within golden batter contrasted by sensually soft crunchiness with flavors of pepper, garlic and thyme all subtly enhanced by the malt vinegar. "Guess I mean like lesbians," he finished, with his mouth very gay.

"How Bohemian," said Annie, managing to look ladylike while indulging in heavenly finger food.

"I knows a lezzy-bean," said Finn, downing his oyster and snagging another.

"Oh, do tell," said Annie.

"He a fisherman."

"Thought lesbians had to be girls," said Willie, popping an oyster into his mouth.

"Come from a island in Greece," said Finn. "Eberbody lezzy-beans dere."

"Must be a real gay place," laughed Spencer.

"Well," said Finn. "I figures we all half boy an' half girl."

"How you figure that?" asked Willie.

"We comes from moms an' dads, doesn't we?"

"What a gay thought," said Annie, dispatching another oyster.

Norman returned with five glasses and a pair of White Rocks, and everyone concocted cocktails. "I'll take your empties," said Dodger, and Norman fetched back a dozen pint bottles, which Dodger stowed in the Gladstone. The lively Charleston ended, the room resounding with cheers and applause, and the cherubic Gypsy kid stepped fully into the spotlight. The band struck up another tune, and, smiling at the pair of boys, the cherub sang in a high, clear voice:

> "Who's that coming down the street?
> Who's that looking so petite?
> Who's that coming down to meet me here?
>
> Who's that?
> You know the who I mean
> Sweetest who you've ever seen
> I could tell him miles away from here.
>
> Yes sir, that's my baby
> No sir, I don't mean maybe
> Yes sir, that's my baby now.
> Yes, ma'am, we've decided
> No ma'am, we won't hide it
> Yes, ma'am, you're invited now

By the way, oh by the way
When we reach the preacher I'll say
Yes sir, that's my baby
No sir, I don't mean maybe
Yes sir, that's my baby now!"

He took up his trumpet to play the coda, and Annie wistfully sighed, "What an adorable angel; he'd be so divine to cuddle."

Dodger took a sip from his glass. "Wouldn't that be robbing the manger?"

"If that's a sin, count me in."

"Must be gettin' near midnight," said Willie, manfully mining his oyster mountain.

"I hope you won't turn into mice," said Annie.

"Nah," said Finn. "We takes off our shirts an' dances with patty-melts on our heads."

"I'll settle for the first two states." Annie touched Spencer's arm. "Care to cut a rug?"

"Me?" said Spencer around an oyster. "You're kidding, right? ...Much as I'd like to."

"Don't you dare say you're too fat."

"That might have something to do with it, but I've never danced in my life."

"I'm sure you have in many."

"...Lives?"

"Bags of 'em," said Finn, chomping another oyster.

Annie turned to Willie, who shrugged. "I might have, but I think I forgot."

"Never been a very good dancer," said Dodger, when Annie appealed to him.

"I would have thought you could do anything."

"Note again my lack of a halo."

"Oh, Finn," said Annie, pleadingly.

Finn popped a last oyster into his mouth. "I knows a few steps."

"My angel!" said Annie, as Finn got up and gallantly took her hand.

"There's a match made in the stars," said Dodger, also dispatching a final oyster and taking another sip from his glass as Annie and Finn departed.

Willie laughed. "Bet you can dance like nobody's business."

Dodger fired a smoke. "Never was much for social graces."

"Finn can sure shake a thing," said Spencer, watching the couple take to the floor amongst the other vigorous shapes. "And Annie's got some heavenly moves."

"They look very gay," said Willie.

The dance ended with a trumpet crescendo to another round of cheers and applause, a lot of it for Annie and Finn, and the cherub stepped down to take their hands.

"Now Finn's in the light," said Dodger. "It's about time he came out."

"What do you mean?" asked Spencer, swallowing the last of his oysters.

"He still thinks he's just a dark angel."

"...Like, not as good as lighter angels?"

"A lifetime of being told one isn't can have that effect in the after."

"He's gotta sing or somethin'," said Willie. "It's a rule when the light's on you. An' Annie, too."

Finn looked very shy as, urged by more cheering and clapping, the cherub drew him along with Annie up into the beam of light. The piano tinkled encouraging notes, and the drummer rolled an intro, backed by the trumpet, bass and sax. Finn swallowed and seemed about to freeze, but Annie squeezed his hand and he suddenly smiled as if inspired, clasped his hands behind his back like a little kid giving a school recital, and began to huskily chant, the instruments joining with back-up.

Little Orphan Annie's come in our house to stay
An' wash da cups an' saucers up, an' brush da crumbs away
An' shoo da chickens off da porch, an' dust da hearth, an' sweep
An' make da fire, an' bake da bread, an' earn her board-an'-keep
An' all us other chillun when supper things is done

We sits around da kitchen fire an' has da mostest fun
Listenin' to da spirit tales dat Annie tells about.

An' da Goblins gonna get you
If you don't watch out.

Oncet dey was a little boy wouldn't say his prayers
An' when he went to bed one night all alone upstairs
His mammy heard him holler, an' his daddy heard him bawl
But when dey turned the cobers down...
He wasn't... dere... at... all!
Dey seeked him in da rafter-room, an' cubby-hole, an' press
An' seeked him up da chimbunny an' eberwheres, I guess
But all dey found was just his shirt an' suchlike roundabout.

'Cause da Goblins gonna get you
If you don't watch out.

An' one time a little girl would always laugh an' grin
An' she make fun of eberone, an' all her blood an' kin
An' oncet when dey was company an' all da folks was dere
She mocked 'em an' she shocked 'em, an' say she didn't care
An' as she made a face at 'em an' went to run an' hide
A sudden dey was... *two big things*... a standin' by her side!
Dey snatched her into nothin' 'fore she knowed what she's about!

An' da Goblins gonna get you
If you don't watch out.

An' little Orphan Annie says when da blaze is blue
An' da lamp-wick sputters, an' da wind is goin' *woooooooo*
You better mind your parents an' your teachers fond an' dear
An' cherish dem who loves you, an' dry da orphan's tear
An' help da poor an' needy ones who cluster all about.
Or...
Da Goblins gonna get you

If you don't... watch... out!

Again the room rocked with cheers and applause, Finn bowing modestly, stepping to the cherub's side and leaving Annie in the light.

"Woah," said Spencer. "There's a lot more to Finn than what you can see."

"The light can be very soul-baring," said Dodger.

Now it was Annie looking shy, but Finn smiled at her and she began, the band joining with accompaniment:

> The sun was shining on the sea
> Shining with all his might
> He did his very best to make
> The billows smooth and bright
> And this was odd, because it was
> The middle of the night.
>
> The moon was shining sulkily,
> Because she thought the sun
> Had got no business to be there
> After the day was done
> "It's very rude of him," she said
> "To come and spoil the fun!"
>
> The sea was wet as wet could be
> The sands were dry as dry
> You could not see a cloud, because
> No cloud was in the sky
> No birds were flying overhead
> There were no birds to fly.
>
> The Walrus and the Carpenter
> Were walking close at hand
> They wept like anything to see
> Such quantities of sand

"If this were only cleared away"
They said, "it would be grand!"

"If seven maids with seven mops
Swept it for half a year
Do you suppose," the Walrus said
"That they could get it clear?"
"I doubt it," said the Carpenter
And shed a bitter tear.

"Oh Oysters, come and walk with us!"
The Walrus did beseech
"A pleasant walk, a pleasant talk
Along the briny beach
We cannot do with more than four
To give a hand to each."

The eldest Oyster looked at him
But never a word he said
The eldest Oyster winked his eye
And shook his heavy head
Meaning to say he did not choose
To leave the oyster-bed.

But four young Oysters hurried up
All eager for the treat
Their coats were brushed, their faces washed
Their shoes were clean and neat
And this was odd, because, you know
They hadn't any feet.

Four other Oysters followed them
And yet another four
And thick and fast they came at last
And more, and more, and more
All hopping through the frothy waves

And scrambling to the shore.
The Walrus and the Carpenter
Walked on a mile or so
And then they rested on a rock
Conveniently low
And all the little Oysters stood
And waited in a row.

"The time has come," the Walrus said
"To talk of many things
Of shoes and ships and sealing-wax
Of cabbages and kings
And why the sea is boiling hot
And whether pigs have wings."

"But wait a bit," the Oysters cried
"Before we have our chat
For some of us are out of breath
And all of us are fat!"
"No hurry!" said the Carpenter
They thanked him much for that.

"A loaf of bread," the Walrus said
"Is what we chiefly need
Pepper and vinegar besides
Are very good indeed
Now if you're ready, Oysters dear
We can begin to feed."

"But not on us!" the Oysters cried
Turning a little blue
"After such kindness, that would be
A dismal thing to do!"
"The night is fine," the Walrus said
"Do you admire the view?"
"It was so kind of you to come!

And you are very nice!"
The Carpenter said nothing but
"Cut us another slice
I wish you were not quite so deaf
I've had to ask you twice!"

"It seems a shame," the Walrus said
"To play them such a trick
After we've brought them out so far
And made them trot so quick!"
The Carpenter said nothing but
"The butter's spread too thick!"

"I weep for you," the Walrus said
"I deeply sympathize."
With sobs and tears he sorted out
Those of the largest size
Holding his pocket-handkerchief
Before his streaming eyes.

"O Oysters," said the Carpenter
"You've had a pleasant run!
Shall we be trotting home again?"
But answer came there none
And this was scarcely odd, because
They'd eaten every one.

Again the sooty rafters rang with spirited applause, and of course more oysters were called for, Louis assisting Norman to pile golden mountains on trays.

"Shall we have a second round?" asked Dodger, as Finn and Annie returned hand-in-hand.

"Oh, yes!" said Annie, "how very gay!" as Finn gentlemanly seated her.

"I'm in," said Willie. "It's swell eatin' somebody else's cookin' instead of my own for a change."

"Yours is still divine," said Annie.

The oysters had been plentiful, and added to all he had eaten at home plus the triple cheeseburger at Willie's, Spencer was feeling massively stuffed but nodded in agreement.

Then, suddenly he was bathed in light. Blinking his dazzled eyes, he saw the cherub up on a ladder aiming the lamp at him, and Louis had taken the stage. "Introducin' Spencer! Who created the upliftin' spirits what may be raisin' yours tonight!"

Again there came applause and cheers, including from his four companions; and Dodger said, "Go to the light."

"...But... I don't know what to do."

"I'm sure you'll think of something," said Annie. "You've already altered universes, space, time and everything; surely a simple poem or song is not beyond your powers."

"G'wan, earn your oysters," said Willie.

Spencer hesitated, but, smiling, Finn and Dodger rose and hoisted him to his feet, the spotlight trailing amid more cheers as he was escorted to the bandstand, where Dodger lifted him onto the boards. For a moment his mind seemed a vast empty place, but then he remembered a poem he'd read, and the band joined in as he began:

"Come hither, my lads, with your tankards of ale
And drink to the present before it shall fail
Pile each on your platter a mountain of beef
For 'tis eating and drinking that bring us relief
So fill up your glass
For life will soon pass
When you're dead ye'll ne'er drink to your king or your lass!

Anacreon had a red nose, so they say
But what's a red nose if ye're happy and gay?
Gad split me! I'd rather be red whilst I'm here
Than white as a lily and dead half a year
So Annie, my miss
Come give me a kiss
In hell there's no innkeeper's daughter like this!

Young Harry, propp'd up just as straight as he's able
Will soon lose his wig and slip under the table
But fill up your goblets and pass 'em around
Better under the table than under the ground
So revel and chaff
As ye thirstily quaff
Under six feet of dirt 'tis less easy to laugh!

The fiend strike me blue! I'm scarce able to walk
And damme if I can stand upright or talk
Here, landlord, bid Annie to summon a chair
I'll try home in a while for my wife is not there
So lend me a hand
I'm not able to stand
But I'm gay whilst I linger on top of the land!"

Bottles and glasses had been waving to the rendition's rollicking rhythm, and more applause rang out when he finished. The cherub smiled and kissed his cheek, and the band struck up another dance as Dodger and Finn helped him back to the floor.

"The poem from *The Tomb*," said Dodger. "By H. P. Lovecraft. But, wasn't the innkeeper's daughter named Betty?"

"Yeah, but I changed it for obvious reasons."

"Very *apropos*."

"Fittin' too," said Finn.

Norman was at the table laying out more oysters, but just as Spencer was about to sit down, Harvey burst in from the alcove.

"Raaaid!"

CHAPTER SIXTEEN

Spencer's first thought was a bug-spray commercial. But the band crashed to silence in mid-note and all the figures around him were suddenly in frantic motion, dropping glasses, pocketing bottles, throwing cigarettes on the floor, snatching coats, jackets and wraps and running for the rear of the room, where Louis flung open a big wooden door.

The band members scrambled to disassemble and scurry off with the drum set along with their own instruments – the old piano left to its fate – and Norman abandoned his oysters to join the jostling exodus, while Harvey assisted Louis in keeping a little rough order so no one, especially younger patrons, were trampled in the stampede.

Dodger grabbed his coat and bag. "Time to amscray, gang!"

"How exciting!" cried Annie, seizing her jacket and purse.

There came a massive iron clank as what must have been a battering ram was brought to bear on the alley door.

Spencer snagged his coat, Finn and Willie following as Dodger gripped Spencer's arm and towed him toward the other door, while Finn took Annie's hand.

Spencer managed a ponderous trot like an earthquake in ebony Jell-O. "In case you forgot, I can't run!" he puffed.

"You're doing a good imitation," said Dodger, tugging Spencer faster.

There was another resounding clank against the alley door, but most of the figures had disappeared through the second doorway, the piano player one of the last helping the small Chinese boy with his bass.

"Thought you were shining the buzzers?" Dodger called to Louis while towing Spencer past.

"New buttons, I guess," said Louis. "But I get it level upstairs an' we be back in no time."

"Cops?" panted Spencer.

"Or moonlighting demons," said Dodger.

Again there came a brutal clank, and this time a crackle of splintering wood as Dodger pulled Spencer through the portal into what first looked like black starless space but resolved into some sort of huge empty room echoing with the scuffle of feet as half-phantom figures funneled through another doorway into mist.

Spencer, though barely retaining his jeans, sweating, and panting for breath, managed a glance over a shoulder, seeing Willie close behind followed by Annie and Finn; and caught a glimpse of a blue-coated cop with a revolver in hand as Louis and Harvey slammed the door and barred it with a timber. Then, with Dodger dragging him on, he lumbered through the other doorway into the softly-swirling mist where dimly discerned was weedy dirt, scattered junk, and the rusty corpse of a truck on blocks. The rest of the figures seemed to have vanished, maybe through sagging half-open gates in a tall but tottering board fence. There must have been a street out there because the mist was illuminated by an incandescent glow that might have been a light on a pole.

"How exciting!" cried Annie again, emerging from the doorway with Finn behind a puffing Willie.

"Glad you're still gay," said Dodger.

"I sure ain't," groaned Finn. "Dem cops gonna confuscate Luli-belle!"

"Oh dear," said Annie, pressing his hand.

Louis and Harvey appeared. "Maybe you can save her," said Harvey. "The cops got their car an' Black Maria blockin' the alley behind, but ain't nothin' in front. If me an' Louis extract 'em, you should be able to get away."

"Yeah," said Louis. "Most of 'em inside wreckin' the joint an' busy bustin' bottles... what they ain't stuffin' in their pockets. We'll go 'round front an' come up the alley makin' noise an' throwin' rocks.

That should give ya time to scram."

"I'll do the cranking," said Dodger to Finn. "You and the gang get aboard."

"Give us a little time," said Louis. "When you hear the ruckus, skedaddle."

He and Harvey disappeared around the side of the building while Dodger led the way through the gates out to a shadowy fog-shrouded street with railroad tracks down the middle, where a lamp on a telephone pole cast a cone of light at the alley entrance. Dodger peered around the corner. "Louis was right," he whispered. "Most of the flatties must be inside making the requisite mess, but there's probably one still out with their car. ...Come on and make like mice."

Slowly regaining some of his breath, Spencer, trailed by the others, followed Dodger up the alley where the truck's headlights still burned. From inside the building came sounds of destruction as what had been mostly junk to begin with was systematically ravaged, the old piano battered to bits in the name of enforcing morality.

Dodger unfolded the crank as Finn scrambled into the driver's seat and adjusted the throttle and spark, while Annie and Willie helped Spencer aboard. Spencer looked back though the hatch, the gap in the van's rear canvas revealing a touring car with its top folded down and a cop sitting on its running-board casually smoking a cigarette and taking a nip from a flask. Behind the car was a boxy truck of the type he'd seen in old movies for hauling off gangsters and prostitutes, though apparently empty tonight without a cargo of youthful scofflaws.

Finn switched on the ignition and poised with a hand on the gear shift lever while Dodger stood ready to crank. Then there came teen-age curses and taunts from the other end of the alley, and rocks began thunking the Black Maria, some flying over and clunking the car, one bopping the cop on a shoulder.

"The divil!" he cried, jumping up and grabbing his whistle. Another rock smacked it out of his hand, producing a yelp and blasphemy; and Dodger pulled the crank.

The engine started instantly, Dodger dodging out of the way as

Finn engaged the clutch, then leaping onto the running-board as Lulibelle roared down the alley.

"Hey!" the cop yelled. "…Stop! Police!"

Annie blew him a raspberry.

The cop unstrapped his holster and started to grab his gun, but another rock whizzed his cap away and he scrambled for cover in front of the car.

That was the last of him Spencer could see as the mist closed in behind them and Lulibelle burst out of the alley skidding sideways into the street – Spencer remembered reading somewhere that solid tires skidded on "dew" -- as Finn wrestled the steering wheel and double-clutched up through the gears.

"How exciting!" cried Annie, clinging to Spencer's arm.

"Pretty gay, too!" said Willie.

"I's back to feelin' gay," said Finn, manipulating the spark-advance and feeding the engine more throttle, the headlights tunneling into the mist, creating a pocket-effect again as they jolted along the shadowy street. Except for the thundering engine, clattering drive chains and rattles and squeaks, the night was otherwise still… but then came the yowling wail of a siren.

"Could that be the cops?" said Annie.

Finn wiped mist from the mirror. "I sees a red light!"

Dodger leaned out from the running-board to peer around the van box, Willie holding his arm. "Yeah, me too!"

Spencer rearranged himself to look rearward though the hatch and saw a crimson glow in the fog. It was maybe still a block behind but seemed to be gaining fast, and the cat-mating squall of the old-fashioned siren was getting louder every second.

"Might be a fire engine," said Willie.

"Don't wanna find out!" said Finn, making a skidding right turn onto another, darker street and flooring the accelerator. The boxes of fish in back slammed against the side of the van, spilling out several specimens; and Spencer saw the scarlet light slew around to stay in pursuit, accompanied by the squeal of tires.

"Shit!" he said. "They're still behind us! …Pardon my French."

"That would be *merde*," said Annie.

"*Les petites sophistiquées,*" said Dodger.

"No thanks to Miss Penelope."

"*Kaka!*" said Willie.

"*Skatá!*" said Finn, skidding the truck into an alley and flooring the gas again. "Learned dat from da lezzy-bean."

"How Bohemian," said Annie.

"How fast can Lulibelle go?" asked Spencer, still peering back through the hatch, seeing more fish bouncing out of the boxes and flopping onto the floor, a few abandoning ship, so to speak, past the flapping canvas.

"Had her near thirty-five oncet, but her rods won't take it for long," said Finn, guiding the truck up the narrow passage, though sometimes clipping a garbage can, which erupted nasty stuff while tumbling away.

"Wow!" said Spencer, pinching his nose. "That garbage really stinks!"

"Discarded detritus," said Dodger, "from those who've left the lower planes... hate, greed, intolerance, and more than a little self-righteousness."

"How fast can the cop car go?" asked Spencer, seeing the crimson light still behind, the glow of headlamps fluorescing the fog, the siren echoing painfully between the rows of buildings.

"Maybe fifty," said Dodger, now pressed against the side of the cab with Willie's arm around him as walls of brick went flying past.

"Shit!" said Annie.

"Help me!" puffed Spencer, squirming out of his coat and squiggling into the hatchway like a blubbery cork in too small a bottle. The opening had looked large enough, but he felt like Pooh stuck in Rabbit's hole before he'd struggled halfway in.

"What's up?" asked Willie, holding Dodger as Annie assisted Spencer with pushes and shoves on his now bare bottom and undulant tuckings and stuffings of fat to squeeze his middle through.

"Bring 'em closer to cod!" yelled Spencer, finally ejecting into the van thanks to a last mighty shove from Annie, and tumbling onto the fishy floor.

"What fun!" cried Annie, doffing her jacket and scrambling after, joining Spencer in grabbing fish and flinging them out the back.

"Dere go da profits," lamented Finn, concentrating on holding course as Lulibelle burst out of the passage, bashing over railroad tracks across another foggy street and burrowing into another alley.

"I'll cover that," said Dodger.

"'Preciated," said Finn, mostly dodging garbage cans.

Meanwhile back in the van, Spencer and Annie were flinging more fish. The police car was clearly visible now behind the electric glare of its lights, loaded with half a dozen cops, the driver fighting the steering wheel as the vehicle bounded over the tracks, becoming airborne for a moment, another cop half standing beside him determinedly cranking the siren as if trying reel in the criminals, the others in back with revolvers drawn and trying to aim at the fleeing truck. But then the rain of fish began, one slamming into the siren-cranker, who almost tumbled out of the car, another smashing the windshield, another smacking the driver's face so he took out a row of garbage cans with offal spattering everywhere, including onto the officers, who hastily holstered their firearms in favor of fending off flying piscines.

"They seem to be floundering," laughed Annie, gaily tossing another cod.

"Let's school 'em some more!" yelled Spencer.

"Give 'em a load of carp!" laughed Annie, grabbing one of the boxes and dumping its contents onto the pavement, a slimy shower of slipperiness the police car's tires didn't like... the vehicle skidding sideways, crashing into more garbage cans with a spray of multicolored mess and smashing its nose into a wall amid a cloud of spew-ing steam.

Dodger called back, "Sorry we didn't have any loaves!"

"Bet that's one fish story," laughed Willie, "we won't be herring about in the Trib."

"Now dem's soiled soles," chuckled Finn.

"Oh my!" cried Annie, clutching Spencer as Lulibelle thundered out of the alley and bounded over more railroad tracks across another street. "Now I'm all hot and wet!"

"...Huh?" said Spencer, steadying her.

"From throwing fish, silly."

"...Oh."

Finn put another pair of streets between them and the cod-floundered cops, then stopped beneath a haloed lamp, dismounting along with Dodger and Willie to help the fish-flingers back to earth.

"Think they radioed for backup?" asked Spencer, as Dodger bear-hugged him down, while Finn assisted Annie, who'd abandoned her gloves for obvious reasons.

"A radio in a *car?*" said Willie, raising an incredulous eyebrow.

A little while later, Finn brought the truck to another stop at the corner of Shafter and College. All was peacefully still once more except for the slow-loping engine, and there were no vehicles plying the streets or figures of people on sidewalks, which glimmered wetly under the lights like late-night city scenes in old films.

Dodger hopped down from the running-board and consulted his watch. "The train will be coming soon."

Willie and Annie dismounted, all helping Spencer descend, and Finn offered Willie a ride home, then smiled down at Annie. "Den I drives you home, if you like?"

"That would be swell," said Annie. "This has been a night to remember full of exciting adventures and fun."

"Pretty gay, too," said Willie.

"We must do it again some time."

"Second star to the right," said Dodger.

Annie turned to Spencer. "And a frolic in your pond?"

Spencer smiled. "If it's in the stars."

"If it wouldn't seem *risqué*," said Annie, "might I have a memory? I'm sorry I didn't bring my Brownie."

"Careful with that clasp," said Dodger.

"I'll blame it on the oysters."

"How about it, gang?" said Dodger.

"Oh, sure," said Willie, shedding his coat and wiggling out of his shirt. Spencer followed suit, and Finn and Dodger joined them, lining up beside the truck. Annie regarded them for a time as if taking a photograph with an old-fashioned camera. "Is touching the merchandise allowed?"

"Handle with care," said Willie.

Finn laughed. "Does girls only want one thing from boys?"

"I'm sure boys have many practical uses." Annie embraced each of them and gently kissed their cheeks, her lips – an unexpected bonus -- meeting Spencer's a moment and sending a tingle of warmth through his body.

Out of the misty distance came the faint hoot of a locomotive. The boys re-donned their raiment, and Finn helped Annie back up in the cab, Willie following. "Let me know about dat frolic," said Finn, climbing up and taking the wheel.

"Whenever Spencer wishes," said Dodger, and pulled a wallet from a pocket. "How much for the fish?"

"A Tom will do."

"Here's a fin, no pun intended."

Finn gave Spencer a wink. "Careful 'bout alterin' universes, dey's kinda like kettles of fish." Then he engaged the clutch and Lulibelle clattered down College, her tail light fading into the mist, which was glowing slivery pearl in the light of the slowly oncoming train.

"Right on time?" asked Spencer.

"Always is," said Dodger, kneeling on the sidewalk and offering his back. "Your trusty steed at your service."

Again, the train was only moving at a walking pace, and Dodger loaded Spencer into an empty boxcar, tossed in the Gladstone and scrambled aboard. The surrounding lights grew fewer and dimmer as city receded to suburbs, the engine audibly laboring as they began to wind around curves climbing back into the hills where trees and foliage shadowed the tracks. Dodger offered cigarettes and lit them with a wooden match as they sat side-by-side in the doorway, their feet swinging over the railbed as the car swayed and click-clacked along.

"This has been the best time in my life," said Spencer, puffing out a spirit.

Dodger smiled. "I'm sure many spirited times await you."

"But, I guess life can't be fun all the time or how would you know if it was?"

"A very enlightened perspective."

"Mom and dad say I'm mature for my age... most of the time, anyway."

Dodger exhaled a ghost. "One may be mature at any age and still have childish fun."

"Think we'll see them again?" asked Spencer. "Annie, Willie and Finn?"

"The possibilities are infinite."

"All that... back there where we were," said Spencer. "How long has it been going on?"

Dodger looked up at the stars, now visible above the trees as the train ascended out of the mist. "Everything that ever was is always going on."

"...I don't understand."

"Understanding, like flying," said Dodger, "comes later in the program. But..." He leaned out and scanned ahead. "For the moment another small leap will suffice."

As when they had disembarked in the city, Spencer landed ungracefully, stumbling and almost losing his jeans on the leaf-covered gravel along the tracks, Dodger taking his arm as the rest of the train went rumbling past tailed by a caboose with a ruby rear light, crossing over the trestle and vanishing around a curve.

"Can I ask you a question?" said Spencer, as they proceeded onto the trestle, the pond glistening in starlight below.

"That's a question already," laughed Dodger. "And wouldn't the proper form be, 'may I?'"

"May I remind you that 'can' may denote a request for permission as well as an ability. Both are proper in modern English; and the difference between the two is that 'may' is perhaps better suited to a formal occasion."

"*Touché*," said Dodger. "What's the question?"

"Did you kiss me when I was sleeping... I mean on the first afternoon I was here?"

Dodger flipped his cigarette away, pausing on the trestle's mid span to watch the ember spiral down to the pond. "You were as awake as you are right now."

"I couldn't have been or I would have remembered."

"You must have remembered or you couldn't have been."

"I wasn't sure what I remembered."

"Then you can't be sure what you forgot."

"Maybe I was dreaming and you only thought I was awake."

"Maybe you were awake and only thought you were dreaming."

"Sometimes tonight I wasn't sure which."

"Do you dream when you sleep?" asked Dodger.

"Of course."

"Do you sleep when you dream?"

"If I slept when I dreamed, how would I know?"

"Inversely, how would you know you weren't?"

"Sleeping or dreaming?" asked Spencer.

"It might less vexing," said Dodger, "to assume you're awake whenever you dream even if you are asleep, because if you're not you won't remember whatever you think you may have forgot."

"...But, if I was asleep in a dream, how could there be anything to remember?"

Dodger laughed. "I know you believe you understand what you think I said, but I'm not sure you realize that what you heard was not what I meant."

"Something like that," said Spencer.

"Surely you don't accept the notion that if a tree should fall in a forest it makes no sound if you're not there? Which, by logical extension, implies that nothing exists anywhere unless you're there to participate... which would be rather pompous of you."

"I assume that has something to do with everything always going on?"

"Including whatever you think you forgot."

"Like the tree falling," said Spencer. "It happened, therefore it was."

"It happened, therefore it *is*," said Dodger. "And therefore always will be."

"But in the past," said Spencer.

"The past is always present," said Dodger. "It's purely a matter of perspective." He pulled the last of a pint from a pocket and offered it to Spencer.

"Maybe that's also like flying." Spencer accepted the bottle and drank while regarding the pond, which looked like a child's wading pool from his present perspective. "I think I can make it going down so you don't have to carry me."

"No bother," said Dodger, finishing the flask and putting it back in his pocket. "But, shall we take the simple way? The shortest distance between two points generally being a straight line."

"...Huh?" said Spencer. "You don't mean...?"

Dodger laughed. "Must I dare you?"

"Darers go first."

"Except if I double-dog dare you. But, it will be much more fun if we go together."

"Is this the part of the program where the fat lady sings?"

"More accurately, when the fat boy flies."

Spencer looked down at the pond again. "Are you going to make the Peter Pan reference?"

"I should hope that would be understood."

"Have we had enough coffin varnish?"

"Mr. Barrie added fairy dust after parents expressed concern that if only 'thinking lovely thoughts' enabled children to fly, some might launch themselves into the æther with less than enlightening results."

"Not all my thoughts are lovely," said Spencer, while thinking of scenes in old cartoons where circus performers launched themselves from frightening heights into buckets of water... often with less than enlightening results.

"No one's thoughts ever are," said Dodger. "But, if we didn't have unlovely thoughts, how would we know they were?"

Almost before Spencer knew it, Dodger had divested him of every-thing but jeans and sneaks, packing all the period clothing back into the Gladstone, then stripping himself to the careless jeans state in which they had first made acquaintance. Then he pressed a palm to Spencer's chest. "Bear but a touch of my hand there."

Spencer clasped Dodger's hand to his heart. "Think we could have another kiss?"

"A lovely thought." Dodger smiled, embracing Spencer, who

drew Dodger into his arms, enfolding his muscular paleness into enveloping ebony. It seemed like an infinity – or simply a peacefully timeless time – as they stood together on the brink. Then, hand-in-hand, they leaped into space.

CHAPTER SEVENTEEN

"**S**pencer! Breakfast!" called his mom.

Spencer awoke to morning sunlight shining in through the pond-facing window sensually warm on his bare-bodied self, and sleepily answered, "Coming."

Then he muttered, "Damn!" finding he already had... again.

The deed being done, so to speak – though he wished he'd been there to enjoy it -- and the aftermath feeling lazily pleasant, he lounged on his back, head on crossed arms, and sought to recall what had happened last night.

He glanced at Wiggins. "*Déjà vu.*"

But, he found he remembered most of it, from waking to Dodger's "The game is afoot" in the misty twilight, to their last starlit kiss on the trestle, but...

Nothing more after they'd leaped into space.

He heaved himself to a sitting position and looked at his jeans on the chair, seeing they were soaking wet, as were the old Keds on the floor, so presumably his flight with Dodger had ended enlighteningly in the pond... though considering the height of the trestle it seemed doubtful if he'd recall anything if it had ended anywhere else.

"Guess it wasn't a dream," he said to the looking-glass boy. "Unless we went swimming in our sleep."

Wiggins reflected a cavalier smile; and Spencer would have further pondered the mysteries of last night's adventure but for his father calling, "Come and get it or we'll throw it away!"

"Coming," Spencer repeated, avalanching out of bed and snagging another pair of jeans from a dresser drawer. He turned again to Wiggins... there seemed to be something different about him, though Spencer didn't know what, but he didn't look a bit bleary-eyed from the nocturnal sojourn; and Spencer was a little surprised to find he was feeling fully refreshed as if he'd slept peacefully all through the night instead of hopping freight trains, swilling gin, fleeing the law, and pitching piscines at policemen.

Again he scanned the other boy: they looked exactly alike. ...But why should that have seemed different? After all, it was a mirror.

"How do you want your eggs?" asked his mom, as he lumbered to the bathroom.

"Preferably cooked... scrambled as usual, please."

After a wash and donning his jeans, he waddled into the kitchen, where his mom in one of her aprons was tending frying pans at the stove, and his dad at the table was sipping coffee while reading yesterday's *Tribune*.

"Do I look fat?" asked Spencer, pausing to spread his arms in a pose.

"Is that a trick question?" asked his dad, smiling up from the paper.

"Guess I mean fatter."

"In relation to what?"

"...Well... yesterday."

His mother glanced over a shoulder. "If the question relates to an ATV..."

"Mom."

"Horizontal stripes will do that, dear."

Spencer loaded himself on his chair, a place already set for him, along with tumblers of orange juice and milk. He chugged the juice and muffled a burp. "Say... hypothetically... the universe was altered last night and I got a lot fatter?"

"I would think," said Jenny, piling a plate with scrambled eggs, a mountain of golden hash-browns, a half-dozen hefty hot links, and setting it before Spencer, "whatever could alter universes might have greater designs in mind than blessing us with more of you." She kissed his cheek and added, "But we're grateful for all we have."

"Food for thought," said Nathan, as he was also served. "But, if all things were relative, no one would notice a change."

"...Yeah," said Spencer, attacking his food. "If I thought anything was different it would be like the Mandela Effect."

"Or maybe a glitch in the matrix." Jenny studied her son. "You look like your usual cherubic self, but you would if all was relative." She gently palmed one of his breasts and wobbled it like a water balloon. "Mine were once so perky and high before you had your way with them."

Spencer set down his glass of milk. "How thoughtfully therapy-making. But, without getting Oedipal, I'd rate your endowment as presently perfect."

"Hear, hear," said Nathan, raising his coffee cup in toast.

Jenney chucked Spencer under his chins. "You still owe me a used unicorn."

"Let's try another perspective," said Spencer, spicing his eggs with Tabasco sauce. "How much did I weigh last time at the doctor's?"

Jenny prepared her plate and sat down. "That wouldn't prove anything if everything was relative."

"...Yeah," said Spencer, regarding himself. "If everything altered was relative, the past would also seem relative to the altered present." He put down his fork and again spread his arms. "How much would you guess I weigh?"

"Our quarter-ton son," said Nathan.

"Has a nice ring to it," said Spencer, again appraising his rolly vastness.

"Of course," continued Nathan, "an altered universe pound might be more or could be less than before the alteration."

"That really muddles things," said Spencer, taking up his fork again.

"Disregarding an ATV, any particular reason for suspecting an expansive event?"

Spencer worked at depleting his plate. "Just searching for the answer to life, the universe and everything."

"I thought it was 42," said his mom.

"Only in base thirteen."

Nathan salted and peppered his eggs. "Moving on to less weighty

169

matters, I'll be working more overtime tonight. Linda Lancaster called yesterday confirming that Mr. Darkmoor is paying for new utility lines, but we're going to need a refrigerator, a water-heater and a furnace."

Spencer stabbed a link and deftly dodged a juicy spurt. "We've got a cool fireplace, if that's not a contradiction in terms."

"But we can't just go around chopping down trees after we've used up the wood pile." Nathan sipped his coffee. "Best water I've ever tasted, but we should check out the spring house; for all we know something dead fell in."

"Thank you, dear," said Jenny, putting down her cup, "for sharing that cheerful thought at breakfast."

"Sparkling refreshment," said Spencer, raising a glass in salute, "from the center of a corpse."

"Let's bury that subject please," said Jenny.

Nathan asked, "Could you take a hacksaw, cut off the lock and have a look inside?"

"I think the key's in the shed," muffed Spencer around another mouthful. "On a nail by the door."

"Good sleuthing, Sherlock." Nathan consulted his watch. "I should be home by midnight. And nice job on your mom's garden; you'd make a good grounds-keeper."

"Or a Grim Reaper," said Jenny. "I remember my childhood days on the farm, and I know good scythe work when I see it."

Spencer laughed. "I don't have the figure to be a Grim Reaper."

"His young apprentice," suggested Nathan. "The Jovial Reaper."

"The Grim Dishwasher," sighed Spencer, glancing at the stack of plates and related utensils by the sink.

"I'll be leaving at one again," said Jenny. "And also should be home by twelve. I brought some veal Parmesan for your lunch, and I'll fix you something for supper. Any requests?"

"How about hamburger smothered with spaghetti?"

"That's a golden-oldie. One of the 'hot-and-a-lot' dishes working-class diners used to serve."

Spencer finished his breakfast. "You know a lot about food, huh?"

"More than a Masters, less than a PhD."

"When were cheeseburgers invented?"

"According to what I've read, sometime during the 1920s. The most widely accepted story is a cook in Pomona, California came up with the idea."

"I assume he was white?"

"That, of course," said Jenny, "is why it's the most accepted story."

"Like potato chips," added Nathan. "They were first said to have been invented by George Crum, a black chef, but over the years the story was altered and now a white cook gets the credit."

"Big surprise," said Spencer, after gulping the last of his milk. "Altering the past to appropriate the present."

"'He who controls the past, controls the future,'" quoted his dad.

"What if cheeseburgers were really invented here in Oakland?" said Spencer. "By a black kid named Willie Watson who worked in his father's diner."

"Wouldn't surprise me," said Jenny. "But, 'who controls the present controls the past.' To complete the quote."

Nathan added, "And those in control of the present are always trying to alter the past to stay in control of the future."

"But they can't really alter the past," said Spencer. "The only way the past could be altered would be by altering it in the past."

"But," said his dad, "since we can't go back to the past to see what really happened, most people accept an altered past as presented by those who control the present."

"To stay in control of the future," said Spencer. "Which, of course, explains the outrage over Critical Race Theory."

"Such an enlightened young man," said his mom.

"Just be careful," added his dad. "The powers of darkness who profit by keeping people in the dark aren't fond of those who show their light."

"I'll take that under advisement," said Spencer, "from my enlightened parents."

"Who," his mom reminded, "...or would that be 'whom?'"

"Whom is on its last legs as far as modern usage," said Spencer.

"Thank you, dear. ...Were held at gunpoint by the police for showing off their enlightenment by moving up to these still shady hills."

"Which alters the present," added his dad. "Which, hopefully, alters the future in an enlightening way."

"Which would mean," said Spencer," we altered the future by being present."

"I love the smell of enlightenment in the morning," said Jenny.

"Back to the present," said Spencer. "Aside from my usual Little House chores... carrying wood, clearing the acres, pitching hay and churning butter... what's required of me today?"

His father finished his coffee. "I bought some rolls of fencing wire to keep critters out of the garden. Also posts to put it on."

"Swell," sighed Spencer.

Nathan got up. "I'll unload the stuff out front." He kissed Spencer's forehead. "Have an enlightening day, son."

"I was hoping to, but a shadow has fallen."

Jenny smiled. "You don't have to do it all today. Have you gone swimming in the pond?"

"A couple of times, it's cool."

"Maybe we'll join you this weekend," said Nathan, going into the hall. "Now that we have a nice place to live, we should start enjoying it."

"A picnic by our pond," said Jenny.

"With beer, I hope," said Spencer. "Although, according to what I've read, I'm supposed to be too old for happy family activities, for which I should be expressing disdain."

Jenny began to clear the table. "Maybe you could wait a few days before your metamorphosis into a moody, rebellious, sarcastic and generally very nasty thing who will make us wish you'd been snatched by goblins while still in swaddling clothes?"

"Guess I can put off morphing till Monday."

CHAPTER EIGHTEEN

After further fortification with a cup of coffee, Spencer went to his room to don the Keds, a task which required much straining and struggle since he could barely reach his feet over the blubbery bulk of his belly. Putting on shoes, like sitting up from a prone position, had been getting more difficult over the last few months but he couldn't remember it being *this* hard in the recent past.

"Or what we presume is the present past," he puffed to his equally rolly reflection puffing in the cherub mirror while battling the paradox of trying to get himself out of his way. "Assuming it wasn't altered last night by our buying a soda with a nickel that didn't belong in that past... if I may take the liberty of inferring you were with me in spirit, since we seem to be kindred... which would make this present an alternate future."

He paused to fondle his torus of middle and thoughtfully bobble a breast. "Though the only thing that seems to be altered is this seem-ingly new abundance of us... assuming it is an alteration."

He took a moment to ponder that and reflect on the looking-glass boy. "We don't appear to look any fatter than when we first met, but it sure feels like we are, huh?"

The boy in the mirror regarded himself, patting and plumping here and there while also looking reflective.

"Moving on to weightier thoughts, we *couldn't* have actually been in the past," Spencer continued to muse. "Even assuming, as Dodger proposed, 'the past is always present.' And the combination of coffin varnish and the mystically misty night probably altered our perspective of where we were and what we saw. ...Wouldn't you agree?"

Wiggins looked circumspect, and Spencer went on to convince him, "Old Oakland couldn't be *that* big, or as elaborately staged with all those actors and old-time things, or it would rival Disneyland and be famous all over the world. ...Like, 'see a classic silent film, eat at Watson's Diner, join the gang at Hogan's Alley, flee a Prohibition raid and take a wild ride with Finn.'"

Again, Wiggins looked non-committal.

"Of course," Spencer continued, "you recall in a Sherlock Holmes story a man being driven at night in a closed and curtained carriage, who thought he had traveled a long way while actually it was just a few blocks the carriage kept traversing to give the *impression* of distance? Which could have been us in the mist last night riding around in Lulibelle, so we only thought the place was much bigger. A deception perhaps not deliberate, as it was in the story, but merely required by geography."

Wiggins looked reflective again.

Spencer considered. "Our theory of a present place being acted-out as the past does, however, contain some flaws; the underage drinking an obvious one. ...On the other hand, we can only be certain that those in our gang were actually drinking. And, maybe Dodger's juvenile gin... and he as much said so himself by suggesting it could be dream-inducing... is possibly hallucinogenic, as such concoctions reputedly were, which rendered us suggestible to an altered perspective: we might have been 'seeing' the 1920s because Dodger *suggested* we were there in speech, behavior and mode of dress. The trains we may presume were real, because something obviously transported us to and from the city, and there is a trestle above the pond. But, not being familiar with trains, and those we rode electrically-powered... as opposed to the clearly discernable difference of present-day diesel locomotives and early twentieth-century steam... we couldn't have judged to what age they belonged. And, after continued consumption of gin with Dodger assuming the character of a streetwise 'twenties bootlegger boy, our perceptions were suggestively altered once we arrived in Oakland. ...For example, the 'streetcars' may have been busses. And everything else we thought we were seeing was modeled upon our own recollect-ions of *Our Gang* films, other old movies, and descriptions read in books. In 1960s hippie parlance, we simply went on a trip... down the rabbit hole, so to speak... and Dodger was our guide. ...At least a working hypothesis?"

Again, his reflection looked reflective.

"And," laughed Spencer, "wasn't it fun?"

Wiggins grinned in agreement.

Shod at last, Spencer glanced at his laptop: it still had battery power, but of course couldn't access the Internet without a service provider, so he couldn't do any investigation into the places he'd been.

"Or *thought* we've been," he qualified to the mirror boy. "Assum-ing, for sake of argument, it wasn't all just a dream... no matter how sure we are it wasn't."

His mom was boiling a kettle of water as Spencer emerged from his room. "Dad freak you out about drinking dead things?"

His mom made a face. "Your 'center of a corpse' remark was a vivid embellishment. I'd appreciate it if, first on your child-labor list today, you'd report on the state of the spring house."

Spencer caught himself before saying he'd already been in there and the water looked perfectly pure... his mom would ask why he hadn't said so. "I'll do it now."

"My responsible cherub."

The morning was growing warmer on what promised to be an-other hot Indian Summer day as Spencer, surrounded by soothing sounds of splashing water and chirping birds, waddled his way to the grounds-keeper's shed, opened its creaky door, and saw a rusty bar-rel key hanging from a nail.

Dodger must have had a duplicate, because his key had been shiny from use while this one had clearly been in here since the 1920s. Taking it, Spencer waded through ferns across the dell to the path by the brook and stopped at the mossy old foot-bridge to study the gate in the wall where Dodger's unpleasant uncle had made his appearance yesterday. As seemingly proved by that nasty event, the lock was apparently functional and, assuming one had its key, the gate could be opened any time.

He proceeded to the base of the dam and bulldozed his belly up to the spring house after pausing by the pond to confirm the trestle was actually there... again in daylight and he wide awake.

The climb seemed a lot more arduous than it had been yesterday, Spencer grasping vines and tree trunks to battle his bulk up the slope, but of course he'd had Dodger's assistance last night. The padlock, looking a lot more aged and tarnished than he remembered, resisted the rusty key, and he considered -- despite the effort of having to make the ascent again -- fetching the WD-40; but the wards finally surrendered. The door was also reluctant, seemingly stuck in its frame, and he used his mass to advantage to gently batter it open.

The interior was softly lit by gentle greenish forest light filtering in though the narrow screened slits between the walls and roof; and the water trinkling into the font made a restful sound. Dodger had been true to his word about removing the gin mill... well, not quite all of it; the Agrocosta and Plymouth bottles, both empty, stood on the basin's rim.

"Presumably," said Spencer, "because they don't belong in the past from the present perspective."

But there was nothing else remaining except the Ivory Soap box on the dusty stone floor. Dodger must have taken the stuff last night, and it seemed remarkable he could have carried the bathtub... though maybe not so surprising since he'd been able to pony-back Spencer. The box's lid was in place, and Spencer knelt to open it, finding the *Whiz Bangs* and *Weird Tales* neatly wrapped in an old white shirt like Dodger had worn on their misty adventure, but this one yellowed like old bones by time. The magazines, though well-preserved, also looked a lot more aged than he remembered from yesterday. The gentle splash of water seemed to echo Dodger's voice... *consider them yours.*

Spencer thanked the echo, put the magazines back in the box and replaced the lid. This would be a good place to read them, like Dodger in his secret hide-out, and...

Despite what had happened in his recent past, he felt the mood coming over him to actively reenact the act as Dodger must have frequently done, but there was plenty of time for that, and he had chores to perform. Gruntingly getting back to his feet, he inspected the font, finding the water crystal clear without so much as a spider's corpse... probably due to the diligent screens and tight-fitting door.

Again he was tempted to sprawl on the floor and diligently daydream a while, but he should reassure his mom their water contained no deceased denizens. He took the empty bottles, then a Sherlockian thought came to mind, making him stop in the doorway and critically study the dust-covered floor: the only signs of disturbance were the prints of the ancient Keds on his feet from when he'd just opened the box. He couldn't recall seeing this much dust on his previous visits... and where were his other footprints -- and Dodger's – from yesterday? And surely there would have been much disturbance when Dodger removed the gin-making stuff.

Maybe Dodger, being artful, had spread this dust to make it appear undisturbed since the 1920s? ...Why? ...In case Spencer's dad had come to inspect and might wonder what had been going on? A bit of broom brushing would have sufficed.

"'Once you eliminate the impossible...'" Spencer quoted aloud.

He tugged the door shut, re-locked the lock and descended the slope to the pond. The morning was still growing warmer and, sweating from his exertions, he considered a swim... but there was work to do; and maybe Dodger would show up later. He pondered what to do with the bottles – his parents would assume he'd purloined the gin, even if it was technically his, but that, like filching cigarettes, was probably best not confessed – so he filled them with water and flung them to sink in the darkest depths of the pond. Then he went to inform his mom -- who was making hamburger smothered with spaghetti for his future supper -- about the pure state of their water supply. Then he returned to the tool shed, hung the key back on its nail, and considered the wheelbarrow as a means of transporting the fence mesh and posts from the front of the cottage. The barrow's wheel was stiff from disuse, but there was a brass oil can on the workbench, and he soon had the wheel turning freely. Then he noticed the Grim Reaper scythe, rusty and covered with dust on the wall. He'd assumed Dodger had cleaned it to do his reaping yesterday, but he must have brought his own, deadly sharp and gleaming… and he had walked away in the evening toting it over a shoulder.

Out of curiosity, Spencer donned the headphones and clicked the Radiola's switch, but of course the dusty tubes stayed dead and there was no skeletal Charleston capering out of the æther.

There was a post-hole digger amongst the other tools, and he loaded it onto the barrow and went to begin his work.

The rich black loam was soft in the clearing Dodger had made, and the holes were easy to bore, Spencer using his weight to advantage to drive the blades into the ground. The posts were eight feet long, so he sunk them twelve inches into the earth, which left plenty of overhead room for his mom to do her gardening. Of course he was soon pouring sweat and puffing again like a steam loco-motive, but his mother appeared with an icy pitcher of homemade lemonade. By the time he'd planted all the posts and started hanging the mesh, using staples his dad had bought and a hammer from the shed, his mom reappeared in the cottage doorway and called him in for lunch.

The veal Parmesan was delicious, even being warmed-over from yesterday's restaurant fare, and he devoured two heaping platefuls, washing them down with more lemonade to finish by politely half-muting the bombastic blast of a burp.

Jenny laughed. "I'll take that as a compliment." She added Spen-cer's empty plate to the other dishes stacked by the sink. "You've done a lot this morning; the garden fence looks almost finished."

"Just have to put the mesh on top and make some kind of door," said Spencer, after gulping a last glass of lemonade.

"I'd say you've worked enough for one day improving the family homestead, so take the afternoon off."

Spencer yawned. "I'll start with a nap."

"I'm leaving now," said Jenny. "Your golden-oldie supper is wait-ing in the ice box, and I'll bring home more cannoli."

"Lots, I hope," said Spencer.

"Find the phantom railroad?"

"Well…" said Spencer ambiguously, not sure how to reply lest it bring questions to which the answers were still in a questionable state. "There's a trestle above the pond, but you can't see it from down here."

"You can always tell when a train has gone by," said his mom, after kissing his cheek.

"How?"

"Elementary, dear, you can see its tracks."

CHAPTER NINETEEN

Spencer awoke in evening twilight to scents of tobacco, boy-sweat and gin, finding Dodger barefoot in jeans -- as seemed his most natural state of being -- leisurely lounging beside him while reading one of his junk shop books and smoking a Fatima... which made Spencer think of Captain Picard waking up with Q in his bed.

"Hi, Dodger," he yawned, and lazily stretched. "Just meant to take a nap after lunch, but looks like I slept all day. Guess 'cause of all the fun last night."

"More fun than a frog at a funeral." Dodger lay the book on the window sill and pillowed his head on his arms. "And most of all having your company."

Spencer mirrored Dodger's pose, also only clad in jeans, which the mirror boy mirrored beside a looking-glass Dodger. "Like I said on the train coming home, kinda wished it could go on forever."

"But you realized," said Dodger, passing the cigarette to Spencer, "that everything can't be fun all the time, or one would have nothing to measure fun by and thus could not appreciate it."

"Like having friends."

"I'm glad you're my friend," said Dodger, taking Spencer's hand.

"Likewise," said Spencer, and clasped Dodger's hand. "And it's swell waking up next to one."

Dodger smiled mischievously. "Assuming you're not waking up in a dream."

"Even if I am it's still swell." Spencer passed back the Fatima and, after a second of shyness, boyishly bussed Dodger's cheek. "Feels like at least one of us isn't dreaming."

180

"Or perhaps we both are," said Dodger, returning the cheeky intimacy, then giving up a last ghost of smoke before flipping the cigarette stub out the window. "I hope you'll forgive my liberty in borrowing one of your books."

It seemed typical of Dodger that borrowing a book was a liberty while invading a bed apparently wasn't. "Books should be shared," said Spencer. "Like anything else good in life. That's a collection of Lovecraft stories."

"Quite good ones," said Dodger. "He seems to be improving with age, perhaps at last trusting his own spirit instead of... if I may say so... rather badly imitating the style of Lord Dunsany."

"And no more atrocious poems," said Spencer.

"I take it you've read *On The Creation Of Niggers*?"

"One of his most atrocious, at least to me for obvious reasons."

"Yet you forgave him for it."

Spencer shrugged. "I'd say the good things he did in life outweighed what was basically ignorance and maybe not having the wisdom or will to rise above the wrongs of those times."

"A very enlightened perspective," said Dodger. "I finished *The Strange High House In The Mist* just as you awakened. It's one I haven't read before and has a happy ending; rare for Mr. Lovecraft."

"One reason it's one of my favorites," said Spencer. "I don't think ghost stories have to end badly with people being snatched into nothing, or losing their souls, or going insane, or suffering horrible fates worse than death."

Dodger donned his impish smile. "Those might seem like happy endings to ghosts."

"Only if the ghosts are bad."

"I take it you don't think all ghosts are bad?"

"All people aren't bad when they're alive, so why should they be when they're dead?"

"Or merely reverting to spirit; the higher, having learned from life, more enlightened and therefore good."

"Which implies," said Spencer, "lower spirits who didn't learn and therefore are bad."

"Now you're on the trolley," said Dodger.

Spencer indicated the book. "I'm surprised you hadn't read that story; it was published in 1926."

"November of 1926, according to the footnote. This is October, relatively-speaking."

Spencer laughed. "Maybe you altered a universe."

"Perhaps no one will notice. ...Speaking of which, are you rested enough for another adventure?"

"Like going back to Watson's Diner? Guess Hogan's Alley is down for a while?"

"Relatively-speaking," said Dodger again. "We can go wherever you wish, but would you care to dine with me?"

"'Dine' always raises my spirit," said Spencer. "Did you bring another Water Rat basket?"

"I thought in my home," said Dodger. "My father is away on business, so I have the haunts to myself. And formal dress is not required, so feel free to come as you are."

"What about your uncle?"

"He is also away... thankfully... no doubt plotting nefarious schemes with others of his unpleasant ilk, ultimately doomed to fail but not before stirring up toil and trouble for many innocent souls."

"Sure," said Spencer. "Mom made me supper, but I can have it for lunch tomorrow. ...But, I should wash the dishes."

"I also took that liberty."

"That's what I call a friend. Thanks."

"Friends share their adversities as well as times of fun," said Dodger. "Perhaps an appetizer?" He pulled a candy bar from a pocket.

"A Chicken Dinner," said Spencer. "Thanks." He unwrapped the bar, broke it in half and returned a portion to Dodger. "Will we be back by midnight?" he asked around a mouthful of chocolate.

"We can return any time," said Dodger, likewise dispatching his share and urchin-like licking his fingers.

Spencer laughed again. "Even before we left?"

"Time can messed about with," said Dodger, "Though messing may sometimes muddle it in paradoxical ways."

Spencer struggled to reach the Keds on the floor, but Dodger took the liberty, slipping lithely from the bed and kneeling to put them on Spencer's feet.

"I'll leave a lamp for mom," said Spencer.

"And your physical form," said Dodger. "In case you're not back before you left."

The shadows had deepened in the dell, the sky now dimming to gunmetal dusk and stars beginning to sprinkle themselves, as Spencer arranged his "physical form" with blankets and pillows on the bed, then squiggled into the window frame, Dodger already waiting out-side.

"Guess I didn't get fatter, 'cause I can still fit," said Spencer. "Or almost still as much as before."

"Before what?" asked Dodger, taking Spencer under the arms and, with a few wiggles and jiggles, pulling him bottle-cork out through the portal into a bear-hug embrace.

"Guess before yesterday."

"It's all relative," said Dodger. "If you could almost still fit before, you can almost still fit in the after." Then, still holding Spencer aloft, he began to recite:

"'Between the dark and the daylight...'"

"I know that one," said Spencer:

"'Between the dark and the daylight,
When the night is beginning to lower,
Comes a pause in the day's occupations,
That is known as the Children's Hour.'

Longfellow." He laughed. "Like Dreyfus' feet."

Dodger quoted the poem's last lines:

"'And there will I keep you forever,
Yes, forever and a day,
Till the walls shall crumble to ruin,
And moulder in dust away.'"

183

"That part always made me sad," said Spencer, with Dodger's heartbeat chest to chest indistinguishable from his own. "But I know it was about loving." He kissed Dodger's cheek. "I love you."

Dodger returned the kiss. "And I love you... and love is not a word to use lightly."

"I know," said Spencer. "I've never said it to anyone except mom and dad."

"I'm sure you will to another," said Dodger. "As I'm sure another will say it to you."

"Think so?" asked Spencer.

"Why ever not? You're smart, cool, and fun to be with."

"Seriously."

"Nothing is preordained, *mon ami*, so the future is never fore-seeable and one may say it's all in the stars. But, when you're search-ing for someone, someone is also searching for you."

"Like looking for light."

"Indeed, never stop, though it may take some time." Dodger set-tled Spencer to earth and drew a flask from his jeans. "For now this may lighten your spirit."

Spencer took a tentative sip, then a full-size swallow. "This is more like the real McCoy with sort of a fairy dust finish." He took another gulp. "Don't misunderstand, but it's almost good."

"Inspired by your formula; your past impression improving the present." Dodger drank, pocketed the bottle, and led the way to the brook, which sparkled a bit in the strengthening starlight as they cros-sed the bridge.

The gate in the wall didn't seem to be locked because he simply pushed it open. The path delving into the foliage beyond didn't ap-pear as overgrown as it had looked in daylight, but Spencer couldn't see much in the shadows except the shadows of other shadows, and even less the farther they went beneath the overhanging trees. "We could bring one of my lanterns."

"Just follow the Wild Child," said Dodger, offering a hand.

"Doesn't this go to the old Shade mansion?" asked Spencer, tak-ing Dodger's hand.

"Wherever you go depends where you want to," said Dodger,

forging confidently into ever-deepening darkness with Spencer wad-dling beside him like Pooh on a quest with Christopher Robin into The Hundred Acre Wood.

Spencer laughed. "Sometimes I'm not sure where I want to go."

"Sometimes you have to go to be sure."

"What if it's somewhere I don't want to go?"

"Then you probably won't want to go there again."

"But, how would I know?"

"You won't till you get there," said Dodger. "Unless you knew before you went; in which case you probably would or wouldn't depending on whether you didn't or did."

Spencer tried to work that out, but gave up and asked, "How can you see?" as the blackness around them kept increasing into a fea-tureless Stygian void as if they were trekking through infinite space in a timeless time before stars had been born, and Dodger now only a phantom suggestion of paleness in the absolute dark; though the clasp of his hand was strong and his earthy scent reassuring. It also seemed strangely silent here… and had been, Spencer realized, since they'd passed the gate; there was no chirping of crickets; no whooing of owls or the other sounds he'd heard on previous nights. Dodger's bare feet made no sound at all on what must have been a carpet of leaves, and the only things audible to Spencer were his own huffing breaths and the trudge of his Keds, until Dodger replied:

"Look for light and you'll never be lost, though you may find a dark labyrinth intervening for a time. …There, do you see it?"

Spencer peered into the blackness ahead, searching for any ghost of a glimmer, and finally did see a faint spark of light… then a few more as Dodger led on, appearing at first like a cluster of stars pos-sibly seen from light-years away but gradually defining themselves as lights in the windows of a huge house as the path at last emerged under trees at the manicured edge of a gigantic lawn that looked as large as a storybook meadow beneath the soft glow of the rising moon now peeping over forested hills behind the enormous dwelling. As during their adventure last night, he felt a sort of slipping sensation, but this like the final slight adjustment an elevator sometimes made when aligning itself with a floor. And, like

185

a sound-track fading in, there returned the rhythmic keening of crickets, the inquisitions of an owl, and the occasional chitters and squeaks of little things afoot.

Dodger took out his White Rabbit watch as there came a faint rumble of a train descending the slopes above the house and the flickering glow of its headlamp slowly winding its way around curves. "Right on time as always." Then he quoted from *The Wind In The Willows* while gesturing toward the heavens: "'The moon, serene and detached in a cloudless sky, did what she could, though so far off, to help them in their quest.'"

Spencer couldn't have said how far they had come, seemingly having lost track of time without anything to measure it by, though with sweat now sheening his body along with the effort to recover air, it felt like more than a mile. He recalled his dad's words about the Shade mansion sitting on several acres: he wasn't sure what an acre comprised, but it seemed they had walked much farther than one and presumably passed the old Shade place somewhere in the dark, so this mansion – and that's what it was – must have been somewhere else.

The mammoth house looming across the vast lawn was perplexingly hard to describe, its architecture belonging – at least from what Spencer had read of such things -- to no recognizable age or time as if a fanciful compilation of many archaic designs. The images of mansions that usually came to Spencer's mind were mostly Victorian structures stereotyped in ghostly films, or Antebellum southern styles from the days of slavery, but this building, made of stone and shimmering pale in the silvery light, three stories tall, not counting two towers, resembled a sort of anomalous marriage of hoary Gothic cathedral – there were gargoyles glowering down -- and Baskerville Hall in the Sherlock Holmes tale.

"Wow!" he said. "I knew you were rich, but this takes the cake!"

"There will be cake for dessert," said Dodger. "That at least is foreseeable."

"Lay on, MacDuff," said Spencer, tugging up his jeans.

The path, becoming neatly graveled, its grassy borders perfectly trimmed and lined with what might have been lavender lilies – their color indeterminate in the illusive lunar light -- continued toward the gargantuan house past shrubbery which Spencer first thought were topiary animals but then discerned as the moonlight grew were ancient gods of Egypt – Anubis the jackal, Set as a donkey, Sobek as a crocodile, and many others he couldn't name, except Taweret as a hippo, so massively fat he was often portrayed with a sort of mystical walker... which Spencer was starting to feel like he needed.

And there were abundant living things going about their nocturnal affairs and not seeming bothered by human intrusion, instead only pausing an affable moment as if bestowing a welcome – several raccoons, a sly-looking fox, a pair of coyotes seemingly questing, a pos-sum, a skunk, and a daint-footed deer – along with ever-inquiring owls and a fluttery flicker of bats on the wing.

There were also many statues of stone interspersed with the foliage forms, most of rolly-poly cherubs often engaged in ecstatic feasting and quaffing from tipsy amphoras of wine; others of boy fauns in various poses – one hunting with a bow-and-arrow, another poised with a broad-bladed knife as if in defense or about to attack, another peacefully playing pipes, another seemingly just daydreaming lounging lazily on his back, and one sitting reading a book -- along with a mistily-glistening fountain splashing a liquid lullaby into a pond where more cherubs frolicked, while in its midst and shrouded in spray as if an incongruous lifeguard, stood a cheerful-looking Grim Reaper who somehow, due to a sculptor's skill – or maybe just the oversize scythe casually slung on a shoulder -- gave the impression of being young.

"Fancies of my father," said Dodger, answering Spencer's impending question as they passed the misty fountain with its paradoxical Death.

"Does he have many?" asked Spencer, as they finally reached the house after crossing a wide graveled drive beneath the gaze of guardian gargoyles, where an imposing staircase flanked by a pair of reclining stone lions led up to a pillared portico lighted by a bowl-like lamp suspended from an iron chain above a tall set of mahogany doors fitted with Marley-faced knockers, their jaws bound up with bronze handkerchiefs.

"Not an annoying abundance," said Dodger, "though he indulges them Puckishly."

"I take it he designed this house?"

"A charming little horror, as he fondly calls it." Dodger pointed to one of the towers. "I used to pretend a beautiful princess had been imprisoned up there, and I as a gallant knight was on a quest to save her."

"That would work," puffed Spencer, pausing at the foot of the steps to hoist his jeans again. "Speaking of roles, those fauns all kinda look like you, except the horns and furry legs."

"I modeled for them," said Dodger, posing Panishly. "My father's *enfant sauvage*, you know." He gestured toward the fountain. "I also stood in for him."

Spencer recalled the image of Dodger with his scythe yesterday. "That must have been hard to do with your skin on."

"The skeleton," said Dodger, "is always there in any skilled form of portraiture, and is what a true artist creates upon, being both the alpha and omega of every spirit's earthly stay." He smiled. "And you might have modeled our cherubs."

"Apparently someone like me did." Spencer noticed a great, gleaming car, a long-hooded, box-bodied four-door sedan of obviously very vintage design, parked a little way down the drive and seemingly surveying him with owlish twelve-inch headlights mirroring the moon. "Is that what I think it is?"

"Whether something is or isn't what you think it may be," said Dodger, "often depends on perspective."

"From my present perspective," said Spencer, "I'm thinking a Roll-Royce Silver Ghost… saw one in a book. Is that what we would have ridden in going to the movie last night?"

"If you had wished."

"That would have been cool, but the train was fun."

"We can go for a drive any time," said Dodger. "But for the moment…"

Taking Spencer's arm, Dodger helped him up the steps – climbing stairs, for obvious reasons, not being one of Spencer's *fortés* -- but paused beside the left-hand lion to delve between its stony paws and draw out a big brass skeleton key. "Our doors are presently open to all, but should you ever find them locked, the key will always be here for you."

"That would seem like a liberty," said Spencer, thinking that having a key to this place might be like having a key to heaven... or maybe at least Disneyland.

Dodger returned the key to its keeper. "Friends are welcome any time." He assisted Spencer the rest of the way up to the lamp-lit portico, grasped the doors' ornate bronze handles to swing them majestically open, spilling forth a fan of light, and bowed him into a foyer that itself was as spacious as many houses Spencer had seen. Its plaster walls were a pleasant peach color above wainscoting of tongue-and-groove wood, and there was a sparkling chandelier suspended from the lofty ceiling. The polished floor was possibly oak with a runner of rose-patterned carpet; and off to the left stood a coat and hat stand, along with a sort of receptacle probably meant to receive umbrellas and gentlemen's walking sticks... though, and perhaps yet another of Dodger's father's fancies, was occupied by a grim gleaming scythe that may have been what Dodger had swung when reaping the garden yesterday.

Against the right wall was a long settee upholstered in wine-purple plush, where, as Spencer had read, callers perhaps with commercial or possibly conversion intents – Jehovah's Witnesses came to mind -- would be politely requested to wait upon the household's convenience... probably by a butler. A free-standing ashtray was provided if they cared to smoke while cooling their heels. Opposite that was a claw-footed table whose only apparent purpose was serving a candle-stick telephone of black Bakelite and yellow brass. The phone had no dial, Spencer noted, and might have been just for display, though its fabric-covered wire connected to a black box on the wall. Maybe some sort of retro phone in keeping with the obviously early twentieth-century theme? Another fancy of Dodger's sire?

The ambiance was so opulent that -- at least to Spencer's mind -- he and Dodger looked in this place as grubbily disreputable as Baker Street Irregulars paying a call on Mr. Holmes. He almost expected

Mrs. Hudson to fluster in through the doorway beyond with an order to wipe their street-urchin feet on a square of cocoanut matting.

A quartet of paintings adorned the walls, each as large as a mural, and Spencer went to study them: three were the sort of dreamy landscapes popular in earlier times, of golden summer afternoons in uninhabited countrysides, their distant features ethereally hazy, mountains rendered in mauve and blues; though the fourth portrayed a boy faun, again very much like Dodger, playing a span of wooden pipes to a gang of abundantly chubby cherubs -- one of whom was African and did resemble Spencer at an earlier age -- lounging by a sunlit pond.

The air, though some might have said was sullied by Dodger and Spencer's spirits, was otherwise mostly neutral except for hints of lemony polish and lingering tobacco smoke.

Spencer indicated the phone. "May I take the liberty?"

"Call whomever you wish any time," said Dodger, closing the entry doors.

Spencer unhooked the receiver and put it to an ear, recalling a picture he'd seen in a book of a cherub statue in London using a similar phone. There was a rustle of static like he'd heard in the Radiola's headset and sounding very far away, but after a moment a woman's voice asked, "Number please?"

Spencer considered calling his mom just for the experience of using the antique instrument, but she would be busy cooking. And she might think he was lonely "all by himself" in the night. "Um," he said. "Never mind… but thanks."

There was a click and more static, and he put the receiver back on its hook.

"Long distance?" asked Dodger.

"Sure sounded like," said Spencer.

"Welcome home, Master Dodger."

Spencer turned as a portly black man of possibly early late-middle-age, clad in a butler's livery perfectly cut to his ample contours, seemed to materialize. For a moment the "Master" jarred Spencer, until he remembered the context, confirmed when the man addressed him: "Master Spencer, if I may presume?"

"Good evening, Barrymore," said Dodger. "Indeed we have Spencer with us in the flesh."

If Barrymore thought *quite a lot of it*, he gave no visible sign.

Although it probably wasn't proper, Spencer offered a hand, which Barrymore took in a genial grip.

"Delighted, sir," said Barrymore. "I hope you'll find your stay pleasant." Then he added to Dodger, "All is arranged as you wished."

"Swell," said Dodger, and smiled at Spencer. "I hope you're hungry."

"One of my natural states of being."

"If you please, sirs?" said Barrymore, bowing them through the other doorway into a mammothly cavernous place that epitomized the term, hall, in Brobdingnagian proportions.

The vaulted ceiling, cathedral-like, arched three stories overhead, and a trio of brilliant chandeliers lighted the enormous space, where almost a daunting distance away – at least to Spencer who already felt like he'd hiked to the moon – at the far end of the gigantic room, a grand stairway rose to a gallery encircling the second floor. The décor was an oddly eclectic mix of mostly mediaeval museum pieces suggesting an Olde English manor, from Knights Of The Round Table suits of armor with halberds poised in respectful salute, to stuffed boar's heads looking ferally fierce, interspersed with jousting lances, swords, crossbows, battle-axes and shields. There were venerable flint-lock muskets, along with massive "pirate pistols" and a bell-muzzled blunderbuss. Many paintings lined the walls amongst the armory relics; most appeared to be Renaissance art but only a few Spencer recognized; the enigmatic Mona Lisa, the Birth Of Venus on a half-shell – which made him think of oysters – along with The Portrait Of Gerard Andriesz and one of Eugenia Martínez Vallejo -- which he'd discovered on the Web and admired for obvious reasons -- and a roundly-rotund Cupid in recline on a pile of skulls. There was a young Dionysus, whom Dodger may also have modeled, beautifully buff by both definitions, carelessly well into his cups and attended tipsily by another plump gang of grape-swilling cherubs.

"I take it those are copies?" said Spencer, indicating the works he knew as they proceeded across a floor so highly polished it looked like a mirror, as if they were walking upon reflections of another universe.

"They will be in time," said Dodger.

"Copies or copied?"

"Both, I should think."

"How many... servants... are there?" asked Spencer, not sure of the proper way to inquire and mindful of present company.

"Barrymore, of course," said Dodger. "And his wife, Eliza, who graciously graces our table with lavish legions of luscious delights. And Dawkins, their son, presently our page." He flashed his foxy smile. "Then there is Mrs. Hudson, head of our housekeeping staff, which consists of Flopsey, Mopsey and Topsey."

"Surely you jest," puffed Spencer, noting with more than a bit of dismay that despite what felt like a marathon they were only halfway to the staircase... which he assumed he'd have to climb.

Barrymore chuckled. "Master Dodger's appellations from his childhood time."

"And Fishy, our footman," said Dodger.

"No doubt," said Spencer, in the spirit, "another of your juvenile tags?"

"Fondly meant," said Dodger. "And Mr. Toad, our chauffeur."

"I assume for obvious reasons," said Spencer.

"If I may," offered Barrymore. "He might give Mr. Oldfield an exhilarating run for his money."

"And how," agreed Dodger. "And, last but not at all in the least, there's Joe, our capable grounds-keeper, along with his charming wife Biddy, and The Avenger, his son; though most of the staff, in my father's absence, have this time to themselves."

The staircase had looked like a challenge when viewed from across the enormous hall, and seemed to ascend to Olympian heights as they finally reached it. The newel posts of its balustrades were topped by life-size twin bronze cherubs profusely plump in every proportion, each holding aloft a guiding torch with sculptured glass electric flames; and Spencer recognized them from a picture as the cherub recovered from the *Titanic*, though these boys were complete with both feet. He then regarded the stairway itself, and not enthusiastically, but Dodger knelt and offered his back. "All aboard."

Barrymore asked, "Shall I see you up, sir?"

"I'm sure we can manage," said Dodger, rising with Spencer pony-mounted. "Thank you for the arrangements, and enjoy this time with your family."

"A fun time for us all, sir. And very nice meeting you, Master Spencer; I hope to have the pleasure again." Barrymore bowed and walked away.

As on the night before when climbing the path above the pond, even Dodger was puffing a bit as they ascended the stairway, proving he wasn't invulnerable to the laws of this universe. Finally reaching the gallery, where Dodger set him back on his feet, Spencer saw a grandfather clock – though the name, he'd read, hadn't come into being until 1876, inspired by the song, *My Grandfather's Clock*, previous to which they'd been called long clocks – this one a magnificent example and possibly eight feet tall, its case carved with very fat frolicking cherubs, though like the scene in the fountain, a Reaper watch-ed over them from above, cheerfully crowning the finial. The clock's ornate hands stood at 3:13; and Spencer remarked:

"I know we seem to have come a long way, but it can't be that late."

Dodger donned his Puckish smile. "Inversely, it could be early."

Spencer noted the pendulum motionless behind its glass door. "...Oh. Guess it's not working."

Dodger only smiled again. "It's always 3:13 sometime."

Then Spencer heard lively music begin; and though the tune was new to him, the band sounded very familiar, as did an angelically youthful voice:

> "Take in the sun
> Hang out the moon
> And rock me in a cradle of dreams."

Spencer looked Dodger a question while tugging up his jeans, but Dodger only smiled once more and led him along to a doorway as the heavenly voice sang on:

> "I want to see
> So clear to me
> It's the only time I'm happy, it seems
> Let my little train of thought go rolling back once more
> To a place I'm always longing for
>
> Oh, won't you take in the sun
> Hang out the moon
> And rock me in a cradle of dreams."

The portal was of course grand, its frame and lintel cunningly carved with a bountiful grapevine and harvest design, its tall double doors invitingly open, though the light beyond was subtly soft as they entered a dining room... which Spencer had expected in keeping with Dodger's invitation. From what he'd seen of the house so far, it also wasn't surprising to find this chamber palatially huge, its ceiling almost lost in space above chandeliers which were tastefully dimmed as if for an intimate supper.

The surroundings slowly materialized as Spencer's eyes adjusted after the brilliance of the great hall: first discerned was a titanic table pleasantly lighted by gold-flamed candles glowing in stately silver stands, and which might have seated a court, though only its far end was occupied by a trio of hazily indistinct figures. The first form to come into clarity was the chubby, long-haired Gypsy boy, the trumpeter and vocalist he'd seen at Hogan's Alley, who looked even more cherubic tonight, his baby-rolled body mostly bare in only jeans and old-time sneaks, his jeans, like a carelessly innocent child's, baring half of his pubescent shaft, because he now stood on a real stage bathed in a cone of immaculate light.

His band was also *sans chemise* – the moppy blond-haired wiry kid tintinabulating time on The Lost Boys drums; the slender Indian boy blowing sax; the small Chinese lad thrumming his bass; and the almost Spencer-sized ebony youth skillfully tinkling the ivories of a gleamingly great grand piano. This exhibition of young male physiques had probably been -- Spencer surmised -- prearranged by Dodger for one of the already seated guests, who now became viably visible... Annie, dressed as she'd been last night, her jacket draped over the back of her chair, and poised with a cigarette in holder while looking raptly appreciative of the sights and sounds on stage; though she was probably just as pleased by the also shirtless presences of Willie and Finn at the table, which Spencer noted appreciatively – after appreciating Annie – was lavishly loaded with platters of food. He started to make an inventory when Annie spied him and Dodger.

"Well, look what the cat dragged in... and both of 'em dressed to the nines."

Champagne seemed to be the beverage *du soir*, as evidenced by magnum-sized bottles ensconced in silver buckets of ice, and effervescent crystal glasses in possession of all the guests -- the band, Spencer noted, also supplied -- as Annie, Willie and Finn raised theirs in salute of their host, and The Lost Boys paused a moment in play to smilingly do the same.

"Swell seein' you again, Spence," said Willie, as Spencer and Dodger seated themselves and the band resumed.

"Likewise," said Finn.

"And to your best advantage," said Annie, her eyes appreciating both as if optically treasuring twins.

"Back at you all," returned Spencer, as Dodger poured him a bubble-brimmed glass.

"I like that," said Willie. "'Back at ya.' Mind if I borrow it?"

"Maybe you invented it. ...Did you all drive up in Lulibelle?"

"Dodger sent a Silver Ghost," said Finn.

Spencer took a tongue-teasing sip of what tasted a bit like cream soda with sort of a fairy dust finish; and Annie tinked her glass to his. "My father allowed me a bit of this stuff at my last birthday party."

"Guess he's got connections," said Willie.

"I asked how he'd obtained it, but he told me not to trouble my head... which he seems to assume is vacuous in matters of the world."

"Dis world, I 'sumes?" said Finn.

"As I assume he assumes."

Dodger poured a glass for himself after topping-off Annie's. "One misses a lot assuming assumptions." He indicated the banquet with a wave of a hand. "Dig in, gang, before it goes cold; I'm afraid it must be self-service this evening."

"Ain't nothin' to be shamed of," said Willie. "An' saves a lot of time."

Finn turned to Annie. "An' what would da lady like?"

It seemed assumingly apparent, despite the unexpected thrill of Annie's lips meeting his last night, that she and Finn, as Dodger had said, were indeed a star-matched pair; and though on a possibly primal level Spencer felt a bit thwarted, he also, on some higher plane, was happy they had found each other, and turned his attention back to the food.

He'd presumed, in light of Dodger's wealth, that supper might be grandiose and possibly beyond his ken with fare heretofore only read of in books – perhaps caviar, *filet de bœuf, pheasant au vin, canard à l'orange, escargot, ratatouille* and haggis -- but was relieved as well as delighted to find a spread more suitable to the egalitarian tastes of youth: piled upon silver warming trays, beneath which flickered blue alcohol flames, were big juicy cheeseburgers worthy of Watson's lavishly loaded with all the trimmings, and beside them a mountain of French-style potatoes, with bottles of Blue Label ketchup for cloaking. There was also a great golden heap of fried oysters, with pepper and vinegar ready to spice. But, Dodger had not restrained the menu to merely encoring the treats of last night; there was a blatantly unabashed platter – impertinently thumbing its nose, so to speak, at any specter of racial *faux pas* -- of crisply-crusted southern fried chicken. Also a platter of fried fish fillets, which, accompanied by the potatoes, would comprise the obvious dish beloved by those of Britannic persuasion. And there were several well-topped pizzas, which -- perhaps in keeping with the period ambiance -- had risen to popularity during the 1920s.

And so, without further ceremony, all began piling their fine china plates with prodigious potions of finger-foods, with Finn gentlemanly serving Annie; and Spencer, as if in one of his dreams of ecstatically eating to blubberous bliss, was for a second overwhelmed as to where to begin. But then he chomped a huge crescent of burger, followed it with a succulent oyster, then a big bite of crispy fried chicken, then a fillet of fish with chips, to finish with a portion of pizza all chased with a gulp of sparkling champagne, which titillatingly temped his palate into an eager repeat of the process.

"I shoulda thought of that," muffed Willie, around a busy mouthful of burger, while reaching for an oyster.

"Maybe you did," said Spencer, commencing another massive migration of vivacious victuals into his mouth, while noting the walls of the vast dining room were hung with more portraits of fat feasting cherubs of every racial origin and color rolling and tumbling over each other in unabashed childish gluttony amongst every manner of glorious grub.

The band struck up another tune, and the living cherub came down from the stage to mingle while singing amongst the diners, laying a hand on Willie's shoulder, playfully bussing Spencer's cheek, clasping his arms around Annie and Finn as if confirming their star-coupled status, and finally alighting in Dodger's lap where, held like a rolly-poly teddy cherished by a loving child, he sang in his seraphic voice:

> Am I a passing fancy
> Or am I the one in your dreams
> Am I a passing fancy
> To love while the pale moonlight beams
>
> The night is so romantic
> The whole world's in love so it seems
> Am I a passing fancy
> Or am I the one in your dreams.

CHAPTER TWENTY

Spencer awoke in silver starlight to the soothing song of the brook, finding himself barefoot in bed and still barely wearing – they had slipped mostly off -- the jeans in which he'd lain down after lunch.

Yesterday?

He reached for his phone and thumbed it on... yes, it had been yesterday, because it was presently three in the morning on what had been yesterday's tomorrow. As he had upon waking several times in the recent past, he wondered if he'd only been dreaming all the out-though-the-window adventures; but then he fondled the bulk of his belly, feeling its bulbously bulging bloat from all he had eaten while dining with Dodger – cheeseburgers, fish-and-chips, oysters and pizza, along with ice-cream and cake for dessert -- and began to recall the events of the evening... at least as clearly as he could considering they were progressively clouded by the effervescent veil of champagne.

He remembered dancing -- *dancing!* -- with Annie to another slow and romantic rendition of *Am I A Passing Fancy* celestially crooned by the cherub. Then he had danced with Dodger, and just as charmingly cheek-to-cheek. In fact, everyone had danced with each other, and his last had been with the cherub; but details became indistinct after that and he wasn't sure when the party had ended. He vaguely recalled the streets of Oakland – again, as on the night before, softy shrouded in swirling mist – had been serenely empty and quiet when Dodger had driven his spirited guests, still supplied with bottles of bubbly and everyone gay in the past-present sense, along with the jovial band of Lost Boys, to various dimly discerned destinations in the stately Silver Ghost... "Mr. Toad," apparently, having been given the evening free after collecting them.

Still, it must have been before midnight when Dodger had lastly chauffeured him home -- the car purring powerfully up the steep lane -- because neither his father's GMC nor his mother's Subaru had been present in front of the cottage... which had saved him an explanation of how he'd returned in the grand old Ghost when he'd ostensibly never left. He could have entered by the front door, but they had gone around to his window and, after a long hug and kiss in the moonlight – Spencer having laid to rest the notion that loving another boy could conjure him into someone he wasn't -- Dodger had boosted him into bed, where, after saying goodnight to Wiggins, he must have fallen asleep.

"And here we are," he murmured to Wiggins, who also reclined with head on crossed arms illuminated by starlight. "Because, as Dodger might say, we always are wherever we go and therefore always whenever we've been."

Then he added, "damn," softly because his parents were – at least presumably – home, finding for the third time in a row his sometimes seemingly spiritual pleasures had manifested materially.

The event had been warmly recent, and there lingered the blatantly shameless sensation of self-indulgent carelessness and indolent urchin indifference to matters of propriety. In fact, thinking wryly of clichés, he took a Fatima off the night table, fired it with his lighter and exhaled a languid ghost, which of course Wiggins mirrored; and both did nothing more for a time than bask in the peace of the moment.

But, like many earthy pleasures, this was also fleeting; and though he wouldn't have called it concealing as if he'd committed a sin of omission by having a nocturnal emission, still required a cleansing atonement. On most other such occasions he would have simply gone back to sleep and dealt with that laborious chore before partaking of breakfast, but found he wasn't sleepy. He flipped the cigarette stub out the window and turned again to Wiggins. "We have to do it sometime, so why not now, I propose?"

Wiggins seemed to agree.

His jeans, being mostly already off, had not been inundated, so he wiggled out of them and avalanched to his feet. Quietly opening his door, he looked down the hall to the living room. The moon had long passed zenith, now beaming its glow on the front of the cottage and showing his parents' vehicles beyond the ivy-framed window. A glance into the kitchen confirmed that Dodger had indeed done the dishes... if Spencer had needed any more proof he hadn't dreamed this adventure. He turned once more to Wiggins and whispered, "Unless we went dishwashing in our sleep."

That made him recall his remark yesterday of going swimming while asleep· the night was still comfortably warm, and he considered a dip in the pond as an alternative to washing, and less labor-intensive. "You're welcome to join me in spirit," he added to his reflection.

He could have departed by the back door, but windows, as Dodger had said, were more fun... though in his case a struggle to egress without the assistance of Dodger, squiggling and wiggling through the portal like a bottle cork pulling itself, and finally clumsily cascading out to almost fall in the ferns. Rather ungainly regaining his balance, he proceeded across the shadowy dell, hearing the rhythmic keening of crickets and the inquires of an owl as he made his way to the brook along the new path he had scythed under Dodger's mentorship. At last he puffed past the base of the dam and up the slope to the pond. The trestle, he saw, was there – but why wouldn't it be – though he paused to consider something that seemingly should have been obvious... that, even though the trains were quiet, he'd never heard any passing despite the stillness of the nights, except when he'd been with Dodger.

"Another mystery," he murmured, and waded into the glimmering water, becoming lighter with every step as his mass buoyed up around him, until he reached the drop-off and launched himself into weightlessness. "Who needs a spaceship?" he laughed. "When you remember you can fly."

Employing a leisurely back-stroke, he propelled from under the shadows of trees into the pond's star-sparkled center and over the deep dark place below to placidly float beneath the night sky to the soothing splash of water tumbling over the dam. For a time his mind wandered at random; he supposed, as a young black male born in such a time and place, he'd been more fortunate than many, not only blessed with loving parents but also given a chance -- perhaps by a combination of fate and the whim of an unknown someone in England -- to rise above, and literally, what might have been a curse for others.

"Thank you," he said to the stars.

For another time he reflected on the added good fortune of meeting Dodger, not only an actual physical friend who apparently liked him for who he was – his "spirit," as Dodger would say – but also someone who shared his interests, not to mention opening what seemed like infinite vistas into other universes, The Great Beyond and everything.

For a while longer he drifted like that as if he possessed no material self and was only *I am* in consciousness and the pond could have been a vast sphere of his spirit, the "bowl" perhaps surrounding himself, or the radiance of his aura, but gradually seemed to return to his body and present earthly surroundings. He was in no danger of drowning, and probably couldn't have fully submerged if he'd wanted to, but began to feel a sense of unease... a creep, perhaps, of something impending which probably wouldn't be welcome. He pictured a scene from *Jaws*, and imagined what he might look like suspended here on the mirror surface to anything watching from down in those depths. He also recalled reading somewhere that "naked" had once meant vulnerable, weaponless and unprotected.

But, that was ridiculous; there certainly weren't any sharks in this pond; and even if, as Dodger had said, there were any big fat fish, he'd never heard of a trout attack.

Still, though relatively warm, the water was cooler than his blood and despite all his insulation he felt a chill seeping into his bones. He turned to paddle back to shore when he saw something pale in the blackness below slowly rising toward him.

His logical mind first thought of a fish... but, if so, and as it ascended, growing ever larger, it surely couldn't have been a trout.

Then he saw what it was!

He thrashed frantically out of the way lest it should horribly *touch* him; and a moment later it sluggishly surfaced clad in an old-fashioned suit and revealing the dead-white cadaverous face and now sightless staring glassy eyes of Dodger's uncle Ebenezer!

And, if it could have looked any worse, the throat had been shockingly slashed, the head all but decapitated, lolling gruesomely undulant on an almost-severed spine.

A Sherlockian observation flashed for a second across Spencer's mind... that one savage swing of a *scythe* could have done such a thing.

But, that was the last of his detachment as, now with a blundering breast-stroke, he swam as fast as he could for shore, his feet finally finding the stony ledge where he lumbered gasping back to dry ground under the moon-shadowed trees. His thoughts were shooting around in his skull like bees trapped and bashing about in a jar: there was, of course, the chilling shock of seeing an obviously murdered man, along with the natural prompting of panic to run to his parents for refuge.

...But then the cops would have to be called; suspicious eyes in mostly white faces would try to probe his soul for guilt; the story-book innocence of the dell would be ravaged by crackling radios, cynical seen-it-all voices, luridly flashing red and blue strobes, and starkly glaring halogen lights illuminating the scene of the crime while a CSI team searched for clues.

But, what scared and confused him more was knowing -- or at least presuming, based upon logical deduction -- *who* had killed the man!

Slowly regaining his breath, standing head down and panting, one hand propped against a tree in the place where he and Dodger had shared their sensual adventure, and not wanting – or maybe not daring -- to face the floating thing in the pond, he tried to throttle his runaway thoughts.

"Tut, man," he puffed, "get hold of yourself! ...Could it have been self-defense?"

A Holmesian coolness came to his aid cranking the Babbage Engine of reason: it seemed clear that Dodger's existence had stood between that despicable man and the inheritance of a fortune. And, Dodger had been on his guard -- watching his step in dark places – perhaps why he'd walked away with the scythe after his uncle had made an appearance the day before yesterday's afternoon.

Had the man tried to kill Dodger tonight, maybe in the mansion, after Dodger had returned from driving Spencer home? It would have been an opportune time with all the servants absent. If so, the logical means of murder would have been a gun – as David Balfour's wicked uncle had almost used on his nephew -- but maybe this Ebenezer hadn't known Dodger's skill with that blade?

Having no real-time references, Spencer resorted to TV scenes; the man maybe waiting in the foyer, taking aim as Dodger entered, but Dodger proving too fast for him, grabbing the scythe out of the stand and swinging before his uncle could fire.

"A possible scenario." Spencer wished Wiggins was with him to help formulate other theories. For a moment he even pictured the boy looking out of the looking-glass… which of course was absurd since how could there be a reflection without him to reflect.

"Or, maybe," Spencer went on as if sounding Wiggins in spirit, "Dodger's uncle missed the first shot? Or, maybe the gun misfired? …But, assuming his uncle wanted to kill him, how could Dodger's death be explained without suspicion falling on him? For surely, given what we know, the uncle would be the most likely suspect. …An attempted burglary, and Dodger confronted the perpetrator? That could play with the police. …Or, a kidnapping gone wrong? The kidnap for ransom of a rich kid. An equally plausible explanation. The man might have gotten away with those. …But apparently didn't."

Spencer boarded that train of thought but soon arrived at a junction: "If Dodger acted in self-defense, why would he try to conceal the corpse?"

Becoming at last possessed of full breath, his heartbeat subsiding to less than a gallop, he straightened his posture as much as he could and let go his grip on the tree, though his eyes still shied from the pond. "He might have feared being suspected of murdering his uncle, and for the same reason his uncle may have tried to murder him. We certainly know he's strong enough to have easily carried the body..."

That put a picture in Spencer's mind of the corpse slung across Dodger's bare shoulders, its half-severed head hanging hideously and perhaps still dripping blood, as Dodger toted it through darkness along the path beneath the trees.

"But why bring it here?" Spencer went on. "To sully this peacefully innocent place he associates with a happy childhood? ...And, being well-read in the genre of murder-mystery lore, he would know, unless securely weighted, a body, due to gasses forming in the process of decomposition, will invariably rise to the surface, and sometimes within a few hours after death."

He forced himself to face the pond.

There was nothing to be seen but shimmering star-lit water.

He roved his eyes along the shoreline, thinking the corpse might have drifted, but again saw nothing. Going back to the water's edge, he carefully scanned the pond... nothing.

Dismissing horror movie scenes where corpses rose up to grab people, he waded in up to his navel and, shading his eyes from the stars with a hand, repeated his visual search, looking for any shadowy shape that might be a body just under the surface, but again saw nothing.

"This is strange," he murmured. "Once a body has risen... at least according to what I've read... it usually remains afloat until it decomposes enough to let the internal gasses escape, which might take days or even weeks. ...It must be there somewhere."

Returning to shore, he carefully crossed the top of the dam, its mossy stone rim maybe twelve inches wide, recalling a comment by a book critic that "teetering" in literature was too often teamed with "precariously," but which in this case *was* apt since he couldn't see his feet and his caution enhanced his customary arms-extended balancing pose.

Safely attaining the other side, he scanned the shadowy strip of shore along the base of the mansion grounds wall, but again there was nothing. Then he began to wonder if he'd actually seen a body, and finally looked up at the stars. "Wish you were here to pinch me."

Reprising his ponderous tightrope performance, risking on one side a six-foot fall to the stone-jumbled bed of the brook or a plunge into the pond on the other, where the corpse *might* have been lurking – even if only a direful dead thing and harmless except in nightmarish appearance -- he made another successful crossing while teetering precariously.

"Well, Wiggins," he said, when back on firm ground and for lack of a looking-glass addressing his watery reflection, "I suppose we *could* have imagined it. ...Or, perhaps the champagne, like Dodger's gin, has more than mere alcoholic effects. In any case, if there is a corpse, I presume, like myself, you're not sad whose it is?"

Wiggins did not appear so.

"If it's real," Spencer went on, raising his eyes past Wiggins for a final scan of the pond, "it's not going to get any deader. Nor, despite many ghostly tales, do I think it's going to go anywhere. ...And, if Dodger did kill his uncle, we should get the story from him before making any more assumptions. ...And, need I add, as history has shown, it has usually been very unlucky for we of darker persuasions to become involved in a white person's death."

Wiggins reflectively seemed to agree.

Spencer turned to the west where the moon had set leaving the dell mostly in darkness except for silvery shades of starlight. "I therefore propose a return to bed and, hopefully, a few hours of sleep despite what we saw... or thought we saw. I'll set the phone to wake us at dawn, when we can search the pond by daylight. And, whatever the future may bring, we'll feel better facing it after breakfast."

CHAPTER TWENTY-ONE

"**S**pencer! Breakfast!" called his mom.

Spencer awoke in warm sunlight feeling both hungry and refreshed despite the fabulous feast with Dodger and having already risen at dawn to again search the pond for a corpse. Thankfully he'd found nothing, not even a taint of blood in the water, though his Holmesian aspect admitted the body might have bled-out while being transported from the mansion... *if* that had actually happened.

Of course it had been reassuring, without finding contrary evidence, to regard what he thought he'd seen as a dream – he *could* have dozed off while afloat in starlight – and it had been with a less-troubled mind when he'd re-settled into bed serenaded by the song of the brook for another hour or so of sleep.

On first returning from the pond at close to four o'clock in the morning he'd intended to enter by the back door, but had found it locked, no doubt by his parents from a lifetime of habit. His window was only four feet from the ground, but that might have been four-hundred for him, not only trying to hoist himself but having to squeeze his middle though without Dodger's tucking and stuffing. The front door would have also been locked, but he'd rolled the wheelbarrow to his window, which gave him sufficient elevation to squiggle, wiggle, squirm and scrooch his undulant entrance into the egress. Of course he'd used the back door when going out again at dawn to search for a grisly discovery.

"Coming!" he called to his mom, finding that hadn't happened this morning for probably obvious reasons, while avalanching out of bed and snagging his jeans from the chair. Then he added to

Wiggins, "Hopefully, Dodger will wake us as usual from our after-lunch nap, and we'll know one way or the other."

Wiggins seemed to reflect that logic.

His father smiled up from his *Tribune* as Spencer came into the kitchen. "Find the meaning of life, the universe and everything yet?"

Spencer loaded himself on his chair. "No, but I'm pretty sure the answer is more than 42." He gulped from a tumbler of milk as his mom set a plate before him with scrambled eggs, crispy hash-browns and a sizable slab of juicy meat. "*Steak* and eggs?" he said. "Did somebody croak and leave us a fortune?"

Nathan laughed as Jenny served him an identical dish. "We haven't become the Shades yet, but I was promoted to foreman, which means a little extra green."

Jenny prepared her plate and sat down. "We'll celebrate on Sunday with that picnic by our pond."

"And, yes, there will be beer," said Nathan.

"Um, swell," said Spencer, not wanting to lower his parents' spirits, though he'd forgotten about the picnic after his real or imagined encounter with the ghastly thing the pond. Prior to that he'd been hoping to début Dodger at the event, his new and charming friend; and while he knew that "white and rich" wouldn't further enchant his parents, it wouldn't be off-putting either. He'd been planning to ask Dodger yesterday, but it had slipped his mind during the dinner party.

"Any menu suggestions?" asked Jenny.

Spencer made a smile. "Remember The Water Rat's lunch?"

*   *   *

Spencer spent most of the morning completing the bird and beast barrier around his mother's garden, climbing onto the wheelbarrow to hang the mesh above, and finally building an entry door from boards he'd found in the shed. His mom gave her hearty approval and served him an equally hearty lunch of more golden-oldie hamburger smothered with spaghetti accompanied by fresh lemonade.

"This stuff is the oyster's earrings!" said Spencer, after gulping from his tumbler and pouring it full again from a pitcher. "A seven percent solution of something?"

"A few drops of rose oil," said Jenny. "Since you seem to have taken an interest in 1920s food, lemonade flavored with rose oil was one of the potions used to disguise the nasty taste of bathtub gin. …Speaking of which, I noticed your Plymouth has vanished."

"A passing fancy," said Spencer, fork-lifting a load of buttered spaghetti surrounding a chunk of juicy ground beef.

"Flaming youth," said Jenny, kissing Spencer's cheek. "Your dad and I should be back by midnight. And, keeping with the present past theme, there's mutton chops and mashed potatoes in the ice box for your supper. And feel free to take the afternoon off, my hard-working garden cherub."

Spencer politely muffed a burp after downing the last of the lemonade. "I'll start with a nap."

Going into his room, joined by Wiggins reflectively, he mounted his bed in a comfortable sprawl, hearing his mother's Subaru start up and murmur away down the lane, leaving peace and quiet again except for the subtle sounds of small life and ever-present song of the brook. Turning his head on the pillows, he regarded the sunlit dell through the window, his gaze going, naturally, up to the pond.

"I'm sure you agree, Wiggins," he said, settling himself and closing his eyes, "our state of being will be more serene should we find what we thought we saw we didn't."

He awoke to the spirits of scruffy-boy sweat, tobacco and gin, expecting Dodger beside him, perhaps having taken the liberty of borrowing another book, but found himself alone. Absurdly, he turned to the mirror, but Dodger wasn't with Wiggins, either. Yet, Dodger's scents were as strong as if he was physically present, and couldn't have been just the lingering traces of his liberty last night.

Warily, Spencer peeked out the window lest Dodger, perhaps in a Puckish mood, be lurking enshrouded in sheet below to give him another scare, but there was nothing but ferns.

"But, he *must* have been here; don't you agree?"

Wiggins looked enigmatic, which was uncustomary for him.

"He could have woken us," said Spencer, feeling disappointed. "He's never regarded that as a liberty."

He consulted his phone for the time, finding it nearing 2:30 on yet another hot afternoon, then struggled to a sitting position and swung his still-Kedded feet to the floor. "I would suggest a swim, since we're begrimed from our morning labor, but as I'm sure you concur, would rather not venture into that water until getting Dodger's explanation of what we may or may not have seen. Nor, as it came to me during breakfast, would I feel at ease with my parents picnicking there on the shore not knowing if we wouldn't be joined by very unsavory company."

He noted again Dodger's spiritual essence, a sort of signature in scent. "...Or maybe a calling card," he mused. "Though we were obviously home for him and certainly always will be. ...Do you think," he added, after a moment, "that his absence today despite an apparent visitation could be connected to what we saw... or, again, only thought we saw? ...A subtle clue, perhaps, like the dog who did nothing in the night?"

Wiggins seemed to reflect on that; and Spencer cascaded to his feet. "I propose we take the liberty of paying a call on Dodger, who said we were welcome any time."

Wiggins accordingly tugged up his jeans.

Spencer went first to the kitchen and fortified himself with a Coke, then left the cottage by the back door, carefully crossed the foot-bridge and pushed, as Dodger had done last night, at the iron-barred gate. Not only did it not give way but seemed as solidly rusted shut as when he'd first examined it on his first afternoon in the dell. However, its state of being proved to be an advantage, because when Spencer applied his bulk the corroded bolt snapped and the gate burst open, its spooky movie sound-effect stilling the bird-song a moment.

Spencer peered up the ghost of a path that dwindled into sun-shafts and shadows beneath the overhanging trees. It was hard to believe he and Dodger had made their way along it last night, and in total darkness.

"Of, course," he said to Wiggins, assumably with him in spirit, "he would have known the way. …Still," he added, after a moment of scanning the wildly overgrown trail, "it looks like Mowgli's jungle in there, so maybe we should equip ourselves for herbicide if necessary."

Re-crossing the bridge, he went to the shed. A machete would have been useful, but apparently hadn't been required when the grounds were groomed in the 1920s. The sickle he'd used previously didn't seem up to the task of cutting heavy underbrush, and the axes clumsy overkill. He was about to select a hatchet, when his eyes were drawn to the scythe, which he took down from pegs on the wall and felt comfortable in his hands from Dodger's mentoring. Though rusty, its blade was still scarily sharp, and though not created for clearing pathways, might serve well for that purpose. A few minutes' work with a wire brush, a rag, and WD-40 had it clean and ready for reaping, if not pristine and gleaming like Dodger's wicked weapon – here a natural pause in thought to recall the reason for this expedition – then, toting it over a shoulder, Spencer proceeded back to the gate and made his way up the remains of the path.

The trudge of his Keds was softly muffled on the thick carpet of long-fallen leaves, though unlike the journey last night there were abundant forest-life sounds – the shrill of blue-jays, the chatter of squirrels, the caws of a curious crow – though the rush of the brook soon faded away into the tree-tunneled shadows behind. The going was not as difficult as he'd anticipated, the foliage yielding without much resistance to his determined material mass, and only occasional tangles of vines, which he slashed with the scythe. Of course he was puffing and shiny with sweat by the time he'd advanced very far, and pausing often to pull up his jeans, but was feeling rather adventurous as if on a storybook quest and prepared to dispatch any big bad wolves with a single swing of his enchanted blade.

"I must warn you, though, Wiggins," he panted, while slicing another web of vines, "based upon my impressions last night, we have quite a distance to travel, apparently across the Shade grounds to Dodger's dwelling somewhere beyond." He managed a laugh. "Guess this is exploring the Great Outdoors."

His mind thus framed for a lengthy ordeal as he'd once girded his loins, so to speak, for the battle of walking eight blocks, it was with more than a little surprise when he slashed through another entanglement and emerged into relative openness at the edge of what once may have been a meadow and which, though heavily overgrown with bushes, ferns and trees, was obviously of more recent origin than the woods he'd been forging through. For a minute he stood blinking in the golden afternoon sunlight, his eyes having grown accustomed to the green-lit gloom of the forest, sheened with sweat, softly panting, jeans about to abandon his bottom and only retained by his frontal fat, leaves and bits of twigs in his hair, a few crimson scratches scoring his body from bulling through a briar patch, and scythe in hands still ready to swing. Gradually, his sight grew less dazzled and he looked around.

"This must be the Shade estate."

But then a sensation of *déjà vu* began to creep into his consciousness, and he lifted his gaze above the trees now growing wild and long-untended on what had been an enormous... *lawn*, to see the topmost story of three, along with the two looming towers, of the perplexing anomalous marriage of hoary Gothic cathedral – complete with gargoyles glowering down -- and Baskerville Hall in the Sherlock Holmes tale!

His mouth would have fallen open, had it not already been so for breath; and though he infrequently used the term, it seemed the appropriate cat's meow:

"No fucking way!"

Naturally, his mind tried for reason... perhaps Dodger's father in fanciful whim had copied this "charming little horror," and Dodger's actual domicile was still some distance away? This explanation seemed reinforced by the length of their journey last night.

In his surprise and bewilderment he'd forgotten he had Wiggins in spirit with whom to share speculations. Still staring at the gigantic house, at least as much as could be seen from his present perspective, he stood the scythe upright beside him, its blade at easily twice his height curving halo-like overhead... albeit a rusty one. "What *could* be an explanation? *Is* there another house like this maybe about a mile away, though of recent construction and upon well-tended grounds?"

Of course he didn't expect a reply, but pausing as if waiting for one gave him time to reflect.

"But," he continued after a minute, "if Dodger's father had wanted such an eccentric home, surely it would have been much cheaper to buy this one than build another. ...Unless, as Linda Lancaster said, Mr. Darkmoor wouldn't sell. ...And apparently at any price, considering what it would have cost to duplicate such a palatial place in present-day coin of the realm."

He paused again to let Wiggins ponder, and was startled for an instant when a deer strode casually past -- no, it wasn't a unicorn – and seemed to regard him affably. He watched it vanish into the foliage overgrowing the long-lost lawn, and a new thought came to mind.

"Perhaps we are searching for explanations which, though not impossible, do seem very improbable, when the real solution may be simple?"

He wished there was reflective surface in which to reflect on Wiggins' reflection and arrive at what suddenly seemed might be a probable conclusion.

"Dodger's coffin varnish!"

Leaning the scythe against a tree, Spencer recovered his jeans. "Surely you agree that if, as we have already surmised, the concoction *is* dream-inducing and rendered us suggestible to seeing Oakland as it was in 1926, it's likewise very probable that our adventure of last night, The Adventure Of Dining With Dodger... you recall we imbibed before embarking... was also perceived from an altered perspective?"

He turned to study the structure again: though apparently intact -- none of the masonry had fallen -- there was obvious weathering; ivy shrouded much of the walls, and oaks and redwoods shot their branches over the mossy ramparted roof, while several lofty eucalyptus overtopped the towers.

"As we have learned from Dodger," Spencer continued to muse, "he seems to have spent much time in childhood roaming the Shade estate, and would, of course, have explored the house, as would any adventurous boy. Indeed, he probably knows it well. So, again assuming an alternate perspective, it takes no great cognitive leap to reason he led us *here* last night, having already prepared the place with lighted lamps and candles... surely the power cannot still be on. And the rest, as the saying goes, was left to our imagination."

"Furthermore," he added, after scanning around, "you will note the trail we have followed continues only toward *this* house; there is no trace of another route to anywhere beyond these grounds, which would seem to indicate there is no present-day clone."

"Of course," he went on, "there are still many questions. Assuming our gang at the dinner party, and with whom we adventured in Oakland, wasn't imaginary, or, dare I say, composed of ghosts... in which I am not yet inclined to believe... who in reality are they? We might concede the existence of an actual gang of Lost Boys... with apologies to Annie... perhaps a pack of like-minded friends obviously intelligent, very well-read in literature, and inclined to naughtiness, who, perhaps inspired by this setting, act the roles of flaming youth in the 1920s. ...Or, possibly homeless kids who've found a refuge here; and Dodger, like Dickens' Artful, is their clever leader."

He turned to regard the house again. "But, as Mr. Holmes would say, conjecture without the possession of facts often leads to false conclusions."

He slung the scythe over a shoulder. "I therefore propose an investigation of the premises in question." He indicated what remained of the gold-graveled path ahead. "Shall we follow the yellow brick road?"

CHAPTER TWENTY-TWO

"**F**eel free to lean on my shoulder if you feel fatigued," said Spencer, beginning his lumbering trudge up the trail, which, though wildly overgrown, wasn't as thickly entangled as the forest path.

"I don't know why I seem to recall you being much fatter than me," he added, "but friends are always there for each other no matter their color, shape or size."

Again he felt *déjà vu*, finding the path encroached upon by lavish ranks of lavender lilies, the sort often pictured on funeral announcements, though -- as he was relatively sure -- he *had* been here before. Still, he felt that sensation again when, through a curtain of ivy, he caught a glimpse of a stone boy-faun poised like Peter Pan with a knife as if confronting Captain Hook; and again when spying a gang of fat cherubs swilling from an amphora of wine and tipsily tumbling over each other half-obscured by ferns. It was the same with other creations of rolly-poly cherubim engaged in feasting and rowdiness, along with the youthful fauns playing pipes, hunting with a bow and arrow, and sitting peacefully reading a book; though he found the recumbent Panlet he'd thought last night to be day-dreaming in a leafy bower was doing so dynamically with a lustful-fisted grip, his expression ecstatically euphoric, his back just beginning to arch, as if poised forever in time on the brink of a celestial surge.

"He would make an impertinent fountain," Spencer remarked to Wiggins. "And more *apropos* in my opinion to expressing the audacious spirit of youth than a perpetually pissing boy; though prone to priggish perceptification by those who see smut in everything except when they look in a mirror."

The resemblance of the fauns to Dodger, though amazingly accurate in both face and figure – except for furry legs and hooves – could, as he added to Wiggins, be attributed to a sculptor choosing a handsome teen model of Caucasian descent.

As he continued toward the house, bulling his way through greenery and occasionally plying the scythe, he began to hear the splash of water above the chirping and twitter of birds, so assumably the fountain, probably gravity-fed from the pond, was still in centuried play. He scanned for what he'd believed last night to be topiary Egyptian gods, but though a few shapes were vaguely suggestive of having once been trimmed as such, only inspired imagination, as in creating constellations, could have rendered them visible.

Of actual animal life there was much in addition to avian and bees droning over the flowers; a trotting fox, a questing coyote, another deer – or perhaps the same one – and none apparently discomfited by Spencer's perambulating presence; as well as squirrels in the trees, rabbits amongst the shrubbery, and a few lizards and snakes in the grass, which seemed perfectly natural since these walled and undisturbed grounds would be a sanctuary. Moreover, many of the trees, though long gone wild, were heavy with fruit – apples, pears, plums, cherries, and others he couldn't identify, though quinces came to mind… along with a runcible spoon. All offered sustenance to creatures of herbivore inclination, which in the natural order of things – as the coyote demonstrated by catching an unwary hare – provided for the carnivores. To one perhaps less-enlightened or clinging to Beatrix Potter beliefs, that might have sullied this storybook scene, but, after all, it was part of life, the universe and everything.

There were also walnuts and almonds, which the squirrels were gathering; and Spencer paused to pluck an apple from an overhanging branch, the variety unknown to him but crisply juicy and sweet, which he munched as he progressed.

Slicing through a wisteria thicket, which had once merely shaded a marble bench on which to rest in company with a slumbering cherub, he came at last upon the fountain sparkling in the sunlight and splashing a liquid lullaby into the pond where more cherubs frolicked, while in its midst and shrouded in spray as if an incongruous lifeguard, stood the cheerful-looking Grim Reaper who somehow, due to a sculptor's skill – or maybe just the oversize scythe casually slung on a shoulder -- gave the impression of being young; and was also suggestive of Dodger.

"Or rather," Spencer reminded Wiggins, "a boy very much like Dodger from a long-ago time. ...Though he may very well look like that now."

The gigantic house loomed ahead against the forested slopes at its back and across the graveled drive, which was filled with ferns like an emerald moat. Spencer almost expected the rusty corpse of a Silver Ghost to be parked nearby, but of course it wouldn't have been left there after Gilbert Shade's demise.

"And, besides," Spencer puffed, "Dodger drove us home last night, and probably put it in the garage... I assume there is a garage somewhere."

He added while wading through greenery, "Which brings up another of many questions... *did* he actually drive us home, or did we only imagine he did?"

That brought a childish picture to mind of kids creating a "car" from chairs and pretending to motor.

"*Very* dream-inducing," he said, proceeding on to the staircase, which though heavily carpeted by many years of fallen leaves, was nevertheless still majestic with its great guardians of reclining stone lions.

He stopped at the foot of the steps under the grumpy gaze of gargoyles to study the dwelling in detail: as he'd noted from afar, it seemed in good condition for something abandoned a hundred years. Nor was there any evidence of the usual cretinous vandalism one might expect to have been inflicted; though frosted opaquely with decades of grime, none of the windows were broken; there were no spray-painted tags or graffiti; and the front doors looked unviolated.

"Shall we continue?" said Spencer. "And again feel free to lean on my shoulder."

Once more recovering his jeans, and using the scythe as a staff, he began to climb the stairs. Strangely, or maybe interestingly – or perhaps intriguingly – he did feel as if his mass had increased as if Wiggins had accepted his aid.

Finally attaining the summit and puffing prodigiously, he plodded across the vast portico to the immense pair of doors.

"At least," he panted to Wiggins, "we didn't imagine the Marley-face knockers. ...Speaking of which, do you think we *should* knock? Proper form and that sort of thing? ...And, as we have speculated, what if the house *is* occupied by an actual gang of Lost Boys? Again, apologies to Annie."

"Discretion being... you know?" he added, and lifted a heavy bronze handkerchief ostensibly binding a Marley jaw to let it fall with a resounding BOOM.

After waiting what seemed a courteous time and receiving no response, he grasped one of the brass door knobs green with verdigris. "Of *course*, it would be locked." He turned to regard the lions. "Do you suppose, as Dodger said, the key *is* always here for us?"

Again with support of the scythe, he descended the stairs to the left-side lion and delved a hand into the leaves accumulated between its paws. "Right where he said it would be."

Bulldozing himself up the stairway again, he inserted the key into the lock, which though stiff, didn't resist, and applied his bulk to the doors, which, with appropriate sound-effects, gave way to his weight and slowly swung open.

He hadn't thought about what he might find, having presumed what he'd seen last night had been enhanced by gin-induced glamour, but except for dust and spider webs softly shrouding everything, the enormous foyer looked the same, though now lit by the westering sun beaming through the doorway instead of the big chandelier. There were the pleasantly peach-colored walls above wainscoting of tongue-and-groove wood and, though layered with silver-gray snow, also the runner of rose-patterned carpet. There were two switches inside the doorway, the push-button type of the period, set in a tarnished brass plate, one perhaps for the portico lamp, and he tried them both with no result except their unenlightening clicks. As when he'd tested the generator, he wondered if it had powered the house, but it hadn't been running last night.

"Though, if there are Lost Boys," he said, "Dodger might have had an accomplice start it after we left the dell."

Spencer's Holmesian observation, as it had manifested when inspecting the spring house, noted the lack of footprints or other signs of recent disturbance, but filed it for future reflection. His sneaks were haunted by infant ghosts swirling up from the floor as he entered, his back-lit shadow with scythe in hand preceding him like a rotund Reaper. Against the right wall stood the plush settee and the free-standing ashtray. Opposite was the claw-footed table, and on it the candlestick telephone. Feeling a little childish, he took the receiver off its hook, breaking a net of spider web, shook out a ruffled arachnid, and put the receiver to an ear.

There was only dead silence.

Hanging up, he looked around, again seeing all the same as last night -- with deference to the spider art and plushy profusion of dust -- though it seemed surprising to find the paintings still on the walls.

"I admit," he murmured to Wiggins, "they would have been hard to imagine in such accurate detail, but I wouldn't have thought such beautiful things would have been left to gather dust after Gilbert Shade died."

As he had done the previous night, Spencer went to study them: again seeing – though dimmed by dust -- three were dreamy landscapes of golden summer afternoons in uninhabited countrysides, their distant features ethereally hazy, mountains rendered in mauve and blues; and the fourth portraying a boy faun, also very much like Dodger, playing a span of wooden pipes to a gang of abundantly chubby cherubs -- one of whom was African and resembled Spencer at an earlier age -- lounging by a sunlit pond.

"Not being well-versed in art," he said, "I can't identify the artists, but all are obviously masterful works and, I would think, very valuable. And the table and settee I suspect are Chippendale... no relation to the Disney chipmunks... while even the vintage telephone is probably worth a chunk of change."

He performed a ponderous pirouette to take in all the furnishings. "I would guess there are many thousands of dollars of antiques and art in this foyer. Which prompts another question…"

He turned to the doorway through which last night he and Dodger, butlered by Barrymore – real or imagined? -- had entered the Brobdingnagian hall. He'd expected only darkness, but saw there was a pale light; and the magnificent staircase, appearing a daunting distance away, was bathed in a soft radiance.

"Shall we continue?" he said. Then he noticed there *was* a slight difference -- again with allowance for webs and dust – between what he'd seen in here previously and the present perspective.

"No scythe in the stand." Then he laughed. "But of course we have it now."

Another thought came to mind: "Do you think we should complete the décor as a wizard might finish a spell by leaving it like a walking stick? …On the other hand…" He faced the great hall. "While it seems a doubtful defense against ghosts, I suppose there could be someone 'at home' still possessed of mortal coil who might resent our liberty; and since we are not inclined to run, perhaps we should stay armed."

He moved to enter the doorway, but paused. "Which brings up yet another question: while possibly… and hopefully… we didn't find Dodger's wicked uncle mostly decapitated last night, but just an illusion glimpsed in starlight, who was that *actual* odious man appearing at the gate in full day to challenge and threaten Dodger? True, we had been imbibing at our pond-side picnic, but I'm almost sure *he* was real. Could Dodger in fact have such an uncle and be in the danger he described? …Or alternatively, if there is a gang of Lost Boys… apologies to Annie… or maybe a band of homeless kids directed by Dodger as the Artful, could that man be their Fagin?"

After hoisting his jeans again, he took the scythe in a two-handed grip and cautiously entered the egress… or maybe vice-versa.

Looking up after passing the portal, he found the source of the pale radiance… far overhead were skylights above the trio of huge chandeliers, which would have provided ample daylight if not obscured by decades of dust, fallen leaves and pine needles, and the shadows of lofty trees; though apparently lesser debris had gathered over the staircase, leaving it lit by a brighter glow.

Again, his mouth would have fallen open, had it not already been so, as he saw – allowing for webs and dust – all he had seen the night before.

The light from above was adequate, and more than enough as his eyes adjusted, to confirm, whatever else he'd imagined, everything here was physically real… a very oddly eclectic mix of mostly media-eval museum pieces suggesting an Olde English manor, from Knights Of The Round Table suits of armor with halberds poised in respectful salute, to stuffed boar's heads looking ferally fierce, interspersed with jousting lances, swords, crossbows, battle-axes and shields.

The space was so vast there seemed little chance of anything still possessed of breath creeping up to attack him, so again with the scythe employed as a staff, its thumping echoing hollowly, he continued toward the stairway, taking in all the incredible sights while baby specters haunted his Keds and swirled around his dragging cuffs.

There were the venerable flintlock muskets, along with the massive "pirate pistols" and the bell-mouthed blunderbuss. And, many paintings did line the walls amongst the armory relics, and most appeared to be Renaissance art but only a few he recognized; the enigmatic Mona Lisa, the Birth Of Venus on a half-shell – which made him think of oysters – along with The Portrait Of Gerard Andriesz and one of Eugenia Martínez Vallejo, and a roundly-rotund Cupid in recline on a pile of skulls. There was the young Dionysus beautifully buff in both definitions, carelessly well into his cups and attended by a gang of rolly grape-swilling cherubs.

"Another logical question," he proposed to Wiggins. "Since it appears to be same boy who also modeled the fauns, as well as, somehow, the youthful Reaper, could he have been Gilbert's son, Gavin Shade?"

Pulling his eyes from all the wonders, he found he was nearing the grand staircase with its plump *"Titanic"* cherubs still well-illuminated, though the light was growing gold as the afternoon aged. The air in the hall, smelling mostly neutral, though dry and suggestive of ancient things in a crypt-like way, was a bit warmer than that of outside, probably due to the skylights creating a hothouse effect, and he was shiny with sweat again, droplets disturbing the dust on the floor like tiny atomic explosions, his cave of a navel dribbling like a leaking boiler, as he puffingly paused to lean on the scythe and surmise to Wiggins:

"I assume we are in agreement that all these relics and artwork are probably worth several millions at least... though it seems incredible they would have been left here all this time, and presumably unguarded. We may assume the known paintings are copies... I would not, in light of the late Gilbert Shade's obvious wealth and sophistication... descend so far as to call them fakes." He spared a bit of breath for a laugh. "Unless they are originals from another universe. ...But even copies so masterfully done must be valuable."

He lifted his gaze to the stairway and the second-floor gallery, noting many doors, all closed. "In light of what we have thus far seen, I suppose it's logical to assume the rest of this house is still furnished... and, 'in my father's mansion there are many rooms.'"

He added after considering, "If one were to think less of Dodger in terms of integrity... or just be realistic in the event he is homeless... having free reign of these premises could explain his expensive spook sheet, as well as his ability to so profusely provision our picnic." He fingered his cherub necklace. "As well as giving this gift. Though if he has been purloining things and possibly pawning some for cash... presumably with greater success than young Copperfield and his weskit... his needs and wants are apparently simple and seemingly unmotivated by greed, which would fit his carelessly child-like and live-in-the-moment mien."

He looked down at the dust-covered floor, which last night had resembled a mirror reflecting another universe, and noted his cuff-dragging footprints from the now faraway foyer. "I suppose, as he must have done when removing his gin mill from the spring house, he could have covered his tracks in here. Surely, despite no vehicular access, *someone* must inspect this place and report to Mr. Darkmoor."

He thought for a moment and added, "And if that someone was Dodger's father, an actual watchman living nearby, since the cottage is supposedly haunted… despite our experience to the contrary… that would explain many things; certainly Dodger's freedom to roam, his extensive knowledge of this place; and the house may have its own generator, having been built when electric power was still fairly new and prone to failure, which of course would explain it being well lighted last night."

He regarded the stairway again, not enthusiastically. "There must be over a hundred rooms in this peculiar Thurnley Abbey… upstairs, downstairs, attics, basement; drawing rooms, sitting rooms, servants quarters; bedrooms, kitchen, parlors; and of course a library, which I would love to see… all of which to explore would probably take a full day. Or more likely several for us. And while I am not yet ready to grant the existence of ghosts, I would… no offense intended… prefer some physical company; and hopefully we'll see Dodger tonight." He glanced to the foyer. "The sun, you note, is sinking, and we have a long journey home. …Still, there should be another few hours of sufficient daylight. Are you up to an ascent? And, again, feel free to lean on me."

CHAPTER TWENTY-THREE

Using the scythe again as a staff and grasping the dusty banister to heave and ho himself along, Spencer quakingly climbed the stairs and finally, panting profusely, pouring new sweat and losing his jeans, attained the gallery. He saw the hands of the grandfather clock still stood at 3:13, and as he'd noted from below, there seemed to be at least fifty doorways all around the colossal hall possibly leading to even more wonders, but it seemed most sensible to first examine the dining room to ascertain if all he had seen there last night hadn't been imaginary. Accordingly, after a minute or so to recover breath and raiment, he proceeded to the portal whose frame and lintel were cunningly carved with a bountiful grapevine and harvest design. The grand double-doors were shut but not locked, and with only slight resistance and the requisite spooky squeals, bowed, so to speak, to his belly bulk, swinging slowly inward. The enormous chamber, having no windows -- as would befit a breakfast room -- could only be dimly discerned in the glow fanning in from the hall, but there indeed stood the titanic table that might have seated a court. Spencer had been prepared for a scene like old Miss Havisham's wedding supper with age-rotted, dust-shrouded, spider-webbed fare, but this board had been properly cleared. An acre of cloth still covered it, though probably for protection instead of in preparation for another phantasmagorical feast, the many chairs all neatly drawn up.

Little else could be seen in the shadows, though when Spencer fired his lighter its yellow flicker faintly revealed a stage with a great grand piano with keyboard cover and lid closed. It was too dark to see any footprints, which might have confirmed he had danced...

but on his long list of things last night that may have been imagined, dancing was in the top ten. He also noted two massive sideboards below the big portraits of fat, feasting cherubs, which seemed to confirm the house was still furnished.

"One would think," he remarked, "Shade's English relations, the Darkmoors, would have had it all shipped to them, or maybe brokered or auctioned here. They have to be rich beyond my comprehension to just leave this place and the land as it is. ...Which, of course, makes me wonder why they would sell the cottage to us, and for only the price we could pay?"

He returned to the gallery and pulled the doors creakingly shut. Just before they met, he seemed to scent a lingering spirit of deliciously deep-fried oysters. He opened the doors again, but there was only the dusty dry smell suggestive of undisturbed crypts.

He closed the doors. "Let us continue our exploration while we still have light."

He scanned the doorways around the huge hall. "We assume servants quarters on the top floor with surely much less lavish décor and only prosaic artifacts... nor do I feel like confronting more stairs. And the towers are probably vacant... and if there was once a princess imprisoned she would look like the Reaper by now. The best rooms should be on this level, and the finest of those with a view of the grounds."

Slinging the scythe over a shoulder, he started toward the front of the house and randomly paused at a portal a few doors from the dining room. "The lady or the tiger?"

The knob, like the others, was reluctant, and he had to apply some weight before the door shriekingly surrendered. This chamber was also windowless and shrouded in shadowy gloom, but a flick of his lighter revealed an opulent parlor or smoking room furnished with armchairs, tables, a sofa, many spider-webbed *objets d'art*, vaguely-seen pictures adorning the walls, and a glass-fronted cabinet containing the shapes of bottles. And there was a small candelabra, blackly-tarnished and probably silver, holding a trio of tapers.

"I suspect the 'Noble Experiment' did not inconvenience... or not very much... those in the social class of the Shades."

Crossing the room to the cabinet, he applied his lighter to the candles, whose long-dead wicks resisted a moment, first only glowing a ghostly blue but slowly arising to warm yellow-gold and banishing shadows to cobwebby corners.

"A-ha!" he exclaimed, leaning the scythe against a wall and opening the cabinet to find no dearth of Prohibited drink. Probably in keeping with Gilbert Shade's English ancestry, there were many brands of expensive scotch, along with various rums, and both Plymouth and London gins. There were also Cognacs, brandies and sherries, and the fabled forbidden absinthe glowing an evilly arsenic green. For presumably American tastes there were bottles of pricey bourbons and ryes.

"And no doubt champagne and fine wines in the cellar. ...Which of course begs the question, if Dodger has access to all these spirits, why bother making his coffin varnish... unless, as he might say, it's more fun?"

He studied the many scotches again, some of which he'd read of, and uncapped a bottle to sample the contents. "This one is too peaty."

He tried another. "This one is too malty."

Of a third he proclaimed, "This one is just right."

Feeling jovial, he laughed. "I'm tempted to try the absinthe so often regarded as sinister, but perhaps we risk angering spirits by imbibing theirs, and absinthe may make their hearts grow fonder."

He closed the doors and regarded the candles. "Though we plan to be out of here before dark, I suppose we should be prepared for unforeseen contingencies."

Recovering the scythe and snuffing the flames, he retained the candelabra, which was probably worth a few hundred oysters, and said to any suspicious specters, "Just borrowing it to enlighten our visit, if you'll excuse the liberty."

Returning to the gallery and closing the drawing room door, he continued toward the front of the house, curious but not inspecting the many other rooms he passed, and stopped at last at another door where a slit of daylight showed underneath. "This one must have windows," he said, grasping and turning the knob.

Once again using his mass to overcome recalcitrant hinges, he bulled the door open to relative brilliance compared to the light in the hall, his eyes overloaded for a moment. Then he exclaimed, "Eureka!"

He'd hoped to find a library appropriate to a long-past time when one of the signs of sophistication -- besides an appreciation of art -- was being well-read in literature, and was not disappointed in regard to the Shades. The room was splendidly spacious, and three of its walls were lined with shelves that towered almost to the ceiling… he noted a wooden ladder provided to access the upper regions. The fourth wall boasted a quartet of windows to furnish good daytime reading light – there were also electric lamps -- and there were several sofas and chairs which, though palely dusted, still looked invitingly comfortable to settle upon and read for hours… or possibly a lifetime considering the number of books, which must have been several thousands.

Setting the candle stand on a table and laying the scythe on a chair, he began to peruse the gilded spines of what were mostly leather-bound and otherwise finely-crafted volumes. There were the works of Shakespeare; also Hawthorne, Dickens, Poe, Cervantes, Kafka, Homer, Tolstoy, Dostoevsky, Stevenson, James Joyce, Oscar Wilde, Charlotte and Emily Brontë, and Mark Twain to name just a few, but he was soon overwhelmed, like being at some lavish buffet with far too much fabulous fare to devour… though, logically, he found nothing published after the mid-1920s. There were also tomes of Philosophy, religion and spiritually, as well as metaphysical works and some devoted to alchemy; and he could have spent hours just reading titles. Many books had slips of paper inserted into their pages, and he inspected two at random, finding

ASS!

in a work by Aleister Crowley, and

RACIST!

in an O. Henry collection, both emphatically pencil printed as if stating informed conclusions... Dodger having confirmed the former and Spencer's own reading the latter.

Stopping to gaze around again, he recalled a *Twilight Zone* episode, but fortunately he didn't need glasses; though after maybe another ten minutes decided there wasn't time at the present to take in even a fraction of this bibliophilic banquet.

"But, can you imagine," he sighed, "the days... nay the weeks, the *months*, we could spend here; and all the while being transported to infinite other places and times?" He laughed. "Of course well supplied with provisions. ...And oh," he added, spreading his arms, "what a glorious gluttony!"

Except for the cigarettes filched from his parents he'd never stolen a thing in his life, but found himself sorely enticed to abscond with at least a few volumes he'd always wanted to read... *The Divine Comedy*, *The Devil On Two Sticks*, and Oliver Onions' *Widdershins*, all of which beckoned like The Fair One.

"We'd bring them back, of course," he rationalized to Wiggins. "But, we should ask Dodger, who at least in spirit, seems to be custodian here. ...Which could also explain him being well-read but not beyond 1926."

Nevertheless, it was with reluctance and only the scythe and candles in hands when he drew the door shut behind him out on the gallery. The light seemed to have waned in the cavernous hall with shadows enshrouding distant perspectives, though that impression may have been due to leaving the brighter library.

"It can't be much more than around five o'clock," he remarked to Wiggins, his voice, though echoing, sounding small. "And since we cleared the forest path, it shouldn't take long to get home. In any case we have these candles should darkness descend upon us. ...Ghosts, you may say? Despite much literary lore, I see no logical reason why spirits would be restricted to only appearing at night. Therefore, if we were to be haunted for disturbing these premises, as in a case of Trespassers Will, we should have already been spooked, don't you think?"

If Wiggins didn't acquiesce, neither did he disagree; and Spencer proceeded past other doors along the front of the gallery to finally choose one on the opposite side, beneath which a slit of daylight shone. Again he applied material mass while turning the age-stiffened knob, and again the panel yielded with supernatural sound-effects, and again his eyes were dazzled by sunlight slanting though dusty windows.

The first thing to come into clarity, though in an eerily hazy way, was a *very* rolly-fat ebony boy shirtless in belly-bibbed dungarees with a scythe and candelabra in hands!

"YOW!" Spencer yelled, his first impulse to run... despite the futility of that on several different levels. Then another instinct cut in and he dropped the candelabra and poised to swing the scythe... as did the other boy!

"...Oh," said Spencer, after a second, then lowered his weapon and smiled. "Hello, Wiggins."

The other boy reflected his smile, looking out of a looking-glass, a full-length rectangular floor-standing type mounted in an ornate wooden frame, his spectral haziness due to dust.

Spencer regarded him for a moment, a silver cherub also nestled between the opulent orbs of his chest. "As I mentioned earlier, I don't know why I seem to remember you being much fatter than me... or me maybe being less fatter than you... but hail fellow well met, and good to see you again in the flesh."

Then he scanned the room, which was cheerfully lit by the evening sun. In keeping with what he'd read of mansions, located here with a view of the grounds, it was a noble bed-chamber containing a no less princely bed of sufficient size for a quartet of Spencers – or a pair of him and a duo of Wiggins – its head and foot boards of possibly cherry and carved with lavishly chubby cherubs celebrating the careless freedom of youth -- at least for the classical upper-class – with nothing to do but eat, sleep and play, which Spencer discovered was apt because this was clearly a boy's lair.

"Must have been Gavin Shade's," he surmised.

Sinking ponderously to his knees, he recovered the trio of candles, which had scattered on the floor, re-seated them into the holder, then using the scythe for assistance, got back to his feet and entered the room.

"So this," he said, gazing around, "was the den of a thoroughly modern boy... though some might say a privileged one... in 1926."

The space indeed befitted a prince, its volume vaster than Spencer's whole cottage, its ceiling soaring high overhead. In addition to the regal bed, there was a kingly chest of drawers, a majestic sideboard, a grand *armoire*, and a royal roll-top desk. A carpet covered much of the floor, very probably Turkish, and there was a great wooden trunk – possibly a Spanish Chest -- that may have served as a toy box. A relatively small chandelier – compared to those in the gigantic hall – graced the central ceiling; and the walls were warm-white plaster above more tongue-and-groove wainscoting. There was a glass-fronted bookcase stocked with a personal library easily thrice the size of his own; and while framed pictures were hung here and there – a clipper ship, a cargo steamer, various idyllic landscapes, some suggesting fairytale scenes -- other adornments were movie posters – Charlie Chaplin in *The Tramp*, Buster Keaton in *Sherlock Jr.*, Mary Pickford in *Little Lord Fauntleroy*, Lon Chaney in *The Phantom Of The Opera* – though, as in the main library, Spencer's eyes were overwhelmed by having too much to feast upon.

"Begin at the beginning," he said. "Go on to the end, then stop."

Leaving the scythe inside the doorway, the candle stand on the chest of drawers, and his jeans in their natural state, he waddled past Wiggins to check out the bed, which stood between a pair of windows affording a dust-misted view of the grounds with its Reaper-supervised cherubs frolicking in the fountain. It was neatly turned down as if by a maid, its spread of indigo velvet – complimenting the window curtains – properly folded at the foot, the sheet turned over the blankets, which were partially drawn to receive someone, the pillows presumably plumped in the past, though presently looking underfed. On the wall above was another framed picture of yet another chubby cherub, his skin of classical peaches-and-cream, a tousled mop of sunny curls, at play in a pond in a forest. The setting seemed familiar, and Spencer said, "We assume Gavin Shade in his diaper days, and that's surely our pond at the cottage."

Then he added, "Oh, pardon me," and went to turn the mirror around so Wiggins could participate, bringing him into focus by brushing dust off the glass. The room was very warm, having had the afternoon sun, and Wiggins glistened like polished onyx, his navel leaking silver drops.

The head of the bed was flanked by night-tables, upon which stood a pair of lamps with tasseled gold-cloth shades. Several books lay on one of the tables, all displaying respectful cloth markers indicative of a gentle boy who would never dog-ear pages. The topmost tome was *The Wind In The Willows*, a first-edition from 1908 and obviously many times read. Eclectically, the book underneath was Bram Stoker's *Dracula*, also a first-edition from 1897, while another was a book for boys appropriately titled *The Aeroplane Boys* and published in 1912. Spencer also frequently read two or three books at a time, switching from one to another as his mood and appetite varied, and it seemed cool to have found someone with apparently similar tastes... though, sadly, dead for a hundred years.

"Of course," he said to Wiggins, "it's highly unlikely we would have been friends in 1926... and probably just as improbable now."

Even more eclectically was the "latest" issue of *Whiz Bang*... October, 1926. Also on the table was an open pack of Fatimas, a box of Radium Silent Matches, and an ashtray of bronze with another fat cherub holding a bowl for ashes aloft. On the other table was a crystal pitcher and water glass, both of course bone-dry, and a brass alarm clock, the cartoonish kind with bells on top, its hands like those of the clock in the hall, indicating 3:13.

"Rather like old Miss Havisham's house, her clocks stopped at twenty minutes to nine." He glanced at Wiggins. "And, like her house, this room seems preserved as if awaiting Gavin, perhaps on the day he never returned... or maybe the night, since his bed is prepared... something a loving parent might do. It also appears as if his father did not object to Gavin smoking, nor his reading of racy humor, though I suspect a boy of fifteen would have wanted more stimulation. A proper maid or valet would never look into personal spaces, nor would a respectful parent, so..."

He opened the table's drawer and laughed. "Indeed a normal boy of his age… or, one might say, of all ages."

There were magazines titled, *Follies*, whose covers were graced with pretty young women displaying much more than *Whiz Bang* allowed… though a lot was still left to imagination. And, underneath were some "French Postcards," which though almost tastefully tame compared to what could be found on the Web by any present-day pubescent, had no doubt provided Gavin Shade with many hours of pulsing pleasure. …Spencer pictured a naked boy very much like the ecstatic faun lying upon the princely bed and indulging as might any common young pauper.

"I could get inspired," said Spencer, shuffling slowly through the stack and feeling an awakening warmth along with a sudden Puckish temptation to sprawl on the bed despite the dust and have his wobbly way with himself. In fact, the urge became quite compelling and he finally had to resist by remarking, "This is a dead boy's bed."

Reigning in his randiness, he added, "This is interesting," returning the cards to the drawer and taking out a flat pint bottle partly filled with clear liquid, which he uncapped and sniffed. "Smells like one of Dodger's early attempts at gin."

There was a little *ex-librīs* label, and printed upon it in fountain pen ink was

DRINK ME

He took a sip and made a face. "Tastes like it, too." He put the bottle back. "Curious, don't you think? I can't imagine Gavin's father forbidding his son responsible access to the fine family liquor, and I'm sure champagne and vintage wine were normally part of Gavin's repasts; so why would he want coffin varnish, which would have to be obtained in less than genteel company and possibly dangerous places?"

Closing the drawer, he went to the bookcase. In a sort of chronological order a childhood of reading was revealed, beginning with *The Crocodile Book* and many other toddler tales – *Peter Rabbit, The Velveteen Rabbit, Peter Pan And Wendy* – then the first fourteen *Oz* books, *The Adventures Of Alice In Wonderland, Through The Looking Glass, The Magical Land Of Noom, Doctor Dolittle, Just*

William, The Boxcar Children, The Jungle Book, The Complete Tales Of Uncle Remus, The Adventures of Remi, Just So Stories, Moby Dick, The Phantom 'Rickshaw And Other Eerie Tales, The Adventures Of Huckleberry Finn, likewise, those of Tom Sawyer, *Kidnapped, Robinson Crusoe, Uncle Tom's Cabin, Lord Jim, Typhoon, Kim, Gulliver's Travels*, and *Carnacki The Ghost-Finder* being only a few. There were several sets of series books including Dave Dashaway, Tom Swift, The Motor Boys, and Pee Wee Harris, which featured brave and manly young males -- always Caucasian and never fat -- in often dangerous situations but who didn't drink or smoke, would faint at the sight of a French Postcard and probably be struck by lightning if putting it to practical use. But, there was *Patches The Paperboy*, who, thirteen, scruffy and street-wise, was more of a *Little Rascals* type hero. There was also *The Complete Sherlock Holmes*.

The light had dimmed perceptively by the time he concluded he didn't have time for any more bibliography, and a glance out a window showed the sun nearing the treetops across the grounds. "So much to see, so little time. Too bad we can't mess about with it."

A large table stood in a corner, possibly Federal furniture and probably worth several platters of Hogan's Alley oysters, but devoted to an electric train, a literal example featuring overhead wires. Though a little clunky and crude compared to modern layouts, its setting rather childishly made of cardboard buildings and *papier-mâché*, with foliage and trees of organic sponge painted shades of green, it depicted an infinity loop descending from a hilly landscape into a city and back again. Spencer recognized some of the structures on what was surely Shafter Avenue – at least as he thought he'd seen them on his misty Oakland adventure – as well as the trestle above the pond, though from an angel's perspective. Confirming the setup was modeled upon an actual age and place was

OAKLAND ANTIOCH & EASTERN RAILWAY

on the flanks of the locomotive.

Of course he tried the throttle control on a dangerous-looking transformer, which no twenty-first century child would have dared to touch, but the train stayed frozen forever in time crossing over the trestle.

He turned his attention to the sideboard, seeing a casket-like Grebe radio with a trumpet-shaped speaker. Naturally he switched it on, but naturally no Charleston came capering out of the æther. Beside it stood a gramophone of the type often teamed with a curious dog, and there was a rack of records. He perused the time-faded titles, careful with the brittle old disks and their fragile paper sleeves, finding the tunes The Lost Boys had played at Dodger's dinner party. Selecting *Am I A Passing Fancy*, he blew dust off the turntable, mounted the record, cranked the handle and flipped a lever to start, then gently lowered the needle arm. Dust puffed out of the speaker horn like an evicted spirit, and slightly skeletal music ghosted around the room:

Am I a passing fancy
Or am I the one in your dreams…

He recalled the plump golden cherub cuddled to Dodger and singing that song in his innocent angel voice. "Much better live," he said to Wiggins.

Leaving the music playing, he examined more of Gavin's possessions, which of a boyish nature included a railroad lantern, its font still full of oil, and bearing a brass tag, O A & E. There was a wooden model schooner, precisely detailed, gaff-rigged, and possessed of generously buxom beam suggestive of comfortable cruising, which might have been about forty feet long in actual incarnation, with the name, *Spirit*, on bows and stern. There were also some cast metal vehicles, obviously sophisticated above the level of toys. One of these was a Key System streetcar, another a Rolls Royce Silver Ghost and…

"Whose dream are we dreaming?" he said, picking up a Mack AC truck and showing it to Wiggins. It was a C-cab box-bodied type, chain-drive with six solid tires, and on the van was

FINN'S FRESH FISH
YOU'LL WANT TO SLAP THEIR FACES

and the impertinent piscine.

He brushed away dust to find

Lulibelle

on the sides of the hood.

"Not just food for thought," he said, "but rather like being force-fed a feast."

Returning the truck to its place, he next inspected two cameras, one a simple Brownie box, the other an expensive Graflex with a flash attachment often seen in vintage films in the hands of news reporters. It was also fitted with a clockwork device that could be wound and set to automatically take a picture.

"A boy of many interests," he said. "Of course one might be cynical and say he could afford them."

He proceeded to the *armoire*. "Perhaps a skeleton in the closet?"

However, opening the door revealed no osseous occupant but instead an extensive wardrobe of swellish garments and suits, including tuxedos, a jaunty top hat, and a silver-knobbed ebony walking stick. The white cotton shirts were yellowed with age, reminding him of what Dodger had used to wrap the *Weird Tales* magazines. There were also casual clothes, mostly tweedy jackets and trousers respectable youth would have worn at the time, along with several "newsboy" caps. There were three pairs of black court shoes properly preserved with trees, as well as everyday oxfords and – looking disreputably out of place like Baker Street Irregulars -- a shabby pair of well-worn Keds.

Closing the door, he continued on, turning the mirror as he passed so Wiggins could accompany him. Reaching the impressive desk, he found two photographs on top in tarnished silver frames. Both were faded with time and further obscured by dusty glass, but a swipe of hand showed one to be of a Knickerbockered boy, possibly around thirteen and crowned with a newsy cap. He was standing beside a Sliver Ghost parked in front of the mansion, and with him was a well-dressed man somewhere in handsome middle-age, tall, blond, and doubtless blue-eyed, a hand upon the boy's shoulder and both smiling cheerfully as if about to go motoring.

Spencer displayed it to Wiggins, who likewise showed it to him. "I think we would be correct in assuming this is Gavin and his dad."

He glanced at the portrait above the bed, then back at the photograph. "Gavin still has his cherub mop, but even in those baggy clothes appears to have lost his chubbiness, though we shan't hold that against him."

He cleared the other picture partially of dust. "Woah! Check this out!"

Gavin was maybe fifteen in this photo but, seemingly like a changeling, transformed from Little Lord Fauntleroy into a scruffy Huck Finn. He was clad in nothing but dungarees drooping carelessly little-kid low, his early childhood chubbiness indeed morphed into a muscular shape in a slenderly-sculpted way, and looked very grimy and sweaty, almost enough to actually smell. Despite the time-faded photograph, his resemblance to Dodger was haunting – or rather Dodger's resemblance to him – though Spencer remembered reading that everyone had at least one double, sometimes called a doppelgänger, somewhere in the world, which would also apply in the past.

Turning to Wiggins he said, "Perhaps an instance of similar genes like the boy or boys in the portraits? ...Or, I suppose it's possible Dodger could be a Shade relation, which would explain his being here and also why he knows so much about the family history."

But a second swipe of dust from the picture revealed another boy, and Spencer could only stare for a moment because it might have been himself!

There was a chair at the desk, fortunately a sturdy one because he plopped down in something like shock and it didn't disassemble. For a time he continued to gape at the photo: like Gavin, the black boy was only in jeans, though belly-bibbed and bottom-baring like the usual state of Spencer's. The boys seemed to be on the shore of the pond, and were obviously friends, Gavin's arm over the other boy's shoulders and the boy's around Gavin's waist, looking like *Little Rascals* pals and smiling mischievously, though cornered cigarettes in their mouths enhanced their impish expressions.

After a minute scanning "himself" as perfectly mirrored as Wiggins, he said, "It's one thing to see a doppelgänger of somebody else in the past, but even more amazing to see one of yourself. ...Though that boy's resemblance to us, like that of Dodger to Gavin, can again be explained by genes, even if it's extraordinary that doubles could be doubled in the same time and place."

Then he added thoughtfully, "Of course, on a metaphysical level, and as Annie suggested, we may have met in a former life... one must, after all, keep an open mind if one hopes to expand it."

He noted the black boy was holding a scythe in his free hand, its blade curving halo-like over their heads as if they'd been reaping together, which could explain their grubbiness; then the record ran out and the music ended

Or am I the one in your dreams?

leaving a rhythmic rustling sound of the needle repeating the final groove. He heaved himself out of the chair, put the picture back in its place and went to turn off the gramophone. After returning the disk to its sleeve, he said, "I think this calls for a bit of Drink Me and a Fatima, don't you?"

Wiggins seemed to concur, and Spencer procured the inspirations and settled back into the chair, taking a hearty swallow of one despite its incredible vileness, and firing the other with his lighter, though it was dry as mummy dust and tasted like smoking the wrappings.

"Their friendship is obviously genuine," he said, after sipping more casket coating and resurrecting his face from its formaldehyde-addled expression, "judging by body-language alone. Of the sort I would imagine... never having had such a friend... bonded by years of companionship and probably many childhood adventures, so the picture wasn't staged." He meditated a moment, fingers steepled on his chest in a Sherlockian pose, smoke ghosting up from the cigarette, then turned to Wiggins again.

"Do you think Gavin's friend was the butler's son, who might have served as a page? And his mother might have been the cook, which would account for his awesome size... imagine all the fabulous food in a grand house like this! ...But, if so, why the scythe, sweat and dirt? ...Shall we investigate further?"

Wiggins looked agreeable, and Spencer rolled the desk cover open, revealing an undusted work space equipped with a leather-bordered blotter. There was a silver inkstand with pens, also a stack of expensive note paper, with other stationery items pigeonholed above. Spencer examined a sheet of the paper.

"The same, you observe, as the note in the box; and the family crest is an S with what appears to be two jackals rampant... possibly representing Anubis since Gavin's father seemed interested in ancient Egyptian gods. ...But this seems to create a conundrum: if the Shade's page boy was Gavin's friend and would have lived in this house, why would they have been reaping? ...And why the note in the grounds-keeper's shed arranging a rendezvous at night?"

He sipped more coffin varnish, made the natural nasty face, and chased it with mummy dust smoke. "If we return to our first speculation that Gavin's friend was the grounds-keeper's son, possibly called The Avenger... perhaps a Dickensian reference to the impish boy in *Great Expectations*... and add to that, based upon this picture of indisputably intimate friends, the premise of Gavin's father approving of such a mixed-class, as well as mixed-race association... which refutes our initial conjecture that he denied his own urchin roots after making his fortune... and further allow that Gavin Shade helped his friend with earthy tasks, perhaps to give them more leisure time, it still leaves the question of why a note?"

He laughed. "Unless, as Dodger said, it was left for us... which, however improbable to a ridiculous extreme... would also beg the question of what night was it referring to?"

He glanced to the windows; the sun now touching the western treetops. "Perhaps another ten minutes of sufficient light in here." He turned to the doorway. "The hall is growing dark, as is, I imagine, the forest path. But I think we may take the liberty of borrowing Gavin's lantern, which will be safer than candles to light our way home through the woods."

He opened one of the desk drawers to find a leather-bound

photo album. "One picture, as they say..."

He placed it on the blotter. "Home photography, thanks to Kodak, becoming popular during those times, I'm sure there must be family albums elsewhere in the house, but this one probably contains Gavin's most meaningful memories and, I think we may assume from the cameras, mostly taken by himself."

He opened the cover. "Unlike a family album starting with infant and toddler photos featuring stupid-looking things with blank bovine eyes and grotesque gassy smiles and of no interest except to their parents, this one begins when Gavin had reached the age of full self-awareness and cognizant memory-retention, generally around five or six." He patted his chest while turning to Wiggins. "Though I, being somewhat a prodigy... as I do say so myself... attained that stage rather early, as I suspect did you." He examined the first few pages of black-cornered neatly pasted-in pictures. "And indeed this album begins with the kind of photos a boy of that age would take with a simple Brownie."

Logically there were images of Gavin's first ventures out on the grounds; of the many rolly stone cherubs he would have resembled at the time, though most were far fatter than he had been in the portrait over the bed. There were several shots of the cheerful young Reaper, and many more of the muscular fauns, including the one ecstatically poised on the verge of a surging sensation.

"Apparently Gavin's father regarded *all* aspects of boyhood as perfectly natural states of being... though, contradicting our first conjecture, the fauns could not have been modeled after teenage Gavin because they were there in his younger days."

He mirrored smiles with Wiggins. "Not having the Internet to enlighten youth of his age, I wonder if he wondered... at least in his early years... what that stony boy was doing to be looking so joyous?"

There were photos of OA&E trains, one with the engineer waving, another the train crossing the trestle. Spencer perused a few more pages of Gavin's earliest image captures, along with others of childhood Gavin, possibly taken by his dad, of Gavin in various settings and many different states of dress ranging from a snazzy tuxedo complete with top hat and walking stick at an affair at the Oakland Hotel, and others in Knickerbocker attire in the mansion, his room, and outside, to wearing only his birthday suit while frolicking in the fountain smilingly supervised by the Reaper. Despite his silver spoon origins he seemed to be an outdoor boy with nothing but droopy dungarees his seemingly natural style. And, probably because of frequently roaming wild and free, his chubbiness passed with the passing of pages until at possibly seven another photo of him in just jeans displayed a boyishly muscular chest above a still-prominent tummy, and looking very street-urchin scruffy while standing waist-deep in funeral lilies and smiling with a sickle in hand as if ready to reap them for somebody's service.

The next page introduced The Avenger at maybe six-years-old when Gavin would have been eight. And again Spencer stared in something like shock at the resemblance to him at that age, already extraordinarily fat, boy-breasts bulbously ballooning, belly well on its way to his knees, and possessed of more rolls than an average Sharpei. He sat filling the cottage's rear bedroom window, now Spencer's window, smiling at the photographer – presumably Gavin Shade – as if emerging for an adventure.

"Which does seem to indicate," said Spencer, "Gavin's friend *was* the grounds-keeper's son."

The light was fading with sunset, and the pictures becoming harder to view. "I suppose we could bring the album home… I hope we'll see Dodger tonight and he could take it back. Or, we could return it tomorrow."

The dimming Wiggins looked noncommittal.

"It *would* be a rather large liberty, being such a personal thing instead of utilitarian. …Speaking of which, shall we light the lantern?"

Wiggins seemed to think that prudent, growing more vague as daylight waned; and Spencer dismounted himself again to take the lantern off the sideboard and open its top to fire the wick. Like the candles, it resisted at first, then only glowed ghostly blue, but finally awakened to cheerful gold. He closed the top, adjusted the flame, and brought it to the desk. "Since we're now prepared for the dark, shall we return to the past?"

The restored Wiggins, with glistening highlights, looked ready to take on the dark.

From the time of The Avenger's début the boys seemed to be inseparable, pictured mostly outdoors, only in jeans, and usually looking adventurous. There were photos of them on a home-built raft fishing in the pond, The Avenger just landing a big fat trout and Gavin poised to grab it; others of them swimming buck-bare, and likewise sharing a huge picnic lunch, as well as relaxed side-by-side on the shore seemingly contemplating the heavens. There were photos of them armed with knightly swords and storming the castle-like mansion, possibly to rescue the princess, and challenging the guardian lions; others of them with pirate pistols possibly vanquishing Captain Hook. There were photos of them in loincloths – which The Avenger didn't need – as if enacting *The Jungle Book*; though there were also winter shots in 1920s casual clothes, The Avenger's belly often escaped from underneath his shirts; and Gavin topped with a newsboy cap, The Avenger with a derby. But there were also images of them here in Gavin's room, several of them constructing the layout and running the electric train, others of them on Gavin's bed maybe reading aloud to each other and well supplied with sumptuous snacks including a bowl of potato chips possibly made in-house by the cook, as well as cream puffs, cakes and pies, chocolate éclairs, and sandwiches, with a pitcher on one of the tables that may have contained lemonade. There was also a Christmas morning photo taken in the cottage, the boys with presents on the floor beside a modest tree, a cheerful fire in the fireplace, and stockings – as Spencer had imagined – hanging with care on the mantle. The photographs by this time had vastly improved in quality, probably due to the Graflex; and since it had the timer, the pair were usually pictured together instead of photographing each other, or someone else taking their photo – possibly their parents? -- as they seemed to have done with the Brownie.

Besides the idyllic childhood scenes – a seemingly picture-perfect place in which to live one's youthful years -- of mansion, grounds and pond, there were photos of them in urban Oakland, at the

Chimes Theatre, also at the T&D, purchasing books at De Lauer's Newsstand, roaming the grassy shores of Lake Merrit, as well as down on the waterfront apparently aboard the schooner whose model was on the sideboard, with steamers and sailing ships in the background… and naturally no Oakland Bay Bridge, which hadn't been built until the '30s. Not surprisingly, considering The Avenger's obvious inclination, there were many images of eating – hot dogs from a street vendor, oysters from a fisherman, the duo in various restaurants suggestive of blue-collar atmosphere with plates of hash, potatoes and chops, spaghetti, cod cakes, and slices of pie, one in a Woolworth's luncheonette chomping juicy hamburgers…

Spencer smiled. "Before we introduced cheeseburgers and possibly altered a universe."

…and others in ice-cream parlors partaking of sundaes, banana splits, and frothy-looking shakes or malts. There were also pictures of the pair dining with Gavin's father at the titanic table, which was lavishly loaded with food – steaks, a roast turkey (or possibly goose) southern fried chicken and egg-battered oysters – enticing even in shades of gray. The boys were clad in white shirts *sans* ties in seemingly token formality, and equipped with goblets of sparkling champaign, the serving being done by a footman possessed of a pleasant but fishy face.

As the past progressed with the passing of pages like time-lapse photography, The Avenger grew ever fatter, while Gavin morphed into what some might call an idol of young Caucasian perfection, becoming, at least on the physical plane, and even disregarding their color, as different – or, maybe as opposite -- as two boys could possibly be. …And yet they seemed to grow more alike in something Spencer might have called spirit.

The album had been left uncompleted, probably due to Gavin's death, but nearing the last of the pages -- Gavin now possibly fourteen when The Avenger would have been twelve -- were images of Gavin pony-backing his flubbery friend up the mansion's grand stairway, a rather remarkable show of strength since by now The Avenger was fast approaching becoming a quarter-ton kid.

The final photo in the album, the boys now probably thirteen and fifteen, displayed a view either natural or naughty -- depending upon perspective -- of the pair lying naked beside the stone faun and joining him in joyousness, though The Avenger's version was naturally bowderlized by blubber.

"I should have let it happen," sighed Spencer, gazing at the photo and feeling something like regret. "That afternoon by the pond." He closed the album cover and reflected to Wiggins, "I don't know why I didn't. ...Maybe I'm not enlightened enough to accept what was offered in innocence without thinking it meant I was giving up mine."

He put the album back in the drawer and took a last sip of coffin varnish. "We have learned much about Gavin Shade, not to mention his childhood friend... and I wonder what became of his friend after the Shades were gone? But, we have yet to ascertain if what we thought we saw last night... both our happy experience here at Dodger's dinner party and the nasty dead thing in the pond... were at least partly real or just dream-induced."

Bathed in the golden glow of the lantern, he'd forgotten the oncoming dark, the windows now portals to deepening dusk. "I suppose we had best be getting home, where, I remind you, our supper awaits, and where, hopefully, Dodger will come to shed some light on both matters."

Unloading himself again from the chair, he adjusted the lantern's flame a bit higher, returned the flask to the bedside table, surrendered his cigarette stub to the cherub, then went to the doorway and took the scythe.

The enormous hall had become very dark, its distant reaches lost in black, the skylights only a faint pale glow, as Spencer emerged from Gavin's den. "See you tonight," he said to the now spectral shape of Wiggins. He closed the door, and as when leaving the dining room and sensing the spirit of oysters, he suddenly scented scruffy-boy sweat, juvenile gin, and tobacco. The smells were so strong it *must* have been Dodger just beyond the door! Had he been hiding all this time and watching Spencer explore?

Spencer flung the door open, the shriek of its hinges echoing, but there was just a perplexed-looking Wiggins scanning around from his mirror perspective, the lantern held out like Diogenes in his seemingly futile search. Even Dodger couldn't have dodged fast enough to conceal himself, yet his scent was blatantly bright; and there was a strong perception of *presence.* But then both sensations faded away.

"Two ships in the night?" he said to Wiggins.

The air in the room hadn't grown any cooler with the passing of the sun, and Wiggins still glistened with sweaty highlights. "I suppose we just smelled ourselves," said Spencer. "Which is perfectly logical since we had a smoke and imbibed the gin. ...Again, my friend, see you tonight."

Closing the door again, and islanded in lantern light amid the ever-deepening darkness, he proceeded around the gallery back to the head of the stairs. He paused to tug up his jeans in preparation to make the descent, when the grandfather clock gave a single TICK.

He'd many times read the expression, "jumping out of your skin," which brought to mind a skeleton performing like a party girl bursting out of a cake, but came as close to doing that as any corporeal creature could.

He spun around to face the clock... which only impassively faced him back with its timeless 3:13. He held his breath for a minute, waiting for a TOCK, but there was only silence.

"...Well... we're not light on our feet," he said, his voice sounding small though echoing, "so maybe that could have triggered a tick."

He regarded the clock a few a moments more, but it seemed to have nothing else to say. Then he transferred the lantern to his scythe-holding hand and, grasping the banister with the other and feeling each step with unseeable feet, made his quaking way down the stairs.

As far as his memory reached back he'd never been afraid of the dark, but nevertheless felt a rush of relief when, after what seemed an eternity of trudging past phantom-like figures and shapes just beyond the edge of his light -- presumably the suits of armor – he finally attained the foyer, which was still faintly lit by the gloaming beyond the open front doors.

Just as he entered, the telephone rang!

For the second time in his life he felt like a party skeleton, and almost dropped the lantern. In the following silence he stared at the phone – long-obsolete, spider-webbed and dusty -- not sure if he'd actually heard it.

It rang again.

Many thoughts flashed through his mind, though the only one that seemed to make sense was someone had seen his light and wondered who was in the house. Maybe an actual caretaker? Was this a trap to keep him here until the cops arrived? ...Which would not bode well for a black boy caught in a mansion lavishly loaded with millions of dollars of things.

But, what was he going to do, run?

He dithered until a third ring, then set the lantern on the table, leaned the scythe against the wall, picked up the phone, unhooked the receiver and put it to an ear.

"Hello?" he said into the transmitter, recalling a joke he'd read in *Whiz Bang*

If this is the wrong number, why did you answer?

"Long distance calling," replied a voice that sounded like any operator ever since there had been operators, though possessed of a British accent. "Have we reached Mr. Spencer Dray?"

Spencer reconsidered a trap, but trying to flee seemed futile since somebody knew his name. He thought again of the body he *might* have seen in the pond. Had Dodger actually killed his uncle and hopped a plane to England? He remembered reading that a flight to London might take around thirteen hours from Oakland, so if Dodger had left very early he could have just arrived.

"...Um... speaking," he finally said.

"Go ahead, please," said the operator to someone else on the line.

Spencer half expected Dodger, but the next voice out of the æther sounded like a young English girl... and a rather cheerful one:

"Good evening. ...It *is* evening there in your time?"

"...Um, yeah," said Spencer. "Good evening. What time is it in your time?"

A pleasant laugh. "I'm never quite sure when it stops being late and starts being early. ...May I call you Spencer?"

"...Sure... But you have the advantage."

"Terribly sorry. Daphne Darkmoor. But please call me Daffy."

At least Darkmoor was logical. "Um... are you sure?"

"Oh, of course, everyone does, if not before then after."

"Hi, Daffy. ...Um, guess you know where I am? ...But I'm not... I mean I wasn't..."

Again a pleasant laugh. "Of course you didn't, and I'm sure you wouldn't."

"I am kinda borrowing a lantern."

"Quite all right, and think nothing of it." There followed a mischievous giggle. "Only 'kinda?'"

Spencer laughed. "*Déjà vu.*"

"How interesting," said Daffy. "I often feel like I've been before, so it seems as if we can never be sure whether we are or whether we were."

"I guess we could be both," said Spencer, "if everything that ever was is always going on."

"You're quite a perceptive person, though I was sure you would be because you wouldn't be there if you weren't."

"I try to keep an open mind."

"Far more useful than a closed one."

"Um, if it wouldn't be rude to ask..."

"Quite all right, I'm thirteen."

"Swell!"

"I seem to have the advantage once more, having seen your photograph."

"...You have?"

"Yes, in front of the cottage with your mum and dad. Linda Lancaster sent it. Rather dreadful woman; but I think you're charming."

"Thanks. I'm sure you're charming, too. ...Um, if it wouldn't seem forward of me, could you send me your picture?"

"Of course, if you like, I have your address."

"Swell, but I meant on the phone."

"I'm afraid I don't have a Belinograph."

"...Huh?"

"I believe you call them wire photos. I try to keep up with the times, but I haven't progressed that far."

"...You don't have a wireless phone?"

"Of course, I'm just being silly."

"Which is why everyone calls you Daffy?"

"Now you're in the after."

"...Um, I came to pay a call on Dodger, but he wasn't home. ...If this is his home?"

"I've heard he pops in now and then," said Daffy, "when he's not having adventures. May I take it you've met him?"

"On the first night we moved into the cottage. I'd like to think we're friends."

"I'm quite sure you are," said Daffy. "And, forgiving his Puckishness, I doubt you'll find a better friend in all the universes."

"I do get that feeling," said Spencer. "So, I assume you know him?"

"I feel as if I know him quite well, being a part of our family lore."

"...Oh," said Spencer. "Then I guess he isn't there?"

"Why would you think...? Oh dear." There was a pause and a rustle of static, then Daffy said, "I seem to have called ahead of time... or perhaps before."

"What do you mean?" asked Spencer.

"Let me think for a moment; I don't want to muddle things any more than I may already have done." Again a pause and a rustle of static. "I presume it's dark there because of the lantern, but what is your time precisely?"

"I can't be precise... around seven, I guess."

"I suppose that can't be corrected now because it shouldn't have happened then. ...Are you armed?"

"...I have a scythe."

"The very thing," said Daffy. "Then all seems to be as it should... though it could still become something it shouldn't; though of course whether it does or didn't, or maybe I should say will or wasn't, is now and then dependent on you."

"…I don't understand," said Spencer.

"Please forgive me," said Daffy. "I fear I may have said too much, which can be worse than saying too little."

"But…"

"I must ring off now. It's been ever so nice chatting with you, and I hope we may meet when the time is right."

"I hope so, too, but…"

There was a click and then nothing. Spencer jiggled the hook and listened but there was only dead silence.

CHAPTER TWENTY-FOUR

The moon was rising over the trees cresting the slopes above the pond as Spencer, puffing profusely again and shiny with sweat in the silvery light, finally got back to the dell, heralded by the *whos* of an owl accompanied by a chorus of crickets and backed by the soothing song of the brook. Even with the lantern's light it hadn't been easy to find his way home on the overgrown path though tree-tunneled darkness, and several times he'd thought he was lost, and more than once had wished for Dodger to take his hand and guide him.

Tugging up his jeans once more, he cautiously crossed the foot-bridge and came down the trail he'd reaped through the ferns. Though weary from more walking than he usually did in several weeks, he was ravenous for supper and quickened his pace to the cottage. He almost left the scythe outside, but, recalling what Daffy had said – which seemed to have dark implications despite her apparently light-hearted spirit – brought it into the hallway and stood it against the wall.

"Hello again, Wiggins," he called, looking into his room at the looking-glass boy. He reflected upon his reflection, glistening from their exertions, streaked with dust from the mansion, scored with scratches from brambles and briars, with leaves like laurels in their hair. "That was quite an adventure. Of course I can only speak for myself, but I wouldn't have dreamed I could do such a thing; and we did it without Dodger's help… though it would have been more fun with him. Adventures, wouldn't you agree, are always more fun with friends."

Wiggins nodded reflectively.

Spencer brushed off the leaves and wiped blood from his wounds. "I trust you're as hungry as I am, so the first thing is to make a fire to warm up our Watson's Diner style supper."

Accordingly, he entered the kitchen, lit the lamp on the table, chugged a Coke from the ice box, blasted a burp and built a blaze, then went to his room while the stove was warming. Setting the lantern on his desk, he consulted his phone to check the time. It was only 8:03, surprising because his trek though the dark had seemed to take several light-years. He also found a message.

"It's from Daffy! Swell!"

About to access it, he paused. "How does she know my number? Linda would have probably given mom and dad's numbers to Mr. Darkmoor... presumably Daffy's father... but how could Daffy have gotten mine?" Then he laughed. "Who cares, she's a girl!"

He opened it. "Woah, check this out!"

He and Wiggins plopped down on their beds to gaze at their respective screens. Being a boy of the present time in a far from enlightened place, it had naturally never occurred to Spencer the Darkmoors might be black. He'd assumed Darkmoor was a family place name, bringing to mind a suitable setting for *The Hound Of The Baskervilles*, rather than literally combining "dark" as in skin, and "moor" as in Moorish with possibly wryly defiant intent. Daffy hadn't sounded black, but neither did most of the British black people on programs from the BBC. And, of course, the Darkmoors were rich.

Which in their case was *really* a case of typical English understatement.

And, "charming" in Daffy's case was another understatement of enormous proportions.

The photo was in color -- which almost surprised Spencer because of Gavin's pictures being black-and-white – of a *very* charming girl as dusky dark as himself. Another oversize understatement would have been to say she was chubby... *voluptuous* was much more apt, and in a most adorable way. Although the term, cherubic, seemed a bit over-used of late, it perfectly suited her plumply round-cheeked, wide button-nosed and full-lipped face, along with winsomely large onyx eyes. Her hair was an ebony halo of ringlets partly subdued by a brown newsboy cap, which lent her an impishly urchin-like air; and her bright white teeth were on cheerful display in a likewise mischievous grin.

After appreciating her face -- which he found very appreciable -- Spencer saw she was dressed androgynously in a heather-toned turtleneck sweater, bulky but not very much concealing the splendidly spherical shapes of her breasts, and an open, knee-length hunting coat of rusty-colored canvas. Enhancing her boyishly-girlish impression were well-worn blue-jeans very well-filled; and half-hidden beneath tumbled cuffs were robust heavy-soled hiking boots. And, perfectly fitting her wild-child persona was a glimpse of mid night tummy chub peeking from under her sweater in a carelessly casual impudent way, which, though probably half his weight, made Spencer recall The Avenger.

The setting also enhanced her aura of just-because-I'm-a-girl... seemingly atop a tor overlooking an uninhabited moor beneath a scuddingly-clouded sky, the sunlight somewhat steely suggesting a blustery day, and standing beside a battered Land Rover -- possibly a Series One -- lavishly spattered with mud. And with her was an enormous hound that could have starred in the Baskerville story, black as coal and fearsomely-fanged, its head about level with Daffy's shoulder, and balefully regarding the camera as if in defense of its mistress.

If the picture had been expressly for Spencer it couldn't have been more perfectly posed, containing all the attributes of what, both consciously and sublime, he'd always dreamed a girl should be... though he was realistic enough to know such dreams seldom came true except in fairytales.

"And," he said, turning to Wiggins, who'd been just as raptly scan-ning his screen, "it's eight PM here, so... let's see... that would be four AM in England, so the photo wasn't taken for us. But the time stamp is yesterday, so we know it's what she looks like now." He smiled. "It's certainly what she sounded like, with the added bonus of color."

Then he sighed. "Of course, with money, social-class, and an ocean between us, the chances of her and I becoming anything more than cyber-friends, seem as remote as..."

He mirrored thoughtful looks with Wiggins. "I was going to say as remote as between The Avenger and Gavin, but that *did* happen a long time ago."

The only text with the photo was, *I hope you still think I'm charming.*

"I want to call her," said Spencer, a finger poised on the pad. "...But it is very early or late there and she's probably dreaming." He considered a moment, then texted, AND HOW!

He waited a minute, but there was no answer, then shut off the phone and got to his feet. "For the present the pleasure of supper awaits."

Returning to the kitchen, he transferred the platter of three hefty lamb chops teamed with a mountain of mashed potatoes, along with a boat of savory gravy, out of the ice box into the oven, and noted his mother had also left an Italian cream cake for dessert. While the main course was warming, he got silverware and a tumbler, and poured the latter full from a gallon jug of milk. The food was soon piping hot and emanating delicious aromas; and using oven mitts, he placed the platter on the table, seated himself and poured the gravy.

"More of gravy than the grave," he said to the looking-glass boy reflecting upon his reflective feast while sprinkling pepper and salt. Seizing knife and fork, he added, "There's no time like the present."

The huge meal, including the cake in all its creamy entirety, washed down with several tumblers of milk seemed at least sufficient to restore himself from the day's adventure and, after a last thundering burp, he dutifully cleared the table and left the utensils by the sink to be washed with the breakfast things. By then it was nearing nine o'clock and, though still hoping Dodger would come, he was starting to feel sleepy. But Dodger would wake him... if he did come. A massive yawn exercised his jaw, and he thought of the sign in Dreyfus' station. "Time to retire."

He took the lamp from the table and left it for his parents in the living room window. Then he returned to his room, set the lantern on the nightstand and subsided onto his bed.

"Should we lose our sneaks?" he asked Wiggins. "We should be prepared for a Dodger adventure… but of course he would shoe us again."

He and Wiggins shed their Keds, then, though it seemed rather silly, Spencer cascaded to the floor and pulled the box from under the bed. The note was still there

See you tonight

but, why wouldn't it have been?

He took a Fatima out of the pack, put the box back in its hiding place, let his jeans slip entirely off and mounted the bed to sprawl on his back. Lighting the cigarette from the lantern, he exhaled a silvery spirit, which drifted out the moon-lit window and ascended toward the stars, then switched on his phone to adore Daffy's photo.

"I suppose," he sighed to Wiggins, "it's perfectly normal to picture her frolicking in the pond, though it seems… well, disrespectful… to be anything more than spiritually inspired." Smiling, he sang in his husky and not very musical voice:

"Am I a passing fancy
Or am I the one in your dreams
Am I a passing fancy
To love while the pale moonlight beams

The night is so romantic
The whole world's in love so it seems
Am I a passing fancy
Or am I the one in your dreams."

Sighing out another ghost, he looked at the looking-glass boy again. "She has my photo *sans chemise*, which still gives her an advantage, but since she thought I was charming it's one I will happily grant."

CHAPTER TWENTY-FIVE

"**T**he game is afoot."

Spencer awoke to the scents of Dodger, though somewhat surprised when he opened his eyes in the golden glow of electric light instead of silver star shine though his window.

"Somewhat surprised" seemed *apropos*, because while a part of him certainly was -- finding himself in Gavin Shade's bed! -- a seemingly other part of him wasn't... as if he was having a dream in which he was a participant yet at the same time an observer, while seeing, smelling, feeling and hearing through someone else's senses.

And, he soon discovered, apparently without any power to direct or affect what his dreaming self did. His still-sleepy eyes roved the room, which though seemingly looking the same as it had when he'd been here in physical form -- Gavin's possessions all in their places; the train layout, the radio, the model schooner and vehicles, the gramophone, the cameras, the movie posters on the walls -- was free of dust and signs of age, the poster colors vividly bright as if they'd been lithographed yesterday, and the chamber cheerfully lit by the bed-table lamps and chandelier. But it was only a casual glance through eyes familiar with everything, and Spencer couldn't focus them on any detail *he* wanted to see. Instead, they went to the brass alarm clock, no longer dead at 3:13 but alive and ticking at 2:06, which was no doubt the wee morning hour as evidenced by star-studded sky beyond the open windows.

These revelations couldn't have taken more than a tick or two of time -- if this kind of time could be measured that way -- though he remembered reading somewhere that it took the same time to do in a dream what it actually took in waking life.

Another observation though the eyes of this someone else revealed he was naked on a white sheet, his body a contrast of blubbery
blackness, a midnight mirror of himself in which he found he felt
quite at home even if not in controlling possession; and the air was
comfortably warm despite the late -- or early -- hour, the spirits of
lingering Indian Summer mingled with those of his earthy friend as
when he'd awakened with Dodger beside him on their last adventure, as well as his own scruffy self.

He also noted the absence of a cherub on his chest, and made
the Holmesian deduction: *I must be The Avenger... or, apparently,
dreaming I am.*

Which raised the proposition: *If I dream therefore am I?*

And he did find Dodger beside him -- or was it Gavin in this
dream? -- an awakening hand on his other self's shoulder, sleep-
tousled mop half-hiding his eyes, smiling his usual friendly fox smile,
and also naturally *au naturel*. "Almost time for the 3:13."

Spencer felt himself smile in return, and heard his voice reply,
"Swell." Then he -- or rather The Avenger -- drew Dodger-as-Gavin
chest to chest and shared a warmly affectionate yet also somehow
boyish kiss; the difference from some other kind eluding Spencer's
definition due to lack of experience... though, allowing a flight of
fancy beyond the one he seemed to be on, he wouldn't have kissed
Daffy quite that way. ...At least he didn't think he would, assuming
that time would ever come.

Nor, as he'd found in regard to acting, feeling, smelling, seeing
and hearing, could he command The Avenger's thoughts or indepen-
dently access them, which, while embracing Gavin, Gavin clasping
him in return as Spencer and Dodger had rafted in peace adrift in the
sun-sparkled pond, went scrolling back though the preceding day. As
with most such memories, they were only flashes and little vignettes,
beginning with breakfast in the cottage, the same sort Spencer's
mom would have made, of eggs, hash-browns and sausages, buttered
toast with strawberry jelly, a tumbler of milk and a mug of coffee...
his parents had taken the Shade estate's Model TT truck to town, his
father to purchase garden supplies, his mother grocery shopping.

Then came a scene of him down on his knees, shirtless in jeans and ferally barefoot, mid-morning sunlight warm on his back, pulling weeds from a flower bed beside the Reaper's fountain and looking up smiling at Gavin, also carelessly clad in jeans, who'd cheerfully come to assist him bearing a big picnic basket. Then he was sweatily scything weeds along the edge of the mansion grounds while Gavin gathered the beheaded ranks and loaded them onto a wheelbarrow. Then another of him upon the barrow like a prince on a palanquin lounging against the treasure chest basket in wobbly bobbly majesty, with Gavin puffing between the shafts down the tree-shaded path through the sun-dappled forest; followed by them on the shore of the pond, presumably partaking of lunch with all the Water Rat's wonders and more, including delightfully-spiked lemonade. Then an intensely pleasurable and hauntingly *déjà vu* vignette of them as he and Dodger had done sensually adventuring, and The Avenger letting it happen without any doubts of who he was or if it might mean he was someone he wasn't.

Apparently having the afternoon free, probably thanks to Gavin's help, they'd spent it swimming in the pond with The Avenger often just drifting buoyed by his undulant ebony bulk with Gavin peacefully resting aboard and speaking of cabbages and kings, the trestle towering high above and a train occasionally rumbling over. Then, fishing from their Huck Finn raft and landing several big fat trout. Then a journey back though the woods amongst the deepening evening shadows, The Avenger again enthroned on the barrow with Gavin providing the power. Then there was a splendid supper, which featured their trout goldenly broiled on richly-buttered beds of rice, though not lacking many accompaniments of equally delicious fare – Cornish game hens roasted with herbs, tender string beans with bits of bacon, baked potatoes and crispy *pommes frites* – pleasantly butlered by Barrymore and adroitly served by "Fishy" the footman, who kept their goblets filled with champagne, in the majestic dining room, both boys in white shirts though lacking ties as token nods to formality.

Gavin's father was absent on business -- as Spencer gleaned from The Avenger's stream of consciousness – and Gavin had given the mansion staff the evening free after supper service. "Mr. Toad" was driving them in the Silver Ghost to see *The Black Pirate* at The Chimes theater... though Spencer suspected the title didn't refer to the buccaneer's color.

The meal was further enriched by Dawkins, the plump page boy of maybe eleven, who expertly played the great grand piano and sang in a heavenly young angel voice:

> I want to see
> So clear to me
> It's the only time I'm happy, it seems
> Let my little train of thought go rolling back once more
> To a place I'm always longing for

> Oh, won't you take in the sun
> Hang out the moon
> And rock me in a cradle of dreams.

Dessert was also opulent with chocolate éclairs, Napoleons, and decadently messy cream puffs, The Avenger so stuffed by the time they finished that Gavin ponied him to his room, where they'd reverted to natural states and napped for a while on the bed. Then they'd taken turns for a time reading aloud favorite passages from *The Wind In The Willows* and polishing off the last desserts – carried up from the kitchen by Gavin – with the warm autumn breeze wafting in through the windows, shared another sensuous quest, followed by a final Fatima, and fallen asleep again.

Now – or was it then? – Gavin got up, donned his jeans and went to get the railroad lantern, while The Avenger also rose and likewise barely clothed himself. Shoes and shirts didn't seem required for whatever adventure lay ahead, though a few seconds later, delving The Avenger's thoughts, Spencer divined the purpose of their after-midnight outing.

Gavin didn't buy bootleg gin, but made the vile stuff in the spring house to sell, though for whatever reasons -- except perhaps the naughty fun of taking risks with like-minded peers – The Avenger didn't clarify. Grain alcohol was the basis of Gavin's ghastly concoction, and of course in this time and place was a strictly restricted substance. But, as in any time and place, it was only a matter of money to get what one wanted in life; and Gavin had made an arrangement with a brakeman on the O.A. & E. to "lose" a carboy once a week – ostensibly bound for medicinal use -- when the train slowed to cross the trestle at around 3:13.

"Shall we gird our loins?" asked Gavin, pulling a flask from a pocket.

"There is nothing so much worth doing," The Avenger paraphrased, "than simply having adventures." He bravely took a hideous gulp and passed the bottle back to Gavin, who likewise fortified himself.

The staff by this time were snug in their beds and assumably dreaming their dreams; and Gavin lit the lantern and doused the lights in the room, then opened the door to the gallery. The gargantuan hall was shrouded in shadows, the only light besides the lantern the soft moon glow through the skylights, as Gavin and The Avenger, accompanied, so to speak, by Spencer, made their way toward the rear of the house where they would descend the servant's stairs and exit through the mansion's back door. The railroad tracks ran near the grounds, winding down the wooded slopes, and there was a path leading to them from behind the garage. From there it was a leisurely walk to the rendezvous point at the trestle, where Gavin's lantern would signal the brakeman to pass him the plunder out of a boxcar.

But, reaching the head of the grand stairway, where the solemn grandfather clock, its ticking funereally slow and stately, showed the time as 2:17, The Avenger whispered:

"I should get my scythe. Gonna need it in the morning to clear some ferns around the cottage."

Spencer "recalled" he'd left it at Gavin's amused suggestion – a nose-thumbing at gentility – in the umbrella and walking-stick stand by the front doors in the foyer.

"I'll get it," Gavin whispered back.

Giving the lantern to The Avenger, Gavin descended the staircase and trotted lightly through the dark hall to disappear into the foyer.

Left alone, so to speak, with The Avenger, whose mind though active and alert now drifted at random like Spencer's had when afloat in the pond, Spencer tried an experiment using a part of his own mind he'd seemingly never known he'd had and found that by intense concentration he could somehow *suggest*, though not force, The Avenger to think of something – in this case the luscious chocolate éclairs he and Gavin had had for dessert – this power of suggestion confirmed when Gavin returned with the scythe and ascended the stairs.

"Any of those éclairs left?" The Avenger asked.

"Should be some in the kitchen," said Gavin, which made Spencer wonder if he'd changed something that might not have happened in the past. If so, that might be a dangerous power, like altering a universe just by dropping a nickel, and maybe he'd better not do it again.

After slinging the scythe over a shoulder, "he" and Gavin went down the back staircase, passed through the enormous kitchen, snagging several éclairs on the way, which they messily shared, and were soon out in the gentle moon glow, crossing a lawn past the garage, where the Silver Ghost regarded them stabled half in shadow. Then Gavin led along the path though gloom under trees to the tracks.

They paused in a patch of lunar light to further fortify themselves with quaffs of coffin-coating; and Gavin pulled out his White Rabbit watch as in the silence of the night a whistle sounded distantly.

"Right on time," he said. "Just coming out of the Redwood Tunnel."

The boys proceeded down the tracks at The Avenger's ponderous pace, Gavin ambling at his side in the swaying lantern light, the rails gleaming sliver under the stars, accompanied by the chirping of crickets and occasional hoots of owls, the train's whistle sometimes wooing behind as it slowly drew closer. The Avenger of course was soon shining with sweat, his jeans growing sodden and heavy, and he retained them with one hand, the other upon the scythe's shaft still slung over a shoulder.

"Haven't seen your uncle this week," he puffed. "Not that I miss him more than a rash."

Gavin laughed. "Don't speak of the devil. He's probably down in Creepmouse Town trying to spawn another scheme to profit by someone else's misfortune. Which will land him in trouble again and, hopefully, father won't save him this time."

The Avenger huskily sang:

> Down, down in Creepmouse Town
> All the lamps are low
> And the little rodent feet
> Softly come and go

Gavin joined in:

> There's a rat in Creepmouse Town
> And a bat or two
> Everything down in Creepmouse Town
> Would swiftly frighten you

The Avenger panted a laugh. "And we know who the rat is."

"Has he been bothering you?" Gavin asked.

"Just spying on me as usual. Which he's not very good at. And he told my dad last week I was getting too fat to work."

"Forever the whispering serpent," said Gavin. "Father said just yesterday the grounds have never looked better." He slipped an arm over The Avenger's shoulders. "Friends come in all shapes, colors and sizes, and you're the best friend in the whole universe."

"No, you are to me."

"Two friends having adventures," said Gavin. "What could be more heavenly in life." He grasped The Avenger's jeans with a hand to retain them as they walked, which though not as symbolic of classic boyhood camaraderie as an arm over shoulders, was in this case more practical.

They emerged from beneath overhanging trees at the moonlit verge of the trestle as the train's whistle wooed behind them again, and Gavin gestured toward the horizon. "And more adventures lie ahead when we set sail for faraway lands."

"Not in this life!" someone snarled.

Spencer recognized the voice; and Dodger's – Gavin's – cadaverous uncle lunged from shadow behind a tree, a massive double-barreled pistol aimed at Gavin's chest!

But Gavin, far from looking scared, only scornfully faced the man. "Have you finally lost your mind... small and foul as it ever was?"

"Shut up, you over-privileged brat! Decadent, dissolute, low-minded thing!"

"So the pot calls the kettle." Gavin stepped between The Avenger and the moon-glinted gun -- which The Avenger recognized as one of the "pirate pistols" from Gavin's father's collection, both its hammers cocked -- crossing his arms over his chest like an angel disdaining a demon, and the man retreated a little despite his deadly weapon, backing onto the trestle as the train's whistle sounded again maybe now only a half mile away.

"You *have* lost your mind," added Gavin, in a calm and steady voice, "if you plan to murder me."

Spencer heard his own voice add, and without any fear, "Yeah, you're nuts! Everyone knows you want all the money, so if anything happens to Gavin the cops are gonna figure you did it!"

Ebenezer's eyes, paranoically rolling, darted up the shadowy tracks apparently knowing he had little time, but he seemed to recover some courage, or maybe rage overmastered his fear, and his hand, which had trembled when Gavin stood proud, now gripped the huge gun steadily. "There will no suspicion about his death! ...And surely not about *yours*, nigger boy!"

"His father will know you killed him!"

Ebenezer sneered. "His father will be so grief-stricken by the loss of his precious spawn he will doubtless take his own life... or so it will appear."

He aimed the gun squarely at Gavin's chest as the train whistle sounded again, and gestured with his free hand to starlit space and the pond far below. "In your usual state of drunkenness you will have fallen to your death. ...Or, under the sway of your own vile creation, you might have believed you could fly." He sneered at The Avenger again. "And you were just as deluded... just as you have been all your life to think *you* and him could ever be friends... to think this world would *allow* you to be when the time came to grow up!"

Gavin laughed... evil things, as Spencer had read, hated being laughed at. Nor did he look down, still calmly facing the man. "You don't know meaning of friendship, which is hardly surprising since you never had a friend." He also gestured toward the stars. "You expect me to jump, you fool? If so, then go ahead and shoot, which may be my end but will also be yours."

The nearing whistle wailed again as the train started into the curve that would bring it to the trestle; and Ebenezer shifted his aim ... Gavin a far from adequate shield for The Avenger's mass. "You *will* jump or I'll kill him now! *Do* you think me such a fool to not have made an alternate plan in which your bodies will never be found wrapped in chains in the depths below, and it will no doubt be assumed you met with misadventure while on another descent into low-life."

Gavin instinctively spread his arms to protect his friend, and Ebenezer lashed out with the gun, bashing the side of Gavin's head. Gavin staggered a moment, then toppled over and plunged into space.

But, also involuntary was the man's turning to see Gavin fall. The night had been clear under moonlight and stars, but a sudden mist seemed to snuff everything out... a mist as scalding hot as steam and as ghastly crimson as gushing blood.

The Avenger swung his scythe.

CHAPTER TWENTY-SIX

"**S**pencer!"

Spencer awoke to silver starlight softly shining through his window. He was drenched in sweat and barefoot in jeans, his heartbeat, at least to his own ears, pounding as loud as in *The Tell Tale*. His bewildered eyes went first to the pond, glimmering under the gentle glow, then turned to see his mom and dad standing in the doorway, both in their naturally natural state. They crowded into the little room, and Nathan gripped Spencer's shoulders.

"You okay, son?"

"...Yeah." Spencer's eyes shot back to the pond. "But I gotta...!"

Jenny stroked Spencer's forehead. "It's all right, honey, you were having a dream."

"Who's Dodger?" asked Nathan.

"...Dodger?" said Spencer.

"You were screaming that name," said Jenny. "Made my hair stand on end."

"...No, it was Gavin!" cried Spencer, struggling to sit up, Nathan giving assistance, and Spencer pointed to the pond. "I gotta get down there!"

"Steady, Spence," said Nathan, gently restraining Spencer, who'd half leaned out the window. "Like your mom said, you were having a dream."

"He might be alive... but he's gonna drown! ...It's so *dark!*"

"Gavin?" said his mother, settling onto the bed, joined in a moment by his dad, who drew Spencer back inside, their earthly spirits of man and woman surrounding Spencer protectively. "Gavin Shade? Gilbert Shade's son?" She soothingly stroked Spencer's hair. "He did

262

drown, honey. I read it in the *Tribune* archives… did a little research on the restaurant computer. He apparently fell off the railroad trestle. Or maybe he tried to dive from it; the coroner said he'd been drinking; and, despite being rich, he was known to be an 'adventurous boy.' …But that was a hundred years ago."

"But why were you yelling for 'Dodger?'" asked Nathan.

"Dodger as in The Artful?" asked Jenny.

Spencer's eyes were still on the pond, recalling he'd said he had to get *down* there, though from here it was up. "…Yeah, but it wasn't him. …I mean, it *couldn't* have been."

"It was just a dream, honey, things get muddled."

Spencer felt very muddled. He looked past his parents to Wiggins, also surrounded with comfort and love within his cherub-framed window, who didn't look any less. "What time is it?"

"Close to three-thirty," said Nathan. "We heard you holler at…"

"Three-thirteen," said Spencer.

Jenny looked thoughtful. "According to the coroner, Gavin died between midnight and dawn, though the engineer on a passing train said he thought he'd seen someone… a shadow or shadows, he said …on the trestle at…"

"Three-thirteen," Spencer echoed.

Jenny studied him. "The grounds-keeper's son found the body. 'Death by misadventure' was the coroner's verdict."

Spencer's eyes returned to the pond, where a deer was daintily drinking while a fox trotted over the top of the dam. "What about Ebenezer?"

"Who?" asked Nathan.

"Ebenezer Shade, Gavin's uncle."

"Didn't know he had one," said Jenny, "but I didn't dig that deep."

"I think I did," said Spencer.

Jenny went on, "Gavin's father apparently never recovered from the shock of Gavin's death; went into what they called a decline and passed-away a month later after consulting spiritualists to try to contact his son."

"In The Great Beyond," said Spencer.

"The servants said he kept Gavin's room exactly like it was, and ordered all the clocks in the mansion stopped at..."

"Three-thirteen," Spencer repeated.

Jenny regarded Spencer again. "That railroad went out of business in 1957 and there hasn't been a train on it since. The tracks were taken out, and the Redwood Tunnel was sealed up."

"...Oh," said Spencer, that revelation adding to his mounting muddle.

Nathan had also been studying Spencer and said half seriously, "I've never been sure I believed in ghosts, but this does seem a little ghostly."

"I've never been sure I didn't," said Jenny. "But Mr. Darkmoor did give us a supernatural deal on this place." She chucked Spencer under his chins. "And probably not to get naked pictures of our charming cherub."

Despite his muddle, Spencer smiled, thinking of Daffy's "advantage," which, though not in the altogether, was about as naked as he could be. He almost said he'd "met" her but decided this wasn't the time. Nor, he also decided, was it a time to introduce Dodger, even in absentia.

Jenny noticed the railroad lantern. "Where did you find this?"

"...Around," said Spencer.

Nathan picked it up. "Looks like it's been inside somewhere." He turned to Jenny. "I suspect our young Holmes has been doing some sleuthing, which might have inspired his imagination." He opened the globe and lit the wick with a Radium Silent Match. "That's enlightening," he said, as warm golden glow filled the room.

Jenny ruffled Spencer's hair. "Want some hot chocolate and a snack? I brought home another cream cake."

"Um... no, but thanks. Besides, we'd have to build a fire."

"Yes, I keep forgetting we're in the 1920s here."

Spencer turned to the pond again. "I'm okay. Thanks for coming to my rescue."

"You're welcome to join us in bed," said Nathan, "if you're still feeling spooked."

"That was swell when I was five, but now it's a little therapy-making."

"How time flies," said Jenny, giving Spencer a kiss on a cheek. "Would an old-fashioned family hug suffice?"

"Like the cat's pajamas," said Spencer, and all embraced together.

His parents got up, and Jenny said, "Speaking of sleeping attire, please lose those grungy jeans before adventuring back to dreamland. I haven't found a laundromat yet, and it smells a bit earthy in here."

Nathan sniffed. "With spirits of tobacco and gin. ...Which seems to solve the mystery of the missing Plymouth."

Jenny smiled. "Not to mention American Spirits... yes, Spence, we've known for years."

"You could have asked," added Nathan. "But of course being naughty is always more fun."

"...Oh."

His parents left hand-in-hand. Spencer waited for them to settle, but instead of shedding his jeans he took the lantern and puffingly squiggled out the window. "I have to know," he whispered to Wiggins, cascading to earth amongst the ferns.

Except for the restful rush of the brook and gentle keening of crickets, the starlit dell was silent as Spencer hurried up the path and pantingly climbed to the shore of the pond. By this time, although still muddled as to what might be real and what – maybe -- wasn't, he'd just about resigned himself to finding nothing at all, which would confirm he *had* been dreaming since waking up in Gavin's bed, "inspired," perhaps, as his dad had said, by yesterday afternoon's adventure into the centuried realm of the Shades.

But he froze in shock for a second when at last attaining the shore and seeing a slenderly-muscular body, naked except for dungarees and wraith-like pale in the spectral starlight, floating face-down in skeletal shadows cast by the trestle above!

"Dodger!"

Dropping the lantern, he lumbered frantically into the water and almost reached the deep dark place when a cheerful voice behind him spoke:

"The game is afoot."

Spencer spun around to see Dodger, barely clad as he usually was, lounging with his back to a tree, a bottle of juvenile gin in one hand, a cigarette ghosting silver smoke between the fingers of the other, and smiling his enigmatic smile.

Spencer spun around again to face the star-sparkled pond… and there was nothing but placid water mirroring the universe.

He turned back to Dodger and sloshed back to shore, retaining his sodden jeans with a hand and picking up the still-burning lantern. "What part of this am I dreaming? …Or should I say, was I dreaming?"

"There is no was because was always is, and therefore ends are only beginnings." Dodger made room against the tree, and smilingly offered the bottle as Spencer subsided squishily down.

"Sort of like the train layout."

"Now you're on the trolley."

Dodger's shoulder to Spencer's was solid and warm, his familiar scents boyishly earthy as always, as Spencer took a hideous gulp and made a naturally nasty face; but Spencer, after returning the flask, and after a Holmesian moment of eliminating impossibles, said, "I don't know how to tactfully put this, but you *do* know you're dead?"

Dodger only smiled again and offered a Fatima, which Spencer accepted and Dodger lit with a Radium Silent Match. "In return I mean no offense," said Dodger, "but don't you think that's a bit pretentious from someone with presently only five senses… or in your case let's call it five and a half." Then, slipping an arm over Spencer's shoulders in Little Rascals camaraderie, Dodger gestured toward the stars. "It's all a matter of perspective."

CHAPTER TWENTY-SEVEN

Spencer awoke in golden sunlight shining through his window pleasantly warm on his mostly bare body, his jeans as usual during a nap having slipped more than halfway off. He picked up his phone to find the time, but decided that kind of time didn't matter in the present perspective: it was another Indian Summer dreamy Elysian afternoon, the rush of the brook a soft serenade; a timeless time in an ageless place. Instead he checked his messages but there was nothing new from Daffy.

He opened her picture and smiled, regarding the girl of his dreams for a time -- though that was probably all she would be -- and glanced at his reflection reflectingly doing the same, then shut off the phone and settled back with arms crossed under his head.

"We knew the meaning of life last night," he said, while gazing out at the sky, "the universe, and everything... which of course we always knew but for the present have mostly forgotten because it wouldn't be any fun to know the beginning before the end."

Still, he savored a few memories, fading though they were... having a picnic in silver moonlight on the forested shore of the pond, though the star-sparkled water had shimmered away seemingly into infinity without any sight of another side.

He'd been with Gavin under that moon -- Gavin Shade, the Artful Dodger -- and there had been the fabulous food conjured from Water Rat's bottomless basket, along with a jug of iced lemonade enchantingly spiked with juvenile gin; another beauteous *déjà vu* banquet, not only in the incredible volume of vivacious victuals consumed, but also in the palate pleasure of seemingly infinite textures and tastes, every one tantalizing his tongue into a rapturous raving for more. And finally after delicious desserts consisting not only of caramel-cream pie but including shamelessly messy cream puffs, Napoleons and chocolate éclairs, he'd drifted afloat in sea of stars, belly bulging in blubbery bliss while the part of him deeply buried below was also engorged to the verge of explosion.

And, as the perfect climax, he and Dodger had sensually shared what Gavin and The Avenger had shared, and this time Spencer had let it happen divinely enlightened in innocence and understanding why the faun looked so joyous doing the same, because what was only a fleeting moment for spirits sojourning in physical form could be an eternal ecstasy in The Great Beyond.

Now, in this peaceful afternoon, his mother having left for work after serving him another lush lunch of 1920s flavored food – consisting of meaty roast-beef hash crowned with a butter-fried egg – he languidly fondled material mass creating an undulant ocean motion in all the softness surrounding himself awakening earthly approximations of supremely celestial sensations and could have leisurely continued, drifting in daydreams as long as he liked until another sensuous surge, but again pillowed his head on his arms and regarded the heavens beyond the tree tops.

"For the present time," he finally said, "our mission as responsible boys is to hoe the rows in mom's future garden."

Avalanching out of bed, he tugged his jeans up to their belly-bibbed level and was about to go to the kitchen to fortify himself with a Coke, when he heard the murmur of a motor slowly ascending the lane. It was neither his father's GMC nor his mother's Subaru, though there seemed to be something familiar about it, but he surmised to his looking-glass self, "Maybe it's a PG&E truck coming to put in the power lines?"

Lumbering into the living room, he opened the front door and stood looking out. There were sparkles of sunlight on metal and glass as a vehicle emerged from shadow under the overhanging trees and approached the little bridge above the rainbow-misted falls.

Yesterday he might have exclaimed "No fucking way!" or something like that, but now though his mouth was indeed open, and a bit more than it usually was, he only watched as a grand Silver Ghost, gleaming midnight and bright polished nickel, crossed the bridge and purred to a stop.

It might have rolled up through a time warp or out of a portal between universes -- though Spencer noted its number plate was a black-and-white British type – and its high-booted, silver-gray liveried chauffeur, a plump black man of possibly thirty, could have come from an earlier age as he dismounted, opened the back door and offered a hand to a passenger...

Assisting Daffy Darkmoor to earth!

"Swell!" Spencer did ejaculate, and hastened out to meet her.

She looked every opulent cubic inch as she had in her digital photograph, and even more of her on display since she was dressed for this atmosphere instead of a blustery day on a moor in Levis, big sneaks, and a plain white T-shirt, a charming glimpse of dusky chub peeking from under the latter, and the splendiferous spheres of her breasts only restrained by its straining cotton; while her untamed abundance of ebony curls was boyishly crowned with a brown newsy cap... maybe the same as in her photo and evidently a favorite thing, looking very well-worn in both senses.

Spencer couldn't recall ever smelling heather but he seemed to scent it now, a sort of wild and woodsy bouquet; and, as he'd noted in her picture, there was something of The Avenger about her, though she was probably half his weight and therefore half of Spencer's. She was, he also observed, taking advantage of her advantage and seemed quite favorably inclined to his present state of being.

"Hi," was all he could think of to say, feeling like a bashful boy depicted in some old-time tale and regretting he had no flowers to offer, until a new thought came to mind, which though seeming absurd on one level, also seemed logical on another since he had spoken with her on the phone -- and she presumably in England -- less than an earthly day ago. And there was the Ghost, so he said:

"If it wouldn't seem stupid of me, may I ask if you're here in spirit?"

Daffy Puckishly pinched his arm.

Spencer laughed. "As I've learned in recent times, that's neither proof of physical form nor that one might not be dreaming."

"I quite understand," said Daffy, offering a chubby hand featuring dimples in lieu of knuckles… which Spencer was tempted to kiss in French fashion but merely pressed in what he presumed would be a proper restrained English way.

"And neither, of course, is this," said Daffy, clasping Spencer's hand in return. "But I assure you it's me in the flesh. …And what a charming cherub," she added, taking the unabashed liberty of palming the pendant on Spencer's chest. "I have one just like it, a family heirloom." She drew it from under her shirt to display. "But, presuming whatever adventure you may have had since last we spoke didn't turn out to be something it shouldn't, I could ask the same of you."

"I'm pretty sure I'm here," said Spencer. "Assuming one can ever be sure of not being somewhere else. And I remember some of it, but a lot is getting misty."

"As it probably should," said Daffy, "since we're here because we're here instead of there whenever we aren't." She indicated the car. "Dad owns an air-cargo company so it was no bother to bring it. I would have preferred my trusty Rover, but it's been rather bashed-about and one must keep up appearances, especially we of color. …This was the Shade's, in case you wonder. …And, I'm forgetting my manners." She turned to the chauffeur. "This is Dawkins."

Spencer shook hands with the man, and Dawkins said, "Pleased to meet you, sir."

"Likewise," said Spencer, and turned back to Daffy. "Would you and Dawkins like some tea?"

"A Coke would be nice if you have one," said Daffy.

"Of course," said Spencer. "Please come in."

"Thank you, sir," said Dawkins, "But I must attend to business… the lane to the mansion, as doubtless you know, is too overgrown for access, so I must arrange for it to be cleared." He smiled. "I'm sure Miss Darkmoor will be in good hands until I'm able to return."

"I'm quite sure I will," said Daffy. "Hands being handy to have, hold and handle. And please don't rush on my account. …This is a very pleasant place," she added while gazing around. "As if stepping into a story." She offered a hand again, and Spencer escorted her to the cottage as Dawkins got back in the Ghost and it murmured away.

"Will your mum and dad be back soon?" asked Daffy. "I am looking forward to meeting them."

"Not till around midnight," said Spencer. "...But how do you know they're not here?"

"Elementary," said Daffy, pointing to the ground. "Neither vehicle present... one a large four-wheel-drive as evidenced by its tracks, and probably somewhat vintage judging by the style of tires; the other a small car and, I'll venture, likely Japanese."

Spencer laughed. "A deduction worthy of Mr. Homes."

"One of my favorite reads."

Spencer said, "Um..." as they entered, and indicated the couch, not at all sure despite all he'd read of how to properly entertain a girl of such sophistication... or any girl for that matter. "Would you like to sit down?"

"What a charming cottage," said Daffy. "It's every bit as I always imagined. I'd love to see it if you wouldn't mind?"

"Oh sure... well, this is living room, and that's my mom and dad's." Spencer continued up the hall. "The bathroom, my room... please excuse the mess... and this of course is the kitchen." He went to the ice box for Cokes. "Um, there's also beer."

"Just the thing," said Daffy, "on such a balmy afternoon... our moor weather at this time of year can be rather bracing. And please don't bother with glasses."

"I hope you're not disappointed; I've read what English people think about American beer."

"Fairy piss it's often called, but I've never had."

Spencer opened two Rolling Rocks and presented a bottle to Daffy, who took a tentative sip. "Not too dreadful," she pronounced, and followed with a hearty swallow. "Though we must have a pint of pub draft in the future, and with fish and chips."

"That would be charming," said Spencer, still not quite sure he wasn't dreaming as Daffy looked into his room.

"What a lovely library. You have the complete Sherlock Homes. I do admire men who read."

271

"Um," Spencer asked before thinking, "do you know many?"

"None, I regret, of your age," said Daffy, "being rather isolated from those of my own in the wilds."

Spencer felt, maybe absurdly, relieved. "You seem to have the hound of the Baskervilles."

"In the picture? That's Akela, my trusty companion. Very stalwart company, but of course he doesn't read, though I'm sure he would if he could. ...You also have *The Wind In The Willows*, *Alice*, and *Through The Looking Glass*. ...And all the Dickens books. How nice!"

"It's nothing compared to what's in the mansion... I did take that liberty, you know."

"And quite all right, as I said," replied Daffy, also taking a liberty by entering to inspect Spencer's den. She added, regarding the looking-glass, which now mirrored herself, "I understand Gavin's room was kept as it always was."

"Yeah, he had a lot of books... or should I say has? I'm still not used to the past being present, even if it always is; but I meant the main library."

Daffy reflected a curious look. "You saw books in there?"

"And all the other stuff in the house... all the antique furnishings. Not to mention the artwork and all the artifacts."

"Perhaps things got a bit muddled," said Daffy, after reflecting a moment. "Dodger does seem to have that effect with his mischievous messing about. ...Is this the lantern?" she asked, taking it from the nightstand.

"I was going to return it."

"I'm sure he'd want you to have it." Daffy looked out at the dell. "This must be the window?"

"The entrance to the egress."

"And there is the pond. May we see it?"

Both finished their bottles of beer and left the cottage by the back door proceeding along the bubbling brook and up to the tree-shaded shore of the pond, where Daffy regarded the sun-sparkled scene. "One rather expects to see cherubs and fauns, and perhaps a unicorn."

"Frolicking," Spencer improved, before thinking that might not be proper despite being pleasant to picture.

"I do love a frolic," said Daffy. "This world, I think, would be far better off if people spent more time frolicking and less in mucking it up. ...And that must be the trestle."

Spencer followed Daffy's gaze to the vine-tangled timbers high overhead. "I take it you know what happened last night? Which is why you couldn't tell me before, because I wouldn't have let it happen and that might have altered a universe."

"Which may not have been a bad thing," said Daffy. "There might have been more frolicking."

"And maybe cheeseburgers for all."

"What a lovely thought," said Daffy. "I do dote on burgers with cheese: Dawkins and I lunched at a Maccies. ...But, of course, we'll never know, because one can't take a road not taken if they never took it."

Spencer regarded the trestle again. "But, like said, I'm forgetting a lot... like what happens in dreams. I remember swinging the scythe, but then I'm having a picnic with Dodger."

"The latter must have been fun," said Daffy. "I've heard the story timeless times beginning when I was very small and sitting upon my grandfather's knee... he passed-away yesterday."

"Oh, I'm sorry," said Spencer.

"Thank you, but as he assured us, he'd learned quite a lot in this adventure as well as having bags of fun and was looking forward to infinite others. He was a hundred-and-thirteen."

"Guess he was ready for something new."

"Precisely as he put it. ...As to the after," Daffy went on. "After wicked Ebenezer met his appropriate end and fell, The Avenger made his way down here hoping Gavin might have survived, but of course, and sadly, he hadn't, being rendered unconscious after Ebenezer struck him and so unable to save himself. As to Ebenezer's remains... a nasty sight, I'm sure... a black boy in those times killing a white man, even in self-defense, wouldn't have gone over well. Even if not convicted of murder, he and his parents might have been lynched; so he weighted Ebenezer with the very chains Ebenezer had left for his dastardly alternate plan and sent him to the deep dark place, where we may assume the big fat trout dealt with most of his physical form, while time eventually did for the rest."

"A fitting end," said Spencer.

"One, as grandfather said, gets the beginnings earned by their ends, so perhaps he is still somewhere in the dark. The Avenger 'found' Gavin's body at dawn, which was his story to the police, but gave Gavin's father the true account. Though devastated by Gavin's death, Gilbert Shade, being a kind man and knowing there would be talk and suspicion about his brother's disappearance coinciding with the death of his son… it being well-known and remarked upon that despite their 'differences,' as 'proper people' put it politely, the boys were very fond of each other… made arrangements for The Avenger and his parents to move to England, where he owned a bit of moor land left to him by his father." Daffy smiled. "With a little stone cottage. Well-financed, of course; enough for a flock of sheep to sustain them, a Thornycroft lorry, and plenty of food to see them through the winter."

"Another beginning," said Spencer.

"And a very happy one… imagine their astonishment when, after grief-stricken Gilbert died, they found he'd left all his fortune to them."

"Wow!" exclaimed Spencer. "Did they buy a castle?"

"Merely an old manor house, appropriately Darkmoor Hall."

"So they became the Darkmoors," said Spencer. "And you're The Avenger's granddaughter."

"A deduction worthy of Mr. Holmes."

"Elementary actually with all the facts at hand." Spencer pointed to the wall. "Have you come for the stuff in the mansion?"

"Grandfather left the house to me and advised I come forthwith to inspect it in regard to its future, which is why Dawkins is making arrangements for the lane to be cleared; but since you've already been, I assume there's a way to get there from here?"

"There's a path from that gate."

"Lay on, MacDuff."

A short time later found Spencer and Daffy emerging from the forest path at the edge of the mansion's overgrown grounds. At first on the way after passing the gate, Spencer had tried to muffle his puffing, not wanting Daffy to think he might not be up to adventuring, but his need for air had grown too great and now, shiny with silvery sweat, he pantingly paused to recover some breath; though Daffy, despite her T-shirt having become enchantingly damp – no doubt due to the climate rather than what, for her, was probably just a leisurely stroll – didn't seem at all critical of her quarter-ton companion.

The scene before them, Spencer saw, was *déjà vu* of yesterday as, raising his eyes above the trees, he beheld the topmost story of three, along with the two looming towers, of the perplexing anomalous marriage of hoary Gothic cathedral and Baskerville Hall in the Sherlock Holmes tale.

Daffy gazed around. "I've seen many old photographs, but they don't convey the whimsical wonder. What a charming place for Dodger's childhood."

"And The Avenger's," said Spencer, "despite their difference in station."

"A mere physical formality; they were always equals in spirit."

"When in Rome?"

"Precisely." Daffy offered her hand. "Shall we follow the yellow brick road?"

They proceeded up the path between the ranks of lavender lilies, passing the statue of the boy-faun poised like Peter Pan with a knife and then the gang of fat cherubs swilling from an amphora of wine and tipsily tumbling over each other, and the many other creations of rolly-poly cherubim engaged in feasting and rowdiness, along with the youthful fauns playing pipes, hunting with a bow and arrow, and sitting peacefully reading a book, which Daffy took in with delighted expressions; though Spencer found himself embarrassed when they came upon the teenage faun poised in eternal ecstasy. But Daffy only remarked with a smile, "He would make an impertinent fountain."

"My thought, too," said Spencer.

"We seem to be kindred spirits," said Daffy.

They continued toward the house, the soothing sound of rushing water now becoming audible above the chirping and twitter of birds. As on the afternoon before, animal life was abundant in addition to avian and bees droning over the flowers; a trotting fox, a questing coyote, a browsing pair of daint-footed deer, and none apparently disturbed by Spencer and Daffy's presence; as well as squirrels in the trees, rabbits amongst the shrubbery, and a few lizards and snakes in the grass.

"I can still see the gods," said Daffy, scanning the feral topiaries, then pausing to pluck a pair of apples and passing one to Spencer.

Emerging from the wisteria thicket, which had once merely shaded a marble bench on which to rest in company with a slumbering cherub, they came at last upon the fountain sparkling in the sunlight and splashing its liquid lullaby into the pond where more cherubs frolicked, while in its midst and shrouded in spray, stood the cheerful Grim Reaper.

"Quite the likeness of Dodger," said Daffy, "in the performance of his chores... he fills in for Him now and then, I'm told."

The gigantic house loomed ahead against the forested slopes at its back and across the graveled drive, which was filled with ferns like an emerald moat, all seeming the same as yesterday.

Spencer stopped at the foot of the stairs to once more uplift his recalcitrant jeans. "The key is always here."

Taking it from the stone lion's paws, and with Daffy at his side, he ascended to the front doors and fitted it into the lock. Then, with appropriate sound effects, he swung the portal majestically open. But then he stood and stared.

Except for dust and spider webs, the magnificent foyer was empty.

Gone were the settee and paintings, the free-standing ashtray, the walking-stick stand, and the table for the phone... though the latter now sat on the floor, its wire still attached to the wall-mounted box.

"What the...!"

"Fuck?" Daffy suggested, a hand going to Spencer's shoulder as he remained looking baffled. "As I mentioned in your room, Dodger tends to mess about, leaving enigmas and paradoxes, metaphysical mysteries, little vignettes of time out of time, and things not back in their proper places, though he seems to have tidied up here."

"…Then, everything else I saw yesterday…?"

"I'm sure it's still there, but of course we're here."

"…It's all a matter of perspective."

"Now we're on the tram."

Spencer noted the dust on the floor, lying as thick as silvery snow, showed no signs of his previous visit. Still somewhat bewildered, he went to the phone and picked it up, then after evicting a ruffled arachnid, put the receiver to an ear.

Only dead silence. He jiggled the hook but there was still nothing. "How could you have called me on this?" he asked, returning the phone to the floor.

"Grandfather told me to ask for long distance." Daffy took Spencer's hand again. "Shall we continue?"

As on the day before, the gargantuan hall was palely lit by the skylights above the chandeliers, but now was devoid of everything but spider art and dust, their footsteps stirring up the latter and awakening long-sleeping echoes magnified by the emptiness as they approached the staircase.

The *"Titanic"* cherubs were still in place, but they were part of the balustrade. Seeing Spencer regarding the stairs with a less than adventurous expression, Daffy said:

If it wouldn't offend your spirit, may I offer a shoulder?"

Spencer laughed. "My spirit is willing but my flesh is fat."

"Charmingly cherubic," said Daffy.

"Seems to be a recurring theme."

With an arm over Daffy's shoulder, his other hand grasping the banister, Spencer heaved and hoed himself upward. There was no grandfather clock, he noted, pausing to pant at the top of the stairs while Daffy adroitly adjusted his jeans. They went around the gallery, and Spencer stopped at the dining room doors. "Out of curiosity…"

"Call me a cat," said Daffy; and Spencer bulled the doors open to a dark and echoing space, a flick of his lighter revealing no titanic table or great grand piano, no sideboards, no artwork adorning the walls. But, as he drew the doors shut, Daffy said:

"Do you smell that?"

277

"Deep-fried oysters," said Spencer.

"If they taste half as good as they smell, they must be food for the gods."

"At least for young angels."

They moved on toward the front of the house, where Spencer, for further verification that Dodger had indeed tidied up, opened the door to the library and saw nothing but empty shelves.

At last they came to Gavin's room, and Spencer was surprised when, after opening its door, the first thing he saw was himself reflected in the free-standing mirror. Then, gazing around, he exclaimed:

"It is as it was… except now it's then!"

Indeed the room was as it had been on Spencer's physical visit, but now there were no spider webs, no dust, or any signs of age; the movie posters vividly bright as if they'd been lithographed yesterday, the bed still turned expectantly down but its pillows and sheets looking virginally fresh.

"It *is* his room," said Daffy, reflecting over Spencer's shoulder.

"For when he pops in now and then?" said Spencer.

"Perhaps he anticipated our visit." Daffy paused to scent the air. "It does smell scruffily boyish… not that I have vast experience in young male aromatics."

"That's probably me," said Spencer. "Like a Baker Street Irregular."

"Earthy, I'd say in a word," said Daffy. "Which I find not at all unpleasant."

Spencer followed Daffy, who marveled at Dodger's past-present things, delighting in the electric train, the model schooner and vehicles – laughing while looking at Lulibelle, "You'll want to slap their faces." -- the radio and gramophone, the cameras and the many books; though Spencer saw the lantern was absent… being now in his room. He asked as Daffy opened the *armoire*, "Would you care for some music?"

"That would be jolly," Daffy replied, inspecting Dodger's wardrobe while Spencer cranked the gramophone and put on a record.

Am I a passing fancy
Or am I the one in your dreams…

"One of my all-time faves," said Daffy, as the slightly skeletal sound ghosted around the room. "Though it must be much better live."

"Especially when sung by a spirited cherub."

Daffy continued her tour of the chamber, spending some time at Dodger's desk looking through the photograph album, in which the pictures were clear and bright, and remarking upon the resemblance between The Avenger and Spencer as the last line of *Passing Fancy* faded away in the æther, then went to the princely bed as Spencer returned to the gramophone and selected another record.

Take in the sun
Hang out the moon
And rock me in a cradle of dreams.

Daffy inspected the magazines, smiled regarding the French post-cards – "Ooh la la" -- then took up the DRINK ME bottle. "I've wondered how Dodger's gin might taste."

"The term, coffin varnish, is *apropos*," said Spencer, after joining her and noting the alarm clock stopped again at 3:13. "And it may also be dream-inducing."

Nonetheless, Daffy uncapped the flask, took an experimental sip and made a charmingly frightful face. "How perfectly horrid!"

She passed the bottle to Spencer, who also took a taste. "Just as I always remembered."

Daffy picked up the Fatima pack. "Perhaps one of these might cleanse the palate."

Spencer flicked his lighter for Daffy and fired a cigarette for himself as Daffy sat down on the snowy sheets where Dodger and The Avenger had lain a hundred years ago. Spencer subsided beside her, both creating smoky ghosts while sharing more sips of casket coating as the music played, then Spencer said:

"A Holmesian thought just came to mind: while, as you said, your

279

grandfather, aka The Avenger, told you of his time here with Dodger... which was, so to speak, the before... but how do you know about Dodger's after?"

Daffy snubbed her cigarette in the cherub ashtray. "Grandfather simply passed, you know, he didn't cease to exist... after all, one never does... and though he was looking forward to having new adventures, he was kind enough to stay a while and tell me some of what he'd forgotten now that he remembered again... life, the universe, and all that... most of which, as you described, seems to be fading into mist, but I'll always remember Dodger."

"He is pretty hard to forget," said Spencer, also snuffing his smoke.

"Do you love him?" Daffy asked.

"Yes," said Spencer with no hesitation.

Daffy smiled mischievously. "You aren't going to qualify that?"

Spencer turned to the photograph of Gavin and The Avenger standing by the pond. "Love never needs to be qualified when it comes from the spirit. And it's the same love we can give anyone, anywhere and any time."

Maybe it was the gin, but Spencer leaned close and kissed Daffy's cheek.

"That was fresh," said Daffy.

"I hope you don't want to slap my face."

"Fresh as in refreshing, and quite the contrary," Daffy replied, and kissed Spencer's cheek in return.

Feeling only slightly unsure, Spencer gently embraced the girl and pressed his lips to hers. Her arms went around him – at least as much as possible – and time was timeless for a time, both sinking back on the plumply-plumped pillows to innocently adventure, though on the purely physical plane their questing didn't take them as far as Spencer and Dodger's explorations.

Daffy sighed when finally they parted and sat up again. "That indeed was spiritual, you've obviously had experience."

"A very spiritual mentor." Spencer regarded the photo again. "Life, as Dodger told me last night... or whenever it was and always will be... will provide the experience needed to uplift a spirit.

…Maybe that's the meaning of it?"

"Makes more sense than 42." Daffy kissed Spencer's cheek again. "You've uplifted mine here and now."

But, Spencer's spirit lowered a little. "Um… I should tell you…" He patted the vastness surrounding himself. "Like… if there were expectations… they probably won't be great."

Daffy smiled. "Expectations, like roads yet not taken, are never known until they are. We should always expect the unexpected, because if we could expect the expected there wouldn't be any expectations, so why shouldn't they be great." She kissed Spencer's cheek once more. "To put it more materially, and as we both have observed, you might be The Avenger's twin."

"…Yeah…" said Spencer.

"And I am his granddaughter."

"…Oh… yeah."

Another short time later found them again in the sun-dappled dell where, though time must have certainly passed, it still seemed endless afternoon. Daffy gazed back at the overgrown path as Spencer closed the gate; and noting her thoughtful expression he said:

"On the material plane, I imagine the mansion and grounds are worth many bushels of oysters these days."

"I'm sure Linda Lancaster," Daffy replied, "would love to see the house torn down and the land butchered into plots for 'dwellings for the discriminating,' but wouldn't it be ever so nice transformed into a boarding school to give underprivileged children a chance in the present to better their future."

"That's the spirit," said Spencer.

Spencer taking Daffy's hand, they made their way down the scythed path, entered the cottage by the back door and came into the kitchen, Spencer drawing a chair for Daffy and seating her at the table.

"Would you like anything?" he asked. "Perhaps another beer?"

"A Coke would be nice," said Daffy. "Dodger's coffin varnish has raised my spirit to heavenly heights… along with your charming company."

"Mom left an Italian cream cake."

Daffy smiled. "This must be a dream."

"If it is, it's fun dreaming with you." Spencer was reaching for the cake when a voice called, "The game is afoot."

"Indeed what fun!" exclaimed Daffy, coming with Spencer into his room, where Dodger stood outside at the window in just his jeans as usual.

But, he wasn't alone… at his side stood The Avenger in all his ebony opulence just as Spencer had seen him last, with Dodger's arm over his shoulders. …And beyond in the sun sat Lulibelle, with Finn helping Annie down from the cab, while Willie unloaded a huge picnic basket, both boys also shirtless in jeans, and Annie clad in a bathing suit of daring design for the 1920s.

"Another star-matched pair," said Dodger, regarding Daffy and Spencer with his friendly-fox smile. "Would you have time for a frolic?"

The Avenger added, "And a movie?"

Daffy laughed. "That would be swell, grandfather."

"And then," said Spencer, offering a hand to assist Daffy out the window, "the best oysters in any universe."

THE END

Or the beginning

ABOUT THE AUTHOR

Jess Mowry was born in 1960 near Starkville, Mississippi. When he was only a few months old his father took him to live in Oakland, California. Mowry's father was a voracious reader who introduced his son to books at a very early age. Jess attended a public school, but despite his love of reading, dropped out at age thirteen, part way through the eighth grade and worked with his father in the scrap-iron business. In his late teens, Jess moved to Arizona to work as a truck driver and heavy equipment operator. He also lived and worked in Alaska as an engineer aboard a tugboat and as an aircraft mechanic on Douglas C-47 cargo planes, as well as at a children's refuge in Haiti.

Mowry has written twenty-five books and many short stories about black children and teens in a variety of genres, ranging from inner-city settings to the forests of Haiti, the wilds of Alaska, the Arizona desert, the Caribbean Sea, and the African veldt. While some of his novels are set in Oakland and deal with social issues, such as poverty, violence, drugs, gangs, teenage sexuality, and school drop-outs, Mowry has also written ghost tales, as well as novels featuring Voodoo and African magic, in addition to sea stories, and compiled an anthology of Victorian ghost stories.

Jess Mowry lives in Oakland, California.

THIS BOOK IS ALSO AVAILABLE IN A KINDLE EDITION

OTHER ANUBIS BOOKS

AVAILABLE ON AMAZON

www.ingramcontent.com/pod-product-compliance
Lightning Source LLC
Chambersburg PA
CBHW051530260626
47170CB00003B/860